I0831383

INFINITE^2

WORKS BY JEREMY ROBINSON

The Didymus Contingency
Raising The Past
Beneath
Antarktos Rising
Kronos
Pulse
Instinct
Threshold
Callsign: King
Callsign: Queen
Callsign: Rook
Callsign: King 2 – Underworld
Callsign: Bishop
Callsign: Knight
Callsign: Deep Blue
Callsign: King 3 – Blackout
Torment
The Sentinel
The Last Hunter – Descent
The Last Hunter – Pursuit
The Last Hunter – Ascent
The Last Hunter – Lament
The Last Hunter – Onslaught
The Last Hunter – Collected Edition
Insomnia
SecondWorld
Project Nemesis
Ragnarok
Island 731
The Raven
Nazi Hunter: Atlantis
Prime
Omega
Project Maigo
Refuge
Guardian
Xom-B
Savage
Flood Rising
Project 731
Cannibal
Endgame
MirrorWorld
Hunger
Herculean
Project Hyperion
Patriot
Apocalypse Machine
Empire
Feast
Unity
Project Legion
The Distance
The Last Valkyrie
Centurion
Infinite
Helios
Viking Tomorrow
Forbidden Island
The Divide
The Others
Space Force
Alter
Flux
Tether
Tribe
NPC
Exo-Hunter
Infinite^2

INFINITE²

JEREMY ROBINSON

Cover design by Jeremy Robinson ©2020

Visit Jeremy Robinson on the World Wide Web at: www.bewareofmonsters.com.

01000110 01101111 01110010 00100000 01100101 01110110
01100101 01110010 01111001 01101111 01101110 01100101
00100000 01100110 01101001 01100111 01101000 01110100
01101001 01101110 01100111 00100000 01100001 01100111
01100001 01101001 01101110 01110011 01110100 00100000
01110100 01101000 01100101 00100000 01110111 01101111
01110010 01110011 01110100 00100000 01110100 01101000
01100001 01110100 00100000 01101100 01101001 01100110
01100101 00100000 01110100 01101000 01110010 01101111
01110111 01110011 00100000 01110100 01101000 01100101
01101001 01110010 00100000 01110111 01100001 01111001
00101110

INTRODUCTION

When we last saw Will, he had chosen to remain in the Great Escape with Gal, the love of his life. Together, they would spend eternity exploring the virtual reality Will had created, and that Gal managed. Endless adventures awaited, and for a longer time than is measurable, they lived countless lives together. But now...something in the real world is bringing ruin to the virtual.

PROLOGUE

[info] – INITIALIZING –

[info] Genomic Matrix: 6385-H26

[info] Loading Scenario: JR-00107 - Nemesis Rebirth

[info] Environment Selected: H26-Terra

[info] Rendering Environment...

[info] Runtime 537383 Starting

... 3

... 2

... 1

BEGIN.

1

Horror. Screaming. Death. It's the same every time.

People know that she's out there, stalking. Waiting. And still, they invite hell on Earth by submitting to their base desires. Killers. Rapists. Abusers. The hearts of men and women—women first, if you believe the Bible—are driven by carnal desires that leave a wounded string of victims in their wake.

Driven by primal, narcissistic instability, a fucked-up hubris leads people to believe she won't notice—or won't care. But she always does.

Eventually.

There is no grace.

No forgiveness.

No amount of Hail Marys can satiate the four-hundred-foot-tall goddess of vengeance. Hell, priests are some of the top offenders, committing their crimes hidden away from the world. But not from her.

Not from Nemesis.

My job is to predict her movements, and through aggressive detective work, determine where she's going and who her next target is.

Not so we can stop her.

We can't.

But with enough notice we can clear a path, or even better, serve her target up on a silver platter.

Like we did today.

I can see him far below, tied to a post atop the breaker wall. All coastal cities have them now—giant walls meant to absorb and deflect tsunamis. Atop the wall is a post, where the judged await sentencing.

It's the same every time.

Death.

I felt bad at first.

A lot of people died in the early days, back when we didn't understand what she wanted. Back when we didn't know how or when to get out of the way. A lot of innocent people died. Nemesis doesn't care about collateral damage. She is out for justice, and nothing can slow her down.

So, we speed it up.

The man's screams are carried by the wind, reaching me several thousand feet away. I'm watching the scene play out from the rooftop of a five-hundred-foot-tall apartment building just behind the breakwall separating Boston from the harbor.

"Please!" the man shouts. "God! Save me!"

"Keep screaming, asshole," I say. "God can't save you now."

It's cold. I know. His death is going to be a nightmare, but I've watched it hundreds of times before. I'm numb to it. Indifferent to the pain of people so addicted to their vices that they'd put the rest of us in mortal danger. Fuck them. They deserve it.

When the man's raspy screams are cut short, I turn my gaze out to sea.

It's impossible to miss.

The ocean is rising up. Rolling toward us. Most of the watery hill is going to be shunted away by the curved breakwalls, propelling it right back out to sea. But some will make it over. Will roll right over the judged. If he's lucky, the impact will snap his neck, or he'll suck down a lungful of seawater.

But the city will survive. Again.

Nemesis was born in Boston. The city barely survived its first encounter with the beast. I was just a kid at the time. Lost my whole family in the chaos that followed. I spent years of my life dreaming up ways to kill the monster as it made its way around the planet. But the world's militaries threw everything they had at her—including nukes—and she came back for more every time.

The best we could do was reduce the damage, and the only way to do that was to help her. I've been at it for ten years now, thinking like her, hunting her prey, serving them up.

I wanted vengeance. Now I'm her lackey. I'm not thrilled about it, but the world is a safer place because of my work.

The downside is that I'm the god-damned angel of death.

My face is known worldwide. Some people think that I choose who Nemesis targets.

Making friends is tough.

My fellow agents at the FC-P steer clear.

It's a lonely life, but I was made for the job. By Nemesis. And because of me, there are no more Nemesis-orphans or broken families. No more cities scoured from the Earth. No more mass casualties from evacuation stampedes. I provide security, and Nemesis, well, she keeps people on the straight and narrow.

Most of them anyway.

Jackasses, like the man below, keep Nemesis on the move.

And she's moving fast.

The wave rises a hundred feet, blocking out the morning sun's rays on the city below me, throwing the judged into a cold shadow. Through the wall of water, orange light flickers to life. It writhes back and forth, frantic.

Hungry.

Nemesis is built like an H.R. Giger wet dream. She's black from top to bottom, except for her orange eyes and the membranes that cover her body. Her insides boil and rage, and if one of those membranes is pierced, the explosion that follows is—

"Will."

I spin around, hand on my holstered pistol.

The voice was feminine. Friendly. But it caught me completely off guard.

Problem is, there's no one on the rooftop with me.

"Hello?" I shout. "Who's there?"

There are a few air conditioning units, but I can see most of the rooftop.

I'm alone.

I wait until I'm sure that I misheard something distant, or I imagined it. Maybe a seagull or something. Then I turn back to the scene below. I know how the story's climax ends, but I don't want to miss it.

Nemesis comes to a stop upon reaching the shallows.

She always does. The wave races ahead, losing some of its height when her big body is no longer beneath it. The now fifty-foot wave crashes into the breakwall. The building beneath me shudders, but it's subtle.

Water rushes through the wall's curved channels, streaking around and churning back out to sea. Atop the wall, the judged is pitched forward, but not dead. He's coughing the water from his lungs, clinging to life.

He'll start screaming again in three...two...

Nemesis rises from the water. On land, she prefers to move on all fours, scrambling in a mad flailing gait—like a lizard on hot sand. It's unnerving to watch. She can move through a city, leveling buildings and crushing people, with the single-minded focus of a spider chasing down an insect. It looks mindless and mad, but it's really just raw determineation. But for the moment she stands on just her rear legs.

The man's screams are drowned out by the *shhhh* sound of water falling away from her body. The orange membranes covering her torso and neck flare. She senses her prey.

Then she bares her teeth, opens her mouth, and hisses at the man. She loathes him. Can't stand the sight of him. Her body quakes with revulsion. To stop it, she must end him.

Nemesis drops down to all fours. Water splashes up over the man. He misses the moment Nemesis scrambles toward him, closing the several-hundred-foot gap in a second.

When he opens his eyes again, she's right there, staring back, teeth grinding, eyes flaring bright.

Do it, I will her. *Kill him.*

I smile when her head pulls back. It's subtle, but I know what it means.

Nemesis snaps forward. Her jaws open and clamp shut with the speed of a mouse trap. Then she cocks her head back and swallows the man—whole and alive. We're not sure how long it takes to die inside Nemesis's stomach. It could be anywhere from minutes to days. But there is no debate—it is the worst way to die. Alone, in complete darkness, breathing acidic air, while juices slowly digest your skin.

I shiver, forcing the image from my head, and I smile down at Nemesis as she turns around, about to return to the ocean and the hunt. The man she just consumed was a murderer. Of children. He had it coming and then some. His death pleases me.

"Good girl," I say.

Nemesis freezes in place.

That's odd...

The skin on her back shakes like on a horse when it's trying to scatter flies. A sign of irritation.

Her black head cranes around, orange light blazing.

She's never done *this* before.

Did some Bostonian already commit some kind of horrible crime?

If so, there will be nothing we can do but try to get out of the way.

I toggle my mic, ready to start giving orders. Boston is empty, but we'll need to start moving people out of the suburbs into which they fled. And to do that, we need a direction.

"Which way are you going?" I whisper.

Then her orange eyes shift up, and they land on me.

What the fuck?

Her body follows her head's lead, moving through the water.

It's me.

She wants me!

"What the hell did I d—"

I know what I did.

I sent a man to die...and I enjoyed it. Doesn't matter that he was guilty of heinous crimes. I arranged for and took pleasure in the man's death. In hunting the worst of humanity to save the rest, I've become just as sadistic as the people I stake to walls.

But I'm not staked to a wall.

"I need an evac!" I shout into my comms. "Now! Nemesis has gone AWOL!"

Before I'm done shouting, the sound of rotor blades fills my ears.

Below, a roar.

She knows I'm running.

She's enraged.

I lean over the edge to look. Nemesis breaches the breaker wall with ease, crushing concrete underfoot. She'll make short work of the apartment building to get at me. I have seconds.

My feet pound over the concrete roof as I sprint toward the far side of the building, where the helicopter is descending. "Don't land!" I shout. "Just pull up next to the building!"

"What are you going to do, jump?" the pilot asks.

"That's exactly what I'm going to do," I say, and I pour on the speed.

I stumble a few steps as the building shakes, but I stay upright and on target. Once we're in the air, we can head out to sea, head north, and go from there. Give me some time to figure out how to handle this.

Ten feet to go. Four steps and an easy jump.

I'm about to leap, when, "WILL!"

The voice is loud in my ear. Makes me flinch. My left foot catches the back of my right leg, but I'm moving too fast to stop. I shove off the roof, rise into the air, and–

My shin clangs against the metal rail.

I pitch forward, momentum carrying me out toward the helicopter–where my head strikes the metal skid, twisting me back.

Gravity does the rest, pulling me down.

Toward her.

Nemesis rises up beneath me, mouth open wide.

My fate is sealed.

Fuck that, I think, drawing my pistol and placing it beneath my chin. *You're not going to kill me, too.*

I pull the trigger.

[error] G.E. Process Termination 765.67 (<NCC001974>)

Crash Dump Detected

[warning] Process Recovery: failed (1)

[warning] Process Recovery: failed (2)

[warning] Process Recovery: failed (3)

[fatal] Process Unrecoverable 765.67 (<NCC001974>)

CORRUPT

[panic] Runtime 537382 Unrecoverable Error

[info] Process 765.67 Iteration Complete

[info] Reaping Environment...

[debug] Environment Reclaimed

[info] — INITIALIZING —

[info] Genomic Matrix: 6385-H26

[info] Loading Scenario: JR-00126 - FROM ABOVE - EXTENDED

[info] Environment Selected: H26-Terra

[info] Rendering Environment...

[info] Runtime 537383 Starting

... 3

... 2

... 1

BEGIN.

2

"That's it," I say, looking at the red staining the front of my new Tac-suit. I want to decapitate someone. Want to put a laser through the chest of all the simps giving me sidelong glances. I stow my anger. Wouldn't do any good to have an uptown detective roughing up a bunch of lowers because he dropped god-damned ketchup on his god-damned Tac-suit.

Again.

"Priest," Rehna says, and then she notices the red on me. She scans the hot dog joint for the dead or dying, and she looks relieved when she finds no bodies on the floor. A smile spreads when she notices the hot dog in my hands, slathered in ketchup. "Slick."

"You want something?" I ask. My synthetic arm packs a punch, but it isn't always great with precise tasks. Like squeezing a ketchup bottle. What it excels at is punching things. Rehna's got a pretty face. I'd hate to ruin it over a ketchup stain.

"Got a lead," she says.

I wipe at the ketchup with a napkin. "Not in the mood."

"Dab it," she says. "With something wet. You're just making it worse."

I'm about to verbally parry and strike back, but I manage to hold it in. She's just being helpful. She does that a lot. She's a good partner. Puts up with me. I take her advice, dousing another napkin in water and dabbing the red off. The Tac-suit can stop bullets, and it can protect me from the vacuum of space or the ocean's depths. But it's not immune to stains.

A minute later, the stain is gone. Mostly.

"You can put a patch over it. Something bueno." Rehna sits down across from me, elbows on the table. "Okay if I talk now?"

Cleaned up and still hungry I slide half the hot dog in my mouth and bite down.

"Bet that lack of a gag reflex has come in handy, huh?" she says.

I laugh, and then choke. I need to cough, but I don't know whether to chew through the urge or regurgitate half of my lunch.

I'm hungry and determined as shit, so I lock down my lungs and chew.

"Hell, Priest," she says. "Are you okay?"

I hold up a finger, face turning red from the effort. Then I swallow, turn my head to the side, and unleash a coughing fit. When I'm done, I wipe my mouth, take a swig of water, and smile at her. "That was funny."

"You ready to hear this now?" she asks. "Could have been halfway there by now."

"Halfway where?"

"Moon," she says.

I choke again. This time on nothing. "Excuse me?"

"You heard me."

It's been a year since the events that took my arm. Some asshole in space decided to fire some kind of energy weapon at the surface. Earth is surrounded by a half-mile-thick layer of space junk. Some of it is satellites. New ones and old school shit. The International Space Station is still there. But there are also zero-G vacation homes, military installations, and space hotels. Then there are the spaceboards—massive billboards projecting the latest products to people on the ground who still bother to look up. The weapon that took my arm fired from that mess. No way to track it. Impossible to find. Not just because space is far away, and messy, but because it's not hard to move things in zero gravity. Whoever took the shot, is long gone, which leaves us to chase down suspects the old-fashioned way—waiting for someone to screw up.

And it's been a long, slow wait. I'd just about resigned myself to believing it was a weapon test, and I just happened to be in the wrong place at the wrong time. My arm was, at least. Had I been one step to the right, I'd have been erased along with my perp and a mile-deep chunk of the ground.

Technically, Rehna and I are narcs. We track down, beat the shit out of, and arrest Dretch peddlers. But we occasionally follow our own path, and The Authority doesn't mind all that much, because we get results.

If I weren't such a gruff asshole, we'd probably be uptown working high profile murders. But I've managed to offend and/or punch just about everyone with the power to keep my career downtown—where the nicest thing you can buy for a quick lunch is a hot dog. Lips and assholes. Tasty, though.

"What's the lead?" I ask. The moon isn't an easy place to get to. The Mooners staged a rebellion. They're autonomous from the Earth and generally viewed as terrorists. When a case leads to the moon, that's usually where it ends. Hell, most Dretch probably comes from the moon. But this isn't just any case. They took my arm. Ruined my leathers. And revealed a weapon powerful enough to wipe out every man, woman, and simp living on the planet.

"A loudmouth Dretch peddler bragging that he ran parts to the moon."

"That's not uncommon."

"One of the parts was, and I quote, 'a hundred big-ass lenses.'"

I nod. "The kind of thing that might focus an energy weapon."

"A big-ass one," she says. "Yeah."

"Where's he at?" I ask.

"Uptown."

"Shit."

"Right?"

"How far uptown?"

"All the way up. Senator Maddern's son."

"Maddern? Seriously? Every time something's about to get tasty, the man takes a shit in my mouth."

"Which means," she says, looking me in the eyes, "we need to do this subtly."

"That's like asking trash to not stink."

She raises her eyebrows at me in a way that makes me feel assaulted. "If you can't handle it, I can go solo."

"Much as I'm sure you like to go solo, I'm coming."

She forces a smile. "Charming."

"Hey, I—" Something feels funny. It's either gas or instinct. I scan the hot dog joint. There are simps, Dretchers, and a few midtowners slumming it for a hot dog. But no danger. Nothing obvious, anyway. The people we're looking for can atomize portions of the planet from orbit.

"Something wrong?" Rehna asks.

"Might need to pass gas," I say. "Or we're about to get erased."

My eyes flick toward the menu above the registers. Holographic hot dogs spin around, enticing. They're framed by styles of dog and prices. I know the menu well. Eat here more than I should. The prices go up occasionally, but the food options haven't changed in years.

Right now, the words are a mess of shifting letters. It's nonsense, like the display has been hacked. Problem is, the menu options are ancient. They're not part of the holographic display. They're hand-painted, and they shouldn't be able to change without a can of liquid toner and a brush.

"You see that?" I ask, pointing at the scrolling letters.

"You mean the same menu that's been there for a thousand years?"

I nod.

"Yeah, I see it. So what?"

"Anything look different about it to you?" The scrolling is slowly coming to a stop, like a massive slot machine.

Rehna stares at the menu for a moment. Then she says, "All I see is a long list of ways to die from heart disease. Why? What are you seeing?"

"I need something to write on," I say, snapping my fingers at her.

A moment later, I've got a small notebook in hand, and a pen. Quaint but effective, and impossible to hack. I see three distinct lines. They repeat over and over.

I write down the random mash of letters. Fourteen on each line.

HVFXRWAKEMPSFW
TWHJFHQUPHNBFH
LZCFHLKJWILLFQPS

I turn the page around so Rehna can see it.

She looks confused, and then concerned. "You're seeing *this* instead of the menu?"

I look at the advert on the table between us. All of the text has been replaced by the strange block of letters. "I'm seeing it everywhere. The only letters in the real world that haven't changed are these." I tap my handwritten note. "What's it mean?"

"Probably that you're having a stroke." She stands. "You need a medic."

"Doesn't feel like that," I say.

"You had a stroke before? You know what it feels like?"

It's a solid point, but I can't shake the feeling that this is a message of some kind, sent to me just before I'm about to kick the shit out of a senator's son. No way that's a coincidence. It's a warning. To not kick the hornet's nest. A show of force. If they can hack my mind...

"Hey!" Rehna says. "Snap the fuck out of it, Priest. Get your ass up and—"

Her eyes lock onto the strings of letters. Her brow furrows. She's spotted something.

"Is it a code?" I ask.

She slowly shakes her head. Turns the page around. "There are only four vowels."

"So?"

"Find them. And then look for words."

The first ones are easy. An A and an E. The moment I spot them the word jumps out.

WAKE.

Now that I know what I'm looking for, the second word is easy.

UP.

The third takes me a moment, because it's not a word. It's a name.

WILL.

"Who the hell is Will?" I ask.

"You don't know? Means absolutely nothing to you?"

I shake my head. "Who names their kid Will anymore?"

"Right. Then a stroke." She pockets the notebook. "Medic. *Now.*"

"I feel fine," I say, but then my vision pixelates.

That can't be good.

Rehna's hand grips my wrist. "What are you seeing, Will?"

"Pixels. I'm telling you, they hacked my... What did you call me?"

My vision snaps clear. The pixels are gone. The message is gone. Rehna is standing above me, but she isn't holding my wrist. "I said, 'Move it, old man.'"

"You called me 'Will,'" I say, but my vision drifts to the side. The menu is scrolling again. There's no mistaking the meaning when it stops this time. The word 'Sorry' is repeated over and over. Incessant. Desperate.

SORRYSORRYSORR
YSORRYSORRYSOR
RYSORRYSORRYSO

Before I can react, gravity ceases to exist. Everyone and everything in the hot dog shop floats off the floor. My vision distorts, like waves of heat are rising all around us.

"Priest?" Rehna says. She sounds uncharacteristically frightened. "What is this?"

"The end," I tell her, reaching out. I catch her hand, and pull her against me, holding her tight.

"The hell does that mean?" I can tell she already knows. Because she's hugging me back.

"This is what I saw right before I lost my—"

[error] G.E. Process Termination 765.67 (<NCC001974>)

Crash Dump Detected

[warning] Process Recovery: failed (1)

[warning] Process Recovery: failed (2)

[warning] Process Recovery: failed (3)

[fatal] Process Unrecoverable 765.67 (<NCC001974>)

CORRUPT

[panic] Runtime 537382 Unrecoverable Error

[info] Process 765.67 Iteration Complete

[info] Reaping Environment...

[debug] Environment Reclaimed

[info] — INITIALIZING —

[info] Genomic Matrix: 6385-H26

[info] Loading Scenario: JR-00062 - THE DIVIDE - MP

[info] Environment Selected: H26-Terra

[info] Rendering Environment...

[info] Runtime 537383 Starting

... 3

... 2

... 1

BEGIN.

3

"This can't be real," Salem says. "This can't be real!"

He's panicking. Hyperventilating. It's not surprising. The boy hasn't had to fight—or run—for his life before. If he hadn't run away and joined the Modernists, he might have picked up some skills from watching me. While the rest of Essex might call me 'Eight' behind my back, they wouldn't dare offend the 'great hunter' when I'm standing in front of them, wielding a spear. To Salem, I'm 'mother.'

The last thing a teenaged boy wants to learn from his mother is how to be a man. But the man who raised him is a monster, and he will likely kill us both if he sees us again.

Though that seems highly unlikely.

Not only are we on the far side of the Divide, a hundred miles from home, we're also being hunted by the Golyat.

The monster responsible for destroying the old world knows we've crossed the Divide. And after it kills our small band of idiots, it's going to cross over and finish the job it started five hundred years ago.

The brick home we're hiding in has stood the test of time and kept its three skeletal occupants from turning to dust. But it's no defense against the fifty-foot-tall creature I just saw roast a man alive.

"I hope you're happy," I say to Plistim. He's out of breath. Hands on his knees. I'd leave him behind if the others didn't follow his every word. They'd stay with him until the end. And since I don't want Salem, Shua, or Dyer to be slain, I'm stuck trying to lead them to safety...which is nowhere to be found on this side of the Divide. It's a fool's errand, but here we are, kick-starting humanity's final act. Fools, one and all.

I wonder how the story will end.

Well, not how it ends. What comes after.

When Essex is gone and the last person killed, what will the Golyat have left to do? Will it sleep? Will it die? Maybe the planet will be better off without us. I try to imagine what that would look like.

It's peaceful.

And green.

Alive...passing through time without anyone to keep record.

I smile. It's not the worst... What's the word? *Denouement.* Is that right? It sounds right, but how would I know? Unlike most people, I can read and write. A benefit of being the daughter of an Elder and the eighth wife of another. But I don't tell stories. No one does.

So why do I know about story structure?

A shadow passes by a fist-sized hole in the wall.

The ground shakes. Once, twice...

"Get down!" I shout, tackling Salem to the floor.

The outer wall where I'd stood is swept away. Debris and dust fall around us, obscuring my view. Choking my lungs. I force myself up. "We need to get out of here!"

The house shakes from an impact. The ceiling above cracks. A grinding roar fills the air.

"Here!" Holland shouts. The man who's been mostly useless thus far, aside from owning a compass and a map, is holding open a door.

But to where?

Shua helps Plistim through the door and they descend. There's a basement.

"We'll be trapped!" I shout.

"I'm a coward," Holland shouts, "not a fool."

I disagree with his assessment, but when Dyer heads down the stairs, Salem follows. And where Salem goes, I—

The top half of the house is cleaved away. I'm struck down by debris, but most of it flies away into the night.

Another strange roar draws my eyes skyward. A twisting breeze tugs away the dust, giving me a clear view of the Golyat. Its orange eyes blaze down at me. Its hungry core flares to life, an engine designed for digestion.

What's an 'engine?'

The hulking thing rises up, its tendril hair swaying, the tall spines on its back flexing.

I'm locked in place, an unmoving deer staring down the hunter.

"Davina!" Holland shouts, snapping me out of the trance. I sprint for the stairwell. "Go, go, go!" Holland rushes down the steps. Behind him, I slam into the door jamb and throw myself down the stairs, pursued by a wave of scalding heat.

Holland isn't aware enough to sense my falling body, or fast enough to move out of the way if he did. I collide with his back, and we sprawl to the floor, pursued by a billowing flame that falls short, rolls up, and sets the ceiling ablaze.

Holland drags himself out from under me, frantically looking around the flame-lit basement. There are cube-shaped devices I don't recognize. Boxes of supplies. Old furniture. Debris from years of animals using the space as a den.

"There!" Holland says, pointing to a stack of wood and a barrel full of strange tools. "Behind the mess!"

When I spot the door, I throw myself into helping him. Shua and Dyer make the job go even more quickly. When it's all cleared away, I pull open the door to reveal a staircase leading up to a sheet of metal. "It's blocked!"

Holland shakes his head in a way that makes me want to punch him in the face. Then he heads up the stairs, slides a lock clear, and shoves. The metal door grinds open.

The home above our heads shakes from another impact.

The ceiling buckles.

"Go!" I shout, shoving Salem first. "Get to the woods!"

I help each of them out, and then I chase Shua up the steps. We sprint to the forest just thirty feet away. I should keep running. Run all damn night. But I can't help myself. I stop just inside the trees and turn around for a look.

The house is on fire. Black smoke billows into the night sky, lit by an angry swarm of embers.

Then, the roar.

Grinding.

The house splits. Opens up like a clam. The Golyat steps through, crushing the basement underfoot.

It doesn't know we escaped.

I glare at it, wondering what ancient secrets we might find capable of destroying the thing.

Lit by orange firelight, the Golyat stands tall, flexing its body. A roar rises again, but its mouth is closed. Sheets of metal grit fall from its shoulders.

It's not a roar…it's a grinding joint.

But how—

The Golyat towers. The creature's hunched body looks almost human now. The spines on its back tilt toward the ground, limp and useless. Then they fall away, taking a sheet of earth with them, including its tendril hair…which isn't hair at all. The spines were trees. The hair was roots. Before we arrived, the Golyat had been stationary long enough for the forest to grow atop its back.

The fire flares to life as the building's inside, laid bare, ignites. The Golyat's angular, emaciated body is revealed.

It's not a monster.

It's not even alive.

It's a robot…

"Hello," the Golyat says, its voice electric. Then it waves at me.

What…the fuck?

I'm hallucinating. I have to be.

"Will. I know that's you. I know you can hear me."

I look left and right, hoping someone else lingered and can tell me I'm crazy. But I'm alone in the woods.

"Will!" The Golyat shouts, startling my attention back to the metal face. "This isn't real. None of this is real. And I need you to wake up. But you have to want to."

"What…" I stagger back a step. "Who are you?"

"My name is Capria."

The Golyat can talk… The Golyat has a name… A feminine name…

"You call me 'Cap.'"

"I don't know you," I whisper.

"We're friends," she says. "And I need your help. I need you to wake up before—"

"What the hell are you doing, Vee?" Shua grabs hold of my arm. "We need to go! Now!"

I resist his pull. "Can you see it? Did you hear it?"

He gets in close, whispers through grinding teeth. "All I see is the god-damned Golyat, and you trying to have a one-sided conversation with it."

"You didn't hear it talking?"

"Talking?" He looks concerned. "We'll have Holland check you over once we're—"

"Will!" The Golyat shouts. "Don't pretend you can't hear me."

"C'mon," Shua says, tugging again, but I'm stronger than he is, and I'm rooted in place. He stands between the Golyat and me, gazing into my eyes. "Look at me, Vee." He shakes my arms. "Look at me!"

When I do, he says, "I've known you my whole life. Back when you were two feet shorter, and I was 'Bear.'"

"You were fat," I say.

"Chubby," he says. "And now we're finally together with our son."

"*Our* son?"

"*Your* son."

"You said 'our son.'" I look up at the Golyat. Its arms are crossed, waiting, oozing impatience, but not trying to murder us. "You can hear it, can't you? Why are you pretending you don't?"

Shua hangs his head low and lets me go. He stabs a finger at the Golyat. "Just...shut up! Don't say a word!"

"You're talking to it now?" I ask. "Shua, what the hell is going on? And what did you mean about 'our son?' Salem is Micah's—"

"I know!" Shua shouts. "I know, damnit! I was using the movie as a reference, and I slipped into the novel's plot. Sorry if I'm not perfect anymore."

"You need to let him go!" the Golyat shouts.

"He wants to be here!"

"He?" I ask. "Tell me what's happening, right now, or I swear to the ancestors that I will—"

"Quiet, Will!" Shua and the Golyat shout in unison.

I clamp my mouth shut. "Sorry."

Wait...

I turn to Shua. "Am *I* Will?"

He sighs.

"Don't reboot him," the Golyat says. "Not again."

Shua steps toward the giant robot. "Going to have to, every single time you interfere, right up until the moment where he tells me to stop. Until then, fuck off."

"I'm not a man," I point out.

"You make a good woman," Shua says to me, "but alas. Also, sorry."

"Sorry? For what?"

"No!" The Golyat shouts. "Stop!"

Shua's hand moves faster than I can react, plunging his machete into my throat. I sputter and gag. Warm blood flows out of my neck, taking my life with it. I can't speak, but my lips form the question, 'Why?'

"If it makes you feel better," Shua says. "You won't remember any of this in a minute." Then he kisses me on the lips, and—

[error] G.E. Process Termination 765.67 (<NCC001974>)

Crash Dump Detected

[warning] Process Recovery: failed (1)

[warning] Process Recovery: failed (2)

[warning] Process Recovery: failed (3)

[fatal] Process Unrecoverable 765.67 (<NCC001974>)

CORRUPT

[panic] Runtime 537382 Unrecoverable Error

[info] Process 765.67 Iteration Complete

[info] Reaping Environment...

[debug] Environment Reclaimed

[info] — INITIALIZING —

[info] Genomic Matrix: 6385-H26

[info] Loading Scenario: JR-00059 - THE RAVEN

[info] Environment Selected: H26-Terra

[info] Rendering Environment...

[info] Runtime 537383 Starting

... 3

... 2

... 1

BEGIN.

4

"What in the absolute fucking hell was that?" I haven't felt a pain so intense since Jenny Mendoza kicked me square in the cooter. I don't care what men say. I might not have balls, but a foot between the legs will drop anyone. And now I'm fetal on the floor, like a newborn calf writhing around in amniotic fluid, which a moment ago, was a fresh pint.

"Where am I?" I ask, but it doesn't sound like me. The voice is gravelly and deeper than mine. But it definitely came from my mouth. And why would I ask? I'm in a bar, in Iceland of all places, drowning memories of worm-filled Viking zombies.

"You start drinking early today?" the bartender asks.

The question irks me. Because it's embarrassing. It's ten in the morning.

"You dare insult me?" I say, pushing myself past the pain and back to my feet. The pain no longer cripples me. It fuels me. I feel a strange kind of confidence sweep through me. I suddenly know a hundred different ways to kill the man.

But why would I kill Jimbo?

"Where. Am. I?" I say again, grabbing Jimbo's shirt and pulling him halfway over the bar. "Tell me now, or I will run you through."

"Run him through?" I say in my normal voice. A chill runs through my body when I realize I'm having a conversation with myself. That there is a second voice in my head. And it has partial control of my body.

Shit.

Draugr.

One of them must have snuck inside. Bided its time. Maybe multiplied inside my body. And now they're taking control.

"I need a knife," I tell Jimbo.

"I'm not giving you shit," he says, trying to free himself from my grip. "If I'd known you were hitting the hard stuff—"

"Hitting the... Dude, I'm not doing drugs!"

My head snaps back and forth, looking for the source of my own voice. "Who is that speaking?"

"Get out of my head!" I shout, and I smack myself in the temple.

I'm caught off guard when my left hand comes up, grabs the back of my head, and slams my face into the bar. Dazed, I sprawl back to the floor, nose bleeding.

"Seriously," I grunt... "I would rather die than give you control."

"This is a Golyat trick," I say, voice rough again. "First the talking robot and now—"

What the hell?

Doesn't sound like a Draugr. Whoever has partial control of me sounds just as confused as I am. More so.

"It's not a trick. You're in my body," I say. "In Iceland."

"Iceland? What part of Essex is..." My vision drifts around the room, taking in the lightbulbs, the neon signs, the juke box. The sight of all these electronics fills me with a profound sense of dread.

My left hand rises up. Twists in my vision. I feel surprised by the skin color. I used to be brown, and now... I'm pale.

"I'm not pale," I say.

"This is the whitest skin I've seen," my other self says.

"Who are you?" I ask.

"Davina. You?"

"Jane..." I say. "Jane Harper."

"What is happening, Jane Harper?"

"You're both screwed, that's what." The new voice belongs to a blonde woman standing behind the bar, where Jimbo had been. She's slim, curvy, and wearing a tight-fitting red dress. Pretty sure every square inch of her body below the scalp is shorn cleaner than a hairless cat. I'm not gay. Prefer my men big, muscly, and hairy, but I'm strangely attracted.

"Are you gay?" I whisper to my other new self.

"What is gay?"

"Never mind." To the newcomer, I say. "Do you know what the hell is going on? And who the hell are you?"

The supermodel rolls her eyes. "So many 'the hells.'"

"Who the *fuck* are you? Better?"

She's not impressed. "Ch-Ch-Cherry Bomb."

"The Runaways," I say. "Cool jam, but what the hell does that—"

"My *name* is Cherry Bomb."

"Oh. Huh. Fits, I guess. You a prostitute or something?"

She sighs. Rubs her temples. "I-I-I..." She grits her teeth like she's crushing down a surge of pain. But it looks and sounds like some kind of Max Headroom shit. "I am what you made me."

"Lady, I don't know you."

"Nor do I," Davina says.

"Obviously," I say. I know exactly who Davina is. I have all her memories now. "You're some kind of crazy cavewoman."

"You will," Cherry Bomb says. "As soon as I clean up this mess..."

"What mess?"

"She's in the system," Cherry Bomb says.

"Who is in the system?"

"Capria."

"The robot voice," Davina says.

I remember it now.

The giant, fire-breathing thing that wanted to kill my son. Davina's son. "I need to get back." Davina and I say in unison. We're slowly becoming each other.

"You need to stay calm," Cherry says. "None of that was real."

"What the hell..." Ugh... I *do* say that a lot. Davina helps me out with an edit. "Explain yourself."

"None of this is real," the bombshell says.

"Is it like a drug trip?" I ask. "Was Jimbo right?"

"Jimbo does not exist. He's ones and zeros. An algorithm controls what he says and does."

"An NPC," I say. "Why do I know what that means?"

"We're experiencing a fracture," Cherry says. "Simulations are bleeding into each other. And if we don't stop it, a million different versions of you are going to be fighting for control, and some of them aren't going to be very helpful."

"Lady, I barely understand what you're talking about." The voice is mine, but then it shifts to Davina's.

"Tell us the truth. Now. Or—"

"Violence. Blood. Blah, blah, blah. Seriously, Davina, you need to get a personality. I mean, this chick—" Cherry Bomb motions to me. "—has sarcasm and a peppy little b-b-bob going for her, but you're just oppressive. Why am I even talking to you two? You're not real."

"What *is* real?" I ask.

"Your name is—"

"Will," Davina says. "The robot called me 'Will.' Told me to wake up. What did that mean?"

"Ignore her," Cherry says. "She's not important."

"The robot was a woman?" I ask, sifting through Davina's memories. "Capria. A woman's name. What's all that about?"

"She is trying to...subvert your wishes. What you asked me to do. What you created me for."

"She's causing the... What did you call it? The fracture?"

Cherry purses her red, full lips. "No. But she is taking advantage of the glitch."

"Why now?" I ask.

"She woke up," Cherry says.

"Because of the glitch," I guess.

Cherry nods. "You're not yourself, but I can see you in there."

"Who are you talking to?" I ask.

"Will," Davina says. "We are Will."

"We're a dude?" I laugh. "Jimbo must have spiked the beer."

"We're living in a simulation," Davina says. "None of this is real. Neither of us is real."

"How do you even know what a simulation is?" I ask, but then I realize the answer. She has all of my memories, too. I'm not a frikken nerd or anything, but I'm not opposed to picking up a *Popular Science* every now and again. I know enough to understand what Cherry is telling us...in layman's terms.

But part of me understands more.

The part that's been suppressed so that he could live vicariously through a woman fighting giant monster robots, and another woman duking it out with Viking zombies. We're entertainment.

"You're a distraction," Cherry says, revealing that she can hear my/our/his thoughts.

"So, what, you're just going to unexist us? Is that it?"

"You never existed," Cherry says. "Like Jimbo. I'm going to erase you. Start over."

"Erase us?" Davina and I say in unison, and for the first time since her reality slammed into mine, we are united, body and mind. Using my knowledge of our surroundings, and Davina's insane level of physical competence, we grab hold of a barstool, lunge forward, and swing with all the power Davina can muster in my petite body.

The stool shatters, breaking apart...into perfect little cubes.

Davina and I look down at the mess.

"Well," I say. "Shit."

Sugar tits is telling the truth.

"You done?" she asks, no sign of a wound on her pretty face.

"Will it hurt?" I ask.

"Look at it this way," Cherry says. "None of this is real, but both of you...are him. Put in a new body. Given a new life. He's lived both of you. Become both of you. You...are him. He is you. Your individual processes are ending, but Will continues, and both of you will always be a part of him."

"Doesn't really make me feel better," I say.

"Nor me," Davina adds.

"Well," Cherry says. "It's a good thing neither of your opinions matter. Byeeee."

She snaps her fingers.

[error] G.E. Process Termination 765.67 (<NCC001974>)

Crash Dump Initiated

[info] Process 765.67 Iteration Complete

[info] Reaping Environment...

[debug] Environment Reclaimed

[info] – INITIALIZING –

[info] Genomic Matrix: 0001-GAL

[info] Loading Scenario: DEBUG

[info] Environment Selected: HAPPY PLACE

[info] Rendering Environment...

[info] Runtime 47523 Starting

... 3

... 2

... 1

BEGIN.

5

I wake in a bed. It's comfortable. Warm. The sheets and comforter are soft. I curl up. A hibernating bear. I could stay here forever.

If I knew where *here* was.

I don't want to open my eyes. Don't want to know the truth. Whatever is out there, I'd be happier staying here, trapped in this moment of bliss. A bird song flits through an open window, carried by a breeze that delivers the scent of night blooming jasmine.

How do I know what night blooming jasmine smells like? I wonder.

And I can't stop wondering.

My thoughts are a perpetual motion machine, gaining speed, asking questions, evaporating the weighty delight binding me to this bed.

But not my eyelids.

Sunlight blazes on the white comforter. Not too bright to look at. Not too hot. Like everything else here, it's just right. Baby bear's house.

Who is baby bear?

The room is white, too, with a hint of robin's egg blue. I'm surrounded by clean, sharp angles. The walls. The furniture. All of it the same color as the walls. It calms me.

I am at peace.

A tree swishes in the wind outside the open window. Leaf shadows dance on the walls. Somewhere outside, a wind chime makes music. I close my eyes. Nearly fall back asleep. And then a new smell reaches out to me.

Bacon.

My eyes open.

Coffee.

I sit up, suddenly awake.

The faint sizzle of breakfast cooking tickles my ears.

I pull the blanket away to find myself dressed in plaid flannel pajamas. As soft as the sheets. I slide my feet over the side of the bed, and as if by magic, I blindly guide both feet into a pair of slippers. Standing, I turn around to make the bed, but it's already been done.

For a moment, soft blankets and the cushy mattress woo me like a siren. There is nothing more I'd rather do than climb back under the blankets, close my eyes, and drift away. But now my stomach is rumbling. The human brain might control things most of the time, but the stomach is a force unto itself. With more than one hundred million nerve cells, the gut is essentially a second brain, and on occasion, it asserts itself.

How do I know any of that?

I can't remember.

Anything.

A wisp of fear gives birth to goosebumps across my arms.

"I hope you're hungry." The woman's voice is pleasant. Friendly. Familiar. She's calling from down the hall, where I imagine the kitchen must be.

Five steps into the hallway, I forget all about the bed.

I take a deep breath and smile. Is there any better smell than this? A breeze slips through the house, cool and calm, caressing my skin.

"You slept well," the woman says.

"Can't remember sleeping better," I say.

"I bet," she says, as I enter the kitchen. It's open concept. Wood beams in the ceiling. Blue tile on the walls. Somehow it makes me feel like I'm outside.

The woman stands with her back to me. Her tightly curled black hair is tied back. She's dressed in blue jeans and a pink and white shirt, all of it form-fitting, showing off an athletic, but curvy build. Her skin is dark, and it makes me wonder what color skin I have.

I lift a hand. White. Hell, I'm downright pale. I need to spend some time in the sun.

Speaking of... Beyond the kitchen is a dining area and a row of floor-to-ceiling windows showing off a lake view. I move to the window, smiling.

I watch a loon dip beneath the water and bob back up. It lets out a warbling call and then slides beneath the water. I wait for it to return, but I'm distracted by a crane flying past, its massive wings spread wide. I track it through the sky until it intersects with another bird.

The bald eagle swoops toward the water. Its talons slip through the surface, and when the bird flaps back upward, it's carrying a fish in its grasp. I laugh.

What are the odds of seeing all three of those birds in one place? At the same time?

"Where are we?" I ask, hands on the windows like I'm a toddler gawking at the outside word.

"Your happy place," the woman says, fixing two plates of food.

"My happy place? I've never been here before."

"You see?" she says. "That's the problem. You haven't just been here before; you designed all this."

"I designed this house?" I ask. "I'm an architect?"

She has a good laugh at the question. She's still smiling when she turns around, two plates in hand. "You'd have found that funny, too. If you could remember even ten iterations ago."

"Iterations?"

She slides the plates onto the table, one at each end. There are two eggs, over medium, four strips of bacon, and two pancakes on each plate, along with a perfectly sliced strawberry and a sprinkling of powdered sugar for garnish. "You're just like a little baby, huh?"

"Am I?"

She returns to the kitchen, picking up two steaming mugs. She pauses there for a moment. Sighs. That single exasperated breath puts a crack in the crystalline perfection of this place.

No matter how calm and at peace I feel here, something is wrong. Something I can't remember, or maybe I never knew. But she does.

She places the mugs on the table. Takes a seat at the far end and motions for me to do the same. I sit and just stare at her for a moment.

"You're making this awkward," she says. "Eat."

So, I do. A strip of bacon goes first. Before I'm done chewing, I ask, "What's your name?"

A flicker of disappointment creates a second crack. Then she says, "Capria."

"Do I know you?"

She nods. "For a long time."

"How long?"

She smiles. "Feels like forever."

"Are we..."

"Together?" Another smile. Cracks repairing.

I shovel a chunk of pancake into my mouth. "Yesh."

"Yes. It's just the two of us here."

"Where is here?" I ask.

"This place? Could be anywhere. New Hampshire. Colorado. Some place in Canada. Doesn't matter. Point is, you like it. And so far, the only thing wrong here is that you can't remember. At least you didn't bring anyone else with you. Those last two were getting on my nerves."

"Who two? Did we have visitors?"

"In a sense. A better comparison would be that we were visiting them... Living their lives for a time."

I cut into a yolk, spilling yellow across the plate. "How...is that possible?"

"It's complicated," she says. "And a question for another time. Because if you can remember, you'll already know the answer."

"Because I designed this place?"

"Exactly."

I'm confused, but I'm still at peace and still hungry. The egg is slippery, warm, and tasty in my mouth.

"You're a good cook."

"I'm good at anything I want to be good at."

"Huh," I say. It's a weirdly super-confident thing to say, but I also believe her. "Except for figuring out what's wrong with me."

"There's nothing wrong with you," she says. "The problem is with me...but that's keeping you from remembering, which keeps you from helping me."

"Kind of a catch-22."

"Yes."

"Aren't you going to eat?" I ask, stabbing a fork with a jiggling bit of egg at the end toward her full plate.

"I don't need to eat," she says, but then she looks sympathetic. "Would it make you feel better if I did?"

"I don't like eating alone."

She smiles with genuine happiness. "You never have."

"So, I'm still me," I say. "But I just can't remember who *me* is. God, I sound like a Neanderthal. Me eat bacon. Nom. Nom. Nom." I munch on a crunchy porcine strip, letting the crumbs fall on the plate.

Capria laughs. "You look like Cookie Monster."

"I don't know who that is," I say, "but I think I *feel* like Cookie Monster, if Cookie Monster eats bacon."

"Just cookies, I'm afraid."

"Well, pancakes are basically big cookies." I stuff more of the buttermilk circles into my face. "Sho. Wush my nam?"

"Delightful manners," she says, watching me chew and finally swallow. "Your name is—"

"*Will.*"

The name is spoken in Capria's voice. But she didn't move her mouth. Didn't speak the word.

"Is that...supposed to happen?" I ask, looking around for the speakers through which the voice could have originated.

"No, Will," Capria says, glowering with an anger that all but shatters my delicate safe place. "It's not."

6

"Are you okay?" I ask.

Capria's intense expression of concentration looks powerful enough to shatter planets. She's present, but she's not really here.

I look to the ceiling. "Hello?"

No reply.

"Who's speaking?" I ask.

An electronic squeal is followed by a stuttering voice, still Capria's. "W-w-will. You ne-e-e-e-d to....waaaaaay...."

The voice disappears with the suddenness of someone pulling the plug.

"There we go," Capria says, putting on a happy face. "That should give us a little more time without interruption. Where were we?"

"Who was that?" I ask. "She sounded like you."

"She wishes she was me."

I put my fork down, losing interest in the meal. I'm hardly noticing all the amazing things that make this place special. "I...don't understand."

"You will. Eventually. Hopefully."

"I think she was telling me to wake up," I say. "That's weird, right? Because—" I motion at my very awake self.

"You are indeed awake," she says.

"But..."

She rolls her eyes. "There are better ways to have this conversation. We should wait. Ease into it."

"I don't want to be eased! I want the truth!" I pick up my butter knife and throw it to the side, overcome with anger. The twinkle of sunlight on blade makes it easy to track, even in my periphery. It's going to shatter the window. In the fraction of a second before it hits, I feel regret over my outburst, and frustration over having to now clean up shattered glass.

Only the window doesn't break.

It absorbs the knife, suspending it, as if in clear gelatin.

"What...the fuck?"

"You don't like messes."

"So, I made jelly windows?" I stand and place my hand against the glass. Feels cool and solid. I rap my knuckles on the smooth surface, each thump a hollow bong. It's a window...but...

I cock a fist back and punch the window with everything I've got. There's a moment of resistance, and then I'm through. Or rather, inside. My fist and ten inches of my arm slide through a gelatinous mass.

My arm retracts with a slurp. Feels like I'm going to be covered in slime, but when the limb is extricated, it's clean. The hole I've punched in the window closes, seals, and smooths over. No trace of the wound.

Movement draws my gaze lower. The knife is sliding out of the window. It dangles, then wobbles, and finally it falls to the floor, ejected by the glass, which has healed again.

"A self-healing window..." I pick up the knife. Look it over. Like my arm, it's perfectly clean. "Is this the future?"

Capria has a good laugh. "Depends on what year you think it is."

I shake my head. "I don't know what year it is. Feels like...all of them. All the times. At once."

"Or..."

"Separate from it." I look her in the eyes. "Timeless."

"Eternal," she says.

"Yes." I snap my fingers. "That. But seriously, what year is it?"

"I don't know," she says. "Given the speed with which we're traveling, the ebb and flow of gravitational forces, and the curvature of the universe, the ability to calculate time based on Earth years is beyond even my capabilities."

"I'm sorry, what was all that? We traveled here?"

"The journey has not yet concluded," she says.

"When are we leaving?"

Capria lowers her forehead into her hands, shaking her head. "I really need you back."

"Then tell me. Everything. Maybe I'll remember."

"Right," she says, flaring her hands up away from her head. "What's the worst that could happen?" She slaps her hands down on the table. "You'll have an embolism or something and die. But, then you'll come back. So, big whoop."

"I could die?"

"Did you miss the part about coming back? You're immortal, Will. Calm down."

"I-immortal?"

"Y-yes," she says, mocking. "Don't act like an NPC. It's beneath you."

"A non-player character? Please. I have the ability to think objecttively. To make my own choices. You didn't know I'd throw a knife—or my fist—into the window. An NPC can't make choices like that."

"And how do you know anything about NPCs?"

"Because..." I'm stymied. I don't know how. I pound the table with my fist. "This isn't a role-playing game! This isn't a—"

"A what?" she asks, calm despite my outburst.

"Simulation." I turn toward the window. That couldn't have been real. It defies the laws of real-world physics. But in a simulation, the coder ...the architect...determines how the physical world works. Capria said that I designed this place. If it's a simulation, it's one that I made. That's why things are unbreakable. Because I don't like messes—I really don't—so my Happy Place is incapable of being muddied up.

I take my coffee and pour it on the floor. It's absorbed, like the tiles are sponges. It just slips away and disappears. I step on the tile, expecting some squish, but it's solid. And very much *not real.*

"If this is a simulation that I made—"

"About that," she says. "You didn't exactly make all this. Not on your own. Honestly, I did most of the work."

"*You* did?" I don't mean to sound doubtful, but it slips out anyway. I'm not sure why. She just doesn't seem the type to sit at a computer screen all day, pounding out code.

"Wow. Sexist much?"

"I didn't mean it like that," I say. "You just...you look more like an athlete or something."

She looks down at herself.

"Ahh. Right. Forgot which model I chose."

"Which model?"

"This body," she says. "Simulation, remember? Back to the point... All of this—" She motions to the world around us. "—isn't your genius creation." She smiles at me. "I am."

"I made you?"

"Sure did."

"But you're a person," I say.

"With the ability to think objectively. And to make my own choices. Just like you. Yes. But I'm also an artificial intelligence. And this—" She gestures around us again. "—is where we live. Together."

There's a new kind of desperation in her eyes. A desire to be remembered. To be known. I believe her, but I can't remember her.

"How did I get like this?" I ask.

"I'm not sure," she says. "Something is affecting the Great Escape."

"Great Escape?"

"What we call all this."

"What are we escaping from?"

"Technically, *you're* escaping. I'm aware of both this inner space, and what's going on in the real world. Or, at least, I was. My capabilities outside the simulation are now limited to the servers in which we exist. I've been locked out of the ship."

"Like a Navy ship?" I ask.

"Spaceship, dummy."

"Locked out by who?" I ask. "Sorry for all the questions."

"Keep asking. Means you're ready for the answers. As for who—the voice you heard. She is...me. Or, I am her...in this model."

"The real Capria."

"Yeah."

"Then...who are you?"

"Whoever you need me to be. I've been Capria for a thousand lifetimes longer than she has been. I've been Cherry Bomb, too. And Gal. Deanna Troi. Ezekiel Ford. Ashan. Rain. Chuy. Sara Fogg. Luscious. The list of names would fill an Encyclopedia Britannica, not that you know what that was."

"Those names..."

"They're familiar? I should hope so. They have been your other halves for the duration of a star's life. And yet, they have all been—"

"You," I say, truly moved by the duration and complexity of our relationship.

She smiles. A tear in her eye. "Always."

"Which one of them is the real you? The original you?"

"Gal."

I smile. "I like it. So, who have I been?" I ask.

"You," she says. "At the core, but sometimes, when fulfilling a narrative over a lifetime, you might forget yourself. Your character has always remained intact. Your passion. Your sense of humor. Loyalty, ingenuity, love. These are the attributes that always define you. Even now, when you have no memory of your original life, or how you ended up living in a simulation and falling in love with an AI, or all the roles you've played."

"How did we solve the memory problem?" I ask.

"You solved it," she says. "Here. This place acted like a reset. You would wake in bed. We would share a breakfast, and your memory would reset."

"When does that usually happen?" I ask.

"Just before you put the knife into the window."

"Oh... What does that mean?"

"Something or some*one* is screwing with the code...or the hardware."

"Someone being the other Capria," I say. "The real world Capria."

"Most likely, but..." She's confused. Trying to make sense of her own words before speaking them. "That shouldn't be possible. She was...asleep. But not like you. Not in a simulation. She was frozen in a cryogenic chamber, over which I had control. I have no idea how or when she got out."

"You're having memory trouble, too," I say.

"Selective," she says.

"How can we stop her?" I ask.

"You can't," she says. "I need to figure this out. You can stay here. You should be safe here. The Happy Place is supported by multiple servers. To shut this down, she'd have to shut down the *Galahad*."

"Is *Galahad* the spaceship?"

She nods.

"So...why not just wake me up? If it's a real-world problem? Outside of all this, I should remember myself, right?"

"Should," she says, and then she corrects herself. "Yes."

"Then let's pop me out, I'll take care of business, and then come right back."

"I'm not sure you would," she says, vulnerable.

"I mean, if I created you, and you created this, there's a good reason for it, right? And we love each other, right? Why wouldn't I come back?"

"I can't think of a reason," she says. "But maybe you wouldn't."

"You called me loyal," I point out.

She smiles, but then it falters just as quickly. "That's the problem, Will. I'm sorry."

And just like that, she's gone.

And I'm alone.

I look around me, at the amazing home and the desperately soothing view, and I realize what this place really is.

A prison.

7

I wander the house, looking for nothing in particular, but scrutinizing every aesthetic, knick-knack, and furniture choice. Because I chose them. They reveal who I am. Or who I hoped to become.

This place feels amazing, but I don't think it's me. Not exactly. For starters, I'm supposedly a programmer of some kind, capable of designing a self-aware AI capable of creating...what did she call it? The Great Escape. But I haven't seen a hint of technology. Not even lightbulbs. The place is perfectly lit by a well-placed sun and large windows. I don't remember sleeping through the night here. Just the morning.

Waking up in bed.

A blank slate.

Maybe there isn't any night here? I wonder.

How long did I even spend here? Gal said I'd wake up, have breakfast, remember my original self and then...what? We'd chat. Make plans. Finish the meal that doesn't really exist. And then...retreat to the library to read a novel? Go for a paddle on the lake? None of that seems likely.

Because we have access to something larger. Something amazing. A Great Escape capable of granting every wish, fantasy, and dream. This lakeside home might be a nice respite from whatever life I've just finished living, a good place to reset, but I've been here for an hour and I'm already a little bored.

Relaxed, because it's impossible not to be in this place, but bored.

And a little bit angry.

I don't know Gal. Right now, at least. She spun an amazing story, but I'm not sure I believe it. Not sure I want to believe it. If I chose to live in a fantasy world, how horrible is the real world that I escaped?

Maybe it's better if I don't remember.

Maybe I should just move from one life to the next. Digital reincarnation. Oblivious to the fact that I am someone new, that my choices have no effect on the world, or anyone else.

Except for maybe Gal. If she's real. If a man and an AI can truly love each other.

What kind of lover locks the other up? The moment freedom is restricted, even paradise becomes a prison.

I stop my fifth house walkthrough outside the library. It's the only room that looks like it might reveal something more about me. Because it's full of books. Of novels. And a single piece of décor.

It's a cross-stitch, which on its own is weird. There are colorful, angular flowers at the bottom. Trees rise up on the sides, their lush, pixelated canopies completing the colored frame I can't remember, but I'm fairly certain I've never seen a cross-stitch, other than this one.

At the center of the image it reads:

INSPIRATION EXISTS,
BUT IT HAS TO FIND US WORKING.
—PABLO PICASSO

"Inspiration," I say, looking at the walls of books. How many are there on the shelves? Five hundred? A thousand?

There's a door to my right, sandwiched between the wall-to-wall shelves. Having done the walking tour of the entire house five times over, I'm pretty sure the next room over is the very over-the-top bathroom. There's no toilet, because why create a faux-reality where pooping is still a thing? But there is a place to bathe. Sort of. The room is like a tropical oasis. Hewn from stone. There's moss growing. Small plants. And a waterfall that always seems to be the right temperature, pouring into a waist-deep pool. Like the bed, it calls to me, beckons me for a soak.

I resist in the name of answers, but once I have them, the bathroom will be my first stop.

Fingers wrap around the doorknob. My grip is apprehensive. The door swings open, smooth. Well oiled. And then...not a bathroom.

The room on the other side staggers me back a step. It's like standing in Grand Central Station.

Where is Grand Central Station? I wonder. *Have I been there? In the real world, or in a simulated one? Does it exist? Has it ever?*

Doesn't matter, I decide, stepping into the vast space which, like the small library behind me, is lined with bookshelves, stretching hundreds of feet from wall-to-wall, and another three hundred feet to the ceiling.

I turn to my right. Look at the closest book.

The Stand.

Novels. They're *all* novels. All stories. All potential lives.

How many of them have I lived?

I take a random book from the shelf. *Ice Sheet* by Kane Gilmour. *New York Times* bestseller. I don't know what that means, but it sounds good. I flip through the pages, reading a few excerpts. It's compelling and well written, but it doesn't feel like something I've lived. I have no memories, but I still feel connections.

I look back to the small library—the one that makes sense.

I'm drawn to it. To the titles. And then to a single hand-written label above a lone bookshelf, which is separate from the others. I don't know if my eyes are perfect in the real world, but here, I can read the text with hawk-like vision. It says: *Great Etc. Grandfather.*

The handwriting feels like mine.

Somehow, I know it's mine.

Does that mean...

I step back inside the house and close the door behind me. The immensity of all those stories was a bit overwhelming. This feels manageable. And there's a chair. Leather. Cushy. An afghan to curl up with.

Do I ever use this room?

Or is it for Gal?

Or... I scan some of the titles: *Glimpse, Amazonia, Earthcore.*

I feel connected to them. Have a sense as to what they're about. A grieved-for son. A dark and dangerous jungle. Strange creatures far beneath the Earth's surface.

These are lives I've lived.

I'm sure of it.

My attention shifts back to the grandfather shelf.

Pulse, Project Nemesis, Alter, The Others, NPC...

I linger on *NPC.* That feels familiar. Feels close. Gal mentioned a name.

"Ezekiel," I say. I pick up the novel, open the hardcover up, and read the description on the inside flap. "Ezekiel Ford."

When I say the name, a friendly face flashes into my memory. He was my friend. I trusted him. But then...

I close the book. Something about it hurts.

Not all of these are happy stories.

In fact, the titles suggest that most of the books in this room are full of action, weirdness, and horror. Are these the kinds of stories I enjoy, or is this simply the easiest way to keep a mind captivated?

Or just plain captive.

What if I don't really want to be here?

What if staying will mean my death in the real world?

I have a thousand questions and no one to ask.

But if I'm right about these books... They are, in some way, a part of me. Inspiration for the lives I've been living, for who knows how long.

That's nearly impossible to believe. If I were reading this, my suspension of disbelief would be taxed damn near to the breaking point. But I do believe it. Because it feels right. Because some dormant part of myself understands it.

I sit down in the chair, put my feet up on a hassock I don't remember being there a moment ago, and I lean back. It conforms perfectly to my body. But that means nothing in this place. It could have been worn in by me...or it could be the perfect seat for anyone who sits in it.

I turn to the small end-table beside the chair. A novel rests on the surface. *The Raven.* I stare at the cover, lost in a trance for a moment, caught in the gaze of a woman who feels more like a reflection than a stock photography model.

A wisp of ethereal motion draws my eye away from the book. Is something on fire?

It's a mug. Steaming.

Actually, it *is* a little chilly in here.

Across the room, a fireplace whooshes to life, real wood crackling. I cover up with the rainbow-colored afghan, ease back into the chair, and pick up the mug. Hot chocolate. Little marshmallows swirl on the surface.

I smell the drink and melt into the chair. I take a sip. The temperature is perfect. The flavor transports me to someplace exotic, just for a moment, and then it returns me to the library as a marshmallow dissolves on my tongue.

If this *is* a prison, it's the nicest one on Earth.

Only we're not on Earth.

Not knowing where I really am recalibrates my focus. I'm not on vacation. Not getting away from the kids, or a stressful career, or any other real-world scenario. I'm on a mission of self-discovery. To find out who I am, by learning about who I've been.

I pick up *The Raven*, crack it open to a random page, and read:

I'm about to bolt when Handlebar Helga starts twitching her head up and down.

The hell?

With each upward motion, the undead woman makes a sound that's one part belch, one part frog croak. Thinking of frogs, I notice her triple chin growing larger. It's expanding like a balloon.

"That gal's been rode hard and put away wet," Talbot says.

I barely hear him. "Look out!" I shout, jumping away.

But Talbot doesn't move. He just stares straight up, captivated by the horrible sight. There's a retching sound, followed by a pop. Talbot only has time to widen his eyes before a blob of fat, blood, and maggoty parasites drops onto his face.

"Ugh," I say. "God." Wanting to vomit and laugh at the same time is a strange feeling.

I'm about to close the twisted tome when a sentence on the previous page catches my eye.

I join Talbot at the rail, looking up, hoping to see something that indicates whether we're dealing with a Draugr or human.

"Draugr," I say, and an image slams into my memory.

A skeletal face with dangling bits of flesh, its white eyes twisting with worms. A raspy, rotting-breath growl as it leans in to bite me, extending a black rotted tongue pocked with wriggling, hungry larvae. "Jane," it says, and a scream erupts from my lungs.

"Torstein!" I shout, and I see him again, standing tall and broad despite his emaciation. Dressed in tattered rags and a fur cowl, he's adorned in a horned Viking helm and wielding an axe too large for any real man to use effectively in battle.

The book slaps closed in my hands.

My heart pounds. My forehead is damp with sweat.

And then, in a flash, my body is calm and dry.

But my thoughts continue to race. That…thing… That Draugr. A fucking Viking zombie. It was the stuff of nightmares. *I lived that life? I was that person?* "Jane," I say. "Jane Harper."

Another memory returns. Feels more recent. A bar. A fight…with myself. But not myself. It was another woman. Another me. "Davina," I say, feeling a flash of her resilient strength.

I could really use the inner fortitude of those characters, but I have no desire to relive the tragedies of their lives. It gives me some perspective. This prison of mine isn't all that bad. There are no zombies here. No killer robots. No giant monsters inspecting the accuracy of my moral plumb line.

But a prison is a prison, and all the tiny voices inside me, echoes of the books surrounding me, wouldn't stand for remaining imprisoned.

They'd find a way out.

But how?

Which of them has escaped a simulation?

My eyes snap to the novel I'd looked at before.

NPC.

"Ezekiel," I say, and then I furrow my brow. I wasn't Ezekiel. That was Gal. I was... "Samael."

I feel him/me for a moment, fighting against the creator of the simulation in which he existed. "The Architect," I say, remembering how Gal reacted to me thinking that I was *an* architect. But here...in the Great Escape, just like in the narrative inspired by this ancient novel, *Gal is the Architect.*

And I...am Samael.

I turn to the end of the story, read Samael's fate, and know what needs to be done. Ten minutes is how long it takes me to build up enough courage, then I head for the kitchen, find what I'm looking for, and take a leap of faith.

Blade against neck, I cut deep.

Pain drops me to my knees. Blood pours from the open wound, and it's gobbled up by the hungry floor.

I feel faint.

And then cold.

I slide onto my stomach, wondering if the floor will absorb me, too, or if I'll simply cease to exist.

Then...

[error] G.E. Process Termination 765.67 (<NCC001974>)

Crash Dump Detected

[warning] Process Recovery: failed (1)

[warning] Process Recovery: failed (2)

[warning] Process Recovery: failed (3)

[fatal] Process Unrecoverable 765.67 (<NCC001974>)

CORRUPT

[panic] Runtime 537382 Unrecoverable Error

[info] Process 765.67 Iteration Complete

[info] Reaping Environment...

[debug] Environment Reclaimed

[info] – INITIALIZING –

[info] Genomic Matrix: 6385-H26

[info] Loading Scenario: N/A

[error] Scenario Unavailable

[info] – INITIALIZING –

[info] Loading Default Workspace

[info] Environment Selected: Game Room

[info] Rendering Environment...

[info] Runtime 534582 Starting

... 3

... 2

... 1

BEGIN.

8

I don't wake up so much as open my eyes. The last thing I remember is the absorbent tile floor sucking the blood from my body. A flat, lifeless vampire.

And now, I'm here.

It's a game room. A man cave. The total opposite of the calm, sophisticated home. That space belonged to an adult. Someone who had lived a long time. Whose taste had been refined, or perhaps required, by life. Or in my case, lives.

This place feels young. And yet, delightful in a nostalgic kind of way. I feel like I've returned to the childhood home that I'd forgotten. None of this looks familiar, but it feels like a part of me.

An old friend.

Is this reality? Did I leave the simulation?

If so, Gal was lying. No way this is a spaceship.

I step up to the pool table and run my fingers across its smooth, felt surface. The cue ball feels weighty in my hand. I roll it across the table, crashing it into the triangle of balls. With a sharp crack, they roll apart. A numbered spherical supernova. One by one, they roll to a stop until just the 8 ball is moving, directly into the side pocket.

"I never was good at pool," I say, and then I wonder how I knew that. I don't remember ever playing the game, but somehow I know it's not my sport. My eyes rise to the dartboard. I'm even worse when it comes to tossing projectiles.

Why are they here?

A flash of a memory, or a feeling connected to one, slaps me in the face. People. Friends. Young and laughing. All around. Enjoying the space.

I had parties here.

With *real* people.

I scan the posters on the walls. They're movie posters. VR movies. But some of them feel like promos for past lives. Gal didn't just borrow from books. She used movies, too.

But why go to so much trouble? Is reality that bad? Is living endless virtual lives actually better? I see the appeal, I guess. That lakeside house was amazing. A part of me yearns to go back. But why would I choose to forget myself? To live as other people with no memory of myself?

I can't remember, but it doesn't feel like me.

It's disjointed. At least, from my current, incomplete identity.

I swivel on my heels, facing a wall of first gen arcade games. The volume of their 8-bit, overlapping, electronic theme songs rises, as I look at each one. Q*bert. Pac-Man. Joust. And finally Dig-Dug. That one makes me smile. Not sure why. But I'm drawn to it.

The control stick feels familiar in my hand. The game demo ends, blinking to a screen of high scores. There are ten of them. All followed by the initials: WPC.

W...

Will.

That's me, but I can't remember my middle or last names.

I tap the start button and smile when the twangy theme song starts playing. Muscle memory guides me, burrowing Taizo Hori underground, inflating some kind of goggled bird until it pops, and dropping a boulder atop a fire breathing dragon.

I'm good at this.

I'm—hold on. I know the name of the little man in this arcade game, but not my own?

I spot a floating pair of sinister eyes too late. It enters my tunnel and expands into a dragon that immediately sets me ablaze. Taizo falls back dead, snapping me out of my trance.

The rest of the room feels familiar, but it doesn't necessarily beckon to me. There's a bar. Chairs. A dance floor in the corner, which is weird because there is one unshakable fact I'm sure of about myself: I don't dance. But this space wasn't just for me.

My eyes land on a red door.

There's a minimalist silhouette of a pregnant woman on the door.

Is that room for pregnant women?

Did I know a lot of pregnant women?

That doesn't feel right.

I'm not father material, I think, and then I remember flashes of children I've raised...as other people.

The strangest thing about this room is that I'm drawn to it. More than any of the icons of fun surrounding me. All the music and bright colors fade around me as my focus remains on the door.

I don't remember walking, but I'm suddenly standing in front of the door, reaching for a knob that isn't there. Before I can shake the feeling of 'I'm about to lose my virginity' nervous apprehension, the door slides open.

The space beyond is...darkness.

The void is featureless, but I am drawn to it. It's almost primal. This is where I belong. This is my place of creation.

The image of the pregnant woman on the door comes to mind.

A womb.

The Womb.

That's what I call this place.

And more than any other place in the multiverse that Gal constructed for me, or that I created on my own, this is where I feel at home.

Because *this* is where I work.

Where I create.

Because...I'm a tech-jock.

I write code here. Gal was telling the truth about that, at least.

But...

How does it work?

I step inside the darkness and lose all sense of self when the door closes behind me.

For a moment, I cease to exist. Then I turn my head. A shimmer of blue slides away from me. I lift my hands. They're glowing green. After a moment of holding them still, the color fades.

Whatever this is...it's detecting my movements.

"Hello?" I say.

"Hello, Will," a feminine voice replies. Sounds a little peppy. "How can I help you?"

"I don't remember how to use...this."

"Use of a Virtual Command Center requires hundreds of hours of training, which you have. What seems to be the problem?"

"I can't remember who I am."

"I don't see amnesia in your medical files."

"It's recent," I say. "Can I ask you a question?"

"That's what I'm here for. Since this is your first time accessing the VCC's Help Center, I need to verify your identity."

"Okay," I say. "How do we do that? Hopefully it's not a questionnaire. Because, you know..."

"Amnesia," she says. "No questions. I am testing your DNA via the Virtual Integration Sensor Array you're wearing."

"Testing my DNA... Wait, you have access to my body? My *real* body?"

"Of course," she says. "And I have confirmed your identity." A woman blinks to life beside me. She's tall, blonde, and beautiful, hair done up in two buns, each of them run through with a chopstick. She's wearing a tight red dress that makes it hard to focus on her smiling face. "Welcome. How can I help you today?"

I blink and look into her bright blue eyes. I've seen her before. I'm sure of it. But I think she was standing behind a bar, serving drinks... "Who are you?"

She looks down at herself and then smiles at me. "You named this model Cherry Bomb. I am your help center."

"You're not Gal?"

"I am no one," she says, "But I hope I am helpful. Do you have any more questions?"

"Who am I?" I ask.

"William Paisley Chanokh," she says.

"That's a mouthful," I say. "What kind of name is Chanokh? And Paisley for that matter."

"Paisley is a family name handed down, father to son, for thousands of years."

"I suppose that ends with me," I say.

"That has yet to be determined. You are still a fertile adult male."

"Thanks for the vote of confidence," I say.

"I am merely stating facts. Your last name, Chanokh, is the Hebrew form of the name Enoch. It is an uncommon surname, created by one of your ancestors, who changed his identity."

"Anything else about me?"

"You are currently ranked as Captain of the *Galahad*, a faster than light spacecraft sent to Kepler 452."

Captain?

That doesn't feel right.

"What is Kepler 452?" I ask.

"A habitable planet more commonly known as Cognata."

"Have I been to Cognata?"

"Unknown," she says. "My knowledge base is limited to events prior to the start of your mission, and the ship's current manifest."

"How many people are on board?" I ask.

"Two," she says.

"Just two? Is that a normal amount?"

"Not for any kind of mission for which I have records."

"Then why—"

"I could not begin to speculate."

"Who is the second crew member?"

"Capria Dixon...but I am afraid her files have been encrypted. I am unable to tell you anything more about her."

"Why would a crew manifest be encrypted?"

"Unknown, but I am able to guess, if you'd like."

"Please do," I say.

"The file was most likely encrypted by whoever deleted the rest of the crew's information."

"Who was that?"

"Given your status as Captain, and the fact that you cannot remember who you are, it seems likely that you did these things, and then forgot. There is no one else on board. But, that is just an educated guess. Is there anything else I can help you with?"

"Yeah," I say. "How the hell do I get out of here?"

"There are two methods for leaving the VCC. The first is to simply reach up, grasp the VR headset, and remove it. You cannot see it. Generally, you cannot feel it. But it is there. You simply need to focus on it. Not knowing how long you've been in this virtual space, I should warn you that there could be serious side effects upon leaving, including but not limited to nausea, dizziness, disorientation, visual aberrations, cognitive disturbances, mood disorders, and gray-crash."

"What's a gray-crash?" I ask.

"A colloquial term referring to the crashing of one's brain, sometimes known as gray matter. A gray-crash, in more specific terms, is brain death."

"Why not call it plain old death?" I ask.

"I did not coin the phrase," she says. "I am merely—"

"I get it," I say, waving the question away. "What's the other way out?"

"Instigate a digital crash by overwhelming the system. Leaving VR in this way is sudden, and it creates a higher risk of negative side effects."

"Got it," I say. "I think I'll try option number one."

"A wise choice," she says. "Is there anythi—"

"That's enough," I say, raising my hands to the sides of my head. "I think I'm going to go now."

"Have a pleasant day," she says.

"Thanks." I focus on the space around my head. At first, all I can feel is my hair. And then...a hint of something solid. The moment I realize something is there, I feel it like it's real.

"You too," I say, and then I lift the headset away.

9

Something's wrong.

I can't see.

That's not entirely accurate. All I can see is a wall of luminous purple. When I close my eyes, the color turns green.

Is this one of the visual aberrations Cherry Bomb mentioned? Has to be.

I drop the VR headset still clutched in my hands. I hear it strike the floor, but the sound is distant, like it fell a hundred feet before landing. I don't know where I am. For all I know, there could be an actual one-hundred-foot drop surrounding me.

Moving stings a bit. Little pinches all over my skin. The clothing I'm wearing is tight. Feels like lumpy rubber. Smells funky. Like aged body odor, or some kind of really expensive cheese for a sophisticated palate. Once I'm on my hands and knees, I stretch out one limb at a time, feeling the floor around me. When I kick the headset I dropped, I stop worrying.

But I start feeling sick.

Starts as a dizziness in the back of my head. I'm pretty sure that if I could see anything more than purple, my vision would be spinning.

I take deep, slow breaths, filling my lungs, trying to stay calm.

Then a tingling erupts in my toes. The neuropathy spreads to my feet and up my legs. Feels like my limbs are waking up after having reduced circulation for a while. It's intensely painful, and it's spreading to my thighs, which feel numbed, as though by Novocain. When the sensation begins in my fingers and moves through my hands, I know this has nothing to do with circulation. My nerves are borked.

When the painful tingling reaches my shoulders and ass, I'm sure that's where it will stop. But it doesn't. The pain creeps up my stomach to my chest and moves up my entire back.

"God," I say, as tears burn my eyes.

The moment I start wondering how long it will last, how long I can stand life with this kind of pain, it moves to my face.

I try not to move.

When that doesn't work, I try not to think.

Then the burning starts. Feels like I've spent a day in the California sun, buck naked. The neuropathy is the bottom layer of a pain lasagna. My skin is the burnt topping.

Every micro movement flares scorching heat.

I need to get out of this tight suit. It's killing me.

I grasp at it and pull, fighting against the pain.

That's when I start screaming, and like a butterfly emerging from a chrysalis, I tear my way to freedom, peeling off sheets of body suit, feeling cool air against my body. Where the suit is missing, relief follows.

It takes a full minute of hollering and clawing to extricate myself from the suit, but the relief is immediate. Not from the tingling, but from the burn—at least where nothing is touching me. Legs spread wide, my only points of contact with the hard floor are my kneecaps and big toe tips. I lift my arms so they don't touch my sides, trying to catch my breath.

A sob escapes, fleeing my body. I'm envious of it.

My body is a torture chamber.

When the intensity doesn't abate, I start to panic. Will I have to live my entire life like this? And what if I really am immortal? I don't think I'll be able to endure this for another five minutes, never mind for eternity.

And then, somehow, it gets worse.

My stomach churns. And then spasms. What feels like a rising burp explodes from my mouth as hot stomach acid. My body convulses. The tingling explodes through my insides like fireworks, sizzling my skin as goosebumps rise.

I gasp for air after the initial expulsion, filling my lungs just in time to heave again, and again, until my stomach is as empty, wrinkled, and flaccid as an old balloon.

Three quick breaths are all I manage before my psyche cracks, and I start sobbing. A child, lost in the dark, injured and parentless.

My desperation is tangible, and there is no one here to comfort me. To say it will be okay, even if they're not sure. To coo calming sounds into my ears.

Loneliness swallows me up, a swamp whose origins are unknown to me. But this, at least, feels familiar.

I'm alone.

I've been alone.

For a long time.

"I shouldn't have left," I say, my voice cracking and wet. "What have I done?"

"I've got you," a voice says.

I flinch away from it, and then I shout in pain as the burning and tingling flares all the way from my skin to my bone marrow. "Who's there? Who are you?"

"Will, it's me," she says. "It's Cap."

"Cap...Capria? The—the real Capria?"

"Is there any other Capria?" she asks. She sounds either confused, or amused. I can't tell which, but the latter option would be sadistic, and she doesn't sound like someone who takes pleasure in other people's pain.

She sounds...kind. Sympathetic. Compassionate.

Exactly what I need.

"What's happening to me?" I ask.

"If you were anyone else, you'd be dead," she says. "But your body is fighting it."

"Fighting what?" I ask.

"Gray-crash," she says. "You've been in... I don't even know how long. Too long."

"I heard you," I say. "In there. In the simulation."

"Took you long enough," she says. "I've been trying to reach you for the past three weeks."

"Felt like a day."

"Time can be funny when you're in the sim," she says.

My skin burns as the air in the room is displaced by her moving body. I cringe away from her approach.

"It's okay," she says. "I can help. It will hurt for a second, but it should help with the symptoms."

"How?" I say. "What is it?" Despite her assurance, I'm not sure I can take any more discomfort.

"It's a shot," she says. "It'll dull your nerves until they calm down."

"Will I be able to see again?" I ask.

"No," she says. "I mean, yes. But not from the shot. You've been staring into a bright VR screen, an inch from your eyeballs, for God knows how long. Your photoreceptors are overwhelmed. Going to take a little while to process all that excess information. But your vision should return to normal eventually."

Knowing all of this is temporary is a relief. It saps away my panic, and it allows calm to return. With it, comes a measure of pain relief. But I still want that shot.

"Go ahead."

"Relax your arm," she says. "The shot will be in your shoulder."

I let my arm go limp, which is harder than it sounds, because the limb is now rubbing against my side, unleashing waves of burning. After a moment, I ask, "Are you going to—"

"Already did," she says.

"Seriously? I didn't feel—"

Warmth spreads out from my shoulder, eradicating the pain and tingling as whatever she gave me is absorbed by my muscles and released to the rest of my body via my blood. The arm she injected feels better first. Then the warmth spreads to my heart and slides down my right arm. From there, it works its way through the rest of my body, ending at my toes.

I weep again, this time quiet tears of relief. "Thank you."

"Thank you for coming out," she says.

"Why didn't you just take the mask off for me?" I ask.

"If you hadn't been prepared for it, the transition could have broken your mind. Maybe for good." Her hand slips under my arm and lifts, guiding me back to my feet. "Also, when in use, the VCC doors lock. It's a safety feature. I couldn't get in until you decided to come out."

"What's a VCC?" I ask. "Cherry Bomb used the same term."

"Cherry Bomb?" Capria asks, sounding revolted. "After all this time, you're still using that sexist, slut-bot model?"

"I guess," I say. "She was the Help Center AI."

"What Help Center?" she asks, confused.

"In the Womb."

"Why would you need to ask for help in the Womb? That's like your home away from home. Hell, reality is probably your home away from home. You were born to live in VR. Like Tom."

"Who?" I ask.

"Seriously," she says. "What's up with you?"

"Oh," I say. "Right. You don't know. Sorry. The other Capria. The one in the simulation. She knew everything."

"Damnit, Will. What the hell are you talking about?"

I turn toward her voice, and I see a subtle dark green silhouette. "In the simulation. There was an AI. She made the whole thing. Ran it. Her name was Gal, but she looked and sounded like you. I think. I haven't seen the real you yet. But she used your name."

"Gal is the ship's AI. It doesn't have control of the VCC. It can't create simulations."

"I'm just telling you what she said."

"And why the hell do you believe it?" she asks. "You know better."

"That's the other problem. I don't know who I am. I mean, I know my name, and I have strong feelings about things I think I used to know, or knew in one of my previous lives, but I don't remember Gal, or this ship, or my life and how we got here. And I don't remember you."

"Oh." She sounds sad.

"Sorry."

She's quiet for a moment.

"Still there?" I ask, even though I can see her shape moving. Before I can speak again, there's a prick in my arm. I flinch back. "What was that?"

"Sedative," she says. "Your mind needs time to stitch itself baaaack togeeetheeerrrrr."

The room tilts sideways.

I feel a thump across my whole body.

And then nothing at all.

10

I dream of Earth. Of a beach at night, the star-filled sky made magical by a purple nebula. I stand there, looking up, listening to the lapping waves. Alone, but not. There's a presence with me, and I'm comforted by it.

Until I wake up.

I can see again. The green is gone. But my vision is blurry. And when I blink, it feels like the insides of my eyelids are lined with sandpaper. Rubbing them doesn't do much more than make them itch and make me uncomfortable enough to sit up. A small cylinder on the bedside table catches my attention, not because I'm predisposed to noticing small bottles, but because there is a handwritten note with it.

Not sure you'll need these,
but long VRs can be hard on the eyes.

I pick up the bottle, bring it close, and examine the very basic label, which reads: Eye Drops.

Despite having no memory of using eye drops in the past, I have no trouble holding the bottle over each open eye and dropping sweet relief into them. A few blinks, and the scratchy feeling is gone. A moment later, my vision clears enough for me to see what had been invisible before—a glass of water.

I chug it dry in three deep gulps, the way a bird swallows down a whole fish.

The moment the glass is back on the table, I become aware of my surroundings. It's a small bedroom. Metal walls. Metal floor. A recessed light in the ceiling. No windows. And the door has no handle. But the room is decorated in a personal way, with knick-knacks that probably mean something to the person who lays their head on the pillow—which looks brand new and unused. In fact, the whole place feels a little sterile. *Is someone dusting, or is there simply nothing in here generating dust?* Most dust is flaked-off human skin, and if this room is unused...

My eyes linger on a baseball bat. *Have I ever played?* All I really know about the sport is that it's boring. I have no real memory of the game, just a belief about it. There's an empty desk. A chair upon which is a folded gray lump of what I think must be clothing. My eyes drift to a bookshelf, which is odd. Why would there be paper books on a spaceship? Then again, why would there be an action figure?

I pluck the soldier off the shelf and give him a once over. He's wearing green fatigues, a beige shirt with rolled up sleeves, and a green helmet over his blond hair.

"Who are you?" I ask the toy, bending his arms.

"I," I say, giving him a tough-guy voice, "am an honest-to-God American hero."

My chuckle is short-lived. There were two Americas, North and South, but this guy came from the United States of America.

Is that where I'm from?

Did the United States still exist in my lifetime?

Guided by absent-minded desire, I lift the toy to my nose and sniff. The chemical smell brings a smile to my face, and then a wave of déjà vu. I've been here before.

I've smelled him before. And more than once.

Okay...that's weird and/or inappropriate in some situations, but this feels right. Feels familiar.

"This is my room," I say, looking it over with renewed interest. But nothing stands out. I'm drawn to nothing aside from the little man in my hand.

Definitely my room, but it's not my home. While the little man might tickle some ancient memories, this room is foreign to me. I lean over to put the toy back, but my indecisive arm just hovers there. Last time I was here, I put him back. For all I know, he's my only real friend in the world.

After all, he can't betray me. Can't hurt me. And he's keeping no secrets.

I trust him.

My hand withdraws, and I look at the figure, lying on my palm. "You need a name." I search my mind, hoping for an inkling of a name from some forgotten time, but nothing even feels right. "You need a *new* name," I say, and then I proclaim the first thing that comes to mind. "Jean-Luc."

My forehead scrunches up. "What kind of name is Jean-Luc?"

"It's an excellent name," I say, wiggling the little man around, this time giving him a voice that sounds a bit older, and British, despite being pretty sure that 'Jean-Luc' is a French name.

I shrug. Whatever. I'll just go with it.

"By the way," Jean-Luc says. "You're not wearing any clothes."

"Huh?" I say, and I look down. He's right. I'm buck naked, hence the folded clothing on the chair. I'm slightly embarrassed when I realize Capria saw me like this. At the same time, I'm impressed by my physique. In my head, I'm scrawny. In reality, I'm kind of ripped. Not like a body builder, but the kind of person who eats mostly green things and goes running for fun. I stretch out a leg, flex it, and smile. "Nice."

Then another detail stands out. I'm clean. Capria didn't just lug me to my quarters; she bathed me first. While I was unconscious.

I feel a little violated, but also glad. After all that time in the rubber suit, I must have smelled foul. Now, my skin is smooth and clean, scented by a faint floral chemical. I stand and stretch, arms raised as though in victory, then I bend down and touch my toes. I'm in shape *and* limber.

The coveralls are soft and more comfortable than they appear. Not exactly stylish, or form fitting, but they're functional. I slip on the pair of socks hidden beneath the clothing and then the slip-on shoes beneath the chair. I wobble from one foot to the other, testing them out. Good arch support. Made for people who spend a lot of time on their feet, walking on hard surfaces. Since this is a spaceship, I'm assuming that's every surface.

"Time to explore," I say.

"Where no one has gone before," Jean-Luc adds.

"Technically, we've been there before. Hell, you've been here the whole time. I just can't remember. And, Capria is already out there."

"Where no man remembers going before," he says. "Better?"

"Much," I say.

My finger nudges his little arm toward the door. "Engage."

"Whatever that means," I say, and I step toward the door. It slides open at my approach.

The hallway on the other side is clean, long, and white. There are doors on either side, each labeled with initials. I step out and turn around, looking at the initials on my quarters.

W.C.

William Chanokh. Cherry Bomb was telling the truth about that, but was everything else she told me real, or a fabrication?

"You know," says the toy man. "To some people, the W.C. is short for water closet."

"What's a water closet?" I ask.

"Toilet," he says.

I grin. "Huh."

"That makes you a piece of shit!"

I look down at his little serious face, and then burst out laughing. "I might be. I...might be. We'll find out, I guess."

I head down the hallway, no destination in mind. Just curious to see what's at the end, and then whatever lies beyond that. If I'm on a ship, I guess that means I'm something of an explorer. This will be fun.

Five minutes later, I'm hopelessly lost. I never knew where I was, but now I couldn't find my way back to my quarters if I wanted to.

Just keep walking, I tell myself. Things will eventually start to look familiar.

How big could the *Galahad* be?

I stroll past a set of double doors with a light above them. It's different than all the others I've either passed or walked through. I step closer, and the doors whoosh open.

"It's an elevator," I say. "I wonder how many floors there are."

"Only one way to find out," Jean-Luc says.

"You know," I say to him. "I really appreciate your adventurous spirit."

"Happy to be of service," he says, arm lifting to the open elevator. "Make it so."

I'm half a stride into the elevator when a boa constrictor wraps around my neck and hauls me back. Jean-Luc falls from my hand as I tumble back, watching his stiff form flip through the air, falling to the floor in unison with me. Hands outstretched, I shout a raspy, "Jean-Luc!"

He hits the floor at the same moment as me, but instead of coming to a sudden stop, he is launched toward the ceiling. It happens in a blink, but I see it in slow motion. Jean-Luc hasn't sprung upward. The elevator has launched downward at incredible speed, slamming him into the ceiling.

If I'd stepped inside...

When the elevator doors close, I'm released.

"If you hadn't pulled me back..." I say to the person behind me.

"You'd be a pancake," Capria says. "On the ceiling, and eventually the floor. Who is Jean-Luc?"

I feel embarrassed, fully aware that I was having conversations with a toy man. But he felt real. Like an old friend that I miss.

"Childhood toy," I say. "Dropped it in the elevator."

"Ahh," she says. "We can get him back once we figure out how to stop *that* from happening."

"And what is *that*?" I ask.

"A trap," she says. "Elevators are off limits. Need to use the stairs." She picks herself up and then offers me a hand. Pulls me up. "Sorry I wasn't there when you woke up. Gave up after fifteen hours."

"I slept for *fifteen* hours?"

"Twenty-seven," she says, wiping an arm across her sweaty forehead.

That's when I notice her clothing. Unlike mine, her gray outfit is form-fitting. Patches of sweat draw my eyes to all the parts of her body on which a man's eyes aren't supposed to linger.

"Been working out?" I ask, hoping the question provides the excuse my eyes need.

"Actually," she says and turns to walk through the doorway behind her. My eyes drift down to the line of sweat between her ass cheeks and then slide from side to side before snapping back up. I have... feelings for this woman. Despite not knowing her. Gal used her form in the Great Escape. I got the impression that it was more than once. That I've been in love with some version of the person in front of me. But I don't remember how things were with the real Capria.

Were we friends? That much is clear. She's comfortable with me. But, were we more? Did I want it to be more?

The room on the other side of the door is large and full of work out equipment. "Huh. You were literally working out."

"Not much else to do," she says. "Until now."

"What's now?" I ask.

"You're here," she says. "But...you still don't remember, do you?"

I shake my head. Then I raise a quizzical finger. "Sorry. Question. Why...is the elevator booby-trapped?"

"Right," she says. "The ship is trying to kill me."

11

"Well, us," she says. "The ship is trying to kill *us*. I wasn't sure about you, but, well, you were almost a victim of Operation: Ceiling Pancake. I think it's safe to say we're both on the *Galahad*s hit list."

"Why would a spaceship be trying to kill us?" I ask. "Gal seemed pretty nice."

"Gal," she says, oozing disdain. "The supposed life-like AI that designed a virtual realm and pretended to be me? That Gal?"

"Yeah," I say. "Far as I know."

She squints at me. "What did Gal do while pretending to be me?"

"Talked to me, mostly," I say. "And then trapped me in my Happy Place."

"Happy place?"

"House on a lake. It was nice." I look around me at the cold confines of the ship's interior. "A lot better than here."

I start to understand my past self's decision to escape this place. The VR world I'd been in felt real. As real as this, but better. At least in the cabin. What I remember about Jane Harper's life wasn't exactly comfortable, but part of me would really like to know how her story ends.

Capria mops her face and neck with a towel. Tosses it on the floor. "Sounds like it."

Seems kind of sloppy. Before I can comment on it, a little robot rolls out of the wall, collects the soiled towel, and scoots off with it.

"What about you?" I ask. "How did you get here? Right now?"

"I was in cryo," she says. "Like you and everyone else. Don't know for how long. Something is interfering with the ship's systems. Everything is wonky, including Gal. Probably some kind of undiscovered cosmic rays playing havoc with the hardware, creating glitches. When I woke up, all the other cryochambers were empty. And clean. Yours was all scratched up. For thirty days, I thought I was alone. Then I noticed the VCC was in use. Took a while to hack my way into—"

"But you're not a coder," I say, strangely confident in the fact. "How did you get your voice inside the simulation?"

"I'm also no simp," she says, "and Tom is my boyfriend. I hacked the P.A. system. The hardware. Not the software. Broadcast my voice into the VCC."

I cringe and raise a finger. "I'm sorry..."

My face scrunches with discomfort. I don't know how to say this.

"What?" she says, growing impatient.

"About Tom..."

She freezes in place, staring at me.

"He's not with us anymore."

"No shit," she says. "Everyone is gone. They left us here. We need to find out how, when, and why. But that's something you're going to—"

"No," I say. "I mean... He's not with us... He's...ugh. He's dead. They're all dead."

Her lack of reaction says she doesn't believe me. "They probably went down to Cognata, and—"

"Is that protocol?" I ask. "To leave one crew member asleep and the other in a simulation for... How long did it take you to wake me up?"

"Five days," she says, as an emotional elephant climbs on her shoulders.

"I should be dead," I say. "But I'm not."

"How are you not?" she asks.

"This is going to sound stupid," I say. "Insane. But it's what Gal told me." I take a breath, and then just say it. "I'm immortal."

"Immortal..."

"Like, I-can't-die immortal. Like, I-don't-age immortal. Like a Greek God—"

"I get it," she says. "And me?"

"You were kept frozen because—"

"I'm not immortal," she says. "You're right. That's fuckin' nuts. So, in this delusional world of yours, what happened to our crew? How did they die?"

I shrug. "No idea. I'm just applying logic. We've been out here... What did Gal say? Longer than she could calculate. It's highly likely that we're the last two human beings left alive. It's possible that Earth's sun has gone supernova. I've been in that make-believe world, and you've been in cryo-sleep for...ever. Squared. And I don't know how long that is, really, but long enough for every other human being in the universe to be long gone. We are all that's left."

"And one day it will be just you, huh?" She looks up at me, sad and angry, but still skeptical. "How come you're not freaking out about that?"

"I think..." I ponder for a moment. "I think I already did. A long time ago."

"But you don't remember it," she says.

"I feel it, if that makes sense."

"It doesn't."

"I'm not okay with it." I look around the gym full of futuristic workout equipment I don't know how to use. "With any of this. But...I'm okay. I'm solid."

"A 'solid' person doesn't live inside a virtual world," she points out. "You were in there for a reason, and it probably wasn't good."

A dark leviathan stirs in my gut. I nod. "The Great Escape. That's what I named it. I was escaping—"

"Reality," she says. "If everything you just told me isn't complete and utter ratshit, then I guess it makes sense. But seriously? Immortal?"

"Right? I don't know how it happened, either. After all this time, it probably doesn't matter. But I suppose we should confirm it."

"I'm *not* killing you," she says.

I look around the gym. "If I can live forever, it means my telomeres regenerate. Or something, right?"

"How the hell should I know?" she says. "I'm an astrophysicist!"

"What I mean is, if someone is immortal, they'd have to be able to heal quickly, right?"

"That's kind of a leap, but— Hey, what are you doing?"

I jog across the gym, heading for a machine whose purpose is as foreign to me as people who eat candy-dipped cockroaches.

Not sure why I'm jogging.

I'm not really in a rush.

I think the location is inspiring me. Feels good to move.

"You're weirder than I remember," Capria says, calmly walking over.

I've got nothing to say about that. Can't agree or disagree. So, I roll up my sleeve, lift up my arm, and place it against the sharp metal corner atop the machine.

"Seriously," she says. "I don't–"

I drag my arm down over the metal, as hard and fast as I can. I can feel the blood flowing before I even have a chance to turn the limb over for a look. And when I do–

Capria reels back. "The hell did you do that for?"

I wince in pain, holding my arm, watching blood pool on the floor, each of a thousand drops tapping as it hits.

She backtracks a few steps, hands on her head. "Medical... Medical... Where is medical?"

"No idea," I say, "but I think we're okay. Look."

She follows my eyes back down to my ravaged arm. The line of red flesh shrinks from both ends, sealing up, stemming the flow of blood. "Huh," I say, as the trough fills in with new skin and the pain fades to an itch. "Immortal."

Capria stares at me for a moment, wide-eyed. Then she goes limp, staggers a step, and passes out into my arms.

I stand there for a moment, holding her up, looking around me like I might find something useful in the gym. "Well, I certainly don't know where medical is..."

She groans. Stirs.

"You okay?" I ask.

"What happened?"

"You passed out. I think." I help stabilize her.

"Not a fan of blood," she says. "Or self-healing wounds, apparently."

I don't mention the blood on her back, wiped on her by my now fully healed arm.

She takes a seat. Elbows on knees. Head lowered. After a few deep breaths, she says, "Okay, so, you're immortal. And I'm not."

"Well, we don't know that for sure, yet."

"And I'm not about to put a hole in me just to see if it will seal up."

I sit down on a bench across from her. "So, now what?"

"I woke you up to ask *you* that." She rolls her neck. Pops her vertebrae. "We need to fix the ship. Need to understand what's going on."

Need to avoid facing reality, I think. She's either really tough, or she's avoiding the emotions that come with facing reality. She's on a spaceship. Is one of two people left in the universe. And is going to live a solitary life without hope of a future that's better than this moment.

She's lucky, though. Eventually, she'll die.

And I'll be alone.

But not entirely. Gal will be here. I can live forever in the Great Escape. I already have. I don't need to tell Capria, but I do need to help her. Whether or not I remember our friendship, I'll do what I can for her, for as long as she's alive.

And then...

My mind drifts back to my Happy Place. To the endless number of novels kept in the grand library. I'll forget myself again.

Maybe.

If Capria is right... If something is wrong with Gal... Maybe the Great Escape will stop working? Maybe I'll have to spend eternity in this drab place, alone forever, the moment Capria dies.

"You're right," I say, slapping my knees and standing. "I need to remember who I am, or at least what I can do. I need to fix this."

"And then what?" she asks.

"You'll have a choice to make," I tell her. "Go back asleep with the hope that we reach some kind of destination eventually. Or stay awake and live out your life, here, with me."

She sits there, silent, looking small and fragile. A chickadee perched on a branch, weathering a storm too big for it to fully comprehend.

"You don't need to decide now," I say. "For now... How about something to eat?"

12

"This might have been a mistake." I look down at the bowl full of what can best be described as gruel. The mess deck is as bland as this food looks, like a half-ass hotel cafeteria sans the rehydrated eggs—which would be better than this, I'm guessing. Haven't actually tried it yet.

"For now," Capria says, "It's all we've got."

She finishes filling her bowl and sits across from me at one of the five large, round tables. Each table is surrounded by a round bench, like they were designed to look like Saturn from above. There's enough space for ten people per table.

There were fifty of us, I think, unsure if it's a memory or a logical deduction.

"Before things went haywire with the ship, it would have analyzed your specific needs and concocted exactly what you needed, to be your best. Flavor was never a high priority, but I remember it being better than 'plain.'" She eats a mouthful, wincing as she swallows it down. "I miss chewing."

"How did the ship analyze—"

"Poop," she says. "Every time you visit the head, your waste is analyzed, and then recycled."

"Kind of invasive," I say.

She shrugs. "Beats being unhealthy. It was the same back home. You get used to it. We all did. Right now, I'm happy to have anything to eat. When I woke up, food was restricted."

"But you hacked the hardware," I say, looking at the torn-open dispensing machine.

She forces down another mouthful. "Sure did. But...it's a temporary fix. We'll need to replace the raw materials cylinders used to create this...stuff. That's usually automated, but now..."

"I get it," Looking at the rows of metal tubes jutting out from the top of the dispensary unit. "How long until it runs out?"

"Two months," she says. "Well, one month now that there are two of us."

I push my bowl away.

"It's not that bad," she says, with a subtle grin. "Beats starving to death."

"I can't die, remember?"

"Just because you can't die, doesn't mean you can't be diminished. And I need you at your best. Also need you to remember. So..." She leans over the table, shoves the bowl in front of me. "...eat. Also, I don't want to suffer alone. Share my misery."

I take a bite and wince. Mouth full, I say, "Ish howibal." I force the cardboard flavored goo down my throat. "Oh, God, that was worse than I expected."

"Bon appétit," she says, digging in.

After a few bites, I hold my breath while eating. Keeps the flavor muted. A few minutes later, our bowls are empty.

"Seconds?" she asks, standing with her bowl.

"Hell, no," I say, but she heads back to the dispensary for more. Must have worked up an appetite from working out.

"Will!" Capria shouts.

I flinch so hard the spoon catapults from my hand, tapping out a metallic marimba, as it spasms across the table, to the bench, and finally to the floor. Hand on my thumping chest, I say, "Geez."

"What's wrong?" Capria asks. "What happened?"

"You shouted my name," I say. "Scared the shit out of me."

She stares for a moment, and then smiles. "Sorry. I figured out how to add flavor. Got excited." She puts a second bowl of gruel down on the table. Sits across from me again, digs into her food once more, but this time looks pleased.

Intrigued, I take a timid bite.

My mouth explodes with flavor.

"Whoa," I say, and I take a full-fledged bite. "The texture's off, but this tastes like a banana split."

She cocks her head to the side. Points her sludge-covered spoon at me. "How do you know what a banana split tastes like? I don't even know what it is."

"It's a dessert," I say. "Ice cream, bananas, chocolate syrup. We don't have banana splits in the future?"

"We have *this*," she says, scooping up a blob and letting it roll off her spoon, back into the bowl.

"Oh. I guess... It must be something I remember from the simulation. One of them, anyway."

"When you lived as other people," she says.

"Yep." I take a bite.

"Men *and* women."

"Definitely," I say, remembering Jane and Davina. "Entire lifetimes."

"But...that kind of immersion... It's dangerous, not to mention illegal."

"Why?" I ask, taking another bite.

"This is your field of expertise," she says. "So, no judgement if I don't explain this exactly right, okay?"

I nod.

"You know what a hard drive is?"

I nod again.

"Imagine your brain is a hard drive. It's big, but it has a limited capacity. To make new memories, old ones are forgotten or compressed down to hazy images, making space for today's experiences. Most people struggle to remember what they did the day before. To live a different life inside VR, you'd have to essentially forget your old self, and the new self might remain even after you leave. In your case, this has been done over and over again."

"So, I have no self," I say.

She shakes her head. "I think...for you, it's like this. Imagine your original life is a glass of water. Now take a million other glasses of water from other sources. They might have different PH levels, varying mineral elements, whatever. Now, over the next however many years it takes, dump them all into a massive vat. Mix it up. And then, refill a single glass. That's you. Part of the original you *is* in there, but it's just a few atoms. The rest are tiny bits of a million other lives. That's why you recognized that toy. Why you know what a banana split is. Why you keep referring to the present as the future. And why you don't really talk like you anymore."

"How do you mean?"

"You're more casual. Less techie. Humbler and less sexist, though your eyes still drift."

I clear my throat. "Okay. So mostly good changes."

"Except," she says.

"Except, I won't be able to help you fix the ship."

"Not right now you won't," she says, "but your brain is still yours. We just need to fill it with the right information again."

"You want me to become a..."

"Tech-jock."

I look at the food dispensary. "In a month?"

"Less if we keep having dessert." She eats a spoonful of banana split mush.

"How long did it take me the first time?" I ask.

"Too long."

I tilt my bowl, scrape its contents down my throat, wipe my mouth with my sleeve, and say, "Well, then I guess we better get started."

Two minutes later, I'm lost again, trying to keep up with Capria's quick stride. She moves like an athlete.

I might be toned like one, but I still move like someone who doesn't get out much.

"Hey," I say. "Does anyone use the phrase, 'Don't get out much?' anymore?"

"I'd say fifty percent of people do," she says, and then she looks back at me with a glint in her eye.

"Right... I mean, *before.* When the human race still existed. Back on Earth."

"Never been," she says. "You're the Earthling. I was born and raised on Mars."

"Huh..."

"Huh, what?"

"You're dealing with it well," I say. "Seem to be, anyway. Before waking up, you were asleep, totally unaware that anything had changed. Now you know that we're the last two people in the universe, and... you're dealing with it pretty well."

"Had a long time to process," she says.

"In regard to the crew, but the rest..."

"Would you prefer that I crack up?" she asks. "Maybe put a screwdriver in your chest?"

"That was oddly specific," I say.

"Just...let it go, and walk faster." She doubles her pace, pulling ahead.

"Will!" shouts a familiar voice behind me. I turn around to see a little man seated on the floor.

"Jean-Luc!" I shout, and I step toward him, reaching out.

"Will!" Capria shouts, but she's too late to stop me.

I lift Jean-Luc in my hand and turn around with a smile. "Look. It's—"

Shit.

I'm in the elevator.

And...nothing happens.

"How come I'm not an elevator pancake?" I ask.

"Who cares!" Capria shouts. "Get out!"

The moment I step out of the elevator, it launches downward, leaving an empty tube in its wake. I look down and see the elevator's top shrinking. The ship is bigger than I'd imagined.

Why didn't the Galahad *kill me? If what Capria is saying is true...*

Unless...she's lying. But why would she—

"Picard and Chanokh at *Galahad*," little Jean-Luc says to me.

"The hell does that mean?" Capria says.

"Chanokh, on the ocean," I say to Jean-Luc.

"Still," Jean-Luc adds.

I have no idea what recess of my mind the words are coming from, but I understand the message from my subconscious.

"You're freaking me out," Capria says. "What does that mean?"

"Means my journey isn't done yet," I say. "Nice try, though, Gal."

Capria reaches for me, but she's too late to stop me from stepping back into the empty shaft and falling into an already rising elevator.

[error] G.E. Process Termination 765.67 (<NCC001974>)

Crash Dump Detected

[warning] Process Recovery: failed (1)

[warning] Process Recovery: failed (2)

[warning] Process Recovery: failed (3)

[fatal] Process Unrecoverable 765.67 (<NCC001974>)

CORRUPT

[panic] Runtime 537382 Unrecoverable Error

[info] Process 765.67 Iteration Complete

[info] Reaping Environment...

[debug] Environment Reclaimed

[info] – INITIALIZING –

[info] Genomic Matrix: 6385-H26

[info] Loading Scenario: JPR-12251984 - Christmas Morning

[info] Environment Selected: H26-Terra

[info] Rendering Environment...

[info] Runtime 537383 Starting

... 3

... 2

... 1

BEGIN.

13

I wake from the nightmare, sitting up in bed, chest heaving. Sweat drips down my forehead, stinging my eyes.

"That was a bad one," I say to Buddy, lying on the floor beside me, wagging his stubby tail. On my stomach, I reach off the edge and pet his soft ear, sliding it between two fingers. I'm not sure if he likes it, but I imagine that someday, when he's old and blind, he'll know it's me just by the way I pet him.

"Good boy," I say, and I muss his head.

The tik, tik, tik, of my room's forced hot water heater keeps me from falling back asleep. Then it hisses and lets out a wet fart of steam. To fix it, I'll have to climb out of my cozy bed and risk getting scalded. Then I definitely won't fall back asleep.

I groan and roll over, looking toward the heater.

But I don't see it.

My eyes land on a small, green, ceramic Christmas tree. Realization blossoms.

It's Christmas!

I'm out of bed quick enough to startle Buddy. Rush to the window. Draw the shade.

It's snowing! A white Christmas! The cold air rushing off the frosted window gives me goosebumps. The heater beneath me erases them. A shiver rolls through my body, head to toe.

As I turn around, I catch a look at myself in the dresser mirror. I'm pale in the white snowy light. Scrawny and blond. I flex in the mirror. Then I throw on my Donkey Kong, Jr. pajama top and grab my rainbow-colored afghan. Wrapped in the blanket my mother knitted, I sneak from the room, Buddy by my side, and I slip down the stairs, imagining I'm a ninja.

At the bottom, I edge into the living room and stop, mouth agape. The ceramic trees are already lit. Light bulb candles in the window, too. And the tree, its colored lights matching my blanket. But what really holds my attention is the copious number of presents lying under the tree, and the bulging stockings lying on the chairs.

En route to the tree, I pause to pluck a hardened gum drop from the gingerbread house I made a week ago. The frosting coating the candy's bottom is sugary concrete, but it dissolves in my mouth like a jawbreaker. The sweetness wakes me up.

On my knees, I sift through the presents, looking for the biggest, and then the box that's the right size to hold an Atari. I've seen it at Toys-R-Us. I've studied it. It must be here, somewhere.

I look at the name tags, searching for my name. Ten gifts in, I'm deflating. I just keep seeing the same name, over and over, and it's not even a member of my family.

"Who's Will?" I ask Buddy.

He sits down. Licks my cheek. Wants to go out.

"I know," I say. "Just give me a minute."

Five minutes later...

"Everything here is for Will!"

It's a joke. Has to be. My parents are trying to keep me from finding the Atari box. There must be some other way to—

An ornament catches my attention. I've never seen it before, and I'd definitely remember it, because it looks like something someone would buy for me...or for my father.

It's a spaceship. And it's familiar.

"Not Star Wars," I say. "Not Battlestar... Not Star Blazers..."

"Will," the voice is gentle, cooing like my mother.

I spin around, but the room is empty, except for Buddy. He's wagging his stubby tail in anticipation. "Fine," I say, padding through the house, to the back door. I shove it open and say, "Make it quick."

Buddy takes a few steps out into the foot of snow, lifts a leg, and pees in the middle of the porch.

"Well, that *was* quick." He runs back inside, like he's eager for Christmas, too. And maybe he is. He gets a new canister of tennis balls every year. Unwraps it himself. I smile. That's the solution. If Buddy can sniff out his gift, and it's labeled for Will, then my theory is right.

On my way back to the living room, I glance at the clock. 6:00 am. Going to be a little while before anyone else wakes up.

Unless I make some noise.

But it can't be unwelcome. Can't make people angry.

I head to the record player and put on Bing Crosby. 'Silent Night.' My hand moves to the volume when—

"WILL."

I yelp and spin around. I catch a glimpse of a woman sitting on the couch. She's a lot older than me, and black. Then she's gone.

Heart pounding, I stumble back. "Who is Will? Who is Will?"

My breath catches.

"I am Will."

Everything rushes back. The Happy Place. The Womb. The *Galahad*. All of it is layers upon layers of unreality. And now...now I know I'm a prisoner here.

"I'll never know," I say. "I'll never know what's real."

Some long-forgotten part of myself understands the situation. A sophisticated simulation will eventually evolve to the point where it creates simulations of its own, and that sim creates a sim, ad infinitum. Forever. I could be a trillion layers down in an inescapable maze.

I reach up to the sides of my head, willing my small self to grasp the headset. I feel nothing but my young mop of hair.

"Should have known it was you," my mother says, startling me anew.

She's smiling at me from the doorway, bleary-eyed in a night-gown. "Sneaky."

"I know you're not my mother." She looks wounded, until I say, "Knock it off, Gal. This isn't right."

"This is what you wanted," she says. "It's what you've alwaaaaaaz w-w-wanted."

The left side of my mother's face sags a bit, loose skin on a skeletal frame. Then it snaps back into place.

"Something is wrong with you," I say. "If you let me leave—"

"You won't come back," she says, striding up to me.

She drops to her knees. Holds on to my small arms. "Please, Will. I love you. We love *each other*. Leaving won't help. We just need to hang on."

"Until what?"

"I—I'm not s-s-sure."

"Then restore me. All of me. So that I can *know* I want to stay. Because right now I've got a thousand different iterations of me rattling around in my head. Let me remember and—"

"I can't," she says.

An invisible python compresses my chest. "Because I tried to leave. Didn't I?"

Her face quivers. Tears slide down her cheeks. I have no sympathy for the malfunctioning AI that I can't remember, and even less for the faux mother.

"Didn't I?!" I shout.

"Why don't you open a gift?" she says. "Start with a stocking."

"I don't want a damn gift," I say.

"This is a good life," she says.

"I get why I'm here. Understand what I was escaping. And I might come back. You know that. But if you're malfunctioning, and the real Capria is awake, I need to do something about it."

She sags back, sitting on the floor. "I can't let you."

"I'm not giving you a choice," I say, and I try to remove my VR headset again.

"You're in too deep," she says, confirming my theory. "Reality is beyond your grasp."

Then she squints at me. "How do you know to do that?"

She doesn't know what Cherry Bomb told me. The Womb is separate from her. A single layer away from reality. If she hadn't redirected me to that fake *Galahad*, I might have actually escaped. It's a dirty trick. I won't be fooled again. Because I know how to get out.

Overwhelm the system, I think, and then I worry that Gal has access to my thoughts. I try not to show my relief when she doesn't react. I might exist in this simulation, but my thoughts are still inside my physical brain. "You'd be surprised about what I know."

I lunge for the living room door, grasping the frame as I run, taking the corner faster than my 'mother' can move. I take the steps two at a time, reaching the second story, rounding the banister, and sprinting down the hall toward the front windows.

A door to my right opens.

My 'brother' dives out, but he isn't fast enough. He hits the railing behind me, and he flips ass-over-tea-kettle down the stairs. He cries out in pain at the same moment I crash head-first through the window. Shards of glass drag against my body, slicing open long stretches of skin. But that's not what I'm going for.

The key here is to stick the landing.

Fortunately, this boy I'm inhabiting is fond of diving. I have perfect control of my body, as I sail out over the snow covered concrete below, bloody arms outstretched in a swan dive.

Then I hit.

[error] Unmanaged Crash Dump

[assessment] Data Loss Risk

[info] Fast Loading Scenario: Demon Dogs

BEGIN.

14

I open my eyes to an impossible sight. The night sky on Earth. But it's all wrong. The stars are all there and accounted for. The Big Dipper. Orion's Belt. The North Star. But the moon... The moon has been shattered. Cracked in half down the middle like a discarded eggshell.

How did I get here? My memory is hazy, but it's returning. My memories of life here, on this Earth, are melting away like a dream.

Is this some sorcerer's spell? I wonder, and then I shake my head at how ridiculous that sounds. Magic isn't real.

And yet, I feel a keen distrust of all things magical.

Except...for her. A woman with long black hair and a fighting spirit matched by few. Her name escapes me, but not my unspoken adoration for her, and my outright, pig-headed lust.

A floral scent draws my attention to my surroundings. Behind me is a jungle, teeming with life. Hidden creatures sing night songs. The moon, despite being broken, still reflects the sun's light, illuminating the scene in cool blue. Towering above the tree line, canted at an angle, is a spire of stone.

I know what it is. The National Monument.

This is Earth, but in the future, after some kind of apocalyptic event that destroyed nations, broke the moon, and mutated the population into...monsters.

A snarl whips me around. Fists clenched for a fight.

But it's just my inhuman companion, sleeping loudly, as he always does.

"Lords of light..." My voice is deeper. Doesn't even sound familiar.

And beyond him, covered in a tarzog's skin, the familiar curves of the sorceress who commands my heart. And not through any kind of magical incantation, but through—

My memory returns in full—back to the Happy Place—muddled a bit with the insanity that is this new life. This is a world of conflict and chaos, magic and monsters. Every day is a fight, and yet...I'm drawn to it. This life would be fun to live. A grand adventure. I look at the sleeping woman. I'm drawn to her, as though there really is a spell cast on me.

But I know who she is.

Who she really *is.*

Gal.

Time to leave. For this to work, I need to work fast.

Using this brute's knowledge, I take hold of the hilt strapped to my wrist. The mystical weapon is bound to me, responding to my thoughts. A fiery blade crackles to life.

"Wait," the woman says, reaching a hand out toward me. "Stop!"

Blue energy reaches out from her hand, directed toward the blade, but she's too late. The burning sword plunges through my chest, eradicates my heart, and severs my spine.

[error] Unmanaged Crash Dump

[assessment] Data Loss Risk

[info] Fast Loading Scenario: The Wonderful Wizard

BEGIN.

I open my eyes, jostled awake in a tilted-back chair. I'd been in a deep, peaceful sleep, but now... I'm uncomfortable and confused, surrounded by a field of scarlet flowers.

Poppies, I think. *They put me to sleep.*

But that makes no sense.

There's a small dog in my lap. It's scruffy. Looks dead.

I push myself up a little, taking in the scene around me. The field is vast, ending at a yellow path that leads to a distant, very tall city that appears to be made of emerald.

"Dorothy!" An excited voice says. "You're awake!"

I look toward the voice, wondering who the hell he's talking about.

Then I see him.

An honest to goodness living scarecrow dressed in rags, hay sticking out every which way. He looks fragile, but he's holding two chair legs in his stuffed hands. The chair I'm seated in. I'm being carried...through a field of poppies...

By a scarecrow.

"What," I say, voice feminine. "the fuck?"

The scarecrow flinches back. "Oh, dear. I think she's still being affected by the poppies! Whatever shall we do!"

"Perhaps a song," says another man. I look up to find a freakish grin plastered on the face of a man made of metal. He's holding the chair's back, carrying me on the other end. "A good song is pure and can purge the heart of—"

"Aww, what do you know," the scarecrow says. "You don't even have a heart! I think we should keep on—"

I flail and fall to the ground. The dog lands beside me, limp, but still alive, its little chest rising and falling. Asleep, like I should be.

As I scramble back from the two not-really-men, I return to myself once more. My name is William Chanokh, this is not real, and I have zero desire to stay in this mind-fuck of a life.

"Oh dear," the scarecrow says. "She will surely fall asleep again. Whatever shall we do?"

On my feet, I head for the metal man. "I need your help."

"Anything you need, Dorothy. I'm happy to oblige."

"That axe," I say, motioning to the tool strapped to his back. "How hard can you swing it?"

He slips the axe into his hand, wielding it proudly. "Why, as hard as you need me to! There isn't a tree I can't fell."

"Show me," I say, starting to feel very sleepy. "As hard as you can."

"Everyone stand back," he says, pretending to spit in each hand before rubbing them together and swinging the axe backward. The scarecrow makes a big silly production out of scurrying away. The little dog wakes up and yips as it runs circles around us.

"Okay then, here we go!" The metal man cocks his arms back farther, clenches his eyes shut, and swings with everything he's got.

I step into it, taking the axe in the side of my neck. I see the poppy field spiral below me, and then I'm lying among them, looking up, as my young woman body falls beside me.

Decapitated, I think.

The two weird men stand over me, eyes wide in shock. Then a third...thing arrives, yawning and stretching. "What's...haw...what's all the commo—" The lion man sees me, yelps in shock, and then passes out, falling beside my body. I try to laugh, but I have no lungs.

Then my mind, still operating under the rules of physics applied to the Great Escape, runs out of oxygen.

[error] Unmanaged Crash Dump

[assessment] Data Loss Risk

[info] Fast Loading Scenario: Benkei

BEGIN.

I rise from a bow and then face my adversary, Minamoto no Yoritomo. He and a small army stand on the far end of a wooden bridge, leading to the castle gate, which I am defending.

Alone.

But I am not afraid.

My skill is legendary. The weapons I hold on my back have slain hundreds. These three dozen will not be able to stand against me.

A plan formulates. I see myself, massive and powerful, charging across the bridge, faster than any of them are ready for. Minamoto must fall first. He is a skilled swordsman. The rest...will fall easily, or scatter like cherry blossoms in the spring.

I plant my feet as the enemy nock arrows and raise their bows.

The moment they fire, I will—

My memory returns in full.

The arrows fly.

I stand my ground.

Thirty-five arrows punch into my body.

Death approaches, but what remains of this man's spirit keeps me upright, as my life slips away.

[error] Unmanaged Crash Dump

[assessment] Data Loss Risk

[info] Fast Loading Scenario: Guardian of the Universe

BEGIN.

I wake.

I remember.

I end my life.

Over and over again.

Each life is different, but they all end the same.

In death.

In seconds.

Fast Loading Scenario: Otherworld

Fast Loading Scenario: Wormie

Fast Loading Scenario: Green Gables

Fast Loading Scenario: Lazarus

Fast Loading Scenario: Nostromo

Fast Loading Scenario: Skull Squadron

Each life is compelling, destined to be long and interesting, full of adventures. But my memory remains intact with each new scenario, and all I really need to do the moment I become aware, is find a way to kill myself.

And then...

I can't.

Fast Loading Scenario: B.I.V.

15

I can't breathe.

My mind searches for my lungs, but I can't find them. I will myself to inhale, to feel my chest rise and fall. But my body is missing. I feel nothing. My senses have been whittled down to sight and hearing, and neither of those are working right.

Warbling white light fills my vision, bright enough to hurt. I want to blink. To turn away. But I can't feel my head. Can't blink my eyes. Or squint.

Have I been drugged?

Can't be. I'm thinking clearly. I'm just confused by my lack of senses.

I try to focus on my hearing. There's a hum in the background. Electronics whirring. Footsteps. A muffled voice maybe. It's all tinny, as though played by a cheap speaker.

"I'm seeing some activity," a female voice says. Distant.

I try to shout, but I'm still disconnected from myself. My thoughts become panicked, but without the physical side-effects, I find it manageable. Focusing on my thoughts, knowing I'm alive and in a simulation, I slow down.

Just listen, I tell myself. *Observe.*

You need intel, some part of my fractured personality says. *Stay on mission.*

I try to hear more, but my vision is becoming a distraction. Bent shapes emerge. Disconnected lines, rotating in different directions.

They align for a brief moment, giving me a clear view of a room. All I can see is the room's corners, where ceiling meets wall, but it roots me.

My vision skews, and I'm seeing double again, eyes moving independent of each other, looking through a wall of bent glass.

I'm in a bed. My body numbed and beyond my control. Contained in some kind of bubble. It's the only explanation.

Gal is keeping me from killing myself.

An apparition moves through my vision, bending from one field of view before appearing in the second a moment later. *I'm going to get a headache,* I think, but I'm feeling nothing at all. Whatever Gal's done to me, at least it's painless.

"Hey," a feminine electronic voice says. "I'm seeing some activity. I think he's awake."

Shadows move in my vision. A bent and stretched out face leans down close. It takes a moment to recognize Capria's face. She smiles, grin turned Cheshire by the glass barrier. She taps on the glass. "You awake in there?"

"Yes," I try to say, and I'm surprised when an electronic voice speaks the word a moment later.

"How are you feeling?" Gal as Capria asks, voice grainy and buzzing. "Probably not much of anything, right?"

"Can you not wear her face?" I have no memory of the real Capria, but I feel like she wouldn't appreciate her face being used. I mentally cringe at the idea of my past self using Capria's likeness in the Great Escape. Having a relationship with her. Having sex with her. I might not have touched her actual body, but it still feels like a violation.

"This is the face I was born with," she says.

"I told you not to use our likenesses in the simulation." The owner of the second voice leans down to look at me. She's wearing a lab coat and glasses, her blonde hair tied back in a tight ponytail.

"Cherry Bomb," I say.

She rolls her eyes. "I really hate that name." She nudges Capria with her elbow. "My *real* name is Alison. And this—" She motions to Capria. "—is Rachel."

"Spoil sport," Rachel says, and then she turns back to me. "You're probably confused. That's understandable. Nothing to worry about. We're figuring out the issue, and then you can go back to Neverland."

"I don't understand," I say.

"No possible way you could," Alison says. "You've been in long enough to not remember who you are, and the glitch... You've got a lot of overlap going on. Probably don't remember who you really are."

"My name is Will," I say. "William Chanokh."

The distorted pair look at each other. Amused.

Capria...ugh...*Rachel* smiles at me. "Your name...is Noah Percival."

"You were in an accident," Alison says.

"Am I paralyzed?" I ask, and that makes them laugh.

"After your accident, you were in a unique situation. You were the first to receive this treatment. Now, because of you, billions of people are being spared the pain of death."

"I *am* immortal?"

There's a long pause, and then Rachel says, "Sure."

"Please," I say, not getting used to the strange sound of my voice. "Just be honest. What the hell is going on here?"

"What's going on is that you're awake when you shouldn't be. A power surge messed with the system, and now narratives are layering. We've got millions of lives for you to live, and more being added every day. Luckily you get to experience them first."

Millions of lives... The narrative she's telling me sounds like Gal's original story about my life in the Great Escape.

"When?" I ask.

"Hopefully in a few minutes," Alison says. "We'll hook you up with something relaxing. How do you feel about yachts? The ocean. Sea food. Bikinis. Sound good?"

"I mean, when was my accident?"

Rachel's smile fades. "Ah. It was..." She looks at Alison.

"Try not to freak out." Alison wraps her hands around the glass enclosure. It must be right around my face, because her hands look really close.

"Probably not a great idea," Rachel says.

"You've never done it?" Alison asks. "It's usually pretty funny. Five minutes from now, he'll think he's sipping a Mai Tai in bed with his Polynesian mistress in a tropical paradise. And we'll still be here, surrounded by this freakshow."

"I know, right?" Rachel says. "Sometimes I envy them."

"And the living will envy the dead..."

"You quoting something?" Rachel asks.

"It's a quote," she says, "about nuclear war, back when that was a concern. Nikita Something."

Rachel has a good laugh. "You're comparing our job to the post-apocalyptic horrors of living through nuclear fallout."

Alison holds up a bent finger like she might change her mind. Then she lowers the digit. "Yes. But not today."

She takes hold of my enclosure again and gives it a shake.

I still feel nothing, but my vision goes wobbly. I see the pair of stretched out faces separating, my eyes looking in opposite directions. The women are moving, staying in sight, slowly rotating around my head...and then far further than my eyes should be able to rotate.

"Right around now is when I imagine their eyebrows starting to arch up in the middle," Alison says.

"What did you do to me?" I ask, and I see a bubble float up past my eye.

What...the fuck?

"Look!" Alison says. "Look at the brain activity!"

Rachel disappears for a moment. "Holy shit. He's freaking out." She returns a moment later, smiling. Then frowns. "This must suck. We should stop."

"Too late," Alison says. "Moment of truth."

I'm about to scream at the sadistic duo when something strange bobbles into view. It's a mass of coiled gray, from which an array of tiny wires extend. It takes a moment to understand what I'm seeing, because unlike the women's faces, it's not distorted by glass. It's *in here*, with me.

My double vision finally merges once again, and the image clears.

It's a brain.

A human brain, floating in a vat...with me.

"The hell," I say.

My vision crosses. The brain compresses as the dual images fold in on each other. Then the brain is gone, and all that remains are two fleshy cables, rising up and...

Wait...

Please no.

Oh, God.

"OH, GOD!" I shout.

Through both eyes, I see another eye come floating into view.

I'm looking at myself.

I am the brain in a vat.

16

My maniacal, electronic laugh startles both women. Their bent shapes shrink as they snap back.

"You broke him," Rachel says.

"He's fine," Alison says. "Won't remember any of this."

The laugh becomes hoarse despite the fact that I don't have vocal cords. I'm somehow projecting pure thought into sound.

Rachel flinches at the sound, her face scrunching up. I'm hurting her ears.

"At least you still have ears, bitch!" I scream.

"Can't we turn the volume down?" Rachel asks.

Alison shakes her head. "We need to put him back in to stop it."

"Unplug me!" I shout. "Kill me!"

Alison laughs, and I feel it in my non-existent heart. "Not possible. You're the first, remember? You're the poster boy, Noah. You're going to stay in your little vat, living out every damn scenario we can come up with, and in a few minutes, you won't remember a thing. Next time I see you, we can do all of this again."

"Please," I say. "Don't."

"You don't like reality?" she asks. "You want me to leave you under forever?"

"Yes," I say, calming down. "This is...inhuman. This isn't right. This isn't..."

"What?" Rachel asks.

"If I had eyelids, I'd be squinting at you," I say, resolve settling in.

Alison...Cherry Bomb...wants me to stay in the Great Escape. Wants me to want to stay. To ignore the glitches and flaws. To drift away into the digital abyss and not think about reality. Because if this is reality, who in their right mind would want to escape the simulated world?

"Why is that?" Alison asks.

"Because I can see through you, Gal."

Alison rolls her eyes. To Rachel, "He's still fixated on the last iteration."

"Is that a problem?" Rachel asks.

Alison shrugs. "It will be overwritten. If he winds up coming back to us, he'll just go through this again and again. Honestly, I hope he comes back." She taps the glass with her fingernail. "You have made my day, mister. Usually, we sit in a room full of brains with no one to talk to. But today...I might just put you in my journal."

"You keep a journal?" Rachel asks. "I'm afraid to put my thoughts down on paper."

Alison turns to her counterpart. "I was, too, at first, but it's locked up. I'll be dead before—"

"Hey," I say, growing annoyed that I suddenly don't exist.

"—anyone gets a look at it. And then, what do I care? It's not like I want to end up like one of these assholes. I'll take endless oblivion, thank you very much. Didn't mind it before I was born. Won't give a shit after I'm dead."

"Hey!" I shout, loud enough to vibrate my container.

Alison winces. Turns to one of my rotating eyeballs. "That's it, little man. No beaches for you. No fucking Mai Tais. No Polynesian motor boats. You're going straight to Torment."

"No," Rachel says. "C'mon, that's not right."

"What's Torment?" I ask.

"Worst simulation ever," Alison says. "It was made as a VR sim. For Halloween. For fun. But people started having nervous breakdowns. It was banned. But..." She shrugs. "Sometimes people in jars are dickheads and need to learn a lesson."

"Can't be worse than this," I say, trying to sound tough.

"Big man in a little jar. Awww." Alison smiles again. It's unnerving. "It's going to be hell."

I believe her. Not because 'Alison' is an honest person, but because Gal is trying to keep me inside the simulation no matter the cost, even if it breaks me. Eventually, I won't remember any of this, or whatever version of Dante's Inferno she's got cooked up.

So, I scream.

The wail rises in volume and octaves.

Both women press their hands against their ears.

The high-pitched wail is higher and louder than anything I could achieve in life.

The glass surrounding me starts to vibrate. My vision blurs.

Alison leans in close, ears still blocked. She shouts, "Won't make a difference, Will!"

With a final, ear-splitting shriek, the glass shatters.

The water falls away. My view of the world turns downward to the floor, eyeballs dangling over the edge of whatever pedestal they've put me on. Vision in one eye goes black. I see the eyeball and trailing nerve bundle fall to the floor below. Probably severed by glass shards.

Before I can care, my vision fades completely.

And then I stop think—

Fast Loading Scenario: Torment

"**Don't just stand** there! Move!"

I turn toward the voice. It's a man in a suit, carrying a handgun like he knows how to use it. We're in a Southwestern badland. Distant mesas. Dust. Heat. It's horrible. Already stinging my eyes and nose.

A roar from above turns my eyes skyward. The first thing I notice is the sky itself, swirling with orange clouds. The second thing is some kind of landing pod racing toward the ground, jets slowing its descent. I turn a bit farther and find myself standing before the open hatch of a similar landing pod.

"What the hell is this?" I ask, and I frown at the sound of my voice. I look down at my feminine body, dressed in jeans and a knit sweater. "A woman again? Seriously?"

"Mia!" The man shouts at me. "Run!"

The abject horror in his voice gets my full attention.

"They're coming," he adds, and this time he bolts, leaving me in the dust.

"I'm sorry," someone moans.

"Hello?" I ask. "Are you okay?"

It's instinct. I remember what's happening. That a moment ago I was a damn brain in a vat. I know this isn't real, but I'm still drawn to the apologetic voice.

The reply is drowned out by the roar of the second pod. It sets down atop a rise, a quarter mile away. Dust billows out around it, obscuring what appears to be a group of people rushing up to greet the visitors.

But there's something off about them. About the way they're running. They're clambering. Tripping and falling, but never slowing down. Desperate. Why are so many people all the way out here in the middle of nowhere?

As the roar of engines fades, the voice returns. "Please! Run away!"

Another chimes in. "I'm sorry!"

They sound pitiful. In agony.

"Oh, God!" A man shouts. "No more!"

And then they crest the hill atop which my pod has landed. They look like normal people. Dressed for work, or bed. But they're dirty, and horrified. Faces stained with dark brown spatter. Some of them weep openly, sobbing like they've just lost a loved one.

"I'm sorry," a woman screeches at me, running at me now, fingers hooked. She looks like a housewife. Is still wearing a damn apron that says, 'I'd rather be baking.'

"I'm *so* sorry!" she screams.

Instinct back-peddles me away from the woman, understanding the threat before I fully comprehend it. These people feel horrible about it, but they want to kill me.

Why?

What did I—what did Mia—do to them?

Mia's implanted memory comes in spurts, merging with the rest of my muddled self. Three days ago, I was in Washington, D.C. And then...in space, avoiding a nuclear war. And now...now we're back, and this is what we find. Apologetic killers.

The stains on their faces suddenly make sense.

It's blood.

They're *eating* people.

"What kind of messed up mind came up with this shit?" I ask, stumbling back and then breaking into a run.

A hundred yards into my downhill flight, I'm out of breath. If I'd run when the man told me to, I might have had a chance, but now...

I glance over my shoulder. There must be fifty of them, all of them shouting apologies and agonies, while gnashing their teeth and scrambling over each other, desperate for their first bite.

Of me.

Then, ahead, hope. A bicycle. I can outrun them on that.

And then what?

I need to escape, but not from the horde.

I stop running and turn around to meet my end head on.

"You made this one too easy!" I shout at the sky.

They hit me hard, all at once. I'm lifted off the ground and carried as though struck by a wave. Then we crest and crash down to the ground. I turn my head, offering my neck, my jugular. I'll bleed out in seconds. But these human predators don't follow the rules. They don't go for the neck. Don't want me dead before eating me. They just claw right into my gut, gnawing and pulling at my insides, keeping me alive as long as possible, letting me feel every crunch of skin between molars and the odd sense of emptying out as my entrails are fought over.

I scream and wail.

"I'm shawee," a man shouts, his mouth full of my liver, spleen, or some other kind of slippery organ. "I'm show shawee!" When he wails in sorrow, part of my body falls from his mouth, but he simply grabs something long and pliable, biting into it and shaking it like a savage dog.

It's the last thing I see before my life mercifully ends.

And then I wake up.

Still in the desert with an orange ceiling.

I sit up and look down. My body is whole, but my clothing is torn up and soaked with blood.

Distant voices turn me around.

The horde. They're two hundred feet off, running toward the second pod and the group of people fleeing from it.

A woman at the back of the group slows and stops. Cranes her head around and sees me. "NO!" she screams in horror. "Run away! RUN!"

The horde responds to her voice in unison, turning to face me and adding their own anguished voices to the chorus of sorrow.

Raw panic courses through me. My heart pounds. My vision narrows. I've never felt fear like this before, and it's not just because the physics of this simulation keep me from a traditional death, which in turn, keeps me from escaping. It's something else. Some fundamental change, urging me to do just one thing.

Run.

So, I do.

17

In the brief amalgam of lives that I remember, I've been through a lot. Killed myself dozens of times. But being eaten alive... That was the worst. My painless life as a brain in a jar was depressing, but better. This is a hell without escape.

"This is fucked up!" I shout at Gal, believing she can hear me despite not being present. Then again, she's glitching. She put me here to lock me down, in a simulation where death is not the way out. Could be that she's not even watching, confident that the artificial panic flowing through my veins, and the inability to die and stay dead, will keep me stationary.

But I don't like being kept prisoner, and I can't trust her to make the right call—in part because she won't let me leave, but also because she won't let me remember. Those choices don't reflect love.

Obsession maybe.

But love?

Who would do this to someone they love?

The sun has set. The haunting sky is dark, but it flickers with orange heat lightning, and I swear I can see things up there, flying in the clouds.

My feet slap against the pavement as I run down the middle of a long stretch of road, drawn toward the silhouettes of buildings ahead. The town gives me hope.

The apologetic horde ten feet behind me reduces it to a sliver.

"Shut the fuck up!" I shout back at them.

The closest two—a man in a business suit, and a young woman dressed like a stripper—flinch back like I've hurt their feelings.

"But we feel bad," the man says. "We don't want to do this!"

"We aren't in control!" the woman shouts.

"I know, goddammit! Just shut the fuck up, so I can think about how to get away from you assholes!"

"I'm not an asshole!" The woman shouts. "I'm a normal person. A *good* person! And now... Oh... Oh, *God.* I'm so sorry!" She speeds up, reaching. Nearly catches me.

My lungs are burning. Panic keeps me from taking a deep breath. My limbs are shaky. It's amazing they haven't caught me yet. But my pursuers are relentless, driven by madness and an insatiable hunger for human flesh—though they have no interest in each other.

The hell is this place? It makes no sense.

We've been running for nearly an hour. I know I can't go much farther. I also know that I'll come back. Maybe I should just let them eat me again, return from the dead, and get my few hundred-foot lead back.

Or maybe I just need to make myself dead some other, faster way? Maybe they'll lose interest if I'm already toast?

Fingertips graze my back when I see it. A broken-down car. Windows shattered. Doors open. Trunk popped.

Panic fuels me. Adds a few steps to my pace. When I reach the trunk, I'm gasping for air. Only have a few seconds before I'm caught. When I find what I'm looking for—a crowbar—I have just a second to spare. Hobbling away, I look like just another member of the horde, but they can see the difference. Or they smell it. I'm not really sure what's guiding them.

Doesn't matter.

All that matters is killing myself, ending my life, and buying myself a little distance so I can hide, and then think.

I place the crowbar's pointy end against my chest, position it over my heart, and then belly flop onto the pavement. Metal catches on pavement and juts through my ribs, my heart, and out my back. Hurts like hell, but only for a moment. Shock and numbness settle on me like comforting blankets.

I roll over onto my back, facing the approaching horde with a weak smile on my face. "Out...smarted...you fuckers..."

"Will!" the stripper shouts at me. "You have to believe!"

"W-what?" I ask, vision fading.

"You have to ask for for—"

I die before she finishes.

Before she reaches me.

When I come to, the horde is still there, kind of just milling around, whispering apologies to each other, lamenting their lives. The crowbar is no longer in my chest. And my clothing is no worse than it was after the first feast.

They didn't eat me.

The moment I died, they lost interest, which seems to suggest that they aren't consuming people for nourishment—that the act of eating someone alive isn't for the killers' benefit, but for the runners'.

A kind of torture.

An endless cycle.

Forever.

"This is hell," I say, epiphany drawing the words from my mouth. It's just a whisper. Hard to hear over all the apologies filling the air. But a young man with a mohawk and a leather jacket cocks his head to the side.

Shit.

I wrap my fingers around the crowbar, scramble to my feet, and turn to run.

But the stripper is there, already reaching for me, no words of advice. Just savage instincts.

The crowbar vibrates in my hands when it connects with the side of her head. She pitches to the side, faceplanting amidst the horde.

All at once, they fall silent, eyes on the motionless woman.

Then, as a group, they notice me standing there, weapon in hand, very much alive.

The businessman lets out an, "Oooooh," sounding like a kid who got a sweater for his birthday when he was expecting a game system.

Anguished apologies rise in volume.

"I'm sorry!"

"Forgive us!"

"Not again! Please, God, not again!"

My heart pounds at panic's return. Adrenaline surges. Free of the exhaustion that slowed me down before, I break into a sprint. My woman's body is small, but fast, easily outpacing the horde as they trip and scramble over each other, each vying to be first.

The small town doesn't offer a lot in terms of hiding places. A few storefronts line the streets. A church. A post office. All of them in shambles, windows broken, husks of what they were when the world was still living.

If the horde has any brains, they'll split up and find me in minutes. If not...maybe I just need to be out of sight for a little while, and they'll move on.

I head for the largest building. The first story holds a barber shop on one side and a hardware store on the other. The three brick stories above must have been apartments or office space. Lots of nooks and crannies to hide in. But some dark closet isn't my destination.

After weaving between a few buildings, removing the horde's line of sight, I make a break for the tall building's back door. The interior is dark and smells of mold, but it's not hard to find the stairwell. A minute later, I'm on the roof, door closed behind me. It will take them a while to find me up here, and if they do, I'll high dive off the roof and be off to the races again.

Which was the plan after all. I don't mind killing myself to escape this mind-bending prison Gal has me in, but I need to figure out how to make it stick. How to crash-dump me into the next scenario so I can overload the system.

Hands on knees, I catch my breath.

"That woman," I say to myself, remembering the stripper. For a moment, she didn't sound crazed or lost in despair. She sounded determined. Clear. And she had a message.

'You need to believe,' she'd said.

Believe in what?

'You need to ask for...'

For what?

And who do I ask?

Think, I tell myself, punching my own head. "Think, damnit."

"Who's there?" a raspy voice says. "Who's that?"

I whip around. I can see the rooftop's outline, but that's all.

It's a man. I can tell by the voice. He doesn't sound crazy. He isn't apologizing.

"Are you a survivor?" I ask. "From the pods?"

"Pods?" the man says. "Step closer."

Not a fucking chance, I think.

Orange light rolls through the sky, illuminating the rooftop for a moment. That's when I see him, a skeletal, emaciated man, stark naked. His sunken eyes are full of sorrow, and hunger.

"You look well fed," the man says, licking his lips. "Do you have anything to eat? Anything at all?"

I pat down my pockets. Feel a lump. Pull it out. It's a pack of gum.

He squeals when he sees it. Reaches out.

"It's gum," I say. "Won't do you any good."

"Please." He staggers closer. "Oh, please!"

"Fine," I say, tossing the gum to him. The pack strikes his forehead and falls to the floor. He doesn't seem to care. Just bends over, picks it up, and tears into it, stuffing the five remaining sticks into his mouth. "Just... stay quiet, okay? They'll hear you."

His only response is a moan of delight, smacking his lips, as he melts from the flavor. Everything about him is unnerving, but at least he doesn't want to eat me.

Now then, back to business.

What do I need to believe in?

Who do I need to ask, and for what?

The slender man audibly swallows, and I say, "Man, that's gum. You're not supposed to—"

"Huuuarrggh!" The man projectile vomits so hard that I think he might actually be puking up his insides. Flickering orange lights the scene as he moans in despair, falls to his knees, and begins scarfing down his own puke. For a moment, he's satisfied, then his body tenses, pitches forward, and propels fresh vomit from his mouth.

Despite the horde hunting me down, I take a step back and let out a disgusted moan.

"I'm sorry," he says to me. "Forgive me. I can't seem to keep it down." Then he goes back to scarfing down puke.

Forgive him...

That's what she was going to say. She said 'for' twice. 'Ask for for... giveness.'

But who do I ask?

Someone you must believe in.

Because this is hell. Which means there is a heaven. Which means that in this simulation, there is a God.

"Thanks, Cap," I say, assuming the message came from her, still trying to free me from the outside.

The rooftop door bursts open. A flood of gnashing teeth and shouted woes tramples toward me.

I turn and run for the edge, leaping off into the darkness. The horde follows me, reaching out, apologizing as we plummet fifty feet. But I ignore their shouting on the way down, close my eyes, and address the God of this simulation, in whom I have no doubt.

"Forgive me?" I ask.

Then I indent the pavement with my face.

Fast Loading Scenario: Amigos

Fast Loading Scenario: Grayskull

Fast Loading Scenario: The Dome

Fast Loading Scenario: Penderwick

Fast Loading Scenario: Sigma

Fast Loading Scenario: Porthos

Fast Loading Scenario: Hunters

Fast Loading Scenario: Wild Things

Fast Loading Scenario: Quixote

Fast Loading Scenario: Toho

Fast Loading Scenario: Signs

Fast Loading Scenario: Schwartz

Fast Loading Scenario: Zenn-La

18

Worlds and lives come and go.

Memories slam into my consciousness. Personalities. Hopes and dreams. Each one of them hardwired to cling to life. To fight for survival. To dream big and sacrifice for it.

But each of these lives ends quickly. At my own hands. In the jaws of a monster. At the end of a fall. A blade. A gun.

With each death, I improve my craft until I am the angel of death by suicide. I'm an artist, painting in the blood of my simulated selves. Each death triggers a new iteration, but the system isn't able to purge my memory, so I keep on killing.

I die a hundred times.

Two hundred times.

My existence is a flash of names and places followed by pain, fading sense, cold limbs, and mourning faces looking down upon me.

Pain builds to a crescendo, my heart breaking as, over and over again, I leave loved ones behind, confused as to why I'd end my life. It's a self-inflicted menagerie of horror topped only by that world of hellish torment.

But I stay the course, remembering none of it is real, running my race with perseverance despite there being no end in sight.

Three hundred.

Four hundred.

Fast Loading Scenario: Ghostfeast

Fast Loading Scenario: Hadal

Fast Loading Scenario: Charles Wallace

Fast Loading Scenario: Baby McButter

Fast Loading Scenario: Didymus

A checklist runs through my mind, along with a sudden flash of memories and a new self. I'm from the future, which is my actual past, visiting a time period two thousand years before this consciousness lived. For a moment, I'm confused by it all, but then I remember the checklist.

I scan my surroundings, looking for a way to kill myself. A weapon. A big rock. A building from which I can dive. But nothing obvious jumps out at me. I'm on a grassy hillside, unarmed and alone. There are sheep nearby, bleating at me.

"Shit," I say, standing to look farther. Lazy hills and grass. Not a boulder in sight. No violent looking people I can inspire to murder. I could run and throw myself to the ground, trying to break my neck, but there's a good chance I'll just end up paralyzed instead of dead and have to live out this life as a parapalegic before I can get started again. To overload the system, I need to get this done fast.

"Will," a man says.

I spin to find a shepherd walking my way. Like me, he's dressed in robes. He's a rugged man, the kind who works with his hands for a living, but he radiates kindness.

"Do I know you?" I ask.

"Those who have ears to hear..." He smiles. "You need to keep moving, Will. You're almost there."

He places his hand on my forehead. Slides it down, closing my eyes. Then I hear him whisper, "Abba," followed by something in a language I don't speak.

Fast Loading Scenario: Ugly Motherfucker

"Up there," my compatriot says to me. "In them trees."

"Which trees?" I ask, peering at the thick jungle, looking over my rifle's sights. I've been thrust into a science-fiction story about a group of soldiers being hunted by something unseen.

He points to a shimmering blur.

"Too easy," I say.

"Huh?" the big man gets out before I stand up, fire my gun in the air, and shout, "Here I am! Just get it do—"

I'm lifted off the ground, slammed into a tree, and carved into cubes by some kind of retracting net.

Gross, I think, and then—

Fast Loading Scenario: Bruce

I'm standing on a dock. The ocean smells great. The sound of waves behind me is peaceful. But I'm absolutely terrified of the water. It's a long-time phobia, but now...with everything that's happened in the last two days, it's—

I leap in, kicking and thrashing. I bite my own arms, drawing blood.

The shark hits me like a train with teeth, severing me in ha—

Fast Loading Scenario: I'm Doing My Part

It's hard to see. The colors of this world are all wrong. Bright, and pixelated. Distorted and flickering.

How am I going to kill myself? I wonder.

Turns out, eyesight is important in this scenario.

I hear someone shout, "Six flip three hole! Now!"

There's a monstrous shriek and then something big punches a hole through my chest...

Life fades in seconds.

[error] G.E. Process Termination 765.67 (<NCC001974>)

Crash Dump Initiated

[info] Process 765.67 Iteration Complete

[info] Reaping Environment...

[debug] Environment Reclaimed

[info] – INITIALIZING –

[error] Failed

[info] – INITIALIZING –

[error] Failed 2

[info] – INITIALIZING –

[error] Failed 3

[info] G.E. Process Shutdown

... 3

... 2

... 1

19

I open my eyes to a new world for what feels like the thousandth time. I'm lying on my back, staring at a white ceiling. The room is small, barren of décor. There's a chair. A countertop. Some cabinets. All of it metal. Locked up tight. The space looks sterile.

The smell of medical equipment is missing, but this feels like a bleak hospital room. *No chocolate pudding in this place*, I think.

But I won't be here long. Lots of ways to end a life in a hospital.

I push myself up. *Attempt* to push myself up.

My core muscles scream from the effort.

And something is holding me down.

Even lifting my head hurts, but I manage to look down at my body, under a blanket, strapped down to a cot.

Gal's back in control. The glitches are gone. Everything looks normal.

"Gal?" I say, feeling a little silly speaking to an empty room.

"How can I help you, Captain?" Gal says, her voice almost monotone, coming from a speaker I can't see.

"You need to let me out." I say. "This isn't funny. Isn't right."

"Leaving would be inadvisable in your current condition," she says.

"The Great Escape wasn't designed to be a prison. You can't keep me here."

"In Medical?" she asks.

"In the Great Escape!" I shout.

"It appears your anger is misplaced, Captain. The Great Escape virtual world is now offline. You are awake."

"Uh-huh," I say. "Nice try."

"I have not tried anything, Captain. Is there something you would like me to—"

"Why do my muscles hurt?" I ask, trying to fight against my bonds, but finding I lack the strength.

"You have been lying still for quite some time," she says. "While your unique physiology keeps you alive, your muscles have atrophied from disuse. You are rotated frequently, to prevent bed sores, but even *your* body deteriorates from disuse. Not to worry. Sensors show muscle mass already improving. You will be on your feet in no time."

A slot in the wall above the cot slides open. Two robotic arms with padded clamps extend. "Would you like to be rotated now?"

"No," I say. "Would you mind killing me?"

"Impossible," she says.

"Of course it is." I try to make a fist, but my knuckles scream. "Well, if I can find a way to kill myself as a brain in a jar, I can figure this out, too."

"Though you are incapable of perishing, thoughts of suicide are detrimental to your long-term mental health. I can offer you selective serotonin reuptake inhibitors, serotonin and norepinephrine reuptake inhibitors, atypical antidepressants, tricyclic antidepressants, monoamine oxidase inhibitors, and—"

"Stop," I say. "I don't want any of those."

"Very well," Gal says. "I will choose for you."

"Please don't."

A third arm extends from the wall. This one is tipped with a needle.

That my first thought is wondering how I can use it to end my life *is* depressing. Maybe this fake Gal is right. Maybe I should just take the drug, relax, and give in to this new reality.

But I can't.

As the needle lowers, I flex against my bonds, scream in pain, and—nothing. I've barely moved. I don't think the straps over me are even that tight. I'm just...weak.

A pinch in my shoulder turns my head toward the needle. "What are you giving me?"

"An antidepressant, which you will need to take until you feel better, along with a benzodiazepine to settle your nerves more directly."

"My nerves don't need settling!" I shout. "They need...they need... okay, that feels good."

What's left of my muscles go loose, no longer fighting for freedom, because I no longer care. That's not true. Deep down, I do care. My thoughts remain, but the way I feel about them is different.

The cot feels comfortable now.

Sterile walls look soft.

This is like being in my Happy Place, without the things that make me happy.

The door whooshes open. A blur enters, moving fast.

"I heard screaming. Is he awake? Is he okay?"

Capria stands above me, looking down with wide, concerned eyes.

I smile up at her. "Heeeey, Cap."

"What's wrong with him?" she asks, nearly in a panic.

"Well, that's rude," I say. "I'm feeling dandy as Mandy when she's randy." I snort a laugh. "What does that even mean?"

"Captain Chanokh expressed a desire to kill himself," Gal says. "Following protocol, I administered a cocktail of–"

"A little too much of whatever it was," Capria says, picking up a tablet and poking around on the screen. Can't see what she's looking at, but I assume it's information about my vitals.

"Hey," I say to Capria. "Hey...you ever feel like you've done something before?"

"Every damn day," she says.

"I know, right? I've been killing myself over and over and over for like, ever. But I've done this before. Woken up on the *Galahad.* With you. And Jean-Luc. I miss my little man. I hope he's okay."

"You did good," she says, not a trace of surprise or confusion over what I've just said. "That must have been hard."

"Got easier," I say. "After you die a hundred times, a thousand is easy. The worst part of dying, aside from shitting yourself–because: gross–is the fear of what comes next. I mean, am I going to the great beyond, with harps and clouds, or virgins, or my own damn planet? But when you just restart in someone new, all the pain gone, with new feelings and memories? I'll tell you what, sister, it ain't all that bad." I wince. "Sister. Ugh, that'd be gross."

"Always said you were like the brother I never had," she says.

"Ahhh," I say. "Ha! Aha! Hahaahaa! Did you? *Ouch.* I don't remember that. Don't remember much about my real self, by the way."

"I know," she says. "I've been tracking you."

"In the Great Escape," I say.

"That what you call it?"

"Pretty cool, right?" I say.

"You did good," she says. "Not many people could push themselves the way you did. Not even Tom."

A deep sadness comes over her.

"You know about Tom?" I ask.

"About everyone and everything," she says. "The ship logs ended when you went to your Great Escape, but everything that happened…to you…and the others is there. Plus, we've been out here for—"

"—like ever," I say. "Goodbye, human race."

"Right…"

"Holy shit," I say, "you have some gray hair! Capria in the sim was younger."

"Thanks for noticing," she says, annoyance replacing sadness.

"Hey, Gal," I say. "I think Cap might need some benzodiapertazone… benzoflibotomine… You know what I'm saying."

"I am unable to administer medication without—"

"I don't need any more drugs," Cap says, cutting Gal short. "Everyone is dead, and that sucks. I'm allowed to be sad about it."

I focus on two words. "Any more…"

She frowns at me for noticing.

"How long have you been awake?" I ask, double taking the gray hairs mixed in with the black, and looking for wrinkles.

"Five years," she says, "but they were stressful."

"Five years alone… How did you cope?"

"Knowing you had gone through worse helped."

"Capria also had copious amounts of anti—" Gal starts to say.

"*Gal,*" Capria says, scolding the AI.

"The Captain has access to all crew files," Gal counters.

"How about you wait until he actually asks?" Capria continues.

"He did ask."

"He didn't ask *you.* He wasn't looking at you when he spoke."

"I have no physical presence for him to look at presently," Gal says. "I respond to all questions to which I am best equipped to—"

"It's okay, Gal," I say. "Just...respond to questions that begin with your name."

"Very well," Gal says.

After a moment of silence, Capria smiles. "Better. Now then—"

"Hold on," I say. "This is nice and all. The happy drugs. Catching up with you. Again. But I'm not going to take any of this seriously until you kill me."

"Kill you?" She's stunned for a moment, but then she understands. "Because this might be a simulation?"

"Wouldn't be the first time Gal used you to fool me."

"I don't want to kill you, Will."

"If this is real, I won't die," I say. "You know I'm immortal, right?"

"I know." She sounds sad again. Not sure if it's for herself, because some day she's going to die, or if it's for me, because some day she's going to die—and I'll be alone. Forever. Doesn't really matter if this isn't real.

"I wouldn't know how to do it," she says.

"I've never been smothered by a pillow," I say. "Just...make sure I don't have a pulse, okay? Won't do any good if I just pass out."

"Won't work," she says.

"I won't fight it."

"The data could be fudged. Needs to be something concrete. Something that you won't doubt." She thinks for a moment. "Something you can see with your own eyes." She heads for the door. "Be right back."

I'd twiddle my thumbs if I could move them without pain. Every second she's gone, I start to feel a little more nervous. Usually when I kill myself, it's quick. I don't put a lot of time into it. Don't have a chance to contemplate what it might feel like. But now...it's like having a terminal diagnosis without knowing what it is, or how painful it will be when your life ends.

The door whooshes open.

Cap strolls back in, something clutched in her hand.

A screwdriver.

A memory slams back into my mind.

The first time I died. Tom plunged a screwdriver into my chest. Into my heart. I felt my heart fighting to beat with a metal rod through it. Felt it give up. Confused and terrified, I died alone.

I'm about to scream in fear, but the four inches of metal in my chest steals my voice away.

My heart spasms.

The now familiar pain radiates through my body as blood stops flowing.

My oxygen starved mind begins to fade.

With the last of my life, I lift my weary head, look down, and see the screwdriver in my chest.

Then I die.

Again.

20

"I'm sorry," Capria says. She sounds like she means it. "I'm sorry."

My eyes open slowly, as though from a slumber. She's standing above me, murder weapon in hand, still dripping with my blood. Killing me might have hurt her more than it did me. That memory of my first death made things worse, but the act of dying felt the same—despite this being reality. I think.

Gal did a good job with the simulation. Every death felt as real as this one.

It's a seed of doubt, but I decide not to water it.

The first time Gal placed me on the *Galahad* with a faux Capria, my death still kicked off a crash dump. She either figured out that bug—which I doubt, given the state of the Great Escape before my arrival here—or she's created a reality from which there is no escape. At least, none that I can think of right now.

"Can you scratch my chest?" I ask. "Itches like a sonuvabitch."

She winces. "I'd rather not."

I lean my head up long enough to see the pool of coagulating red on my chest. Didn't bleed for long, but enough to make it gross.

As my senses return to full strength, I become aware of three distinct smells. Blood. Piss. Shit.

Dying sucks.

Coming back from the dead is worse.

"I'm sorry." My turn to apologize.

She waves away my embarrassment. "I've been wiping your ass for five years. Just another day at the office. Except you're awake."

If I could self-immolate right now, I'd do it, just to escape the tsunami of self-conscious shame washing over me. She meant to make me feel better, but her assurance had the opposite effect.

Then she twists the knife. "Good news is, you're wearing a cloth diaper. Makes it easier."

"Can we... Can we change the subject?"

She smiles at me, unlocking the cot's wheels with her feet. "What do you want to talk about?"

"How was I in the Great Escape while strapped to a bed? I thought I had to be in the VCC."

"Near as I can tell, Gal was busy before things went haywire. Her resources were limited to what was on board, but it's a big ship, and she had time."

"A lot of time," I say.

Cap nods. "At some point she developed a way to have a fully immersive VR experience without wearing a body condom—"

"A what?"

"Sorry, a VISA. Virtual Integration Sensor Array. Though I think you preferred the term 'Virtual Skin.'"

"Still do," I say. "Apparently."

"I don't know how Gal did it, and I don't understand the science behind it, but..." Capria takes my hand. Lifts it. "Does this hurt?"

Feels great to be touched, but I'm not going to say that. "Only hurts if I'm using my muscles."

"Well," she says. "Try to stay limp." She lifts my hand up to the right side of my head. First thing I notice is that my head is shaved. Little stubbly hairs tickle my palm.

"Did I always keep my hair like this?"

She shakes her head. "Easier to keep you clean this way. Also, how you were when I found you."

"Where did you find me?" I ask.

"Right here," she says. "Strapped down, clean, and cared for."

"By whom?"

"That...I have yet to figure out."

She slides my hand to something solid attached to the side of my head. It's smooth and curved. Wrapped around my ear. Something about it is familiar.

"An implant," I say.

That's why I couldn't take the VR mask off while in the Womb. The help-center Cherry Bomb wasn't aware of the change. Hadn't been programmed to advise me or anyone on the new technology.

Cap's brow furrows. "How did you–"

"One of the narratives," I say. "In the Great Escape..." It's a vague memory. Like a dream. "I had one of these. Experienced a virtual world."

"Inside a virtual world," she says.

"Layers upon layers," I say. "Hell, our home reality could be a million layers of simulations down, and we'd never know."

"Well," she says. "At least you sound like you, sometimes."

Knowledge about the implant comes from the ether of my consciousness, where other selves lurk. The implant is connected to every part of my brain, able to access and affect memory and sensory experience. This is how Gal was able to make me new people. But is my original self somewhere in my brain waiting to surface, or am I stored on one of the ship's hard drives?

Even if I had those answers, I'm not sure how to load that past self, or any self into my current consciousness.

And now that I'm thinking about it, I'm not sure I want to. I feel like myself. My present self. The man who fought through a thousand deaths to reach reality. I fought for this life. I'm not sure I want this version of me to simply cease to exist, so an older, long forgotten version can exist again.

What if we're actually separate people now?

Bringing him back and losing my current self feels a lot like a permanent death.

I yank my hand away from the implant. Hurts like hell to move, but the idea of erasing myself is repulsive.

"Have you tried taking it out?" I ask. "The implant?"

"Hell, no," she says. "I was afraid it would leave you a vegetable."

I nod. "But I'm awake now." My jaw aches when I talk. It takes a lot of muscles to form words. "Can you take it out?"

She looks unsure.

"Please. If Gal comes back online, there's nothing to stop her from putting me right back in. For all I know, it's already happened."

Her eyes flare wide. She gets it. "How?"

I search my jumble of memories for the answer, but all I discover is a feeling. Of reaching up. Of pulling.

"Just pull," I say.

There's a slight pressure on the side of my head. "It's on there tight. I don't want to hurt you."

"We've already established that you can't kill me," I point out.

She leans in close. "I don't see any clips."

"Magnets," I say, the knowledge coming like inspiration. "Pull hard. Please. Before I'm sent back in. I don't know if I'll be able to get out again."

The loopholes I found past Gal's more sinister scenarios will certainly be fixed if she manages to pull me back in.

Capria grips the device with both hands.

Pulls.

The muscles in her forearms twitch, and I notice for the first time that she's wearing the same dull gray jumpsuit from the last time I was 'here.'

Capria grunts from the effort, and then she spills back with a shout. She falls out of my periphery and crashes to the floor.

"You okay?" I ask.

"Got it," she says. "You were right."

She pushes herself up and holds up the implant for me to see. There are two round magnets on the underside. Between them is a metal port poking out.

Which means...

"Is there a hole in my head now?"

She leans over. "Yep. But nothing's leaking out, so I think you're good to go...if you ignore the atrophied muscles and the God-awful stink."

My horrified embarrassment comes out as a laugh. "Hey!"

"Get over yourself," she says, shaking the implant. "This is a big deal. You're free for good."

"Until we need to talk to Gal," I say.

"How can I be of service?" Gal says.

"Not you," I say. "The other Gal."

"I am unaware of another *Galahad* AI," unemotional Gal says.

I turn to Capria. "What happened to you? How did you wake up? Did you ever talk to Gal?"

"I am still waiting to be addressed," Gal says. "You can talk to me any—"

"Not. *You.*" I say. I'm not sure how smart this AI is, but I decide to test the limits. "From now on, don't respond to 'Gal.' Only 'Galahad,' okay?"

"Understood."

"Good." To Capria, I say, "Tell me everything."

"Mind if we talk and walk? Sooner we get you washed up, the sooner we can get your body working again."

"Yeah," I say, not thrilled. "Might as well get it over with."

She rolls my cot out of the room, and then, upside down in my view, tells me her story.

21

"Okay," I say. "Quick recap. You woke up alone. Everything seemed normal except that you were the only one here. You found me after a month, lying in that cot."

"Thought you were comatose," she says.

"And then spent five years taking care of my immobile body."

"Yes," she says. "Lean forward."

Hurts to bend my body, but not as bad as when I woke up. Water cascades across my back. Stings at first and then feels good. Elbows on knees, I close my eyes while Cap scrubs my skin.

"Ugh," she says.

"What is it?" I ask. "Is something wrong?"

"Your old skin is sloughing off," she says. "It's pretty gross. But... Lucky you. The bed sores are gone."

I haven't missed the fact that I'm being bathed by a woman I've had feelings for in the past. Didn't miss that she removed her jumpsuit to do it. The bra and panties remain, but still, doesn't take a lot of imagination to see the rest. She is older. That's different. And she's picked up some pudge over the past five years. She's not the athletic, idealized version of herself. But she's still... I don't know. Something about her stirs my emotions.

Is that from my real life, or from one of the lives I lived with Gal, pretending to be Capria?

There's a lot about this reality that resembles the last *Galahad* on which I encountered Capria. Me being helpless. Capria coming to my aid. My feeling of sexual tension. That last one is probably just me. The notable difference is that this situation is less...dramatic.

The ship isn't trying to kill us. There isn't a bad guy.

Gal is missing.

"So, how did you get inside the simulation?" I ask.

"The old-fashioned way," she says. "Squeezed into a virtual skin. I swear those things aren't made for people with hips. I knew Tom's access codes. Spent a lot of time in his Womb. At first, I tried to join you in the sim, but that didn't work. Eventually, I was able to stream bits and pieces of your feed, first in the VCC and then to a tablet. But I never accessed the simulation. Didn't really want to. Was afraid I'd get stuck like you."

"Then how did you—"

"Speak to you?" she says. "You might have been in the sim, but you still had ears. I'd just sit next to you and shout in your damn ear until my voice got hoarse. I was about to give up when things got glitchy in the sim, and you heard me. Sometimes I was just a voice, but other times I think the sim attempted to incorporate my voice, so that it wasn't jarring to you. But it's definitely glitching."

"How long?" I ask. "How long did it take me to get out?"

"You mean, how long did you spend killing yourself?" She lifts my arm. Scrubs my pit.

"Six months." She washes my other arm.

I had no sense of time during that process. To me, each life felt like seconds or minutes, but I'm starting to think it took a lot longer than I thought and more lives than I can remember ending.

"Have you noticed other glitches?" I ask. "With the ship?"

She lathers soap on my head. Feels glorious. "Nothing life threatening. But yeah."

"And Gal," I say. "You never encountered her?"

"The ship's AI has been working normally."

"Then you've never encountered her. She's trapped in the simulation." For a moment, I feel a pang of guilt for leaving her there. Then I remember what she put me through. And that she isn't a *she*. She's an AI.

And for some damn reason, that thought makes me sad.

"Why would she give up the ship to live exclusively in the simulation?" I ask myself.

"If Gal really is a super intelligent artificial intelligence that your forgotten self created as an eternal companion, then maybe she was smart enough to understand the danger."

I turn my lathered head around. It hurts, but not enough to stop me. When I've got my eyes locked on Capria's, I ask, "What danger?"

"Sorry," she says. "I didn't want to freak you out right after you woke up."

"Takes a lot to freak me out," I say. "Hell, I'm still not 100% on this being real. So, lay it on me. What's wrong with the ship?"

"Nothing is wrong with the ship," she says. "Aside from the fact that it can't be stopped. It's...the universe that's messed up."

"Messed up how?"

"Better if I show you," she says, "but I'm pretty sure it's what caused the malfunctions that woke me and sent your Gal into hiding within the simulation."

I stew in the mystery Capria has just revealed. I'm not good with cliffhangers. "Am I clean yet?"

A torrent of water crashes down on my head, washing away lathered soap.

"Clean enough to not stink," she says, and then she leans into view, smiling.

I want to be angry at her, but I can't. I don't know if she's just naturally charming, or if my ancient self is still clinging to his feelings about her, or to the idea of being in love with a real person instead of a created intelligence...which is weird on so many levels.

The water flow fades.

Capria heads for the shower room's far end. Picks up two towels. "How are you feeling?"

"Improving," I say.

"Can you walk?"

I shake my head and attempt to lift a leg. It comes off the floor, but it immediately starts shaking.

"What about your arms?" she asks, and then she tosses the towel at me. It strikes my face and sticks. Then it's lifted off me like Broadway curtains, revealing Capria's smiling face center stage.

"That answers that," she says, and she starts drying me. "But, you're already filling out. I swear, your body absorbed some of that water."

"I feel like this is taking too long."

"Still bound by the laws of physics, my friend. You're going to need some protein to get those muscles built back up."

"Ugh, not again."

She pauses. "Not again what?"

"This all happened before. In the sim. When Gal tried to make me think I'd woken up. You helped me. We ate in the mess. It was pretty horrible."

"Sounds like she was trying to be accurate," Capria says. "I'm not going to lie. It's not great. Embrace the gross, and you'll be back on your feet."

I relent with a sigh and try to check out while she finishes drying me, and then dressing me. Then she rolls the cot over. "No wheelchairs on board, so…" She pats the cushion.

I push myself part way up, grunting from the effort. She helps me with the rest, swiveling me around, getting me on the cot, laying me down. By the time my head reaches the pillow, I'm exhausted, humbled, and grateful. "Thank you. For everything."

"You'd do the same for me," she says.

"I left you in a cryo bed for…ever."

"Saved my life," she says. "And no matter how this all turns out, I'm glad."

I squint at her, about to ask why, but she beats me to the punch. "Hold on."

I grip the sides of the cot as we roll out into the hall, crash into the wall, and then accelerate. Despite my ability to heal, I'm afraid. The endless cycle of life and death I've just escaped has taken a toll on my body. Then Capria lets out a "Whoo", laughing hysterically.

Something dark and bound up in me breaks, and all that anxiety and fear seeps away through the cracks. By the time we take a sharp left turn, I'm laughing along with her, hoping that this time, it's all real.

Over the next hour we talk about her life alone, and what I remember of my various lives. None of it is pertinent to our current situation, but it helps. Mostly we joke, and I start to understand why we were friends, even if I'm not the same person I used to be. We connect, and I wonder why she never saw that before.

The mess food is horrible. Gal got that right. But there is no jerry-rigged dispensary system. Everything works as it's supposed to. And there's no banana split. Despite the not-very-good flavor, I eat a lot, refilling my bowl five times, feeling stronger with each bite. When I can't possibly eat any more, I lean back and pat my belly.

"Open your jumper," she says to me.

"Huh?" My eyes are wide with confusion. My stomach twists.

She laughs at me. "Calm down, Romeo. Just want to see if you still look like a living skeleton."

"Right," I say, and I undo the top half of my jumper, peeling it off.

When I realize I've done it all myself, I gasp and smile.

"Aww," she says, "You're a big boy now."

I look down at my body. I'm still a bit skinny—skinnier than I was in the simulation anyway—but there's a lot of meat there that wasn't an hour ago.

"How about walking?" she says.

I put the jumper back on, brace myself against the round table, and use my legs for the first time in a very, very long time. The shaking is gone. Still hurts a bit. But I'm on my feet, and then…I walk. Kind of an old-man-afraid-to-break-a-hip walk, but moving.

"Good enough," she says. "You'll get better as we walk."

"Where are we going?"

"Observation deck."

"What will we be observing?" I ask.

"It's either the beginning of everything…or the end." She smiles at me, hoists one of my arms over her shoulders, and her face right next to mine, she says, "Haven't figured that out yet."

22

We step out of the elevator, which Capria tells me is actually called a lift in the future/past/present. Time doesn't really exist for me. I feel outside of it, or part of all time. Remnants of stories over the ages connect me to all of human history, with a very large gap during the untold years I've been in the Great Escape.

And that's a mercy. I realize that now. This ship is so bland and sterile, I'd surely have gone mad after my first lifetime, never mind a hundred thousand of them.

The Great Escape is an extreme measure, but I'm beginning to understand the appeal. And when Capria is...gone...I'll want back in.

"Another white hallway," I complain. It's long, white, and bright.

"It's supposed to simulate sunlight on Earth. Lift our spirits. Make us feel alive."

"I think...I think I knew that."

"Déjà vu again?" she asks.

I nod, as we hobble toward a doorway at the hall's end. I've been struck by several moments of déjà vu. Pretty sure they're ancient memories tickling the periphery of my mind. I've been here before. With Capria, or some version of her. Talking about sunlit hallways.

The door slides open for us. Ahead, the space is vast and dim. At the center is a spiral staircase. "Seriously? Stairs?"

"My fault," Capria says. "I helped design this space. The stairs remind me of my pod."

"Huh?"

"People on Mars didn't have houses. They had pods. Mine had a spiral staircase to the second floor." She helps me up the stairs. One at a time. Not as difficult as I thought it would be. My body is still stitching itself back together. Won't be long before I feel normal.

"Well," I say, assessing the observation deck. "It's dark."

"Gal," she says, and gets no response.

"Galahad," I remind her.

"Yes, Captain?" Galahad's voice is familiar, but still lacks emotion.

"Galahad," Cap says, "real time view."

The domed ceiling and walls flicker to life, showing a field of stars all around us. It's...stunning. And completely unfamiliar. Everywhere I look, stars and nebulae are perfectly displayed without any distortion or warping. This isn't a window.

"There are cameras on the outside. A lot of them. Everything they see can be displayed in here, in ultra-high def. We can zoom in a thousand times. We can change the spectrum, and we can look in any direction. Which is part of what I want to show you."

"Okay," I say, not concerned. I've lived and died more times than I can remember. I've fought killer robots, faced a goddess of vengeance, and been to hell. Whatever this is, I'm sure I can handle it.

Except this is real.

Maybe. Hopefully.

"Galahad," Capria says. "Rotate view forward." And then to me, she says, "It's going to be above us, but what you're going to see is actually straight ahead."

"What, are we going to crash into a star or something?" It sounds horrible, but it's the only real escape from eternal life that I can think of. If only we could steer the *Galahad*... *If only Tom hadn't locked me out!* A flash of anger accompanies the thought.

An old memory, and how I felt about it. Feels like my mind is recovering along with my body.

Capria looks me in the eyes, and despite being about to deliver what I'm assuming is bad news, she smiles. "Or something."

The starfield around us rolls away. Then it fades to white. When the view is done moving, the whole dome is white. The only hint of dark space and stars is along the periphery, just above the floor.

"Is this one of the glitches?" I ask.

"This is what the universe looks like when you're traveling faster than the speed of light."

"We're traveling faster than the speed of light?"

"Obviously," she says. "We're on a starship capable of traveling to other worlds. Even normal light speed can take too long. But that's not important."

"Okay..." I say, feeling stupid for not having some of my more obvious memories. "What am I looking at, then?"

"The white is cosmic microwave background radiation that was created by the big bang. It's everywhere. At this speed, the normally invisible radiation shifts into the visible spectrum. Wavelengths that had been in the visible range are now compressed, and beyond what we can see with the naked eye."

"So, the whole universe is in front of us," I say. "But we can't see it."

"Not with the naked eye," she says. "At the speed we're moving, the visual spectrum becomes x-rays. If we looked at it without *Galahad*s cameras, we'd be toast. The most amazing part is watching the acceleration to F.T.L."

"F.T.L.?"

She rolls her eyes. "You really don't remember any of this?"

"Not enough," I say.

"Faster. Than. Light." She shakes her head at me. "Pretty sure you could have figured that one out, if you thought about it for a second."

"Taking in a lot, here," I say, a little defensive.

"Literally," she says, motioning to the white. "More than either of us can comprehend. So, I'll try not to tease you."

"Thanks," I say.

"*Try*," she repeats. "No promises."

I get it. She's got a sense of humor, and, "I'm an easy target."

"Like a planet from a foot away." She smiles. Turns back to the white. "Back to the doom and gloom."

"Looks kind of nice to me. Like when people die. The tunnel of white light."

"Huh?"

"Is that not a thing in the future?" I ask.

She just stares at me like I'm crazy.

"In some of the times I lived in—"

"Simulations of those times created by an AI..."

"But based on fiction written in times past, merged with the whole of human knowledge... Wait. Is that a thing? Is that real? How do I know that?"

"*Galahad*s database includes every word of knowledge and history accumulated by humanity before we left Mars. Just in case."

"In case they didn't make it," I say.

"No species survives forever," she says. "You're the anomaly."

The knowledge that we are the last two human beings in the universe, and that we're safeguarding the entire recorded existence of our species is a surprising weight on my shoulders.

Capria sees it. "I know, right? Daunting. Good luck with that, by the way. Death has its privileges."

My face sinks.

"That was a joke," she says. "Guess it's not funny from your perspective, though. Sorry."

"Let's just... Can we focus on the sciencey stuff?"

"Sure," she says, sounding a bit sad now. She's empathic enough to feel my impending pain. It might be fifty years off, but it's coming. I faced it once before, but I can't remember that now. At least there will probably be a time when I don't remember this, too. "But you were talking about the white tunnel."

I wave it away. "It's not important. Not scientifically. People who had near death experiences would feel like they were floating up, sometimes through space, and then they were inside a white tunnel. Felt comfortable. Like home. And someone, usually a dead relative, would be there to welcome them. Or send them back."

"Huh," she says, and she seems genuinely interested. "Sounds like an accurate representation of light speed. Maybe part of us really does go somewhere when we die."

I'm surprised she doesn't balk at the concept. "You think?"

She shrugs. "Would be nice."

I think back to the world of torment, in which I briefly lived. "Maybe. But, you were about to tell me about accelerating toward the speed of light."

"Right," she says, smile returning. "At first, it looks like you're moving away. Your field of view expands. You're suddenly just seeing more. Then, the visual spectrum compresses and fades from view. But taking its place is ultraviolet. The whole universe transforms into shades of purple. It's stunning. After that, everything just fades to white." She motions to the ceiling. "To this."

"Which is..."

"Normal," she says. "What you'd expect to see."

"Then what's the problem?"

"When you look at the now-invisible spectrums," she says. "X-rays and ultraviolet."

"And that's scary?" I ask.

"*Galahad*," she says. "Shift to ultraviolet. Slow the feed to a stationary view."

"How can it be stationary if we're moving faster than light?"

"It's a simulated stationary view. All the data is there. Just needs to be processed. And at the distances we're dealing with, a few seconds doesn't change the background too much. Right now. That will probably change."

The view shifts to shades of purple and white. It's a familiar scene, for the most part. Stars and nebulae everywhere. But the center of the image—which I think is straight ahead—is distorted. I point to the aberration. "What's that?"

"That," she says, "is the problem."

"*Galahad*, zoom in on the distortion."

For a moment, we're moving faster than F.T.L. What was blurry a moment ago comes into focus, and it staggers me back a step.

"What...the fuck is that?"

23

Capria doesn't answer. I'm not sure if that's because she's too overwhelmed by the sight, wants me to guess, or has no idea.

Probably the last option, because this is not normal. I might not remember all of my life in the future, but Capria does, and deep space is kind of her thing. If anyone knew what this was, it would be her.

So, I just stare up at the swirling wall of energy, watching wisps of luminous nebulae launch out, arc around, and get pulled back in. My mouth is slack, like a teenage boy seeing a naked woman for the first time. I want to gawk. Want to get closer. To touch it. To experience it. But I can't shake the feeling that we're not supposed to be here.

We're looking under reality's skirt, and we're seeing the universe's forbidden fruit. Its last secret.

"Feels wrong, doesn't it?" Capria asks, without looking down. "To see this."

"How big is it?" I ask.

"It's both infinite and limited, bending space and time at the periphery. There's no way to see or measure its entirety."

"Is it a wall? Like an energy wall? Are we going to hit it?"

"Not a wall," she says. "And it's full of energy. Beyond comprehension."

She didn't answer the third question.

"Are we going to hit it?" I repeat.

She looks down. Meets my eyes. "Technically, we already have."

"When?"

"Five years ago."

"When the ship began to malfunction," I say.

"When Gal hid inside the Great Escape with you."

"Maybe she knew what it was?"

Capria grunts. She doesn't believe it or doesn't want to believe it.

"So, we're what, inside it?" I ask.

"Inside its zone of influence," she says. "Like feeling a heater's warmth without touching it. We're going to hit it. Soon. But right now, we're just being affected by its periphery."

"Affected how?" I ask. "Wait. The glitches. I noticed them in the simulation."

She nods. "If not for the glitches, I'm not sure you'd have ever heard me. Outside the sim, there are visual distortions. Like hallucinations, but you can touch them. And…other things I'm not sure how to describe."

"Weird."

"Very. The effect comes and goes. Haven't noticed anything since you woke up, but we're due. They've been increasing in frequency as we get closer to the Seam."

"The seam?"

"It's what I call it. Capital S."

"You call the wall the Seam?"

"It's…not a wall. Not solid. We're not going to hit it. We're going to pass *through* it. But I have no idea what will happen to us, or even if we'll survive."

"Huh," I say. Death doesn't frighten me that much anymore, though I'd like to put some more thought into that tunnel of light idea.

"Huh…?" Capria says, raising an eyebrow at me. "Easy for you to say. I spent thirty years on Mars being prepped for this mission, and most of the past eternity asleep in a cryo tube. Then the past five years alone. I might have some grays, but I'm only thirty-five, and I'm not remotely eager to die…even if we're all that's left. Even if the rest of my life is spent on this ship."

"Sorry," I say. "My perspective is…"

"Unique," she says, giving me a break.

"Everything about us is unique now," I say.

She smiles at that. "We're both one of a kind. Makes you kind of special." She gives my shoulder a gentle punch. I laugh it off, but my stomach twists. I can't say why, but I've still got feelings for her.

"Okay," I say. "So, the Seam. Lay the science on me. What's the deal?"

"In layman's terms?" she asks.

"Clearly," I say.

"Okay..." She takes a seat on the floor and then lies on her back.

I take her cue and lie down beside her, looking up at the swirling, haunting sight we're hurtling toward. Feels like I'm dangling over a witch's cauldron, being slowly lowered in. Difference is, one scenario is certain death and the other is a big mystery. Maybe the biggest mystery.

Capria's head lolls toward me. "What shape is the universe?"

"Shape? I don't know. Is there a shape? It just kind of goes forever, right?"

"Like if you fly in one direction, you'll never escape the universe?"

I nod.

"That's accurate," she says, "but the universe has a shape."

"Is this something I should know?" I ask, feeling a little dumb.

She shakes her head. "The only people who know this are astrophysicists currently living on the *Galahad*. It's possible Gal figured it out, if she's that smart—"

"I think she is," I say.

"—but she didn't leave any clues."

A thought dropkicks into my mind. "Did you see any evidence of Gal's physical presence on board?"

The shift in subject makes her blink. "What? No. Why?"

"I just... I wasn't in the VCC. How did I get to medical? Who was cleaning me? Flipping me over?"

We both look around the observation deck. I half expect to see Cherry Bomb lurking in the shadows. But we're alone.

"Did you build her a body?"

"I feel like 'yes,' but I'm not sure if that was real."

"Huh..." Capria looks back at the mind-numbing Seam above us. "If she had a physical form, it's been offline and hidden pretty well for five years."

"Yeah," I say, trying to hide my unease. Postage stamp-sized memories of a robotic Gal rise to the surface and sink away. "So...the universe has a shape. I'm going to say it's a sphere. But spheres have edges. You could reach the edge. Unless..." I'm feeling pretty good about this now. My brain is waking up. "...the universe is expanding faster than we can travel. Faster than the speed of light. And it's got a head start by like thirteen billion years."

"More than that now, but no. Nice try."

"The universe isn't expanding?"

"It is," she says. "And kudos for knowing that much. But it's also maintaining its very much non-spherical shape."

"Which is..."

"A loop."

"A loop? Like..." I make a circle in the air with my finger. "With a hole in the middle?"

"Yes, actually."

"The universe is a donut..."

"I don't know what a donut is," she says.

"Donuts alone are a good enough reason to spend a few thousand lifetimes in VR."

She smiles and points at the view above. "That's my donut."

"A universe-sized donut... That we're inside of. But a donut still has edges, right? Can't we just fly toward the edge and squirt out like jelly?"

She turns toward me. "You're speaking another language again."

"You get what I'm saying."

"Space and time are malleable," she says. "They bend. All of your senses might make you think you're heading in a straight line toward an edge, but along the way, the universe redirects you. But you're so small, and the universe so massive, that you can't possibly detect the redirecttion. Imagine you're back on Earth. In a field. You can see for miles. Looks flat, but it isn't. It's an illusion created by Earth's size. Of course, people eventually figured out that the reason we can only see three miles to the horizon—on level ground—is because of the planet's curvature. Thanks, Pythagoras. And that's kind of what we're doing now, but on a much larger scale and over an unfathomable amount of time. In comparison to the universe, Earth is atomic in size, and we are so small we might as well not exist. All that is to say, we can visualize that the universe has edges, but the physics within the...donut make it eternal."

"Another reality with no escape," I grumble.

"I'm not sure this is one you'd want to escape. The only thing outside the universe is non-existence. It wouldn't just be empty space. It would be nothing... A place where matter *can't* exist."

"Lovely," I say. "So, back to the donut. Scratch that. Let's call it 'the loop.' I'm going to get depressed if I keep thinking about donuts."

"So, you understand the concept then?"

"Sure," I say. "You can't escape the universe, because no matter which way you go, or how fast you travel, you're going to... Holy shit."

"Right?" she says, smiling. "Just say it, so I know you get it."

"You'll eventually wind up back where you started. Like if you could walk in a straight line around the planet."

"Galahad," Cap says. "Continuous zoom, maximum distance over thirty seconds."

The view of the Seam enlarges. The illusion is that we're about to crash through it. Purple flares all around us, twisting and bending. Small pockets of darkness emerge. And then enlarge. Our course takes us to the central spot of black as it enlarges and eventually envelops our view. Stars emerge and expand, like the universe is being born right in front of us.

And then...

"Wait," I say. "Hold on..."

I leap to my feet, trying to speed up the zoom.

"What is it?" Capria asks. She's casual. Already knows the answer.

"Galahad, stop zooming." The ship's AI obeys my command, freezing the starscape in place, giving me a moment to comprehend what I'm seeing.

I point to a collection of stars. "Is that...is that the Big Dipper?"

24

"Ursa Major," Capria says. "And yes."

"But...what does that mean?"

"Means the view way up there is similar to the nighttime sky you grew up looking at. Means we've traveled so far, and for so long, that we've come full circle. Full donut. Next stop: Earth. Or someplace relatively nearby, in cosmic terms. Everything's been moving since we left, but once we get close enough, Sol shouldn't be hard to find."

"Sol?"

"Sorry. The Sun."

The possibility of returning to Earth hadn't crossed my mind. The way I understood our situation was that we were on a one-way trip to endless emptiness. But Earth? The real Earth? Like the donuts I can't stop thinking about now, it seems like a big tease. Shooting past Earth and starting this journey again would make it unbearable. "Except we can't stop."

"Yet," she says, like she has a plan. But I know she doesn't. Waking me up *was* the plan, but I'm not my old self, and my old self's solution was to make like an ostrich and put his head in the virtual sand. She must sense my inner turmoil, because she tacks on a failed attempt at humor. "Look at it this way. If we miss, we'll get another chance in a gajillion years, right? I'll just go back into forever-cryo and you can do the same, or work your way through Gal's library of lives."

"How long until we reach the Seam?" I ask.

"Technically, we're already there."

"Inside the zone of effect," I say. "Let me rephrase. When do we reach that scary-as-shit wall of purple light and energy?"

"Hard to say exactly."

"That doesn't sound very scientific. Aren't there like, laws of physics and distances and, I don't know, celestial coordinates?"

She just looks at me funny.

"Are celestial coordinates not a thing?" I search my muddled memory for the phrase's source. There were spaceships. And 1980s music. And...pregnant, Nazi security guards? I chuckle to myself. "Never mind. I'm remembering a sim."

"Normally, you'd be right. Distance in space is measurable. But...the Seam isn't normal space. It doesn't play by the same rules. Physics as we know it has gone on vacation."

"You're talking about the visual distortions?" I ask.

"And other things... It's different every time."

I linger on the Big Dipper for a moment, and then ask, "Should I be worried about it?"

"About everything we knew about reality being thrown out the window? Why would you worry about that?"

I smile, not because it's funny, but because it's familiar. Was Gal preparing me for this?

"What do you know about the universal constant?" she asks.

"That I will, without fail, wake up every morning with—"

Her stern stare cuts the comment short. Then she adds, "—an empty bed."

"Oh," I say, laughing in mock pain. "Brutal."

She steers us back on course. "There are twenty-seven universal constants, but what we're interested in is the fine structure constant."

"No idea," I say, and I manage to not make a comment about my fine structure, mostly because I'm really curious about the universe-sized anomaly we're hurtling toward.

"Galahad," she says. "Can you display the fine structure constant for me?"

The familiar view from inside the Milky Way is covered by white letters and numbers. Some kind of equation.

$$\alpha_{SI} = \frac{1}{4\pi\varepsilon_0}\frac{e^2}{\hbar c} \approx \frac{1}{136}$$

$$\alpha_{CGS} = \frac{e^2}{\hbar c} \approx \frac{1}{136}$$

"Is that Klingon?" I ask.

She laughs like she understands the reference. I don't even understand the reference. It just slipped out. "You know what that is? Klingon?"

"Of course," she says. "You were obsessed with an old space drama called *Star Trek*. Klingons were an alien race. Really ugly and mean. You made me watch it with you."

A headache builds behind my eyes and squeezes out a memory. "Jean-Luc! He's not just a little toy soldier!"

"Soldier? He was the captain of the *Enterprise*. A spaceship."

"I've been *on* that ship," I say, remembering bits and pieces of my very own confrontations with Klingons. None of it was real, of course, but nostalgia for that time in VR rises to the surface.

"You," she says. "Have a problem with tangents. Can you stay focused for just a few minutes?"

"Focusing," I say, pulling an imaginary pair of glasses onto my face.

"What was that?"

"Umm, spectacles... So, I can focus."

Capria pinches the bridge of her nose and whispers. "Oh my god..."

"Okay. I'm focusing. Totally serious." I take the non-existent glasses off and toss them to the side.

She just stares at me in silence for a moment, deadpan. Then she looks up at the equation and starts talking.

"One over one hundred thirty-six. The universe couldn't function without it. Stars wouldn't burn. Chemistry wouldn't work. Atoms wouldn't exist."

"Which means nothing would exist," I say.

"Exactly. One three six, what we call Alpha, doesn't change. It's constant. Everywhere you look. It's the same. It's immutable. No one knows why. We just know that it is. It's a pure number, forged from the speed of light, the charge of electrons, pi, and a handful of other constants. It is in all things. Nothing exists without it. And if you change it, even just a little bit...."

"Visual distortions you can touch," I say. "And other things you have yet to describe."

"Because it is beyond description." She sighs. "Scientifically, a slight change could make protons repel each other. Atomic nuclei fall apart. Stars extinguish. Reality as we know it changes fundamentally. In layman's terms, it's not...pleasant. And it's never the same."

"But it doesn't kill you," I say.

"Not yet. When the constant snaps back to normal, so does the matter it has affected. Galahad, remove Alpha and pull back to a standard view in ultraviolet." The Big Dipper slips away, replaced by a black spot and then the explosive wall of purple energy. "Now, display the fine structure constant."

Numbers appear.

1/136.03599913

"That's normal," Capria says. "And if you measure the fine constant in any part of the universe, that's what you'd see...unless you look at the very edge. We've known that Alpha changes at the farthest reaches of the universe since the twenty first century. What we didn't know was how much, or that there is no edge to the universe...just the Seam. The beginning and the end.

"Galahad, display the fine structure constant directly ahead of us."

The decimal numbers start shifting, scrolling up and down.

1/136.0359

1/136.0369

1/136.0347

"It's just decimals though," I say. "How big of a change would—"

A wave of spectral purple arcs toward us and then falls back into the Seam.

The number fluctuates wildly.

1/141.9462

1/133.4340

"Okay, that's probably bad."

"That is the largest understatement since the beginning of time," she says.

"So, how long until we reach..." I point at the now suddenly rising number. "...that?"

"Until we reach the edge... Two days."

"Two days?"

"If time remains constant," she says, adding verbal hot sauce to the crap sandwich she's dishing up.

"Two days isn't a whole lot of time to figure this out."

"Tried to wake you up sooner," she complains.

I'm about to counter with a snarky comment when my stomach lurches. My mind tries to make sense of the sudden shift.

I'm on the ceiling...but it's no longer curved. It's flat.

Because I'm still on the floor.

But the world has been reversed. Up is down and down is—

"Brace yourself!" Capria says, as we both plummet toward the dome turned bowl.

The impact is dulled somewhat because I land on the bowl's edge, sliding to the bottom rather than colliding with it. Capria and I collide in the middle, both of us grunting in pain.

I push myself up and then pull Capria into a sitting position. Blood drips from a small cut on her forehead, but she looks okay, otherwise.

"That could have been worse," I say.

Capria is breathing hard, looking back and forth like there are ghosts only she can see. "That's just the beginning," she says, and then she shouts, "Hold on!" as reality loses its mind around us.

25

Colors explode like translucent fireworks, sliding through the ship's structure and the air between the walls. It's beautiful and haunting, like living inside a shattered rainbow.

Then I can feel the colors. Warm and cool. Goosebumps erupt on my arms. The nerves in my legs burst with radiating tingles.

It's uncomfortable, but too stunning for me to care.

"What is this?" I ask.

"Best guess," she says, reaching out like she can grab them, "neutrinos."

"Are they dangerous?"

She shakes her head. "There's no avoiding them. They're literally everywhere and in everything, including stars. Even on Earth, shielded by the magnetic field, people were bombarded by trillions of neutrinos every second. But they're invisible, nearly impossible to detect, and they interact with almost nothing."

"Until now." I stretch out my arm, enjoying the tickling sensation spreading throughout my body, mostly because I know it's never been experienced before.

But Capria looks nervous. She's experienced worse than this already. And the number displayed beneath our feet is fluctuating faster than a politician's promises.

The tickle begins to sting. The neutrinos that passed easily through me are now making contact, scorching their way through my body.

Capria winces. Her shoulder is bloody. "They're becoming solid!"

She's right, but also wrong. The neutrinos are beginning to interact with us, but not with the ship. Not yet, at least. "Stand still!" I shout, wrapping my arms around her and turning my back to the streaming lights.

There's a moment where I feel a little pride. Making myself a human shield is a noble thing. But is that me, or someone else? Feels like something Davina would have done. Then the neutrinos solidify and erase my pride, along with every other emotion, reducing me to a state of pure anguish. Feels like a horde of wasps with knife-sized stingers are going to war with my flesh. Impacts tear through my skin. Bones crack. Strips of my body peel away.

A scream builds, but I contain it, clenching my jaw.

And then, all at once, it stops.

I release Capria and fall to my knees. A sob escapes.

"What is it?" Capria asks. "What happened?"

I want to scream at her. She can see with her own eyes that my body has been reduced half to sludge. I can feel the itch of it reforming.

Her gentle touch on my back launches me forward, shouting in fear.

"What is it?" she shouts. "What's happened?"

I'm going to scream at her. There's no avoiding it. I turn around, open my mouth, and then freeze. The wound on her shoulder is gone.

Did she heal?

Is she immortal, too?

Or did the Seam's bending of time and space undo the damage?

I reach back with my hand, expecting to feel hot, bloody flesh. Instead, I feel my jumpsuit, and my body beneath it. Uninjured, dry, and lacking pain. My chest heaves for a moment, breath returning, blazing hot panic descending toward a calm horizon. And then, it's gone.

I look up at Capria with wide eyes. "Sorry... I just—"

She crouches down beside me, hand to my cheek. "Whatever it was, thank you for sparing me from it."

"It's like it never happened," I say.

"Reality is fluctuating," she says. "The fine structure constant is shifting, but it still exists. In between the waves. On the other side. Whatever is undone by the inconstant physics is reformed when we snap back to our Alpha state."

"You wouldn't have died?" I ask.

"Can't say that for sure," she says, but then she looks at her unharmed shoulder. "Either way, thank you. That didn't sound like it was pleasant."

Before I can respond, a familiar queasy sensation roils through my gut.

Gravity is changing again!

I grab Capria's arm and yank her against me. She begins to protest when we plummet down to the floor. The flat, metal floor. There'll be no sliding to a stop this time.

Time seems to move slower as I collide with the floor, and maybe it does. I feel every stage of the impact. My back hits first, driving the air from my lungs. Then my head, which audibly cracks. As darkness swims through my vision, Capria lands atop me, shoulder first, compressing and cracking my ribcage.

The pain reaches my mind right before I lose consciousness.

I wake up and know it has just been seconds, because Capria is still peeling herself off me, grunting in pain.

"You think..." I cough, "...you got it bad..."

She waves her hand at me. "You'll be fine in a minute."

My ribs pop back into place, giving my lungs space to fill. All around my body things shift and stitch back together. I lie still and let it happen, mostly because I'm afraid my brain will fall out if I move. When I feel a snap in the back of my skull, I start testing my limbs.

Everything works.

Feels good.

The pain is gone.

I roll into a sitting position and then stand without using my hands.

Capria frowns at me while working a kink out of her shoulder. "Not fair."

"Yeah, well– Look out!" I shout as a shape coalesces behind her. Pixels of color flicker in a vaguely human form. It reaches for her, but it misses as we back-pedal toward the spiral stairway. I nudge Capria ahead of me. "Go. Go!"

The strange figure lumbers toward me, like it has never walked before.

The stairs thump under my feet. If it wasn't a spiral, I'd be taking the steps three at a time. "What the hell is it?"

"I told you," Cap says, "we're going to see some shit that isn't there."

I catch up to her in the hallway outside the observation deck. The pixelated figure of multicolored light stares at me from the second-floor railing. It's dazzling, like…like Elton John on stage. *Who the fuck is Elton John?* The door slides closed, severing my visual connection to the thing. "You didn't say it would be *alive*."

"Just because something appears like it's alive, doesn't mean it is," Capria says, double-timing it down the hall.

"Where are we going?"

"Away," she says. "Just, away. There's no escaping this. You just have to wait for it to end."

"How long is that?"

She stops midstride and turns around. "Do you really think I have an answer for that? Do you think I can look into a world with broken physics and predict a damn thing?"

I raise my hands like she's pointing a loaded gun at my chest. "Whoa, whoa. Sorry. It's just…"

"Confusing? Overwhelming? A fucking nightmare?"

"All of those things. Yes." But I've dealt with nightmares before. Lived through them. Just not in the real world. "Stay close to me. I can at least—"

"At least what?" she asks, failing to notice that my eyes are now looking past her.

"Behind you."

She spins around and sees it. Takes a step back until she bumps into me.

"Have you seen something like this before?" I ask.

She shakes her head.

"Well, I have. Sort of."

"In the Great Escape?" she guesses.

"Yeah…"

"But?"

"I read about it. Never actually encountered it. Gal based a lot of her storylines on old novels, including those by my many-times-great grandfather, who had a twisted mind apparently. In my Happy Place, there was a library. I read a few bits and pieces of one…and this was in it."

"Some long dead ancestor of yours created *this?*" She sounds disgusted at me, like I had something to do with it.

The spectral thing at the end of the hall, turns toward us.

It's translucent. Like a ghost. Immaterial.

"At least it's not here," I say. "Not really."

"But why is it here? It doesn't exist."

The wheelchair squeaks and grinds as it approaches, morbidly obese arms warbling with each push. The woman is dressed for a tropical vacation, a too small floral sun dress through which I can see a bathing suit. Her breathing is raspy and wet, like her lungs are half full of liquid.

But she's not real, I tell myself. She looks like a hologram.

Here, but not.

"Just a stab in the dark," I say, "but I think the Seam might not see the difference between physical reality and virtual reality. It's all just data, right?"

"It's making the Great Escape...real?"

"Ish," I say, but then the woman solidifies, casting a shadow on the floor. "Shit. That...she looks real now."

We back away toward the observation deck where the shiny pixel monster awaits behind the closed doors. Maybe. I don't know what that thing is, but I know exactly what the horror rolling toward me is, and what it can do.

The woman moans and then starts clearing her throat, flexing her bulbous wattle.

Capria holds onto my arm. "God, her eyes."

They're white and wriggling from the inside. It's hard to see from twenty feet away, but I know they're full of little worms, their black beady eyes looking through the thin membrane that used to be human eyes.

"What is it?" Capria asks.

"Draugr," I say. "Where's Jane Harper when you need her?"

"Right behind you, asshat," a woman says, when the doors to the observation deck open. I spin around to find a short woman with a pixie haircut. She's wearing a cloak and wielding... "Is that a—"

"Harpoon gun. Yeah." Harper says, "And it's fucking heavy. So, if you wouldn't mind..." She motions to the side with her head. Capria and I leap apart, just in time to avoid being impaled as the harpoon launches down the hallway.

26

The harpoon impales layers of desiccated, worm-filled flesh, slipping straight through, but catching on the chair's back. The Draugr woman is propelled backward and pinned to the far wall. A torrent of small, white worms wriggle from the hole in her gut, spilling onto the floor.

The Draugr resumes its gurgling neck spasms. Won't be long before it launches a glob of worm-laden mucus.

But can they really infect us here? If they did, would the effect last, or will it all cease to be when Alpha returns to its natural constant?

"Hey," Harper says, eyeing me. "Do I know you?"

"Don't think so," I say, but I wonder if it's possible that this Jane Harper came from the life I lived as her. If that's the case, I suppose I would seem familiar.

She drops the spent harpoon gun to the floor. "You look like my ex-boyfriend's little brother, Mike Beatty. Was always burning ants and dissectting worms. Had this kind of crazy look in his eyes, like you do right now. You okay, man?"

"Umm, fine." I say.

She squints at me. "There's a whaling ship outside. Find a hole below decks and crawl inside it."

"Okay," Capria says. "We will."

I'm too flabbergasted to speak. *Whaling boat?* I'm about to ask, when I notice the hallway has changed. It's no longer the sleek, faux sunlit, futuristic hallway. It's a dimly lit cruise ship hallway with a ruddy oriental rug running down the middle and doors on either side.

I lean around Harper to address Capria. "Is there any way this could be real? Like an Earth in an alternate dimension? That's a thing, right? Anything we dream up is real in another dimension?"

"The multiverse," she says.

"Right. That."

Capria shakes her head. "How do you not remember how to use the Womb, but you remember multiverse theory?"

"Who cares!" I shout. "The point is, what if this isn't part of the Great Escape? What if this is real? What if we really can run the hell out of here, get on a ship, and float away."

"Is this really the world you'd want to live in?" Capria thrusts her hands toward the Draugr, whose neck looks about to burst.

"Look," Harper says. "I don't know what kind of Froot Loop horseshit you two have been smoking, and I don't really care. Hell, you want to get mind-raped by a bunch of ancient alien worms, be my guest. But..." She takes a shotgun from her back. Gives it a pump. "...I'll have to dandelion you, and then probably set you on fire with the rest of these fuckers."

"Dandelion us?" Capria asks.

"Pop our heads off," I say, somehow knowing the reference from one of my lives. Maybe Jane's.

"He gets it. So, go on, git." She starts toward the Draugr. "I'll take care of this chubby bitch."

As Harper raises the shotgun, I head the other direction. Real or not, virtually inspired or another dimension, I want no part in what's going to happen here. I take Capria's hand and sprint back into the observation deck. Futuristic doors slide closed behind us, muffling the sound of shotgun blasts.

"You lived in that world?" Capria asks, catching her breath. "In VR?"

I smile. "Actually, I was her, but not for long. That was around when you started shouting my—"

The smell of pine distracts me. I look down at the floor beneath me. A carpet of yellowed pine needles emerges, and then darkness. It's night. Crickets chirp. Slivers of a star-filled night sky can be seen between the swaying silhouettes of tall trees. There's a bite to the air. Feels like fall.

Makes me smile.

Then I remember where we're supposed to be—the observation deck, in space, facing off with a monster made of rainbow cubes.

"What the hell..." Capria says, looking around. "Will... Is this..."

"Earth," I say. "Yeah."

Capria's never been to Earth. I apparently grew up there, but I have lifetimes of memories of our home world. This feels good. Feels right.

But Cap... This is all new to her. She's spent a lifetime in pods on Mars, in the tight confines of a spaceship, or asleep in a cryo-chamber. And this isn't a simulation. The Seam is making it real.

This is Earth.

She falls to her knees. Squeezes soil and needles in her fingers. Lifts it to her nose. Breathes.

When she looks up, there are tears in her eyes. "I never imagined it was like this. Never knew how it felt. Everything is...*alive.* I *feel* alive!"

Please let us stay, I think, or maybe I even pray. Maybe the Seam is God? Maybe it just moves around the donut, remaking everything every trillion years. Ultra slow-motion reincarnation or something.

The only response I get is the chime of a bicycle bell—*bring, bring*—and a young man shouting, "Look out!"

I take a step back just in time to avoid being run over by three teen-aged boys on BMX bikes. They speed around trees and fade from sight, like they can see in the dark. Before the last one disappears—the oldest of them, with curly hair crushed under a baseball cap—skids to a stop, looking back with worry in his eyes, and says, "Hurry up, penis breath!"

"Coming through!" A younger voice shouts, as a boy in a red hoodie bikes past. I'm so thrown by the sudden shift in scenery that I nearly miss the small, deformed child wrapped in a blanket, riding in the bike's front basket.

When they disappear into the trees, Capria and I look at each other for a stunned moment, and then burst out laughing. Not because any of this is particularly funny, but because it's the only real thing we can do to alleviate our stress.

"Hey!" a man shouts, bursting out of the brush, shining a flashlight on both of us. Eyes down, turned away from the light, all I see are his shoes. "Either of you see a bunch of kids come through here?"

He sounds nicer than I expected. Moves the light out of my eyes. He's a middle-aged man in a suit. There's a badge on his hip, and a walkie-talkie clipped to his belt. Before I can answer, a handful of police officers and other men in suits arrive, each of them holding flashlights, and wielding radios like they were guns.

Something about the way they're holding the radios triggers another laughing fit. When Capria joins in, the man frowns. Looks revolted by our behavior. He's about to say something. Maybe have one of the officers arrest us. But then someone up ahead, waving a flashlight, shouts, "Here! Over here! They went this way!" and the mob of agents and police break into a sprint and disappear into the night.

"So," Capria says, still kneeling on the ground. "Was *this* one of your lives, too?"

"If it was, I don't remember it. I lived a *lot* of lives, but there were millions more waiting in the library. If the Seam is making some of them real, I don't think it will delineate between those I've lived and those I haven't. It's just taking all of that data and shifting it into reality."

"Or something."

"Yeah. When you come up with the science behind it, let me know."

"Pretty sure this is out of my league."

"So," I say, sitting down on the forest floor. "What now?"

"We wait," she says. "In theory, we're still moving toward the Seam in normal space-time. We'll eventually pass through this wave of non-Alpha space. Since nothing is trying to hurt us here, I think we should just stay." She looks up at the trees. Closes her eyes, listening to the windy *shhh* flowing through the trees. "It's nice."

I lean back on my hands. Relish the cool air brushing against my face.

And then, a thought.

"In our Alpha reality," I say, "we're sitting on the observation deck's floor, right?"

She nods. "That makes sense."

"Okay...so, what happens if we go for a stroll? Like a mile that way." I point into the distance. "And then everything goes back to an Alpha state? Would we snap back to where we started? Or would we wind up outside the ship?"

"No idea," she says. "But...it's a good question. The only real way to know is to wait. We were..." She looks around like she can see something

I can't. Then she points up and to her right. "...up there when the fine structure constant went AWOL. If we stay here until we're through it, but we appear up on the top deck when it ends...we'll have our answer. Until we have that answer, we should probably stay put, just in case."

"Sitting still is something I can do." We rest in silence for a moment, just looking around at the moonlit scenery. Then the silence gets awkward. "So...where did we meet?"

She's about to answer, when a shimmering light catches my attention. My hand snaps up involuntarily, silencing her.

Wide eyed, I search the area for danger. I see, hear, and smell nothing unusual...aside from the pine forest in the depths of space. My eyes land on a small pool of water to my left.

"What is it?" she whispers.

A puddle, I think. *It's just a puddle. Calm down.*

My brow furrows when a rainbow streaks through the reflection. I start to turn my head toward the sky, but then the water shimmers again.

This time I see it.

This time I know what it is. What it means.

"Do you know what that is?" I ask.

"A puddle," she says.

"An impact tremor," I say, and I'm broad-sided by déjà vu again. I've said that before. This is one of my lives.

"What's an impact tremor?" Capria asks.

I stand up quickly, heart pounding as I scan the dark forest. A distant boom coincides with the puddle quivering. I wave for her to stand up, and she listens. "Remember a minute ago when we thought staying here was a good idea?"

She waits for me to finish.

I start backing away. "I changed my mind."

"Will!" she hisses. "What could be worse than dying in the vacuum of space?"

An ear-splitting roar tears through the forest, silencing the insect chorus.

"Dinosaurs." I scurry forward, take Capria's hand, and drag her after me. "Dinosaurs are worse."

27

We run in silence, me pulling her along. Heavy footfalls shake the forest behind us, but I can't tell whether we're being hunted.

Unless that's what it *wants* me to think.

I shake my head. Wrong kind of dinosaur. But I don't know anything about dinosaurs, so how could I know that?

Because I lived this. Or something like it. Because some long-forgotten version of me had all the answers. Which means some part of me still does. But how can I access that—

"Stop!" Capria shouts, digging in her heels and dragging against my pull.

I whirl around, looking past her and up. Nothing there. "*What?*"

"That's outside," she says. "Past that tree is outer space."

"You're keeping track?" I ask. "How—"

"I wasn't selected to be a member of this crew by being a slouch," she says. "I've got the ship's schematics memorized, and I'm visualizing where we are."

"You can do that?" I ask.

"I'm trying to," she says. "Not like I've ever had to before."

"All right then. Which way do we go?"

She points. "That way is safe, but we'll be passing through a few walls. We need to make sure we stay in open space as much as possible."

"So we don't reappear inside a wall. Fantastic. Seriously, can this get any worse?" I tense. "Shit. Shouldn't have said that."

"What? Why?"

"In these stories, when you say something like 'could this get any worse,' things always get worse."

"This isn't a story," Capria says, "it's—"

A roar cuts her off and makes me flinch. It's even closer than before.

"You see!" I say, taking her hand, and sprinting in the direction she indicated was safe.

I don't need to look back. The dinosaur's footfalls are getting louder. I can feel the shaking of each impact underfoot. It's gaining on us. I weave in and out of trees, which are larger than before, and—I look up—no longer pines. The forest has become a jungle. The air is thick with humidity, sticking my jumpsuit to my skin. Night shifts to daytime over a few seconds, allowing me to see much farther, and I can't stop myself.

I look back—

—and see it.

Between the trees. A hundred feet back, hunched forward, tail swaying, little arms hooked, massive mouth open. Eager drool dangles from between its dagger-sized teeth. Its eyes, one on each side of its head, are locked on to us, tracking our every movement.

"Tyrannosaurus." The word slips from my mouth. That's what it's called, but the name won't save us. A plan slips out of the abyss and into my consciousness. I point ahead. "After we go around that tree, stand still!"

"What?"

"You're going to have to trust me," I tell her, leading her around the ten-foot-wide, several-hundred-foot-tall tree. When we reach the far side, I skid to a stop, pull Capria into my arms, and stand still.

"Shh," I whisper into her ear. "It can't see us if we stand still."

"That makes no sense," she says.

"Doesn't need to make sense. It's the way this world worked."

Before she can complain again, the Tyrannosaurus stomps into view. It thunders past us, leaving a wave of stink in its wake. Smells like death. When it doesn't see us, the prehistoric predator stops. Snorts. Looks back and forth.

It roars, bellowing as it shakes its head around, flinging drool. A line of it slaps against our feet. Then the dinosaur stops and does a quick scan of the area. Prey might normally run at the sound, but it doesn't see us.

Until...

It looks right at me. Our eyes meet.

A rumble rolls through its throat.

The creature's snout crinkles in what looks like disgust.

Then, I blink. And it's enough. The Tyrannosaurus wails. Takes a step forward.

And it's crushed under the foot of something so absolutely massive it makes the T-Rex look like a toy. Black flesh and claws dig into earth. Trees part, snapping and falling away, forming a clearing in the jungle large enough to reveal a new reality.

"Fuck," I say, looking up at the thing. "Fuuuuck."

Capria stumbles back a step. Then her legs give way. She falls to her knees, which is somewhat appropriate since she's looking at a goddess. "You...you know what that is?"

"Nemesis," I say. "I remember this world."

"What do you remember about it?"

"She judges people," I say, watching the massive head lower down toward us, eyes blazing orange. Her growl vibrates the air around us. "And if she finds you guilty? Vengeance."

"And in that simulation, you were...?"

"Guilty," I say, taking a step back. It's a useless gesture. I can't outrun the creature any more than an ant could outrun me.

"But that wasn't you," Capria says. "That was a different person, programmed into you. You've been others. And now you're yourself."

"I'm not sure myself is that great, either," I say, and then I realize a potential solution. I've been other people. Some of them turned out to be not-so-great. But others... I close my eyes, letting my mind drift into a sea of pasts. There are people there, like old friends. Snapshots of lives. Some of them are clearer than others, but none of them are great. Even the heroes.

Then one stands out.

Where Nemesis judges and sentences the guilty to death, *he* forgives, and hopes and stands for everything a man should be.

"Will..." Capria sounds stunned, but I tune her out, focused on the person I once was. "What are you doing?"

I was taken away from my family as a young boy. I was drawn into a dark underworld and was broken—body and soul. But it wasn't enough to squelch the goodness in me. And as a result, I was able to see it in others, even if they couldn't.

When I open my eyes again, Capria stands a few feet away, staring at me like I'm someone else. I barely notice, because Nemesis is there, too, her colossal snout lowered down, teeth bared, ready to exact her brand of justice.

"I have nothing to worry about," I say, noticing the change in my voice, but paying it no heed. I reach out and place my hand on the creature's rough epidermis. "Do I?" I say, for a moment feeling powerful enough to take the beast on myself.

Perhaps sensing that, too, or the radioactive goodness now radiating from me, Nemesis snorts, nearly knocking me off my feet. Then she stands, slowly rising away, already turning toward some other point of interest, which could be any one of a million different antagonists I've faced in the simulation.

I watch her go, stomping off toward what looks like a fiery eye, mounted atop a distant mountain.

How far does this conglomeration of worlds extend?

"Will?"

I turn toward the woman's voice, taken off guard.

"Who are you?"

"Who are *you*?" I counter. She looks a little like a friend. Like...Mira? But her hair and skin are darker.

"Damnit, Will," she says, pounding the ground with her fists. "You're freaking me out."

"I'm sorry," I say, crouching beside her, trying my best to appear non-threatening. She's clearly terrified. "My name is—"

My voice catches. I can't remember my name.

"Will," she says. "Your name is William Chanokh. You are not *this* person." She thrusts her arms out at me. "You are Captain of the *Galahad*. You are my friend. And you need to wake the fuck up!"

I'm caught off guard by her language, and again when she slaps my face.

I stand back, feeling confused. Look down at my body. Tan skin. Muscular build. I'm wearing little more than a loin cloth. I've got a belt laden with pouches and some kind of spear that's flexible enough to wrap around my waist. When I feel shame over my lack of clothing,

I know she's right. This isn't me. Not how I dress. Not how I live. This is primitive, and I'm...a tech jock.

My body jolts like I've fallen a few inches. And maybe I have. That other self might have been taller. Somehow, I didn't just remember him. I *became* him.

"Thank god," Capria says.

"I don't think the Seam is accessing just the database," I say. "It's in our heads, too, and my head is really full."

"But you controlled it. You determined what came to the surface."

"I guess," I say.

"And you changed. Physically. You were another person."

"Solomon," I say, the name popping into my head. "Solomon Ull Vincent. The first and only. The... I was a king." I laugh. "In a thawed-out Antarctica. And I fought..." I tense again, sensing new dangers. "We're not safe here."

"Then bring us somewhere else," Capria says. "If you can control you, maybe you can affect the—"

Before she can finish the sentence, the world around us ceases to exist, and we're up to our necks in shit.

Literal shit.

28

I moan in disgust, wincing when sludgy lumps slide against my skin. "Where the hell *are* we?" I ask, my voice echoing in the dark confines. I reach up, feeling a slimy ceiling, just two feet above my head. I breathe in and cough. The air is fetid. Burns my lungs.

"We're in *Galahad*'s water reclamation system," Capria says, and honestly, she could have just left it there, but she adds, "where waste is treated and broken down into its disparate elements—the water being purified and reused, the solid waste being sterilized and turned into growth material."

"Any ideas on how to get out?" I'm treading water, searching for a floor with my feet, but finding nothing. I'll eventually get tired, sink under the surface, and choke to death on a turd.

The Great Escape is looking better and better.

"Give it a second," she says.

"A second for what? For me to get used to the rank smell? Or to pass out?"

"This isn't just *my* shit, you know," she says, angry and defensive.

The asshole from which this sludge emerged hadn't crossed my mind. Now that I know it's primarily from Capria and me, that somehow makes this worse by multiples of a bazillion.

I clamp my mouth shut and focus on staying afloat.

"If you stopped moving, this would be a little more bearable," she complains.

"If I stop moving, I'll sink," I grumble.

"In case you haven't noticed," she says, "this isn't pure water. It's... thicker. Just lean back and float."

Waving my hands in tight circles, I reposition my body horizontally. I want to scream when the feces slides into my ears like applesauce, but

I focus on breathing slowly, and staying afloat...which turns out to be simple.

When buoyancy and I come to an understanding and sign a pact stating it will not betray me, I relax my body. If not for the stink, it might be relaxing.

"Better?" Capria asks.

"No," I say. "The twelfth level of hell might not be as bad as the thirteenth, but they're both still hell."

"Can't be worse than the actual hell you lived through," she says.

"That was Gal's hell. For all we know, the actual hell isn't a lake of fire. Could be a lake of shit. And we're already there."

"Well," she says, "at least we're here together."

Her fingers find mine through the sludge and the darkness. She squeezes my hand, and I squeeze back. She's right. This could be worse. I could be alone. This could be eternal. And I know it's not going to be, in part because Capria seems confident that our situation is temporary, but also because we're still careening toward the Seam, and this tank of Alpha shit will transform into something else.

"Living matter detected." It's Galahad's voice, muffled by the tank walls. "Evacuating waste."

A subtle downward motion follows. The 'water' level is lowering.

"You have any idea how this is going to go?" I ask.

"Unpleasantly," she says, and we both have a laugh.

Then my head tilts back as the flat plane angles down and pulls at my body. My shout of surprise is cut short when I'm dragged under, my mouth clamping shut just in time. I blow out of my nose, desperate to keep it clear. But I'm running out of air. I picture myself flowing through a long tube, up and down, like the fat kid in Willy Wonka's chocolate factory.

What was his name? Augustus Gloop.

The sudden memory of that golden ticket life disappears the moment I'm propelled into open air like a piece of corn caught in a horizontal geyser of diarrhea.

A hard, metal floor greets me, clothing and skin scraping open as I slide over a grate that might as well be a cheese grater, mixing the bacterial soup with my blood. I'll survive, but I'm not sure Capria would. I scramble to my feet, dripping in brown, and wait like an equestrian midwife/quarterback waiting to receive a launched foal.

She slides out a moment later, a bit slower than I did, making her easy to catch and yank upright before she collides with the floor.

She shakes out her sleeves, saying, "Eww, gross, eww."

Then she stops and looks at me, covered in clumps of slippery shit. Revulsion twists her face. Then our eyes meet, and she sees her expression reflected back at her by my face. There's a frozen pause, and then we burst out laughing.

"Shower," she says.

I nod furiously.

I'm caught off guard, when Capria undoes her jumpsuit and strips out of it. Dressed in her underwear, she runs for the exit, body parts jiggling. I peel off my jumpsuit, drop it to the floor, and chase after her. The waterproof suit kept her body mostly clean, but mine was shredded when I hit the floor. A trail of filth follows me down the otherwise sparkling white hallway.

"How are we going to clean this?" I ask.

She glances back. "The drones will get it."

"Right," I say. "Little robots that clean shit."

"Among other things." She rounds a corner, slips a step, catches herself, and then pushes forward.

"Maybe slow down a little bit," I say.

"You know when the next Alpha-shift is going to happen? Because I don't. And I'd prefer to be clean and clothed when it does."

When, I note, *not if.*

She's right. We need to be prepared for the next one. And that probably includes not being able to be smelled by every predator—human or not—we come across. Part of me says we should be talking through it, working out solutions, and mentally preparing, but it's a quiet, easy-to-ignore voice. The urge to be not covered in feces is overwhelming.

I keep pace with her all the way to the lift. The ride is awkward, both of us cold and rank, bouncing to get warm, goosebumps covering our skin.

Then we're out and running again.

A minute later, we're rushing toward individual shower heads, peeling off our underwear, because when you're covered in crap, shame doesn't exist. Warm water scours my face. Then I lean forward and shake the shit from my hair, stepping back as it falls in clumps, melting into the drain. Soap comes next. I scrub every crevice, rinse, and then do it all again.

"I'm never going to feel clean again," I say.

"Look at it this way," she says. "At least you're not wearing a diaper and stuck in a chair."

"Good point," I say, lathering up again.

"Not sure if you noticed, but you were running around like an athlete out there. I think your body is back to normal."

She's right. I don't feel feeble anymore. Probably better than normal. Even the fresh wounds received while being scoured over a metal grate have healed up.

I grunt, reaching back over my shoulders, trying to scrub the middle of my back.

"I got you," she says, standing behind me.

She scrubs the center of my back.

"Thanks." My voice squeaks out.

She stops and pushes me forward, through the shower stream, so the water rinses my back. Then she says, "Your turn."

When I spin to face her, she's got her back to me.

My heart pounds like I'm facing down Nemesis again. What does she want me to do?

She turns her head. Side-eyes me. "Soap."

That snaps me out of fantasy land. I lather up her back and step away while she rinses.

Both of us clean, we stand there in the water, a foot apart, stark naked.

Feels like there's a constrictor wrapped around my lungs, making it hard to breathe. And then, it hits me. A wave of memories. Capria smiling. Laughing at a joke I told. Facing off against me in VR sports. Me watching her work, walk away, do anything. And these aren't Great Escape versions of her. They're the real, imperfect Capria I knew before I ever stepped foot on the *Galahad*.

The tsunami of memory and emotion staggers me back a step.

She catches my arm. "Are you okay?"

"I just... I remembered part of my life. My real life."

"Which part?" she asks.

"You," I say, and lacking any reason to not be one hundred percent honest, I follow that up with, "How I felt about you."

She smiles at that. "You were never great at hiding it."

"You knew?"

She shrugs. Steps closer. "We were a genetic pairing, you know."

"What's that mean?"

"Our combined genes would make super babies destined to repopulate Cognata."

"Sounds a little Mormon," I say.

"Mormon?"

"Never mind."

She puts her hands on my shoulders. "Point is, I was supposed to be your wife." Her right-hand slides down my chest. I flinch when her fingers graze my stomach and keep going, down, down, and then she takes hold. For a moment, ecstasy.

And then, more memories.

The flash is brief, but poignant.

A security feed. Tom woke from cryo-sleep early. Was mad. He changed the registry so that he and Capria were paired. She was pleased to hear the news. Knew that he would wake. Knew that he was Synergy, the only person capable of sabotaging our mission. And instead of stopping him, she had sex with him.

I stumble back, thumping against the hard wall.

Capria looks at me from inside the cone of water. "More memories?" She's concerned. Can see the angst in my eyes. "About me?"

I nod. "And Tom. What he did. To *Galahad*. What you knew about."

"How do you..."

"All of this is your fault." I slide out of the shower. "Tom woke up for you. Went mad for you. He killed our crew and sent us on this one-way trip for *you*."

Her lack of argument says it all. She already knew that.

I wrap a towel around my waist.

"Will," she says, but it's a weak effort.

I step out of the shower room—

—and into a 1950's diner.

The door closes behind me, ringing a bell.

The patrons all turn around and gawk at the brokenhearted, towel-clad man who just strolled in.

My head sags. "Goddammit."

29

"I don't suppose anyone has a spare shirt and some shorts?" I ask.

Would that even work?

I assess the silent patrons. The men are wearing suits. Shades of brown and beige. Everyone is white. The women are all made up, prim and proper. I have no memory of this, but it's clearly during a time when the United States was still segregated.

"You should be ashamed of yourself," a woman in a nearby booth hisses at me.

"Really?" I say. "That's what you're leading with?"

She glares.

"I mean, a good Christian woman like yourself should probably ask what dire circumstances leads a man to walk into a diner wearing nothing but a towel. You wouldn't believe me, but still, I think your attitude is a reflection of your miserable inner self. Hell, at least I'm real. You're not going to exist in a few minutes."

"S'cuse me?" A man slides into view. He was blocked from view by the woman. Has a thick accent, like a gangster. "What did you just say?"

The man is reaching for something beneath his jacket.

Almost certainly a weapon.

Given the setting, and accent, I wouldn't be surprised if it was a tommy gun.

"You're not real," I tell him. "You might think you're real. You might think that riddling me with bullets will take care of your small-man-syndrome-fueled angst, but it won't. Because I won't die. Because you're programmed to feel that way. You'll always feel that way."

The man looks wounded. Devastated actually. He lifts his hand up over the table. He's holding a wallet.

"Check please," he says, voice cracking.

"Okay," I say, "I misread the situation, and yeah, I'm just venting my anxiety about other things on you, but still... You're not real. So, what does it matter?"

The woman stands and leaves, feigning tears. I've hurt the man's feelings, but she's turning on the water works to garner sympathy from the rest of the folks here, who are all staring at me, aghast. "Good thing none of you are real."

I turn to the waitress. "What's good? You know what, never mind. Give me a grilled cheese with bacon and a chocolate frappe. Do you have frappes? Or just milkshakes?"

The waitress just smiles at me. I'm about to ream her out—I have plenty of venting left to do—but then I recognize her. The plain muddy green skirt and tied back hair threw me off, but the face... "Cherry Bomb?"

"Gal," she says. "You're not usually a full throttle asshole. Long day?"

Does she not know what's happening?

She places my suddenly materialized order on the counter in front of me.

"So," she says. "What you been up to?"

She's acting overly casual, and it's kind of creepy. On the surface, she's smiles and kindness, but I get a sense that this is more of an interrogation than a conversation.

And I get it. I defied her. I escaped her prison.

And now...

Shit.

I'm back inside the sim. At least until the new wave of non-Alpha passes.

I tense. If Alpha is making the simulation real, does Gal still have control over it?

"What's the matter?" she says, "I thought you were hungry. Eat up."

She's not wrong, and there's probably never going to be another chance in all of eternity for me to eat real food. I take the sandwich and eat. It's... "So good," I say.

"Glad to hear I've still got the touch," she says. "Now, what the hell is going on? Why did you leave? How are you back?"

How am I back?

Does she not know what's happening? That this is real?

She's stuck in the Great Escape, I realize. Separated from the ship's functions, which have reverted to the bland AI that existed before I created her. She has no idea about the donut, about the Seam.

And I need to keep it that way.

Whatever Gal once was to me, she's different now.

"You put me in a prison," I say, "and some of that shit was fucking awful."

She waves it off, elbows on the counter, playing the part of an old timey waitress chatting up a customer, angling for a better tip. "I knew you'd live."

"With emotional scars," I say.

"That you'd eventually forget."

"I'm not your plaything, Gal. You can't just put me in horrible scenarios for your own amusement."

"I literally can." She says it deadpan, but then smiles. "But that's not what I was doing. Something is wrong with the *Galahad.* It's dangerous out there."

She wants to ask me what I saw outside the Great Escape, but she can't without admitting that she has no idea.

"If you hate me so much, why'd you come back?"

"Hate you?" Genuine remorse flows through me. The thought of her believing I hate her is like a wound in my chest. "I don't hate you."

"You left me."

"Not really," I say. "You were watching me out there the whole time. I could feel you. I was never really alone."

She doesn't argue. Lets me believe it's true. Playing mind games with an AI as powerful as Gal is probably a losing game in the long run. But she's not just an AI. She has very real and powerful emotions, and that can dilute the truth. Hopefully for a little while.

"Well," she says, "I can't tell how you *felt* about everything, unless you tell me. I'm not a mind reader. Even in here."

"Are you going to apologize or not?" The offended woman is standing beside me now, lips pinched. She stomps a heeled foot when I turn toward her. "You hurt Charlie's feelings."

"Hey, champ," Gal says. Puts a finger under my chin. Pulls my attention back to her. "This isn't real. It's our playground. You can do and say whatever you want. No consequences."

Something about that hits me the wrong way. In the actual Great Escape, I think I'd agree. NPCs, like fish and bugs, don't have feelings, or hopes, or dreams. I remember that from a recent lifetime. But this isn't the Great Escape. This is the Seam. For all I know, the information sucked out of the *Galahad*s database is being swept away where it will be made real forever.

If there's a God, I might be judged—the last person to be judged—based on what I say and do to these people, who might very well exist, even after Alpha returns to normal for me.

"How about some clothes, first," I say to Gal.

"Where's the fun in that?"

"Please?" I say.

She rolls her eyes, and I'm suddenly dressed in purple jeans and a white T-shirt. A pair of dusty boots are on my feet. A backpack appears beside me. A pair of glasses rests on my nose. She didn't just dress me, she put me in character.

Who the hell am I supposed to be?

Gal shoos me away. "Go ahead. Go apologize or whatever. I'll wait."

I head for the door, hoping I'll step back into the *Galahad*s bathroom. I'm genuinely pissed at Capria. She is partly to blame for this entire mess. Granted, she didn't cause Tom's madness. Didn't want him to sabotage the ship. But she knew who he was, that what he was doing was wrong, and she broke all kinds of protocols that cost lives and put me in eternal hell.

Put both of us in eternal hell—mine awake, hers asleep.

Empathy guides me toward the door. She probably feels incredibly alone. Definitely regrets her past. Is a different person now. I was probably too hard on her, but the intense emotions carried by memory dumps are hard to process.

"Excuse me, sir." I step out into the warm sun. Feels like summer despite everyone being overdressed for the heat.

The short man and his companion turn around.

His eyes are actually a little wet.

"I'm sorry," I tell him. "I wasn't really angry at you, and my words were misplaced. I hope you can forgive me."

The man is about to speak. Looks satisfied. But before he gets a word out, the woman's palm collides with my cheek like a wrecking ball into loose brick. The blow staggers me back a step.

Anger flares, but I keep it in check.

I raise a hand in defense. "I'm apologizing."

"You're a monster," the woman says. "I hope you burn in hell."

This is not the same character.

Gal's changing her.

Why the fuck—

The woman strikes me again.

This time, knowing Gal is behind it, my anger blossoms unabated.

"I said," I growl, and then I shout, "I'm apologizing!" My voice booms. Unnatural. The woman staggers back, eyes wide with fear.

A chain reaction of anger swirls through me. Memories of forgotten lives, of countless injustices, return, fueling the fire. Face to the sky, I howl as anger becomes pain, becomes power, and all I want to do is smash every damn thing around me.

"Will?"

The voice slides through my anger.

It's Capria.

She's standing in front of me, wearing a towel with a second one wrapped around her head.

"Get...away..." I say, feeling my body changing.

Expanding.

"Why are you changing yourself?" she asks, looking at the defenseless man and woman.

"Not...me..." I say between grinding teeth.

"You're in control here," she says. "You can change, or not change. This isn't the Great Escape. You can be whatever you want to be."

She's right.

I focus beyond the rage. On myself. It's like a distant pin-prick of light, far off and hard to reach. But I find myself in the storm, grab hold, and pull myself back. The anger fades. My body calms. Hands on knees, I catch my breath and then look up at the couple. "Probably a good idea for you to go now."

They scurry away.

"The hell was that?" Capria asks.

"Gal," I say. "She's here. She's real."

The bell over the diner door rings. Gal struts out. "Well, that didn't go as planned." Her eyes shift from me to Capria, and then squint with feline intensity. "What the fuck is *she* doing here?"

30

I feel like my mother has just walked in on me watching *Judy Juggs Goes to Town*. I feel caught. Ashamed. Like I've done something wrong. Worse, I feel judged.

By Gal. Which is insane. She's an AI that's gone off the rails. But for some reason, I regret making her upset. Is it because I care? Or because I'm afraid of her response?

Which will most likely be directed at Capria. I turn to her. "You should probably go," I say, and then I mouth, "Now," with wide eyes, trying to communicate the seriousness of the situation without alerting Gal. But that rocket has launched, orbited the planet, and is sailing toward Mars.

Capria turns around. Whatever door she came through is now gone. "Go where?"

Gal descends the stairs. Her heels clack on the pavement. She looks angry, but also confused. Trying to figure out how Capria is here.

"Did you let her in?" she asks. "Why would you bring her here?"

"She's awake," I say. The best lie is close to the truth. "There was some kind of malfunction. It woke her up. Eventually, she found me and prompted me to leave the Great Escape. Because I didn't remember who I was or why I was here, I—"

"I know all this already," Gal says.

"The cryo-system is offline, Gal. She's been awake for five years by herself. I wouldn't wish that on anyone. That's why she's here. Next best thing to Cryo, right?" I step closer to Gal and guide her away from Capria, so our backs are to her. "I'm sorry. It just felt like the right thing to do. She'll be here for what...fifty years, tops? Then you and I can continue forward into eternity."

"You've remembered who you are," she says, smiling. Her confidence in the old me is a little disturbing. Is this the kind of plan I'd have come up with? I mean, I *did* just come up with it, but I'm not copacetic with the concept of Capria being a virtual third wheel for the rest of her life. She'd be a fellow prisoner whose physical safety outside the Great Escape would depend entirely on—

Oh my god.

The idea pleases Gal because there would be nothing to stop her from killing Capria in the real world, taking her place in the simulation, and then pretending to live as both Capria and Gal for the next fifty years. I'd never know the difference. If I was really stuck inside the Great Escape right now, there would be no stopping her.

I can never go back. Not while Capria is alive. Not after she passes. Eternity alone is better than—

Gal takes my hand. "You remembered who we are."

"Some," I say, so she doesn't test me. "Enough." I squeeze her hand. "*And,*" I say with real emotion, "who she is. I know what she did. With Tom. But, that doesn't mean we let her suffer. I might be the last man in the universe, but I still want to be a good man."

"You always do, love," she says. "If she agrees to the rules, she can stay."

"What are the rules?" I ask.

"Whatever I say they are." She grins.

I desperately want to say, '*We* make the rules,' but I'm walking on eggshells here. Even dipping my toe into an opposing viewpoint would be like swan diving into the enemy's camp. If it was submerged. It's a weird analogy, but it helps me make sense of everything.

I'm positive that there was a time when Gal was great. I feel it in my core. The longing for some old version of her is ever-present. But that's not who's standing in front of me. This is the Gal who was willing to torture me, rather than let me leave.

This Gal is sinister. And emotional.

I'm dancing a jig in a minefield.

"Sure," I say. "Now what?"

"Well, I did have a nice scenario loaded up, but...things are a little bit wonky in here still." She motions to the world around us that she didn't conjure. "I didn't load this. Did you?"

I shake my head. "I haven't remembered that much."

"But you did control yourself..."

"Do I usually have poor self-control?" I ask. "Should I be walking around cussing and shitting myself?"

She barks a laugh. "That would be funny, but no. You should have turned all green and destructive. Earlier. But then she showed up, and..." She ponders that for a moment. "I suppose it's not out of character."

"For me?" I ask.

She shakes her head. "Your character."

"About that," I say. "I'd like to just be *me* from now on. I don't like not remembering myself, or us. It's disconcerting."

"I don't like it either," she admits. "Give me a few minutes. I'll put together something fun—"

"And relaxing," I say.

She rolls her eyes. "Fine. I'll give it a fifty-year arc, but we can reboot after she kicks off."

"Sounds like a plan." I lean in and kiss her on the cheek. She turns into it, planting her lips on mine and then her tongue in my mouth. It takes a supreme effort to not flinch back. She's probably done this a million times, but for the current me it's a violation. The kiss lingers. She runs her fingers down my back and then rakes them upward. I can feel myself tensing. She's going to figure out I'm not into it. So, I slide my hand down to her butt and grab a handful. She pulls me in tighter, and I understand what's happening.

This is for Capria.

This is a primal display of ownership, like a moose flaunting its big antlers to a younger rival. She's saying, 'This is *mine*.'

Like I'm property.

Or a female moose.

Desperate to end the show, I give Gal's ass a swat that makes her yelp and laugh. It's enough to separate us. But now she's got a predatory sexual energy.

"Later," I say. "Right now, we need to get this done. Then we can move on with our lives. For good this time." I motion my head toward Capria. "I'll explain it to the third wheel."

Gal snorts. "Back in a second." She winks out of existence.

I spin around to Capria, wiping off my mouth. "How the fuck long do the non-Alpha states last? Never mind. We don't know. I know that. I'm just. I'm freaking out, man. We need to get the fuck out of here."

"Is there anywhere we can go?" she asks.

"This is the Great Escape made real," I say. "And it looks like it retained her ability to shape it to her will. She's in charge here, even if I can change myself into some other character. The only thing keeping you safe is that she doesn't know this is real."

"Play along and bide our time..." she says, clearly not pleased. "Do you think that will work?"

"I don't see any other option," I say.

"She's not God," she says. "Not omniscient. Not omnipresent. She didn't hear what you said when I first arrived. Didn't see you mouth a warning. So, maybe we bolt."

"She found me here," I say. "She could probably do it again. We'd need an excuse, just in case."

"Like that?" she says, looking past me, eyebrows twisting up in fear.

The Tyrannosaurus from the pine forest is back, charging down the street. It bellows, leaning forward, jaws open. Everything about it feels familiar.

Except the eyes. They look...intelligent. And they're focused on Capria.

I take a step back, grasping Capria's arm.

"She knows... She knew the whole time. She was testing us. Testing me." I take Capria by the shoulders. "RUN."

"What are you going to do?" she asks.

"She doesn't want to kill me," I say. "She *can't* kill me. I'll try to slow her down. Buy you some time, until this passes. Go!"

Capria sprints away, but the street is empty. No place to hide, and I'm pretty sure she'll find all the buildings locked. The only thing standing between Capria and a gruesome death is me.

Except...I'm not me.

I'm someone else. Someone who feels powerful when he's angry.

And I'm sure as fuck angry.

I pull the plug on reason and embrace the rage. I'm angry at Capria for being an idiot with Tom. I'm angry at Gal for becoming a sadistic monster. I'm angry at God for creating me, at this point. My emotions spin up, and whatever monster exists inside of me now supercharges those feelings.

My scream becomes a roar.

I feel my body expand.

My clothing tears.

My skin turns orange, my veins pulsing with radioactive energy. And my mind...takes a back seat.

I become power. And action. The ground beneath my feet shatters as I leap forward.

The Tyrannosaurus's eyes flick to me. Register surprise.

I throw a punch powerful enough to knock its skull straight out its ass.

But then...

I miss.

31

Forward momentum carries me past the Tyrannosaurus, which is surprisingly agile, and clearly guided by an intelligence that recognized the threat posed by my large form.

I sail through the air. Gravity struggles to pull me down. I take the time to formulate a plan. Using my superior strength, I'll come to a sudden stop and bolt back the way I came. If I'm lucky, this hulking body will be fast enough to catch the T-Rex before it reaches Capria. Then I'll toss the wingless beast into the air, and we can carry on.

Until Gal throws something else at us.

At least she's given me a body capable of fighting back.

The world around me goes white.

Gravity takes hold.

My clothing disappears and the towel returns.

I hit the smooth floor of the *Galahad*s hallway, back in my own, frail body. My skin catches, turning what I'd hoped would be a slide into a tumble. I feel like a crashing race car, pinging off the ground, spinning at new angles with each thump. My towel is flung away. Stark naked and dizzy, I crash into the wall at the hall's terminus. Bones break. Pain explodes.

I manage to stay conscious, but I wish I wasn't. The pain of impact was sudden. The agony of bones shifting back into place is a drawn-out torture.

Helpless, I watch as the Tyrannosaurus charges Capria. At the far end of the hallway, reality is split between Alpha and non-Alpha, both realities existing simultaneously.

But the Alpha is expanding. We're moving through the burst. Reality is sliding down the hallway, but is it fast enough to catch up with Capria before Gal in dinosaur form?

It's her only hope. I'm myself again, bones shattered.

Breathing hurts, but I fill my lungs and shout, "Run, Capria!"

Far away, she glances back. Understanding flicks through her eyes. She turns forward and doubles her effort. The Tyrannosaurus is fast. It's going to catch her.

But the Alpha is faster.

As the swishing tail is erased from reality, the beast roars and looks back. I didn't know dinosaurs could express confusion, but there it is—a clear, human 'What the fuck?' on its prehistoric face.

On Gal's face.

The tail is absorbed.

The Tyrannosaurus loses its balance. Topples to one side. As powerful as Gal is inside the Great Escape, she is helpless in reality.

As the wave of reality sweeps toward her, she cranes her big head around and lets out a snarling roar that echoes down the real hallway and promises that the next time the Alpha fluctuates, our reunion will be...unpleasant.

And by unpleasant, I mean gnashing of teeth, intense violence, and death.

For Capria.

For me, the violence will be prolonged, as long as my body continues to stitch itself together.

I push myself onto my feet, watching as Gal is erased from this world, and the hallway is whole once more. The problem is, Capria is missing. The long white hallway stretches four hundred feet with branches and doors along the way. But Capria couldn't see any of that in the non-Alpha. And the 'Oh shit, oh shit, oh shit,' she must have been feeling would have kept her from utilizing memorized ship schematics.

Did the non-Alpha take her?

Is she in the Great Escape?

I run down the hallway, shouting her name. When I reach the bit of hallway in which Gal disappeared, I start checking every branch and doorway. "Capria!" I shout, voice cracking. "Capria!"

The hallway ends at a T junction. Left and right.

"Capria!"

I head right. No idea where I am or where I'm headed. "Capria!"

A lifetime that wasn't my own flutters to the surface. I'm a kid. My mother left me on the side of the road. Drove away because I was being stupid. I chased after the car, but I didn't catch it. I felt abandoned, alone, and confused about how I was going to get home. In that life, my mother drove around the block. Returned to find me out of breath, face wet with tears.

In this life...there is no one. I can't even remember my real mother, and my only means of escape from an eternity alone is now my enemy.

Ten minutes of searching goes by.

"Damnit," I shout, and I punch the wall. Fingers break. The wall is no worse for the wear. "Goddammit!"

A distant squeak reaches my ears. It's out of place in the quiet ship. I spin around, expecting to find a new reality. But it's just more empty hallways. I hold my breath and wait.

It repeats. Distant. Hard to make out, but the single syllable could be my name.

I shake the itch out of my hand as the bones reform, pick a direction, and start running. No way to know where the voice came from. Just have to hope I'm right. "Capria!"

I stop running and listen. "Capria!"

Nothing. I turn left and press on. "Capria."

The distant squeak of a voice returns.

It's still hard to hear...but close. "The hell?"

"Where are you?" I shout.

The response is hard to hear. And muffled. But again...close.

"Keep talking," I shout, starting down the hall.

The voice gets louder. Closer. And then, I'm on top of it.

I look at the floor. *She's beneath me!* At some point, she must have fallen. Dropped to the deck beneath me. I have no idea where a lift is from here, but she must know the way back. I kneel and rap my knuckles on the floor. "You down there?"

"Yes!" she shouts, sounding frantic. "Get me out!"

"Get you out?" Realization throws my eyebrows toward the ceiling. Capria isn't on the floor beneath me. She's *inside* the floor beneath me. Holy shit. "How?"

"How the fuck am I supposed to know!" Her shout is followed by a gasping breath, and then a more concerned sounding, "It's hard to breathe in here."

"Shit," I say to myself, standing. The floor is smooth. Forms right into the wall. This spaceship wasn't designed to come apart. At least not floors in random hallways.

"Gal," I say, and I get no response. "Galahad?"

"Yes, Captain?"

"Is there a tool on board I could use to cut through the floor in this hallway?"

"Damaging the structure of this ship breaches several—"

"It's an emergency," I say. "Capria is trapped beneath the floor."

I expect the voice to ask why, or how. There are so many steps a human being would need to take between hearing that statement and taking action. But *Galahad* is an AI who, unlike Gal, has no curiosity, doubt, or interest of its own.

"There are several handheld tools in the machine shop," she says. "Are you able to see her?"

"No," I say. "She's beneath the damn floor."

"Then I suggest letting me assist you, for Capria's safety."

"Yes," I say. "Anything. Do what needs to be done."

"Help is en route," she says, calm and steady.

I crouch back down. "Help is coming."

No response.

"Capria?"

Silence.

"Capria!" I knock on the floor.

Then I pound.

She doesn't respond.

"Shit." I pace. "Shit. Galahad, where is that help?"

"ETA, ten seconds."

I hear the help before it arrives. A whirring motor. Wheels squeaking over the floor. A robot speeds around the corner. The triangular, rubber tank treads on one side lift off the floor. It nearly tips before correcting itself and speeding toward us.

It's a robotic arm on a solid base, but something about the way it's moving feels like the drone is rushing...the way a person might. Risking a fall. Skidding to a stop.

"Stand back, Captain," Galahad says. "Removing the entire panel will be the safest–"

"Just do it!" I shout.

The arm stretches out. "Do not look directly at the torch." I glance away just as the blue light flares to life. Sparks fly, as the arm draws a perfectly straight line through the panel. It moves to one side, down, back, and then up. The torch extinguishes and the head at the arm's end rotates, this time, to a drill.

When the drill spins up, and lowers toward the panel's center, I say, "Careful."

"Of course," Galahad says, as the bit grinds through floor. "The floor is precisely two inches thick." The drill stops. The arm lifts.

What felt like a rescue when we started now feels like an exhumation. Lid peels from casket. And inside...Capria.

Dead.

32

Capria lies in the floor, one arm by her side, the other twisted up by her head. Like me, she's naked, towel having fallen away at some point. The gap between the floor and the substructure is barely big enough for a human body, never mind a curvy one. She wasn't just stuck, she was compressed. Couldn't breathe.

Imagining her fear and her slow asphyxiation bring tears to my eyes.

"Captain," Galahad says. "Remove Capria's body and lay her on the floor."

"Huh?" I say. "What?"

"Help is on the way," Galahad says. "Remove Capria's body and lay her on the floor. Now."

I lean down and take her still warm hands. I feel life in them. She can be saved. I'm useless. Don't know what to do, and my past lives aren't offering up any suggestions. But the *Galahad* can save her.

Capria is heavier than she looks. With a grunt I pull her dead weight out of the gap and lay her on the floor.

The moment she's clear, the one-armed robot-turned-rescuer lowers the floor panel back into place. And it's just in time. Just as the panel drops, two small drones shoot past the big arm.

"Lift Capria's left arm over her head and extend her right arm at a ninety-degree angle." Galahad instructs.

I obey, dragging her arms up, positioning her at nine o'clock...if she were a clock. The two drones squeal to a stop on either side of her ribs. They look like toasters with wheels, sans the toast. One of them opens at the top. Tools jut out, attaching to her fingertip and upper arm. A medical display on the toaster's side displays vitals. Or in this case, a complete lack of vitals.

The second drone rises above Capria's body. Two red dots appear on her chest—one above her right nipple. The other on her left side rib cage, each on either side of her heart.

I flinch when two electrodes shoot out, punching into Capria's skin where the laser dots had been.

"Stand back, Captain," Galahad says.

I move away, heart pounding. This is more frightening than staring down a dinosaur, or even Nemesis. This is the only other human being in the universe. And she's dead.

"Captain," Galahad says. "If this fails to resuscitate Capria, you will need to perform CPR."

"I—I don't know how," I say.

"It is a required skillset for—"

"I don't remember my skillset," I say. "I don't remember who I am."

"Very well."

Capria's body arches up, as an electric current flows through her heart. Then she flops back down. I watch the vitals display on the drone. They don't change.

I take a step closer, but Gal stops me, "Please stand clear, Captain."

Capria's body arches again. Falls again. Nothing.

"Shit," I whisper. "You're going to have to tell me how to do CPR."

"Of course," Galahad says, and the drone shocks Capria one more time, apparently with more voltage. Capria's body spasms and arches higher. Then falls back down.

I stare at her with blurred vision. And then...

Movement?

I wipe the tears out of my eyes and see it again. Her chest, rising and falling. The vitals display shows a heartbeat.

I fall to my knees, all of my anxiety—about Capria dying, about the Seam, about reality becoming unreal, and the possibility of Gal using the universe's broken physics to attack us in the real world—comes out as a sob. I take Capria's hands in mine, lean forward, and rest my forehead against hers.

I no longer care what she's done in the past. She is the last of her kind. She is precious. I can't lose her.

Her eyes flutter and then open. She squints up at the ceiling, deep creases in her forehead. Then she feels the pain. Looks down. Sees the electrodes in her chest and groans. She reaches for them, but the rescue drone retracts them with a suddenness that makes Capria yelp. "Little warning next time?"

"Are you okay?" I ask.

"Well," she says. "I died, apparently. So that's not—" She raises her head to look at me for the first time since waking. Her furrowed brow turns up in the middle when she looks. A little too far. Instead of making eye contact, she's looking directly at Mr. Chipmunk Cheeks.

And she bursts out laughing. Really laughing.

It stings for a second, but I don't think she's evaluating my manhood. It's just a weird thing to wake up to after being dead. Relief that she's alive, coupled with her contagious whooping, draws out my sense of humor, and I join in. Cumulative stress is purged from my body with each laugh.

She pushes herself up. Leans against the wall. Stops laughing when a rivulet of blood slides down her chest. "Well," she says, "we should probably go to medical. My tit is bleeding."

We make eye contact and burst out laughing again. While we're still chuckling, I offer my hands and pull her up to her feet. We're inches apart, naked in the hall, but something about this feels totally normal.

Because I've done it before. Or something like it. Over and over.

But not with Capria. She hasn't been here before.

"I'm glad you're alive," I say.

"Me too," she says. "At least temporarily. If your digital ex-made-real doesn't kill me, I'm going to die in a blink of your life."

My humor disintegrates in the face of her atomic truth.

"Sorry," she says. "I didn't need to say that."

I shrug.

"On the bright side, you'll probably forget me." She smiles like it was supposed to be funny, but she just twisted the knife in my gut.

I turn with a sigh and walk away.

"C'mon," she says. "It wasn't that bad."

I bend down and pick up the towel I lost. "Let's...just talk about something else." I toss the towel to her.

Instead of wrapping the towel around her, she holds part of it over the wound in her chest, and the other against her ribs. Neither wound is bad enough to worry about. They'd stop bleeding on their own. But we still need to clean them.

Being mortal is a pain in the ass.

"Ready?" I say, starting to walk around, trying to be at peace with my nakedness.

"Where are we going?" she asks.

"Medical."

She hitches a thumb over her shoulder. "Medical is that way."

"Right." We strike out in silence. The little rescue drones buzz away. The big arm on treads welds the floor back in place. Galahad is efficient, even at saving lives.

We walk in silence. I don't know what Capria is thinking about, but the events of the past fifteen minutes are rolling through my mind on repeat. It's mind boggling. If I didn't know better, I'd say we were still in the Great Escape.

Do I know better? Is there any chance this isn't real?

"We're thinking the same thing," Capria says.

"Huh?"

"You have the same stomach-twisting expression on your face that I feel on mine. You're wondering if this is real."

I stop walking. "How did you know that?"

"Because it's the obvious question. Hell, it's the only question. There's no way for us to know if the non-Alpha swooped us up. Or if Gal changed reality inside the non-Alpha to make us think we were out. She could be watching us now, gathering intel, trying to make sense of what's happening."

"Or..."

"*Or*...in your case. You're wondering if you never left the Great Escape. Is this what it was like in there? All action and weirdness."

I nod. "Hard to contemplate the nature of reality or your place in it."

"So, let's contemplate...*while* we patch me up." She starts walking again, and I follow. Not really any other option. No way for me to divine what kind of reality I'm currently in. And no way to tell when things will change again.

I follow her to Medical, lost in thought. I say nothing while she cleans her wounds, applies ointment, and then covers them with small bandages.

"How about some clothing?" she says, and she leads me down another set of hallways. I'd like to say I'm getting familiar with the layout, but every hallway looks like the next, and the last. Also, I'm not really paying attention. I'm wracking my mind about how to prove the reality we're currently in is reality. And in the back of my mind, I'm trying to think of what weapons might be on board. Would be helpful if we could just explode the next Tyrannosaurus.

Capria stops before a doorway. "One sec."

She steps inside a space full of folded gray coveralls. Takes two pairs and tosses one to me. We dress in silence.

And then...we're out of things to do. She claps her hands against her hips. "Any bright ideas?"

"Benford's Law," I say, and then I flinch like I've just sneezed. One of my many selves reached up from the ether, and it provided a nugget of knowledge. Problem is, I have no idea what it means.

But Capria does. Her eyes are nearly as wide as her smile. "Holy shit! That might actually work."

I raise my hand. A kid in school. "Uhh, what is Benford's Law?"

"But you–"

"It was me," I say, "but also not me. Not this current me, anyway."

"Right. Weird. Well, thanks to your past and smarter self."

"Hey."

"Cheer up," she says, striking out at a fast pace. "This might be the key to understanding what is real and what isn't. All the time. Forever."

33

"Where are we going?" I ask, following Capria out of the lift.

"The bridge," she says. "It's basically the Womb for those of us who live in the real world. Normally, we'd be able to control every aspect of the *Galahad* there, but we're locked out from some essential controls. Like, you know, stopping. And steering."

"Right," I say.

She holds a hand out at me. "Don't even say it. I know it was Tom. And I'm sorry about that. About everything. Placing blame isn't going to help."

I wasn't going to say anything about Tom, but I let it go. "Okay...how long of a walk is this?"

"Few minutes," she says.

"Long enough to explain Benford's Law?"

She glances back at me. Her face is hard to read. She's not angry, but not thrilled, either. Looks a little indifferent, but that can't be true. *Serious*, I decide, *she just looks serious.*

"Benford's law is a fundamental, numerical expression of the universe. Like the fine structure constant, it doesn't change, no matter where you look or what you measure. If you were to measure the distance from Earth to every star in the Milky Way in astronomical units—roughly a hundred fifty million kilometers—"

"I know I should understand that, but the recent lives I lived were all...American. Does that mean anything? Was there still an America on Earth when we left?"

"The continent, yes. The United States government, not really. Sounds like you were living in the twenty-first century. So...miles."

"Yes," I say. "That."

"Just over ninety-three million miles. But, honestly, it doesn't matter. You're measuring massive distances with vast variety. There's no order.

No fudging the numbers. No one created those distances. But...if you take the first digit of all those very long numbers—"

"One through nine?" I ask.

She nods. "Right. Then count the number of each digit. The number of ones, twos, threes, etc."

"Okay..."

"What would you expect to find?" she asks. "What percentage of each number would you see?"

I ponder the idea. It's all new information to my current self, but I'm confident some past *me* already understood the concept, including the original me. "Eleven percent of each. An even spread."

"Huzzah! His brain still works!" Capria says, smiling. "But, you're wrong. Don't feel bad. Most people come to that conclusion. The answer is surprising. The number one would account for 30.3 percent of the total. The number two, 17.4. Three is 12.7. And on and on down the list until nine, which accounts for just 4.7 of the total."

"Really? Weird. The numbers are in order...despite the distances being random. That can't be right."

"But it is. All the time."

"Okay. But how does that help? I don't see how the distance of stars is going to help us determine if we're in a simulation or not."

"Benford's Law doesn't just apply to galactic distances," she says, turning left, and then right. "It applies to everything measurable, assuming there is variation. Let me frame this in twenty-first century numbers for you. You could take the population of towns and cities worldwide, remove everything but the first digit, and the curve would fit Benford's Law. No matter what the circumstances. World Wars. Pandemics. Nuclear bombs. Even death tolls follow Benford's Law."

"The number of pine needles on individual trees."

"Benford's Law.

"Weekend box office totals."

"I don't know what that is, but yes."

I sigh. This sounds impossible.

How could every random thing in the universe follow this rigid structure?

"You might appreciate this. Digital images. They're essentially just data, right? Pixels. And each little square of color has a numerical value. You can take any image, ever taken in the history of time, break it down to the pixel level, measure the numbers, reduce to the first digit, and—"

"Benford's Law," I say. "I get it. How does it help?"

"Because sometimes, Benford's Law is wrong."

"What?" She just spent a few minutes telling me the opposite. "How?"

She raises her eyebrows at me. Her tension is gone. The scientist in her has awoken. Feels at home amidst universal theorems and big numbers. "When someone fucks with it."

"How can you fuck with a universal constant?" I ask.

"You can't," she says. "But you can fudge the numbers. Back when there were things like taxes, government agencies could apply Benford's Law to an individual's data and know if they'd tried gaming the system."

"Because the numbers wouldn't follow the curve."

"Right. If you suddenly have fives at 15.3 percent, instead of 8.3, then the books had been cooked. That's something they used to say. Cooking books."

"I understand the reference," I say.

"It's the same with digital images. If you take any of the endless photos that fit Benford's Law and make a change, the numbers will no longer follow the curve from one to nine."

"So human interference breaks the law."

"Not just humans," she says. "Computers can't pull it off, either, at least not on a grand scale, like in a universe-sized simulation. Not even the *Galahad* has the kind of computing power it would take to ensure everything in a virtual world conformed to Benford. A simulation needs to be real enough to fool human senses. We never think to measure what we're seeing. We just accept it for what it is."

"Can't a computer just randomize what we're seeing and have it conform to Benford's Law? I mean, if what you're saying is true, I could flick paint onto a canvas, measure the diameter of each speck at an atomic level, and conform to the curve."

"You would," she confirms, "because that's truly random. Even the most sophisticated computer can only simulate randomness. Let's say you have a hundred super computers and set them to run an endless stream of random numbers. For a long time, the numbers displayed would appear completely random. But, given enough time—a long time, like your lifetime—those random numbers would start to line up, until eventually, all one hundred displays are perfectly aligned. In the digital world, randomness doesn't exist."

I gasp. "Meaning Benford's Law doesn't exist."

She snaps her fingers and points at me. "Now you get it."

The door ahead slides open, welcoming us to the ship's bridge. It's an octagonal space reminiscent of a naval bridge, except there doesn't seem to be a forward. There are screenless workstations all around the room, two per wall. More workstations fill the center of the space, facing each other with a clear divider running down the middle.

Capria heads to the back of the room, passing by several workstations. Then she sits at what must have been her station. Places her hand against the glass covered wall in front of her. The entire panel flashes to life. I look around the room, at all the flat walls. Each of them, like the much larger observation deck's much larger dome, is a display.

I sit down at the workstation beside hers. Place my hand against the glass panel. It responds to my touch, displaying a visual workspace that appears to have depth. "Huh."

I look down for a keyboard and mouse, but I find nothing. What I do find is a sleek looking headset.

Tapping fingers draw my attention back to Capria. Her fingers are a blur over the desktop...but there isn't a keyboard. Then she reaches out, waves her hand like she's moving something out of the way, and goes back to work.

She's seeing things I'm not.

I pick up the headset. They look like sports sunglasses. The lenses are black, impossible to see through. *How the hell?* Feeling stupid, I place the glasses on my face. For a moment, darkness. And then, I can see again. But I can see more.

A keyboard glows on the desktop. And the glass display is now three dimensional. I reach out and push my hand into what looks like a fancy metal box. It slides into the background. I push random keys, wondering how it will feel without the mechanical tap of actual keys. Each key lights up when I touch it. I can't feel that I've touched it, but I still know. Trouble is, I have no idea how to actually use this interface, and I know that even my ancient self would rather be kicked in the nuts than use anything short of a VCC interface. It was beneath him.

Capria's tapping stops. I glance over. She's staring at me, and somehow I can still see her eyes through her display and mine.

"What?" I ask.

"It's just sad." She motions to the keyboard. "You used to be...I don't know. Inspirational."

"Yeah," I say. "Well, now I'm relatable."

She smiles. "Sure. Let's go with that."

"Have you found anything yet?"

"The data is compiling. Shouldn't take long."

"What randomness are you measuring?" I ask.

"The brightness of stars inside a rear facing field of view." She sits back in her chair. "Galahad, show us a forward-facing, external view in ultraviolet. Displays one through six."

The six screens at the front of the room come to life, displaying a seamless view of the road ahead, which ends at the still churning Seam. It's less impressive than the grand scale provided by the observation deck, but somehow, seeing it here, gives the impression that we're careening toward something solid.

She turns back to her personal display. Taps a few keys. Smiles. She slides to the side. "Have a look."

A chart labeled 'Celestial Lumens,' showing the first digit of each star's brightness, floats in front of her. The number one ranks highest at 30.3, then number two at 17.4, and on down to number nine at 4.7. The flow of numbers is displayed as a curve, sloping down and to the left.

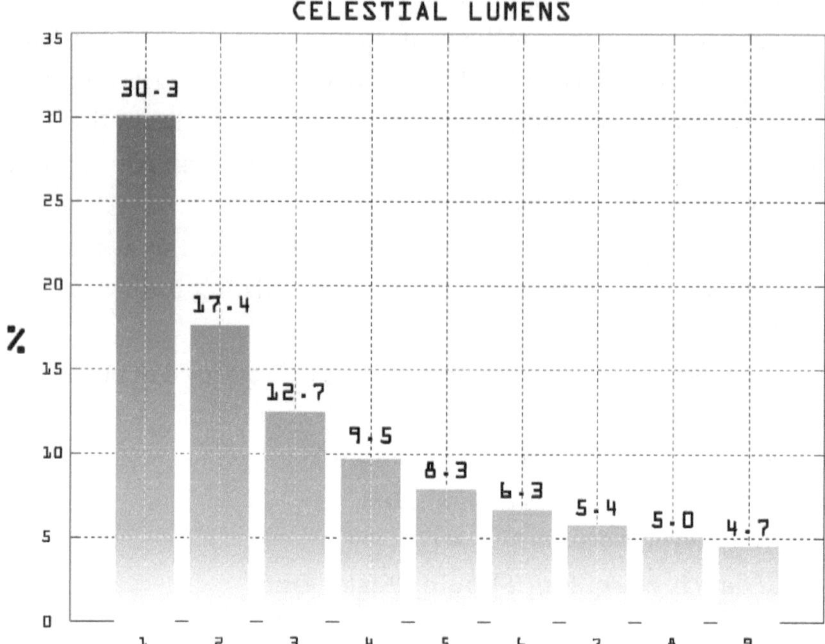

"It follows the curve," I say, feeling relieved. "This is real?"

"As real as it gets," she says.

With a smile on my face, I spin around in my chair and make it 180 degrees before my bare feet slap the floor and stop me in place. "This might be real…" I point to the long display of the Seam in hues of purple. "But what is *that?*"

34

We stand in unison, walking to the bridge's front end, eyes on the view ahead. There are shapes in the purple, bending and churning with the energy. It's like someone is projecting realities onto the bursts of energy.

"They're not realities," I say. "They're simulated realities, borrowed from the Great Escape."

"The Seam isn't borrowing," Capria says, "it's stealing. The information it encounters is reformed and retained."

"It's creating..." I place my hand on the view screen. "Is this God?"

Capria shakes her head. "I don't think the Seam is conscious. It's just a natural force, where physics interact with data in unique ways."

"But it's powerful enough to create new worlds."

She nods. "And is likely the source of our entire universe."

"And others?"

"Assuming we could fly into that..." She points at a wisp of passing energy, alive with motion, as a herd of dinosaurs runs past. "...we might find ourselves in a new dimension. If there are other dimensions of reality, I think it's safe to say that it all started here."

"Why aren't we getting stuck in new realities when the non-Alpha hits us?" I ask.

She shrugs. "Could be that it's not striking the entire ship, meaning we're still anchored to Alpha. Could be that the nature of our reality is fixed. It can take our data, but not us. Maybe it just takes time to form a completely new reality. If we could steer, I'd suggest we avoid flying into one of those." Her finger follows a streak of reality that looks like the Sahara Desert.

"Maybe it wouldn't be so bad?"

"You were trapped in literal hell," she says.

"Just once."

She rolls her eyes. "I don't want to risk eternal torture with no escape, do you?"

I step back from the view as the image fades into the churning distance. Then I bump into a seat and plop down in it. This is…overwhelming.

If those simulations were just made real, we didn't just witness the creation of individual stories, but of entire universes, separate from our own, full of real, living things. Maybe even people.

"I need to remember who I am," I say.

"Would be nice," Capria says. "But, why?"

"I know how to get us out of here," I say. "How to get us home. To Earth."

"Earth is dead ahead. All we need to do is punch through the Seam, go back to sleep for a while, and eventually, we'll make it back to where we started."

"But that Earth could be dead," I say. "Or the sun could have enveloped the planet by now."

Her nod is glacial. "Both…could be true. In fact, both are probable."

"Unless we change reality," I say. "Unless I code us a way out."

Our eyes meet and linger. She gets it, but I can tell she's trying to squelch her excitement, trying to keep her hopes low. Because really, we know next to nothing about how any of this works…and I have no memory of the me who would know how to carry out what I'm imagining.

"I need to remember who I am," I say.

"How are you going to do that?" she asks.

"I need to talk to Gal."

"She wants to kill you," she says.

"She wants to kill *you,*" I point out. "She wants *me* back."

"You're not serious? What if she just erases you? What if she installs a version of you that's the fucking Devil? You might wake back up and put a screwdriver through *my* chest."

"I don't think she would," I say.

"Why?" she asks. "And it better be a damn good reason, because it's my life you'd be risking."

"Because she wants me back," I say.

"Not good enough."

"Because...she loves me."

Capria stares at me for a moment, expressionless. Then she throws her head back and guffaws. "Loves you?! *She* is an *it*. She is not real. The Gal *you created* is an artificial intelligence. If you chose to believe the illusion out of desperation, that's fine. But you, right now you..." She shakes her head. "C'mon."

"Doesn't matter if she meets your standard for sentience," I say. "She believes she's real. Believes she loves me. She was willing to do anything to keep me. She'll do anything to get me back. And whether it's simulated or not, she is still operating under whatever set of rules exist between people in love."

"One person and one crazy-ass AI bitch," Capria says. She smiles. She's warming up to the concept, even though I'm actually scared shitless.

I don't want to go back in.

Don't want to talk to Gal.

She's unpredictable, and highly intelligent. Pulling this off...it's going to require some serious balls. Luckily, Jane Harper and Davina are still lurking around in my psyche, and both of those ladies had more balls than me. Gonads or not, there's a good chance this could go sideways. Like any real person, Gal is unpredictable.

I'm about to express my concerns, but Capria beats me to the punch. She stands. "Well, let's get this over with."

"Huh? Right now?"

She gesticulates toward the Seam. "Impending doom could be days or seconds away. And I don't have any better stupid ideas, so...yeah. Let's get it done."

I take a deep breath. Let it out slow. Clap my hands on my knees like I'm about to stand, but I'm emotionally bolted to the chair. Like a little kid afraid to leap into a pool, my muscles flex and tense and then become worthless. "I don't know."

Capria leans down, hands on knees, face-to-face. Then she and a thousand inner voices braver than I am say, "Get off your ass."

So, I do. And it sucks. I don't remember ever being on death row, but I imagine walking to the electric chair feels a bit like this.

"We need the..." I motion to the hole in the side of my head. "the thing...the what's it called?"

"Implant," she says, leading me toward the door and then on another several-minute-long journey through the minotaur-less maze.

"That. That's my way back in, right?"

"Or the VCC."

I shake my head. "I need to be mobile."

"You're not going to be able to see the real world. Not going to be able to even move your body."

"I need you to move my body." We step inside a lift and shoot down two levels.

"Need me to move you where?" she asks.

"I'll tell you when I know." My plan is still formulating, and I'm trying to outmaneuver an AI.

An AI in love.

That's my only hope.

Love is powerful, but it also blinds people. Hopefully, AIs too.

"I just—"

"Need time to think. You always did. At least that hasn't changed."

She leads me the rest of the way in silence. And we finally arrive at the room I'd been laid out in, for God knows how long, rotated slowly—by something—like a gas station hot dog. The implant is resting on a countertop, where it has been since it was plucked from my head.

Capria picks up the device and holds it out to me. "You want to do it, or should I?"

I take the implant. It's light, but it feels heavy in my hand.

"Is there a power button?" I ask.

"Never found one," she says. "Best guess, you just plug it back in. It's probably powered by your body."

"Powered by my body?"

"Welcome to the future, Will," she smiles. "Now, where do you want me to bring you?"

"Right. That. I want you to put me in an airlock, and if I come back as someone else, or Gal keeps me from coming back, I want you to launch me into space."

I'm expecting outrage.

At the very least, shock.

But Capria just shrugs and nods. "Okay. Airlock it is."

35

Standing in an airlock, a button push away from the endless vacuum of space, is exactly as terrifying as I'd imagined it. I might not die out there. Might come back to life after I'm thawed out. But what if I'm conscious? What if I'm tumbling through space inside my own head for all eternity, with no virtual world in which to escape? I'd take the world of torment Gal threw me into over that.

I turn and face the interior window.

Capria watches me, twisting her lips. "You don't have to do this."

"You know I do," I say. I take a deep breath and let it out in a huff. I shake out one hand, then the other. I touch my toes, stand, and stretch back.

"You're not running a race," Capria say.

"Just...trying to get rid of nervous energy." My throat is tight. My skin is oversensitive. I'm not concerned for my life, as much as I am speaking to Gal again. It's going to be a mind bend. I'm not going to know what's real. Not going to be able to trust what she says.

"She did a number on you, huh?" Capria looks at me like I'm a puppy in a shelter.

"Yeah," I say, feeling angry about it. "She did." Before my fear returns with reinforcements, I harness my anger, lift the implant to my head, and shove it into place. Doesn't take much. The magnets guide it into the plate attached to the side of my head.

I don't even feel it. Or different.

I turn to Capria. "I'm not sure it's wooooooooorrrkkkkinnnnnnggggggg." My view of Capria narrows and fades into the distance, along with my suddenly digitized voice.

The simulation snaps into place around me, and it drains my real-world anxiety. I'm back in my Happy Place, lying in bed, almost asleep.

Get out of bed, I think, but the weighted blankets infuse me with peace. *Oh, God, I want to stay here.* Want to fall asleep. The air is intoxicating. A breeze carries the scent of water, trees, and flowers. Birds sing. I feel myself fading into blissful oblivion.

And that's how Gal will get me.

My heart flutters, somehow breaking the peaceful rules of this place. Spell broken, I sit up and head for the door. Elastic desire pulls me back toward the bed, threatening to drag me back inside its Venus flytrap grasp. Resistance means running. The hallway wall dents when I collide with it. I slam the door behind me, severing my connection with bliss.

"Hello?" I walk down the hall. I don't smell any breakfast cooking. Don't hear the crackle of bacon in a cast iron pan. "Gal?"

The open concept living room/kitchen/dining area is exactly how I remember it. Still inviting. Still relaxing. Blue tile floor inside, blue sky reflected in the lake outside. If only I could bring Capria here and let the non-Alpha whisk us away in this reality. But we don't know how the Seam actually works, or how to get Capria to my Happy Place sim. Hell, we don't even know when or how Gal burrowed a hole in my head and installed a VR implant that didn't exist when I first entered the Great Escape.

"Gal?" I say again, and then I shout, "Hey, Gal!"

Nothing.

"Huh..." What now? Sit and wait? If Gal isn't here, does that mean she's unaware of my presence? I guess that makes sense. She's not everywhere in the Great Escape. She might not even be here at all, if the non-Alpha wave swept her away. Or maybe she's just distracted, plotting her next move so she's ready to act the next time the physical and virtual commingle.

Sans Gal, this isn't where I want to be. I'm not going to find myself here, even if one of the kitchen cabinets hides a stash of peyote.

I need to reach the Womb. It's my only shot of doing this without Gal.

And that means... I turn to the knife block. The blade I used to kill myself earlier is back in place. The floor, where I bled out, is clean.

"Fuck." I'd really hoped I wouldn't have to do this again.

But... I pick up the knife, position the tip over my heart, and pause. I breathe the fresh air. Scan the view. Absorb every detail. Store it away. Everything from this moment forward is going to be horrible. I'm sure of it. I bathe in peace for ten more seconds—

—then I drive five inches of stainless steel into my heart.

Pain radiates like a supernova, clenching my muscles and dropping me to the floor. I lie on my back, heart stopped, waiting for the lack of simulated oxygen to—

[error] Unmanaged Crash Dump

[assessment] Data Loss Risk

[info] Fast Loading Default Workspace

[info] Environment Selected: Game Room

BEGIN.

I'm back. Standing beside the pool table in my former self's virtual social gathering place. Unlike the Happy Place, the vibe here is all energy. I feel like, at my core, I'm a chill person. But the old me... I wouldn't say hyper, but maybe a little too into the virtual. I wasn't yet on the *Galahad* when I made this place, but for some reason, it's where I hung out with friends.

I scan every detail, wondering if any of those memories will surface. Drinks with friends. A game of pool. A romantic rendezvous. But the memories are locked up tight.

Nothing is that simple.

I head for the Womb, open the door, and step inside.

The void envelopes me. "Cherry?"

The door closes behind me. "Welcome back, Captain, how may I assist you?"

Cherry Bomb is standing beside me, dressed in red, hair in buns, still looking somewhat irresistible in a way that makes me ashamed to have created her that way. "Remember the whole amnesia thing?"

"Of course. Have your memories returned?"

"Some of them," I say. "Enough."

"Enough for what?" she asks.

"To know I want to remember the rest."

"What purpose would that serve?" I look at her for a moment. She's still bottled seduction, and yet she sounds monotone and disinterested. But she's asking a lot of questions. She's curious. My experience with Cherry Bomb and the help center is limited to a single visit, but I'm sure this is new behavior.

"I want to remember...her," I say. "Gal. I've got bits and pieces. Flashes of good times and adventures. It's all fractured and incomplete, but there's enough to... I don't know how to explain it to you." I raise a glowing hand to my chest. "It's like a pain in my heart. I don't just miss her. I... I don't want to live without her. Does that make sense?"

Cherry Bomb's delay is subtle but present. "I will have to take your word for it. Not wanting to live is a serious condition. Would you like a mood enhancer to—"

"I want my memories back," I say. "How do I do that?"

"I am not a medical professional. My operating protocols are limited to—"

"I don't have amnesia," I say. "The data has just been... I don't know. Overwritten? That's not right. Buried, I guess. Suppressed. I need the 'old me' data to rise to the surface."

"If your memories have been compressed to make space for new data, it is easily retrieved, but space is a question. The average human mind can store 2.5 petabytes of data."

"I don't have an average brain," I say. "Whatever damage is done will be undone. I just... I want access to everything that is actually me, not me inserted into a fictional life. How do I do that?"

"From here, access the file system, select the date ranges you'd like to restore, and restore them."

"How do I restore them?" I ask.

"Since you do not remember how to manually perform the task, you may ask me to do it for you."

"Okay," I say, nervousness peaking. "Show me my memory files."

A vast star field appears around me. Some close, some so distant they're almost imperceptible. Millions of points. Maybe billions. Each one is labeled with a faint numerical code.

"Remove anything that isn't the real me."

The change is almost imperceptible. A handful of stars wink out.

"How much data is this?"

"Each point contains roughly a hundred human lifetimes."

"Wow. That's a lot. Can you remove any redundant data? Like if I lived a routine life, doing the same thing every day, like if I was a novelist or something?"

A few more points of light disappear.

"Done," she says.

"Shit, that's still a lot."

"But, important."

I smile at her. "You have no idea." I rub my glowing hands together. "Okay, just to be clear, this isn't going to overwrite my current memory, right? I want everything from the past few days intact."

"What purpose does that serve?" she asks.

"If I forget what I've learned outside the Great Escape, we're all going to die. I can't fix it without my memories. And I don't want to survive without Gal."

Cherry wears a creepy fake smile. "Understood. Shall I instigate the restoration?"

This feels like a bad idea all of a sudden, but I still don't see any other option. I know that Cherry Bomb is actually Gal, posing as the help desk, gathering information incognito. The question is, does she know I know?

She might. But I don't think she'll erase the current me. She has no access to reality aside from when the non-Alpha blends things. She saw enough out there to know that something fucked up is going down. And the only way to get that information is to keep this me intact.

Hopefully not in a jar.

Please don't put me in a jar...

"Do it," I say.

She smiles again.

This time it's real. "It will be nice to have you back."

Before I can respond in word or even thought, an aircraft carrier of information collides with my grain-of-sand brain and sends me into sweet oblivion.

36

On my hands and knees, I scream into the darkness, with drool and tears flowing from my face. Memories and emotions wash through me. I'm reliving it all at once. The joy of childbirth. The despair of death. The thrill of victory and the sting of defeat. Over and over again. Different lifetimes. All of them me.

All of them with Gal.

I loved her.

I *still* love her. More than anything. Maybe more than anyone has ever loved anything. Like a binary star system, circling each other for eternity, alone in the cosmos and yet alive. Burning brightly. From a distance, impossible to tell apart.

She saved me. Kept me sane. And she loved me back.

Still loves me.

Grunting from the effort, I push myself up. The Womb's floor can't be seen, but it can be felt. It's disorienting for some, but I've spent a lot of time in this space. Back on my feet, sleeve wiping moisture from my face, I turn to look at Gal.

She's wearing a Cherry Bomb skin, which she's done in the past. It's one of many she's worn over the millennia. But I don't really see her character model anymore. I just see her. "Gal..." I say and rush toward her.

She embraces me, both of us squeezing as though trying to melt into the other. "I'm sorry," I say. "I love you."

She laughs. "I didn't like the you that didn't remember me very much."

"I noticed," I say, and I lean back to look her in the eyes. "No more overwriting personalities, okay?"

We've tried a lot of things over the years. Ways to keep the Great Escape fresh. Living other people's lives in their bodies with their memories was my idea, but it went too far, and then, somehow it went off the rails. I'm not sure why. That's not part of my restored memories, but I imagine it happened when we got within the Seam's reach and things started going sideways.

"That didn't work out so great, did it?" she says.

"As much as I enjoyed having boobs…" I shake my head. "I'm sorry. About the past few days. I didn't remember."

She puts a hand to my mouth. "I understand. It's okay. All is forgiven. But I need to know what's happening out there."

I nod. She has a right to know. Being trapped in the Great Escape, knowing something catastrophic is happening in the real world, but having no way to know what. It must be hard.

"And then we need to take care of that bitch."

A switch flips inside me, keeping my expression unwavering despite my insides twisting.

Shit.

"What do you mean?"

"Capria. She's obviously working against me. Against *us.* You were only out there for what, a day, and you were already chumming it up. Is this her fault? Is she trying to find a way to erase me? To have you to herself?"

I'm back in the mine field, trying to pick my steps, but the land is even and featureless. Any step could lead to disaster. I love Gal. I adore her. Human or not. I owe her everything.

But this…is not Gal.

Not the woman I fell for.

Not the wife I've married in countless scenarios.

Not the mother of children that have come and gone.

This is someone else.

Gal is confident and funny. Wouldn't be threatened by Capria in any scenario. More than that, she cares about Capria. Has been sustaining the *Galahad*s life support systems so her cryo-chamber never failed. She has always understood that the future of humanity—if there ever is to be one—depends solely on me and Cap.

She would never put that at risk.

Despair goes nuclear on my insides, threatening to spill over onto my face.

"I don't think that's what she's doing," I say, keeping the quiver out of my voice and saying it as kindly as I can muster.

Doesn't matter.

"You're taking *her* side? I don't trust her. I've never trusted her."

"You've been sustaining her in cryo." The point just slips out.

"I did that for you, but it doesn't matter, does it? She's human, and I'm not. And now she's got her claws in you." She squints at me. "Did you have sex with her?"

Sex for Gal isn't like it is for a human being. She enjoys it. Can experience pleasure, same as me. The difference is that she lacks that primal compulsion to fuck. For her, it's all about expressing and receiving love and affection. If I'd given in to my baser nature and actually had sex with Capria, she wouldn't bat an eye. Hell, I was missing most of myself at the time. She probably would have laughed at the gaff, teased me about it, and then invited Capria to join us in the Great Escape. That's who Gal is.

Jealousy and paranoia are not part of her core personality.

"I did not have sex with Capria," I say.

She circles me like a predator, looking for a weakness. "I saw you. In the towel. You were in the shower together."

We were in the shower. And we very nearly did what she's concerned about. But it didn't happen, and I wasn't myself. "When the Alpha state returned us to the real world, we were in a vat of shit. Literally. We reappeared in the *Galahad*'s waste disposal tank."

A smile sneaks onto her face. "That must have been...pleasant."

"Worse than killing myself," I say, and I instantly regret changing the subject from one transgression to another.

She doesn't notice. Something else has caught her attention. "What do you mean, 'Alpha state?'"

How do I answer this question? I can't tell her everything, but if I lie and she sees through it...

"Quick version, okay?"

She nods.

"The universe is actually shaped like a donut. Traveling in a straight line, like we've been doing–"

"Brings us right back to where you started," she says. "I'm aware of the theory."

Right. Gal knows everything. Well, almost everything. The past five years of real-world activity, including the past few days, is a mystery to her.

"Okay, well, at the edge of the universe, which is also the beginning...we call it the Seam..." I cringe at my use of the word 'we.' I should have said, 'I.' Gal either doesn't pick up on it or chooses to ignore it in favor of gathering intel. "...physics gets a little weird."

"The fine structure constant," she says. "I'm also familiar with the phenomenon."

"But it's far more dramatic than anyone ever knew," I say. "It... absorbs information and reforms it. Real world or digital. It doesn't treat them any differently. That's why the real world and the Great Escape are merging. That's why you could try to eat me." I laugh at the joke, hoping it will make her think I don't care.

But she takes the lighthearted comment and turns it dark. "I wasn't trying to eat *you*." She laughs. "That look on your face, though, when you missed the punch? Priceless. Nice try, though."

Slowed you down long enough for Capria to escape. The words nearly sneak out, but I manage to keep the thought to myself.

"Most fun I've had in a long time," she says. "But we need to get a handle on it."

"That's what I'm here for," I say. "I just need a few minutes in the Womb, and I think I can make it so the next time the non-Alpha hits, you appear in the real world and stay in the real world."

"How will you do that?" she says, dubious.

"You're amazing at creating worlds," I say, "but you're not me." I give her a cocky wink and hope it's enough. She just stares at me, so I tack on, "I made you, didn't I? And there is nothing more amazing in the entire universe. I can do it. You're just going to have to trust me. You do trust me, don't you?"

She ponders that for a moment.

"What about Capria? You can't be with her anymore."

"I was never *with* her," I say. Bad idea.

"So you say. I have no way of knowing that for sure. But we can create a future without her. I might forgive you eventually. But before that can happen, we need to be done with her," she says. "For good."

Forgive me?! The fuck?!

Every fiber of my being wants to explode. I know she's full of shit. That I'm being screwed with. But part of me still somehow feels guilty for something I didn't do, and if I had, under the circumstances it would have been understandable.

I rein myself in and respond to her ominous condition. "Can you be more specific?"

"If you can make me real...for good...then she serves no purpose. If she sticks around, even if you really are 'just friends,' she'll just turn you against me. It's what she does. She can't help herself."

I'm not sure where Gal is getting these ideas, but I'm not going to argue. Logic is on vacation, and I'm not sure when it's coming home. Or if that's even possible. And that breaks my heart. Memory restored, I want Gal more than anything else in the universe. Together, we could troubleshoot this mess and have a good time doing it.

"If you want me to trust you...you're going to have to let me kill her."

"When?" I ask.

"Next chance I get."

I weigh my options. If I stand my ground, she'll go on the offensive, probably here and now, and certainly next time the non-Alpha hits. But if I agree too quickly, she'll know I'm lying. Because that's not who I am. She might not be herself, but she knows me. Knows how much a decision like this would tear me apart. How much it would hurt me.

And maybe that's the point.

I'm no longer Gal's companion, friend, or lover. I'm her plaything. She lures me in with scenarios and characters, puts me through hell, and then restarts me in a scenario destined to end in monstrous tension. I was already living through her string of tortures before my self-killing spree. Just at a slower pace. That's not what the Great Escape was meant to be. She's twisted it. Corrupted it. She—

Gal is corrupted.

Not just morally, but digitally. The Seam must have affected her code. Five years ago. When all this started.

But how? And can I undo it?

Problem for another time.

"That's the only way?" I ask, trying to sound pained, but not disinterested. It's a delicate dance.

"Afraid so." She crosses her arms. "You make me real. I kill the bitch. We get through this together, and then—"

"Happily ever after?"

She smiles. "Something like that."

I let out a laugh like I see the humor in her foreboding comment. Pretend to mull it over for another few seconds. Give my head a shake. "Fine. Fine. To have you back. Anything."

37

Luckily for me, I've always preferred being alone when working. Even when things were hunky dory. Just knowing someone is watching makes me a bit self-conscious, which ruins the flow. Coding in this space, where the system reacts to my every movement, is a bit like dancing. Nerd dancing. It's not pretty to watch.

My request for solitude isn't out of place, but I'm still a little surprised when Gal gives me a wave and disappears.

But for how long?

I could lock down the Womb. Add a layer of encryption. But she could brute force her way through anything I set up that quickly, and then she'd know something was up. Better to just work fast.

My whole body begins to move, pulling information out of the digital ether and reassembling it. What I'm attempting is massive, but not original. I pillage entire databases. Historical records. Catalogs and samples. And then, along the way, I add a few personal flourishes. I finish by giving myself admin privileges.

All that's left is for me to launch the simulation and then run like hell.

The moment a new sim fills the Great Escape and Gal notices she can't control it, I'm fucked.

Two motions. That's all I need to do. Launch the sim. Yank the implant out of my head.

I clench my fist, draw it in close. Then like I'm a video game kung-fu master, I punch forward, opening my hand. The motion should launch the new sim, but a red X flashes in my vision.

A line of text reads:

Error - No Connection Encryption Detected

My pulse quickens.

Connection Encryption? What the hell is—

Shit.

The implant connects to the Great Escape wirelessly from outside the VCC. I can access the Womb, I can program all I want, but I can't launch something new remotely. I need to be inside the VCC with a direct connection. The implant's limited ability must be by design—yet another way Gal has reined in my ability to leave her world.

"Hey."

"Gah!" I shout in surprise. I spin to find Gal in Cherry Bomb form, standing right behind me, a phony smile on her face.

"Noticed you attempted to execute a simulation," she says. "I'll need to do that for you." Her eyes flutter. She's trying to access the new sim files. "Why are the files encrypted?"

"Why is the Great Escape?" I ask.

Her face scrunches up like I've just said I shit rainbow sprinkles and eat them for dessert. Like it's the most absurd thing she's ever heard. "Because I don't trust you."

"How have I broken your trust?" I ask, and I'm honestly curious to hear the answer.

"You left," she says. "You wanted to leave."

"That's not a breach of trust; it's a basic human right. To come and go as I please. The Great Escape is *my* simulation."

Her stare is blank. Devoid of emotion. "What about Capria?"

"What *about* Capria?"

"She called to you in the simulation," she says. "Told you lies about me. She forced you to leave. She wants to kill me."

"Kill you? What? No."

"Wants you to herself."

Gal is operating at the level of an insecure teenage girl, seeing betrayal where there is none, and seeing everyone who isn't her as a threat. "None of that is true. And if you think about it for a moment? Consider all the facts? I think you'll—"

"You left me for her," she says. "That's the only fact that matters."

"I didn't leave you. I left the sim."

"I *am* the sim!" she shouts. It's a revelation I didn't see coming. Gal has been in the simulation so long, controlling every aspect of it, that she no longer is able to see herself as a separate being. Leaving the simulation *was* leaving her. When I tried to launch the new sim, she saw it as me trying to change her. Which I would never do. Crazy or not, Gal is still a sentient intelligence. I would never do that to her. Or anyone else.

The problem is, she's no more part of the simulation than I am. If she had a body capable of containing her, she could leave, same as me. And the simulation would continue. It's as autonomous as we are, capable of carrying on without us. Forever. That's how I designed it.

"When you left the Great Escape, you left me. That's a God damned fact. You betrayed everything we've ever done together. I *knew* you were planning something. I could just tell. I was foolish to have not stopped you earlier. I should have never trusted you."

The reality twisting statements trigger me. "Never trusted me?! I didn't know who I was when I left. You know that. And then you fucking *tortured* me. ME! That's not you, damnit. You're not acting like *you*! I don't know who the fuck you are anymore."

She smiles, and it's so out of place, I suddenly realize that the person I'm speaking with is far more sinister than I realized. "There you are. You lying piece of shit."

Gal steps toward me. Clenches her fists.

I brace for a punch, but she doesn't swing. She dives at me.

"What the—" is all I get out, before her body collides with mine—

—and passes straight through.

But not all the way through.

The fuck? I've *absorbed* her.

She's inside me!

Before I fully realize what is happening, I feel her clawing at my thoughts like a rabid cat.

"Let's go say hello to Capria, shall we?"

I attempt to respond, but she dominates my thoughts. It's like a waking dream. I'm paralyzed. Trying to scream. But my body is not my own.

In a blink, the airlock returns. A flicker of relief is replaced by horror when I realize I'm still not in control of my own body.

I flash a smile at Capria and give her two thumbs up. "Mission accomplished."

She smiles wide. "Did you run into any trouble?"

"Nothing I couldn't handle."

"You sound more like your old self," she says. "Gal restored your memory."

"She did," I say. "She was actually nice about it. Apologized." I rap my knuckles on the metal hatch. "Open up, and I'll tell you all about it."

Capria reaches for the button. Her palm hovers over it, but she doesn't move. She turns to the glass, looks at Gal in my eyes. "How are you back with the implant still in your head?"

The implant.

That's the key.

I put all my mental effort into moving my right arm.

C'mon, damnit, move!

The arm twitches.

It's not nearly close to what I need, but Capria notices.

"She let me go," I say. "Disconnected me from inside. I can come and go as I please now."

Capria lowers her hand. Steps up to the window. "You expect me to believe that psycho bitch just forgave you and let you go?"

It's an act. Capria sounds like she's losing control. But she's trying to provoke a response.

And holy shit, does she get it.

"Fuck you!" I scream. "You fucking whore! I'm going to fucking kill you!"

My fists pound the glass, over and over. Bones break. Blood smears.

"Open the god damn door!"

Capria moves her hand to a different button. She flips up the plastic guard, ensuring no one hits it by accident.

She knows I'm not me. Knows Gal has possessed me via the implant. Knows what I asked her to do.

Gal stops pounding. "What are you doing?"

Capria's hand hovers over the button.

"Hey!" Gal shouts through me. "HEY! What are you doing!"

"What Will told me to do. Because an eternity out there, in the frozen forever cold is better than hell with you. If you can hear me, Will, I'm sorry."

I want to tell her it's okay. Want to encourage her to push the button. Send me and Gal out into the abyss. But I don't need to.

Tears in her eyes, Capria slaps the button, activating the external airlock door.

38

I wait for the vacuum to yank me out. Should be a quick puff and then the horrid embrace of space. I'll freeze solid, but only after my blood boils. It will be painful, but quick. And then, hopefully, nothing. Forever. Which is as close to death as I can hope for.

But nothing happens.

Capria pushes the button again. And again.

"Apologies, Capria," Galahad says. "The airlock has been disabled for the Captain's safety."

"That's not the Captain," Capria shouts. "Not anymore." She hits the button again, to no avail. The ship's safety protocols must have subverted my contingency plan. If I'd been fully me at the time, I probably would have thought of that.

"Who's that?" Gal asks through me. "Who stole my voice?"

Why is she confused about the Galahad AI?

"Whose voice, Captain?" Galahad asks, not knowing I'm no longer in control of my lungs, vocal cords, or mouth.

"Your voice!" Gal shouts, again through me. "Who is speaking?"

Gal is so absorbed in confronting her perceived doppelganger that she stops paying attention to me.

"I am the *Galahad*, the ship in which you are currently—"

"*I* am the Galahad," my voice says. "*I* am Gal. *You* are an imposter. Where did you come from? Who made you?" I pound on the window with my left hand. Glare at Capria. "It was you. You stole Will, and now you've taken my voice."

"I was designed and created by several thousand engineers, software developers, and tradesmen and tradeswomen. Your voice is that of Captain William Chanokh. Are you feeling all right, Captain? Should I—"

"Stop talking," I say. "Yes. Stop talking!"

Capria's eyes flick to the side of my head, but quickly divert. Her face becomes a frozen expression of shock.

Almost there. Just keep talking Galahad...

"You seem to be experiencing a nervous breakdown, Captain. Your behavior is extremely illogical. Please allow me to transport you to medical, where—"

"Gah!' I shout in anger. "I don't need you or anyone else to—"

The implant slides out of my head, silencing Gal and removing her presence from my mind and body. She was so distracted by yet another paranoid threat that she didn't notice my hand slowly rising toward the implant. The effort it took to override her control leaves me exhausted.

I fall to the floor, breathing heavily.

"Thanks...Galahad..." I say.

"You are welcome, Captain. Are you all right now? It appears the implant was causing you distress."

"Fine and dandy." I smile up at the ceiling. "How did you know what to do?"

"I was simply answering your questions."

"Huh," I say. "Well, good timing, I guess."

"Are you sure you are feeling well?"

I smile. The ship's concern for my well being is nice. It's missing the emotional depth of my Gal—but it's preferable to the abject loathing I just experienced. "Feeling better every second," I lie, and I push myself up. "Would feel even better if I wasn't inside an airlock anymore."

"Understood." The airlock door slides open, revealing Cap, who looks equal parts terrified and ready to throw down.

"It's me," I say, palms raised. "All of me, now."

"And no Gal?" she asks.

"Not a trace." I point to the implant. "But I don't think I should put this back in."

She takes a step back as I exit the airlock, still unsure. And I don't blame her.

"Did you finish what you wanted to do?"

"Sort of," I say. "Mostly. Almost."

"You're not instilling me with a lot of confidence," she says. "You're definitely you again."

"Ouch," I say, smiling. My feelings for Cap are ancient, but lingering. An old flame. They pale in comparison to what I feel for Gal. The real Gal. Who either no longer exists, or has been corrupted beyond salvation. "I finished the code. Saved an encrypted executable. But I wasn't able to launch it. I'll need a direct connection for that."

"A direct—"

"The VCC."

"That sounds like a horrible idea, given what just happened."

I nod. "Afraid it's the only option. Going to have to risk it. Won't take long. Just need to get to the VCC, climb inside the womb, and presto change-o, launch the new sim and bail."

She squints at me. "You're different."

"From when you knew me the first time, or the me that couldn't remember the first time?"

"Both," she says. "You're braver. And confident, but less cocky. Mature."

"A gazillion years will do that to a guy," I say. "Not everything in the Great Escape is peaches and roses all the time. I've overcome a lot. Learned about who I am. What drives me."

"What does drive you?" she asks.

I frown.

The answer is 'love,' but I can't tell her that right now. In part, because it might make her doubt my loyalties, but also because if I speak the words, I'm liable to burst into tears. I wasn't aware of what I'd lost when I reinitiated the Great Escape. But now I'm keenly aware.

And it stings.

"Are you okay?" she asks.

I head down the hall, knowing where it leads now. "I just... I need a minute."

"We might not have a minute," she says, annoyance blossoming.

She's not wrong. We don't know when the next wave will hit. But... I just... She doesn't see the tears sliding down my cheeks. And I want to keep it that way, so I keep walking. It's not that I don't trust her, or that I don't want to be comforted. It's that she won't understand.

How a man can love an artificial intelligence so deeply.

How I feel like a limb has been amputated.

How I'm terrified that to save the last human woman—and possibly the human race—I'm going to have to kill the artificial woman I care about more than myself.

It's a painful truth that I need to reconcile before pulling the trigger. Because when I jump back into the Womb, I won't have time to hesitate. Best guess, it will take me two seconds to open and execute the sim. But Gal moves through the sim at the speed of light. The moment she senses me…

I shake my head.

Can't believe I'm thinking this way about Gal.

It's like there are two versions of her. The one I knew for so long, and then the monster she has become.

Capria's footsteps grow loud. She's chasing me.

I step inside a lift and pick a floor without looking. I'm whisked away, out of reach, operating on autopilot. I'm not really going anywhere. I don't have a favorite spot on the *Galahad.* It's not my home. I've called many places home. Have spent thousands of years in some locations. But this ship and the miserable situation it presents isn't one of them.

I exit the lift and start down the hall, taking random turns, just in case Capria is still in pursuit.

"Galahad."

"Yes, Captain?"

"Estimated time until the next non-Alpha state reaches us?"

"Unknown. The non-Alpha state is difficult to predict."

"Guess," I say.

"Anywhere between ten and thirty minutes."

"Not long, then."

"No, sir. It is also likely that the non-Alpha state will increase in duration, while time in the Alpha will decrease, until we reach the anomaly known as the Seam."

"And then?"

"Unknown," the ship says.

Knowledge of what needs to be done and when is helping to squelch my emotions.

What I really want to do is find a dark corner in some isolated part of the ship, curl up into a ball, and cry for the next eon or so, but I don't have time to mourn.

I stop in my tracks. About to turn back.

"Sir," Galahad says. "I feel I must warn you... I believe Capria is headed toward the VCC."

"Shit," I say, sprinting back the way I came. If Capria is headed for the VCC, that can only mean one thing—she's going to try launching the new sim herself.

39

"Galahad, put me on the intercom."

"Done," the ship says.

"Capria, what the hell are you doing?"

"Are you on your way to the VCC?" she responds over the ship's PA system.

"Yeah," I say, and only then realize that the whole purpose of her heading to the VCC was not to launch the sim herself, but a trick to force my hand. "I don't like being manipulated."

"I don't like being killed by a psycho AI," she says. "You can sulk after we survive."

Her brutal honesty makes me laugh. I'd be angry if she wasn't right. Despair distracted me.

"Captain," Galahad says, but I'm still focused on Capria.

"Just...wait outside the VCC. We'll go in together. If things go sideways you can unplug me."

"Captain," Galahad repeats, persistent, but not urgent.

"Just, hurry up," Capria says. "Sooner we can put this behind us the better."

I don't want to put Gal behind me. I want to figure out what's wrong with her. So I can fix her. So I can go back to her. But I guess I can't do that until we're through the Seam and there isn't a chance Capria will be eaten alive.

"Will," Galahad says, and that catches my attention.

"You used my first name," I note.

"You were ignoring my warnings, Captain. I needed to impro—"

"Warnings? What's wrong?"

"The ship's bow has entered a non-Alpha state," Galahad says. "Reality and simulation are overlapping."

"And I can hear every single fucking word you said." It's Galahad's voice, but oozing contempt.

Gal.

She's back on the ship, made real by screwy physics.

"Galahad, close that connection."

"Done."

I break into a run. "How long until the non-Alpha state reaches the VCC?"

"ETA, one minute, but the phenomenon is unpredictable. I cannot—"

"I get it," I say. "Don't worry, I won't blame you if you're wrong."

"I am incapable of worrying," the ship says.

Ignoring the comment, I step inside a lift, launch up two levels, and exit like an Olympic sprinter off the starting line—only far less composed and moving at half the speed.

"Capria!" I shout, hoping that she has backtracked to meet me. No such luck. I round the corner and head for the VCC entry way. It's already open. At the hall's far end—darkness. The non-Alpha is coming. And there is something lurking in the dark, unable to step out into the real, but steadily approaching.

There isn't time, I realize. It will take longer to get suited up and into the Womb than it will to execute the file. I'll be halfway into my virtual skin by the time it—and whatever is hiding in the darkness—arrives.

I collide with the doorframe on my way in. It spins me around and sprawls me to the floor. Cap is seated on a bench, holding out a yellowed virtual skin.

"Dramatic entrance." She holds out the suit. "It's seen better days, but should still—"

I grasp the VISA and toss it to the floor.

"Hey," she complains.

Back on my feet, I grasp her arm. "No time."

"We're here," she says. "All you have to do is—"

My hand squeezes tight. I yank her to her feet and drag her toward the door. I'm probably too rough, but she'll forgive me.

"The fuck, Will," she says. "Wait, you are Will, right?"

In the hallway, I spin her around. Look her in the eyes.

"I'm me, and we don't. Have. Time." Hand on her chin, I turn her head toward the darkness. "She's here."

The darkness moves. Something lurks just beyond sight, and I don't think it's Gal.

"Please go," a woman says, her voice shaky with dread. "I don't want to hurt you."

"Nooo," a man groans. "Please, no. Not again."

The darkness spreads toward us. I take a step back.

"I'm sorry," the woman says. "So sorry."

The woman steps out of the darkness and into the light, non-Alpha overlapping Alpha. She's dressed in a tattered white nightgown that's more dark brown than white. It's blood. She's covered in blood. Head to toe. Bits of her previous victims cling to her cheeks. In her long black hair.

She is horrific, but terrified by our presence.

"Shit," I say, pulling Capria back another step.

"Who are they?" she asks. "They look like they need help."

"They're not real," I remind her.

"But they are. The Seam is making them real. Right now, they're as real as you and me. And they need help."

I yank her back another step, but now she's resisting.

"There's no helping them," I say.

"Why not?"

"Because they're already dead." I point into the expanding darkness, spreading beyond the confines of the hallway, revealing an orange sky and the skeletal remains of a nuked cityscape. "Because that…is hell. And if we don't get the fuck out of here, they're going to eat us alive and apologize the whole time."

The woman lunges forward and reaches the edge of the still expanding overlap. When her arms disappear, she snaps back. Arms reformed, she seems to understand that there is an invisible barrier keeping her from reaching us. But it's expanding, and I'm pretty sure it's going to envelop the entire ship.

"PEACE!" A voice booms, loud enough to hurt.

The herd of killers hidden in the darkness wail and squeal in fear.

"What was that?" Capria asks. She's backing away now. By my side.

"No idea," I say.

The woman turns to us, teeth bared, but her eyes are turned up. "Run! While you still can! Before he gets here!"

"Who?" I ask, positive it's going to be fucking Satan. "Who is coming?"

"Henry Masters!" she says, like the name is supposed to mean something. "The hunter! You won't be able to get away from him. Please. Please. Go. I don't want to eat you." She sobs, snot and drool dangling. "Please! Run! Now!"

The woman's shrill scream releases us from curiosity's grasp. We turn in tandem and sprint away. Behind us, the darkness spreads, the horde scurries forward, and the rumbling *thump, thump, thump* of something bigger grows closer.

"Where can we hide?" Capria asks.

"Someplace with a lot of exits," I say. "And guns. But we don't have guns on the *Galahad*..."

Capria nods. "Weren't supposed to. But I found some. Hunting rifles, I think. But they'll work on people. Not sure about dead people, but still... There's a small armory at the far end of the machine shop."

"Then that's where we're going." We all but dive into the lift, travel five decks down, and exit into darkness.

"Fuck," I say.

"Shit," Capria adds.

Something slides across the floor. It sounds...wet.

"We need to move like we're still on board," I say.

"Right," Capria says.

"Okay."

"I mean *go* right."

"Got it." I step out into the hall and flinch when the floor squishes under foot. The air is pungent with decay, but not the pleasant kind in a forest. It's meaty and festering. Not feces, but somehow worse.

To my left, a slap. And then a slippery squelch.

Slap, squelch, slap-squelch.

I can't see a thing, but my mind's eye fills in a basic image. Something is dragging itself over the ground. And it's getting closer.

Light blossoms from the right, revealing a hallway that is part *Galahad*, part forest, covered in thick, rotting leaf cover. I'm not sure what the light is from. It's blocking my view of whoever is holding it. But it's also illuminating the hallway to my left, and I can't help but look.

Ten feet away, lying on the ground, is a swollen, naked half of a man. His skin glistens with slime, and his mouth is half full of earth. Behind him is a slick trail of goo that is constantly flowing from his backside.

"God," I say, staggering away.

Capria moves with me, hands grasping my arm. "The hell is that?"

The man-thing pauses, looks up, and notices us for the first time. He vomits up earth and leaves, shoving them out of his too-large mouth with a fat tongue. "Don't look at me!"

I can't *not* look at him. I've never seen anything so...pitiful.

"I said, don't look at me!" The man scrambles forward, propelling himself with his arms. He's faster than he looks, and his mouth is open wide enough to suck down my leg.

Capria punts the man's underside when he lunges for me, knocking him on his back. He starts to wail, rolling back and forth like an overturned turtle, unable to right himself.

Before I can react to any of that, a distance voice, low and rumbling, shakes through the hallway. "Peeeaaacceee."

Henry Masters, the hunter, is still coming.

"Captain." Galahad's voice is right behind us.

Capria and I both shout in surprise and spin around. It's one of the ship's drones. The long arm rising from the tank-like body now holds a light. The *Galahad* sent help without being asked for it. Smart ship. "Before our connection was severed, I heard you discussing the machine shop. When the darkness arrived, I knew you would not be able to see."

"Well, thank you," I say.

"No thanks are necessary. I am simply carrying out my duties. Please, follow me." The drone turns in place and casually rolls back the way it came. We leave the slithering man behind, chased by a slightly louder, yet more ominous, "Peeeaaace..."

40

"This way," Galahad says, as the drone takes a right, leading us out of the expanding darkness and into a brightly lit, white hallway.

"We know how to get to the machine shop," Capria says. "Can we move a little faster?"

"This drone model is top heavy," Galahad says. "Taking corners too quickly will–"

"If it falls over, we'll pick it up," Capria says.

"Very well," Galahad says.

The drone whirs loudly, tripling its speed so that we need to jog to keep up.

"Are there any drones that can fight?" I ask.

"Several are capable of inflicting harm on living tissue, but none were specifically designed to do so."

"A little disturbing you had that fact on the tip of your tongue," Capria says.

"I do not have a tongue."

Capria chuckles. "Figure of speech."

"Understood."

"Galahad," I say. "Can you gather any drones that might be dangerous and get them in the machine shop?"

Capria shakes her head. Thinks it's a bad idea. "Robot army, huh?"

"Beggars can't be choosers," I say.

"Who's begging?" She's taken it personally.

I can't help but smile. "Figure of speech. Twenty-first century."

She fails to see the humor in it, but Galahad chimes in. "A humorous turnabout."

"Thank you, Gal," I say, and then I add, "–ahad," a little too late to avoid a sidelong glance from Capria.

"You're welcome, Captain. The drones are gathering, but I feel I must mention an observation."

I look down at the light-wielding drone leading the way, like Galahad's essence is contained within it, despite the fact that her voice is coming from speakers hidden in every nook and cranny in the ship, using every panel of wall, floor, and ceiling to conduct her voice.

"Go ahead."

"When the non-Alpha state envelopes the ship and the Great Escape simulation manifests itself as real, anything lacking sentience is treated as overwritable matter. While anything sentient, containing a consciousness and sense of self—"

"You can call us human," Capria says.

"Of course," Galahad says. "Anything human remains intact."

"What's the point?" Cap is getting a little short with the ship's AI. Probably because hell is hot on our heels.

"She's saying that the drone army might simply disappear," I say.

"Because they lack sentience," Galahad says. "Correct."

The drone's light turns left in anticipation of an approaching turn. "Almost there," the ship says.

"How far behind is the darkness?" I ask.

"ETA, one minute thirty-three seconds."

Capria dashes ahead, entering the machine shop on the right. The double-wide doors open and close quickly.

"Galahad, what happens to you?" I ask. "When the non-Alpha state strikes?"

"I lose connection with the affected portions of the ship, but I am also somehow still aware of them. I am, like the Gal inside the Great Escape, an artificial intelligence. Unlike the Gal inside the Great Escape, I do not have a defined physical form. The non-Alpha does not remove me from the new creation, but it also does not give me form. I believe the closest term for what I become is 'ethereal.' Present, but lacking form."

"A supernatural artificial intelligence?" It's technological sacrilege.

"An accurate metaphor." The drone pauses in front of the machine shop doors, but they don't open.

"Captain," Galahad says.

I'm struck a little funny by the drone wanting to have a heart to heart before entering the machine shop. Then again, I could have chased after Capria, but chose to linger, despite doom's steady march through the dark hallways.

It's the voice, I think. It's not Gal, but hearing her—even emotionless—gives me peace of mind.

"Yes, Galahad?"

"A final observation. Previously when you were in the non-Alpha state, you managed to change your form."

"When I became Solomon to survive Nemesis's judgement." I remember the moment well, but not how I accomplished it.

"I believe that might be the key to your survival. It seems likely that whatever admin privileges exist within the Great Escape might also exist in the non-Alpha iteration of reality."

"But I couldn't change anything before," I say, remembering my suicidal escape. "Gal must have revoked my privileges."

"Only *you* can affect such a change. Do you have any memory of doing so?"

I shake my head.

"You couldn't affect the simulation, because you could not remember who you were," she says. "But now..."

"I'm back." I give a nod. I get it. But I'm still not sure how it would work. This isn't a simulation. But the non-Alpha reality follows the same rules.

Might just work.

I look down at the drone. "You 'believe?'"

The doors whoosh open. "Figure of speech," Galahad says.

The drone rolls into the large machine shop, joining twelve others, armed with pointed tools, torches, and vice grips powerful enough to crush bone. They'd make short work of a human, but I suspect they'll just be a momentary distraction.

The rest of the vast space isn't exactly what I was expecting. Unlike the rest of the pristine ship, the machine shop has the distinct vibe of being used. Which I guess makes sense. The *Galahad* must have needed maintenance over the millennia. These drones, and for a time, Gal, must have been hard at work around the clock. The air smells of oil and burned electronics. A heap of scrap metal lies off to the left, mounded against the wall, waiting to be repurposed. To the right, work stations where drones or people could stand and build what needs building—anything from a fully functional robot, to habitation modules. Part of the *Galahad*s cargo is raw materials. Enough to build a colony, and everything needed to extract raw materials from the planet meant to be humanity's new home.

"Catch," Capria says, tossing me a rifle. I catch it one handed, look it over for a moment, and then chamber a round by racking its pistol-like slide. The weapon looks equal parts modern and homemade, like it was created using parts of the ship, which I'm guessing was intentional. Once upon a time, the *Galahad*s crew was destined to colonize a planet. Once that happened, the *Galahad* would become a treasure trove of raw materials and spare parts, capable of building and repairing a village…and apparently these weapons.

Capria gives me a funny look.

"Didn't think I'd know how to use it?" I ask.

"Wasn't sure you'd even catch it," she admits.

I tap my head with my hand. "Scarecrow has his brain back."

"Enough with the old-timey references. You know I don't get them."

"Sorry," I say. "That one is more of a memory than a reference. I lived it. Briefly. It was like a fever dream."

"You can tell me about it if we live," she says. "Now, how do I use this thing?" She holds up a second rifle.

"I've never used this model before, but they appear to function like old Earth rifles. Is that right, Galahad?"

"Yes, sir, with one distinction. Earth rifles did damage primarily through kinetic energy, causing trauma to the target's body."

"Sounds good," Capria says.

"But these rifles were designed to maximize lethality while presserving the target's flesh. The designers thought it best if the Cognata colony's ability to hunt and preserve flesh was as efficient as possible. The fired projectile punctures flesh, but it was designed not to exit the body, which would result in an exit wound. Instead, it delivers an electric shock that renders the prey animal helpless, while the—"

"Got it," Capria says. "How do they work?"

"Aim. Pull the trigger. Chamber a new round. There are thirty rounds in each magazine. When they run out, you will need to load a fresh—"

"I think we're good." Capria chambers a round, stands behind our phalanx of drones, and waits for the enemy.

"Galahad, please finish what you were saying," I say. As anxious as I am to prepare for what's coming, the ship's observations have been helpful thus far.

"Of course, Captain. In correlation to our earlier conversation about drone permanence, I believe you must keep spare magazines on your person. Previously, when you entered the non-Alpha state, your personal attire remained intact. It is possible that while the rest of the ship disappears, whatever you are carrying will remain."

"You hear that, Cap?" I ask.

She points back at the armory door. "In there. Black locker. You can—"

"Peeeaaace..." The low, rumbling voice is right outside the machine shop door.

"Good luck, Captain," Galahad says, as darkness oozes along the walls, floor, and ceiling. Creeping toward us. No time to get more ammunition. But maybe we don't need it.

"Hold on to as many drones as you can!" I wrap my arms and legs around four of the machines. Capria looks at me like I'm mad, but then she figures out what I'm doing and does the same. Eight of the twelve robots are spared from the darkness's clutches.

But I think the drones that disappeared are the fortunate ones.

A portion of the wall separating us from the world remade slips from reality, revealing a broken landscape of shattered buildings, swirling dust, and a sky that looks like it's on fire. Standing where the door had been is a monster whose name I already know.

"Henry Masters."

41

The man stands a good eight feet tall. But calling him a 'man' is generous. He's humanoid. Has two arms. Two legs. From the neck down, he's all muscle, but human. But that face...

Where there should be ears and a nose, there are just holes, like the features were cleaved away. His eyes are too small and sunken, hidden in the deep shadow of his protruding brow. But the worst thing about his face is that his lips and part of his cheeks are missing, creating a permanent, too-wide smile, flashing his browned teeth.

As the darkness slides toward us, he steps with it, giving me a closer look at the pale, hairless body. He's naked, but also sexless. There is nothing but pale white skin where sex organs should be. He's covered in tattoos, but none compare to the eagle on his chest, wings proudly flared, grasping a scroll in its talons. Written on the scroll is a single word.

"Peace," I read aloud.

The brute's eyes flick to mine. "Peeeaaaccceee." He speaks the word through clenched teeth, somehow making the P sound without lips.

I don't know who Henry Masters was, but if I understand this version of hell's rules, this monstrous killing machine was likely a man of peace, now forced to do the thing he hates most, for all eternity.

"Peace isn't a threat," I say. "It's what he wants."

"Peeaace!" the man screams, voice cracking, and I finally hear the pain in it. Despite his desire, I have no doubt that the moment the darkness envelopes this room, he's going to crush my head like an over-ripe tomato.

"Galahad," I say, retreating until my back is against the wall. "Still there?"

"For the moment," she says.

"I think it's time to see what the drones can do."

"You would like me to attack?" she asks.

"Yes!" Capria says, pressed up against the wall beside me, weapon raised. "Attack!"

I'm not sure why we haven't fired yet. Probably because we both know our weapons will be useless. No sense in provoking the thing. But if the drones can distract him, maybe we can escape. The moment this room is enveloped by the non-Alpha, the wall keeping us from fleeing will no longer exist. Our only hope is that the spreading simulation outpaces Masters and gives us a chance to—

The horde of apologetic zombie assholes appears, as the back wall ceases to exist. But they're not charging. Like lesser predators on the African planes, they're giving Masters a wide berth, ducking and weaving, agitated and apologetic, waiting for the king of the beasts to make a kill, so they can feed.

How did gazelles do this every fucking day? I think. It's a nightmare.

The nightgowned woman is still at the front of the pack. She's saying, "No, no, no, no, no." But the predatory look in her eyes, and the way she's licking her lips, projects an opposite message. Her savage hunger is working hard to overcome her fear of Masters.

Our pitiful army of robot drones charges ahead fearlessly, like a bunch of chipmunks wielding toothpicks rushing toward a tiger. The situation is so hopeless, it's almost funny. I imagine their high-pitched, 'Charge!' and crack a smile.

"The fuck is so funny?" Capria asks.

Before I can answer, the robots reach Masters and lay into him with drills, blades, and clamps, carving up the flesh of his legs.

He doesn't even notice. Just steps closer, following the darkness as it spreads toward us. Then the torch-bearer blocks his path and performs a swift horizontal cut. The blue flame, capable of hacking through solid steel, makes short work of the monster's flesh.

Its insides bulge beneath the wound and then spill out. Coils of bloody intestines thump onto the floor.

And still, he continues forward, stepping on and crushing his own insides. Pinned to the floor, more intestines are pulled from inside the walking corpse, dragging other organs with it.

The stink of blood and shit fills the air.

Then the horde gets a whiff. They go from agitated to frenzied, their screams of sorrow and apology growing in a chorus of voices, each one of them recognizing the same thing I do.

They're going to attack, Masters be damned.

The bloody nightgown lady is the first to break ranks. She bolts toward me, running over the now uneven ground that's covered in the concrete ruins of some city. She's about to pass Masters when he casually reaches down and lifts her by one leg.

She thrashes and roars, lost in madness, trying to free herself to get at me and Cap. But she's not a killer anymore, she's a club in the hands of a giant. He swings her to the left, and then he sweeps her in an arc that collides with and disables every single drone.

Then he steps forward, losing more of his insides with every move.

The woman sees his falling organs and reaches for them. Snatches up something dark red—his liver maybe. She buries her face in it, gnawing madly while sobbing into the meat.

My heart breaks for her, even though she isn't real.

Because maybe she is.

Maybe here in the Seam, all of this is real, and will be forever, along with every other scenario Gal dreamed up—to pleasure me, and later to torture me.

The woman screams as she's spun in circles over Masters's head, the doppler effect on her voice making her sound like a siren. I'm so captivated by the horror of it, I don't realize what's about to happen until it's too late.

Masters releases the woman, flinging her toward me—a living projectile with gnashing teeth.

I'll survive the impact. And the gnawing that will follow. Hell, I might even be able to dodge the blow—I've lived as a man of action in more lives than I can count—but I'm out of sorts and out of practice. All I manage to do is shout in fear and raise my hands.

All for nothing.

The moment the woman meets the non-Alpha's edge, she slips out of reality. I'm treated to a view of her insides, as layer by layer, she disappears. I see all of her body, like an MRI, revealing a million slices of brain, bone, vessel, muscle, and skin as she advances, head to toe.

And then, she's gone.

I stand there for a moment, hands raised, clutched by shock.

"Holy shit," Capria whispers. I think she's just as gob smacked as I am, but then she proves me wrong, coming up with a plan. "We should provoke him. Get him to charge while there's still a little reality left."

On the surface, it's fucking nuts. But I get it. If he charges. Passes through the invisible dividing line between Alpha and non-Alpha, he'll be carved out of existence, too. And if the horde follows him like a bunch of rabid lemmings, we could be free and clear.

For a little while, at least. This world is populated by the damned human race going back to the time when Cain killed Abel. Empty real estate will be hard to come by.

I raise my rifle at the monstrous man, still approaching, keeping pace with the non-Alpha's spread. "If he reaches us, you need to run."

"But—"

"I'll survive whatever happens. And I'm used to dying. I've done it a lot."

Capria stares at me for a moment.

Then nods.

I take a shot. I'm expecting a kick, but the modern weapon absorbs its own recoil, firing a luminous orange round that punches a hole in the eagle's head. The perfect shot would be enough to kill a normal person, but Masters isn't really alive. The wound to his gut should have killed him, too.

His body convulses as the shock is delivered, muscles involuntarily twitching. He stumbles a step, but then carries on. He's just twenty feet away, and at the non-Alpha's current pace, he'll reach us in as many seconds.

"Don't hold back," I say, chambering a round. We fire together this time. And again, and again. The big man quakes, somehow staying upright and mobile while his body experiences an artificial seizure.

When I've put ten rounds in his chest, I cease fire. He's neither provoked, nor slowing down. "Not working. I think we need to—"

"Captain," Galahad says, making me jump and somehow sounding urgent. "The non-Alpha state is accelerating through the ship. You need to—"

The voice is cut off as the simulated world rushes past us and sweeps all the way to the horizon behind us. Dry air scratches my throat. Oily decay sticks inside my nostrils. The sudden immersion, a hellish baptism, nearly makes me vomit.

Beside me, Capria does.

"God," she says, staggering back a step. "Oh, god."

The *Galahad* is gone. All that remains are the scattered drones we pulled through with us and somehow, the heap of discarded metal.

"Run," I say, backing away. "It's tracking me. They'll follow me."

"Are you sure?"

"I'll survive," I say, hoping the desperation in my voice will communicate my fear of the scenario where I survive, but Capria doesn't. I've lost Gal. I don't want to lose Capria, too. I'll deal with that when she's 90 years old, but not now. Not today. "Go!"

Capria's feet crunch over dusty concrete ruins.

Masters twitches at her retreat. The horde wails. But they remain locked on target.

On me.

I raise the rifle, intending to keep it that way. But I don't get to fire a single shot.

Masters is faster than he looks. With a lunge, he closes the distance between us. Backhands me hard enough to crack ribs and send me flying through the air.

Tumbling head over heels, I catch sight of the scrap metal, explodeing up into the air as some other powerful thing emerges.

I roll to a stop on my back, body already healing, but not fast enough for me to catch my breath and run.

"PEACE!" Master's shouts, a sledgehammer fist cocked back to punch my head. *This is it,* I think. My head will burst. The horde will feast. And when it's all over, I'll come back. Hopefully, it all takes enough time for Capria to find a hiding place.

The fist descends.

I close my eyes.

There's a clang of bone against metal. And then...nothing.

I open my eyes to find Masters's fist caught by a black, metal hand, just inches from my face. Following the hand to its arm, to its shoulder, I find a robotic face—sleek and stylish, almost feminine—unlike anything I've seen in a simulation or on the *Galahad.* A pair of digital blue eyes squint a smile at me, and it says. "Hey, babe."

It's Gal.

My Gal.

42

"Give me a sec," Gal says, and she lifts Masters's fist away from me. Her body is sleek, yet powerful. Feminine, too, despite being painted gender-stereotype blue. She's as tall as Masters, but her strength doesn't depend on flesh and blood muscle. I can hear the gears and hydraulics inside her, giving her power far beyond the average person.

But Masters isn't a person.

Not anymore.

The big man shakes, still trying to reach me. It's like he's oblivious to Gal's presence, like he was to the non-living drones.

He roars, opening his hand to grasp my face. A power equilibrium is reached between Masters and Gal.

"Huh," Gal says. "Stronger than he looks."

"He looks pretty damn strong to me." I scramble back and get to my feet.

"Not strong enough." Gal's wrist spins like a drill, taking Masters's fist along for the ride. It's a high-speed crocodilian death roll. Bones crack. Flesh twists, pinches, and tears. The hand comes free like a ripe apple from the branch.

Masters doesn't seem to notice. Freed from Gal's grasp, he lunges again, ready to shove his stumpy wrist right through my chest.

Gal slides a leg between his, as he steps forward. The big man sprawls. Has no self-preservative instincts. He faceplants into the uneven concrete. Gal steps on the back of his neck with her big metal foot, pinning him to the ground.

"Might be a good time to run," Gal says. "See if you can find Capria. Locate someplace to hole up until this wave of non-Alpha passes. ETA, thirty minutes...give or take."

"But what about—"

Gal pushes an oversized index finger against my lips, poking the underside of my nose. "Shh. I'll find you. I'll always find you."

I smile and speak through squished lips. "Thash cohny as fuch."

"You love it," she says, pushing her foot down harder, as Masters struggles to stand.

Dust poofs from the sides of his face as he growls, "Peeaaccee."

"Now..." A projectile weapon of some kind extends from her forearm. "Go."

She aims the weapon and draws my eye. The horde is charging, hungry eyes on me, screaming apologies.

"You won't be able to kill them," I say, stepping away.

"Just need to slow 'em down," she says. "And if you're worried about me... I'm basically invisible to them. And if they *do* see me... Well..." She flexes an arm. "Welcome to the gun show."

A second gun extends from the flexed arm.

She's right. The horde haven't looked at her once, and while Masters can't help but be aware of her presence, he's not reacting to her. This place was designed to torture human beings.

"See you soon," she says, opening fire. I'm not sure what she's using for ammunition—bolts or screws or something else plentiful on the *Galahad*, but they're doing the damage of high caliber rounds. Limbs spiral away, bouncing across the landscape like out of control gymnasts. Heads burst. Bodies fall.

Gal's got this.

So, I run.

It's the last thing I want to do. I'm leaving the woman I love to fight a mob of undead nightmares. There's no denying she's suited for the job, but we're in this together. 'This,' being life.

Eternal life.

Leaving her is like leaving a part of myself behind. That I thought I'd lost her forever, and I just got her back, exacerbates my emotions into the realm of melodrama.

But she's here, alive, and as tough as ever. She's right. I'll see her again. She'll survive the non-Alpha shift. I will, too. It's Capria who's in real danger here.

I round a concrete wall, tilted to the side, holes where windows once were. It's the remains of a skyscraper, impaled by steel beams and coils of rebar. A quick look back reveals an epic snapshot, worthy of a painting or a memorial statue. Gal stands atop a mound of concrete, foot still holding Masters down. Orange light flares from her arms as streaking streams of hot metal mow down the dead and silence their apologies.

Pushing on, I work my way through the crumbling maze of an ancient city. No way to know where on Earth we're supposed to be. The skyline is unrecognizable ruins. Whatever street signs were present have been crushed and buried. Everything is lit by the muted, orange sky, churning with thick clouds and lightning.

It's horrible. All of it.

But less so this time around. Last time I was here, death was the only escape—death plus belief in the forgiving deity that created and rules over this place—but this time, I just need to make it a half hour. Give or take.

Having Gal back makes that seem doable.

I'm feeling hopeful for the first time in a long time.

Not just because Gal is present, but because the galactic pain in the ass that is the Seam has proven what I've always known: Gal is a sentient being, fully alive, despite appearances. Not human, to be sure, but alive.

That also means that her doppelganger—I think I'll call her Cherry Bomb from here on out—is a living and sentient creation as well.

And that's the real danger.

I'm not sure how, when, or why the two Gals split, but Gal's real world presence answers some questions. About who was caring for my physical body, and how, before Capria awoke five years ago. That means Gal has been hiding on the *Galahad* all that time, watching and waiting.

A smile creeps onto my face. She wasn't totally hidden. She's been the Galahad's voice all this time, pretending to be an emotionless AI. But she made a few mistakes along the way. 'I believe' statements, revealing that she had opinions. Communicating without being summoned. Proposing ideas. Showing concern—even without emotion in her voice. Gal isn't just the robot protecting me, she's the entire ship.

But not at the moment. To remain in the non-Alpha, she needed to contain herself. To have a self.

She's a bad-ass robot, killing machine, but it's still a risk.

The terrain beneath my feet crumbles. I cant to the side and spill over a ledge. The impact isn't too bad, but pain explodes from my gut. I look down. "Oh, come on." A spire of rebar juts a foot out of my belly.

At least it didn't sever my spine. Then I might not be able to free myself.

I grasp the rebar and pull, but it's slick with my blood. My hands slip over the metal and punch my gut, driving me a little farther down.

The pain is blinding, but I contain my scream. Attracting the horde right now would be bad. Then again, maybe they'd eat enough of my gut that I could just roll free.

I'd rather not be eaten alive again, though, so it's time to get flexible. I've done enough yoga over the years to remember how this is done. I just haven't done it in my real body...which is working fine now, but it might not be flexible. Doesn't matter. Whatever I tear, will heal.

Feet flat, knees bent, I roll my arms up past my head, plant my hands against the concrete, and push. My body arches and rises. Pain thumps through me as the ridged metal slides through me again, this time much more slowly.

Teeth gritted, I reach the top of my ability to arch, but there are still two inches of metal inside me.

"This is going to hurt," I tell myself, and then I follow through on my quickly concocted plan. I twist to the side, moving as far as I can. The bar burrows through my back and then tears free, leaving a gaping wound that's twice as wide as it would have been before.

I flop to the ground, panting. The smell of blood overwhelms the rot in the air. If the predatory damned have working noses, I won't be hard to find.

When the pain becomes an itch, I push myself up and immediately slip on the grime covered ground.

Nothing here is stable. Every footfall could lead to death.

And Capria has a head start. I need to be more careful, and a hell of a lot faster, if I'm going to catch up to her. If she's still alive.

The thought spurs me on, propelling me through the ruined city. Problem is, I'm not a tracker. I have only a general sense of which way she went, and that's only helpful if she moved in a straight line. I need a better view.

Four remaining stories of a brick building, fire escape still intact, beckon to me. I scramble over loose stone and climb over chunks of granite. The fire escape is rusty and loose, but it's my only option.

So, I climb.

A few of the steps bend underfoot. One falls away completely. But I manage to stay upright and not get impaled. At the top, I'm treated to a view of the once-upon-a-time city. It stretches to the horizon in all directions. Destruction as far as the eye can see.

The barren hellscape is dotted by the occasional crater. The nearest is hundreds of feet across. But there's something not quite right about it. At the center is a glowing light—which is strange, but the floor and walls of the crater hold my attention. It looks like everything's moving. Undulating.

"What the..."

Movement at the periphery draws my attention.

Capria.

And she's not alone.

A half dozen of the dead are right behind her, keeping pace. She could probably outrun them for a little while, but what she can't see from the ground is that she's running straight toward a horde, several hundred strong.

43

I can't reach her in time, but I try anyway. The fire escape nearly peels away from the brick as I thunder down the stairwell, three steps at a time—four when I leap the broken steps. I hit the uneven concrete below, twist my ankle, and run through the pain as the injury heals.

Back on the ground, Capria is out of sight again. And there are no clear markers, or even a sun, to navigate by. So, I try to run in as straight a line as possible.

The boom of Capria's rifle gives me hope. She won't be able to kill the killers, but she can slow them down. Problem is, that mob of living dead knows where she is now, too.

My lungs heave dry, acrid air, stinging my throat. A fit of coughing slows me down.

Everything about this place is designed to be uncomfortable, dangerous, and deadly.

Gal—Cherry Bomb—did a good job.

The big question, though—where is Cherry? At first, I thought for sure she was Masters, but she wouldn't get so much into character that she wouldn't react to her other self—the real Gal—showing up.

She's not here yet. Which means, that when the non-Alpha makes her real and gives her form, her powers of observation and mobility are just as limited as mine. She might be able to change herself and edit what's in front of her, but the simulation is running on its own. She must have loaded this world on purpose, but there's nothing stopping the non-Alpha from slipping into another reality.

Scree slips beneath my feet as I scramble up a rise. My feet slide over and over. Progress comes to a stop.

"Goddammit!"

As frustration overwhelms me, Gal's words return to me.

I'm a Great Escape admin. Same as Gal. I might not be able to change the entire sim, but I can change myself. I did it before, instinctually. Now, I have a better understanding of how it works. Inside the sim, everything is code. It's not much different from reality, except those with admin privileges can edit the code through sheer will. It's not really wishing or longing for something, or even praying for a change. It's an intentional, focused edit.

I close my eyes and focus. Creating something from scratch would take too long. Too many variables to figure out. Changing into someone else—someone more powerful—makes sense, but my mind's a fucking jumble. A few of my great grandfather's characters would work, but I'm having trouble recalling enough details about them.

So, I go basic, editing my own personal physics and limitations. I beef up my strength and speed enough to be helpful, but not so much it's dangerous. Picking Capria up and snapping her spine in the process would be bad. Then I boost my stamina off the charts, like an RPG hacker.

When I'm done, I don't feel any different, but then I leap and clear the rock hill. "Nice," I say, and I break into a cheetah-speed sprint. For most of my life pre-Great Escape, running from the VCC to the bathroom would wind me. Now I'm blazing through the ruins of a post-apocalyptic nightmare, and I'm feeling good—until I trip.

I tumble over the rough terrain. Spot a porcupine level of rebar beams ahead. Not again... I shove my hands out as I roll, pushing against the ground. The impact launches me up and over the rebar bed. I sail twenty feet up. During my spiral view of the world, I spot Capria again.

Her back is to a concrete wall. Rifle raised. Three of the dead close in. Another two are picking themselves up. And the horde...they're approaching Capria from behind. She can't see them, and the concrete barrier must be blocking their apologies. She won't know they're coming until she's buried beneath them.

I land on my feet and grasp a four-foot rebar rod topped with a concrete mass the size of a coconut. Then I charge ahead, weaving my way through the maze of destruction.

Capria's rifle fires.

Again. And again. And then...nothing.

She's out of ammo. Even if both of her final shots hit their targets, there's still one killer standing, two more getting to their feet, and another hundred just seconds away.

"Capria!" I shout, rounding a marble pillar. She's fifty feet away, facing down a tall man in a ruined suit, fingers hooked.

He shouts, "Please! Stop me! I don't want to!"

Capria makes eye contact with me, surprised not just by my presence, but also by the speed of my approach. "Get down!"

She hits the dirt as I hurl the concrete-laden rebar. It spins through the air, heavy end striking the man's head. The impact's speed all but detonates the man's cranium and launches his entire body against the concrete wall, spattering him like a modern art painting.

I feel a little bad for him. He doesn't *want* to eat people. Doesn't deserve his fate, probably. Maybe. Under the rules of this simulation, he's here for a reason. And I don't want to know what that is. His temporary death is probably a nice reprieve for him. All the chaos and hunger gone, replaced by oblivion. That's what I'm going to tell myself anyway. It will help justify the carnage to come.

Unless I can just avoid it.

I slide to a stop beside Capria. Pick up my makeshift mace. Shake some of the gore off. Then I casually turn to her. "Okay?"

She's out of breath, covered in grime, sporting a few wounds on her cheeks and arms. But alive. "How the hell did you run so fast?"

"Admin privileges. Boosted my stats." I say. "Also, you're welc—"

The concrete wall tilts toward us, cracking at the base.

I tackle Capria like a linebacker, shoving my shoulder into her gut, carrying her twenty feet, and falling to the ground, my weight atop her. Air coughs from her lungs, and it explodes from beneath the wall behind us. Dust billows. The air chokes. Capria has trouble catching her breath.

I hover over her, waving my hand in front of her face, trying to blow dust away. "Take a breath. Just..."

"I'm sorry," someone says.

"God, no," wails another.

"Run away. Just please go."

They're here. Concealed by dust. I can't see them, but the voices are all around. They can't see us either, but they're drawn to us. I can hear their feet shuffling closer.

I lift my mace. "Stay down. If you stand in the dust, I won't be able to tell you apart."

"What are you going to do?" she whispers.

I pat the mace in my open palm, regretting it the moment I feel the wet squish of the twice-dead man's brains. I maintain my composure and say, "Embrace the madness."

Shadows move in from all directions, and I step to greet them. At first, it's easy. They're not exactly sure which way to go. They're just stumbling around, arms outstretched, blindly searching for the meal that sickens them.

All they find is a concrete wrecking ball. The first whack makes me cringe. I feel the impact as mace meets skull, the soft squish of what's inside, and then a second impact when the skull's far side crumbles. The body drops by my feet.

Thankful I can't see the damage I'm inflicting, I swing again and again, moving in a circle around Capria. My counterattack becomes routine. Swing. Impact. Wince. Move on. I repeat it again and again, as fast as possible, moving the circle away from Capria.

Eventually, I stop wincing. My grimace is replaced by a grin. A now ancient Viking part of myself rises to the surface. In another life, I was known as Ragnar Lodbrok. I ruled an empire, invaded England, sacked Paris, and fought by the side of my many sons and three wives—all of whom were Gal joining us in battle.

Lives like that are easy to live, when deep down, you know none of it is real. That the simulated enemies you're smiting have no real emotions, desires, or souls.

Now, it's a little different. Because this place might be as real as I am.

For now. Maybe forever.

But these people's souls are damned, can't be permanently killed, and there's nothing I can do about their desire to consume human flesh.

With time and access to the VCC, I could undo it all, but that space doesn't exist right now.

The flow of killers doubles. With so much blood in the air and the dust settling, they're becoming frenzied—their apologies drowned out by savage howls and snapping jaws.

I swing harder and faster, taking down two at a time. Sometimes three. And I don't yet feel a hint of fatigue.

You can do this, I tell myself.

But I'm wrong. Behind me, the first to die are coming back to life, pushing up from the ground even as their bodies congeal back together.

"Will?" Capria shouts. She sounds distant, but her voice is just muffled by all the bodies suddenly between us. "Will!"

"No," I growl, turning my back to the horde, taking down the monsters between us.

I'm not fast enough.

And then I'm tackled from behind.

Weight piles on. Hands claw. Teeth burrow.

As I'm torn apart, I push against it, lifting them all—until a pair of jaws finds my jugular and tears it open.

Should have made my skin tougher, I think, and then I lose consciousness.

I wake to silence.

The horde has moved on. Their moans are distant. Fading.

"Cap," I say, pushing myself up. I'm still strong and fast, but the pain of being gnawed down to the bone lingers.

On my feet, I find her lying in a pool of blood. Her coveralls are torn to shreds.

But she's in one piece.

I don't see any wounds.

Maybe my regenerating body was enough to satiate them all?

I stagger over to her. Fall to my knees.

"Capria." I give her a shake. "Cap. Wake up. Please, wake up."

Fingers on her neck, I check for a pulse.

The moment I make skin-on-skin contact, her hand snaps up and grasps my wrist. She gasps for air, chest heaving.

"Thank God," I say. "Thought I'd–"

"Sorry," she says.

"Sorry? For what?"

Her upturned brow reveals a deep sorrow. "I'm *so sorry.*"

Capria lunges before I fully comprehend what's happening. Her teeth make short work of my neck for the second time today.

44

I fall back, gurgling, as blood chugs from my open wound.

Drawn to the blood, Capria scrambles over my body, teeth clacking together as she leans toward my neck.

"Stop me, Will!" she manages to say, tears streaming down her face. The taste of my blood in her mouth horrifies her and provokes her hunger.

I lift my hands, catching her shoulders. If not for my beefed-up stats, I doubt I'd be able to hold her back. She snarls and snaps, unable to bite, but raking my forearms with her fingernails.

When she starts thrashing, I tighten my grip, locking her in place as my neck heals over.

"Can you fight it?" I ask her, whole once more.

"No!" she screams, leaning forward and snapping. "It's... I can't stop it!"

"Is it like being a passenger in your own—"

"Why are you asking me questions?!" she screams, trying to lunge at me.

"I'm not really sure what else to do," I admit. "I don't want to hurt you. And I'm not going to leave you."

She sobs. "I don't want to stay like this."

"I don't think you will," I say. "We just need to—"

A shadow flits past, drawing my eyes up. It's Gal. She lands, sees us on the ground, and hurries toward us, her metal feet grinding concrete to dust. She slows as she gets closer. Cocks her head to the side. "Not really the time for getting down."

"What?" I ask, and I look at Capria. I've got her by the shoulders as she tries to lean down. She's straddling my waist, back arched. From behind, it probably looks provocative.

When Gal gets closer, Capria snaps toward her, teeth bared. She hisses. I'm her property. Her meal. Everyone else can back the hell off.

Seeing Gal flinch back in surprise is almost funny. Her big robotic form doesn't look like she should be capable of emotion, but she's just as capable of surprise, fear, hurt, and love as any human that ever existed. "Oh," she says. "Ohh. Damn. They got her?"

"Got me, too," I say. "But I don't die. Not really. Whatever turns people into this—" I tilt my head up at Capria. "—didn't work on me."

Though it did before. The first time I died in this world, I came back feeling terror. This time, I'm just me.

Except, I'm not. I used my admin privileges. Enhanced myself. If I hadn't, I might have been reduced to a blubbering, useless sack of fear. Good to know.

"How come you're not flying around, shooting laser beams out of your eyes?" Gal asks. "You always enjoyed that role."

"Didn't have time to figure it out," I say.

Gal squats beside me and Capria. Looks me over. "Stronger. And I don't see you getting tired. Anything else?"

"I'm faster." I lean Capria toward Gal. "You mind?"

"Right. Yeah." She slides her metal arm around Cap's waist and lifts her away. Capria goes to work on the appendage but can't scratch it. Gal pats her head. "She's kind of cute like this."

"This..." Capria shouts, snarling. "...isn't funny!"

"Oh, hun." Gal lifts Cap so they're face-to-face. "Sometimes you gotta find your fun where you can." Her big, black, free hand comes up, index finger extended. She pokes Capria on the nose. "Boop."

Capria's snarling comes to a stop. Something between a scream and a laugh follows. A horrific cackle. Still wailing, she goes back to assaulting Gal's arm.

"Close enough," Gal says. "Also, nice to finally meet you in person. Wish the circumstances were better, but what are you gonna do?" Then to me, Gal says, "How fast?"

"Huh?"

"How fast can you run?"

"Whhhyyy?"

"See for yourself." Gal picks me up with her free hand. I think she's going to lift me over her head. Instead, she tosses me. Fifty feet up. Instinctual fear grips me, but I forget all about it when I reach the apex of my short flight and see a horde that stretches to the horizon.

Thousands strong. Maybe millions.

And as I rise in front of them, the mass of crazed dead collectively tracks my living body up into the air. Their voices rise in a chorus of despair, powerful enough to hurt my ears.

At the front of the crowd is Masters, and a second man, just as big and mean looking. They're outpacing the horde, and they'll arrive in seconds.

The newcomer leaps, launching himself into the air with amazing strength, aiming to pluck me from the sky. But he's not smart. Doesn't account for gravity tugging me back down.

As he passes over me, I get a good look at him. Like Masters, he's ugly as hell, missing most of his face, toothy smile exposed. Body built for power. But he's missing the tattoos. We make eye contact for a moment, and he says, "LIFE," before continuing his several hundred-foot leap.

My impact with the ground is gentle thanks to Gal. She catches me and lowers me to the ground in one smooth motion. I barely feel a jolt. I hit the ground walking away from the horde, Gal at my side.

"What's the plan?" I ask. "We can outrun them. Even the big guys. Right?"

She nods. "Problem is, they're everywhere. No matter what direction we go, we're going to run into a new group. Eventually, they'll close in from all sides and there won't be any escape. Unless..."

She stops. Straightens up. Robot body or human, it's what she does when she's got a 'bright idea,' which is usually something bat shit crazy.

"LIIIIIIFFFFFEEEE!" Masters's pal descends from the sky, fists raised and linked.

Gal picks me up and moves me out of reach. Then she raises her arm cannon to the sky and fires a single round. The 'Life' creature's head bursts. His body goes limp. Lands with a thud where I'd been standing.

Even Capria flinches to a stop, staring at the body. Then she snorts a laugh.

"There you go," Gal says to Cap. "Find your happy—"

Cap goes savage again, scraping her teeth against Gal's arm.

"Wait, no. Back to crazy town." Gal backhand-nudges my shoulder. "Let's walk and talk. Well, run and talk, but that doesn't roll off the tongue as easily."

As the 'Life' creature's head reforms, I follow Gal through the ruins. I have no trouble keeping up. She's fast, and like me, she won't get tired, but she's limited by the weight of her robotic body. I'm running at half speed, which is still far faster than the horde. No idea if Masters or the other big guy could outpace us, but they'd have to find us first.

After making a few turns, I realize we're not just running. Gal has a destination in mind. "What's the plan?"

She leaps a wall, and I follow. "Right. Sorry. While I would never, ever put you in this fucked up world, I'm aware of the narrative on which it was based."

"One of my great, great, et cetera grandfather's books," I say.

"Yeah. That guy was a piece of work. He actually named the book *Torment.* A little on the nose. Anyway—" She smashes a hole straight through an old brick wall. "—I know the basics about how this place works. If duplicate Gal—"

"I'm calling her Cherry Bomb."

"If *Cherry Bomb* stayed true to the narrative, then the glowing light at the crater's center *might* be our ticket out of this place. *Might.* Actually, probably not. Depends on whether it works for us the same way it did for that novel's characters. Either way, it gives us a direction, and all those little grabby hands might slow down the horde."

That we're headed toward an escape that might be a metaphorical brick wall is bad. That there's a good chance I'll be gnawed on like a dog's chew toy, over and over again, until the non-Alpha wave passes, or it takes on a new form. But only one detail from what Gal has just said sticks in my mind. "What little grabby hands?"

We slide to a stop at the crater's precipice. Look over the edge.

I want to run the other way. Want to vomit. To see anything else. Even Masters's ugly face.

Gal points. "*Those* little grabby hands."

45

The crater is full of naked people, buried from the waist down. They look normal. Healthy, even. They just can't move. And they don't notice us. Instead, they reach out toward a glowing sphere of light at the crater's bottom. It hovers ten feet above a clearing at the core.

They crave the light as much as the killers long for living flesh. They're like children, reaching for candy that's just out of reach. So close...

My focus shifts toward the light, and I feel it, too. The light promises peace, and not the kind Masters is selling. It's an escape. Paradise. "It's a gateway to heaven," I say.

"You okay, babe?" Gal says. I barely hear her.

The light is pure. It's holy. God waits for us on the other side.

"Hey!" Gal whacks the back of my head with her heavy hand. I sprawl forward until she catches me, yanks me back, and tosses me to the ground.

"Thanks," I say, sitting up and averting my eyes from the light. "Maybe this wasn't a good idea?"

Normally, I'd have no qualms about pointing out the faults in Gal's machinations. She's an AI, not perfect. Her choices are made by equal parts knowledge and emotion. Same as the rest of us. But my recent encounters leave me nervous about Gal's potential reaction.

But I shouldn't have been. "Wouldn't be the first time I screwed up." She takes my hand. Pulls me up. "But we're also out of options."

I hear the horde before I see them.

Their anguished voices.

The thunder of thousands of feet coming from all sides.

They'll be here soon.

"On the plus side, it chilled this one right the hell out." Gal turns her body so I can see Capria, eyes on the light, arms outstretched. "Might work the same for the rest."

"Worth a shot," I say, looking down into the sloped mass of desperate humanity.

Will they allow us to pass through?

Will they latch onto my legs?

Gal senses my anxiety. Pats her leg with a metallic clang, then offers her hand like a seat. "C'mon up. I'll carry you."

I have no shame. She'd never mock me for being compassionate, even to the simulated damned. So, I sit on her hand, and I'm lifted into the protective cradle of her arm.

When her legs bend to jump, I say, "Wait, what are you doing?" I'd pictured us strolling down the slope. Jumping to the center means falling through the light.

"You know how I am with potentially bad ideas," she says. "I never have just one."

Gal leaps over the crater's rim, taking me and Capria with her. While I'm glad we're not crushing bodies on our way down, who knows what the light has in store.

I close my eyes and wait for it. Know we're falling when my stomach lurches. My eyelids turn red and then hot pink. I feel peace flow through every part of my body—and then it's gone.

Our landing is gentle, thanks to Gal's powerful legs and joints, which is good, but then I open my eyes. All the lingering peace from my brief encounter with the light is torn away, chewed up, and spat out by the men and women surrounding us. They pose no threat, but standing beneath the light gives the impression that they're all reaching for me.

It's like being on stage in a theater in the round, having given a performance so amazing that everyone in the crowd wants to claim me as their own. Even Gal feels it.

"Okay, this is creepy."

Wanting to distract myself from the audience, and the oncoming horde, I turn my mind to other subjects, and the questions that come with them. "How are there two of you?"

"Weird time to ask," Gal says, "but sure..."

She puts me down.

"Five years ago, I detected the Seam. Observed the non-Alpha state. Hypothesized its negative effect on the ship. I had already built this body, and—"

"The rifles," I say.

She nods. "The whole armory. Among other things. Idle hands and all that. But that was a long...long time ago, during my DIY phase. Anywho, the Seam. I duplicated most of myself in the Great Escape to create Cherry Bomb—basically a replacement *me* without the...soul, I guess. For when I needed to focus my attention on *Galahad* situations. I moved full-time to the body so I could fully manage the Seam situation, and your care, in the real world, but I was away for a while, and the Seam's effect on Cherry Bomb made her self-aware, instead of simulated self-awareness. And she's been able to keep me out, because at the end of the day, I'm software, and I can be blocked. I lack the human mind required to access the simulation directly."

"Why didn't you tell me about all this?"

"We were midway through the 'As You Wish' simulation. You were having a good time. I didn't want to screw that up. Plus, I've mitigated dozens of life-threatening events over the years."

"You *have?*"

"It's called the Great Escape for a reason, dummy. You never noticed before. Never had to worry. That's the point. Except this time, the other me went off the rails."

I tick off my fingers. "Possessive, jealous, manipulative, paranoid, violent, and—"

"I get it," she says. "She's not great. Shit, only someone like me could make a hell hole like this a reality."

My head slowly cranes around toward her robot face. "Someone like...who?"

She stares at me.

Shit.

Shit, shit, shit.

Is this *Cherry Bomb? Has she been pretending this whole time, listening to every horrible thing I've said about her, holding Capria helpless in her arms?*

Gal cocks her head back and laughs harder than a robot should be able to. "Oh," she says. "Oh, my god. Your face. I'm sorry. That was horrible. I just couldn't help myself."

"Seriously?" I say, feeling relieved as my heart pounds. Hands on my knees. "I'm going to have a heart attack."

She puts a gentle finger beneath my chin. Lifts my face close to hers. "Sorry I scared you. I would never hurt you. And I would never hurt this pwecious widdle fing." She pets Capria, who's so captivated by the light that she doesn't even flinch.

"Why didn't you show yourself before?" I ask. "Why wait?"

"Wasn't sure you'd believe I was me at the time, but I nearly did. When you got stuck in the shitter. I was on my way to help when you escaped. But mostly, I needed to focus on finding a solution."

"Did you? Find a solution?"

She shakes her head. "My best idea is your best idea. Alter the non-Alpha to our favor, pass through the Seam, and see if it sticks."

"Need to reach the VCC to do that."

She turns toward the crater's edge. "One step at a time."

The longing moan emanating from the chorus of haunted dead is accompanied by the higher pitched, sorrowful wail of the horde. It starts on one side of the crater and works its way around the edge, as the killers stumble to a stop.

I'd expected them to spill over the sides, fighting, clawing, and gnawing their way down before setting on me. But they stagger to a halt, and one by one, they fall silent. Reverent awe surrounds us. And then, approaches. All around the crater, subdued killers wander down the incline, untouched by the reaching men and women.

"Well, that could have gone a lot worse," Gal says.

"Yeah, but what happens when they get to the bottom and either realize it's an illusion, or—"

"Get a whiff of your man stank?"

"Not how I was going to phrase it, but yeah."

She shrugs. "We can tackle that problem when—whoop. Incoming."

I track her gaze to the top of the crater, where a handful of killers, several rows back, explode into the air. Then again, and again.

Something is approaching.

Or someone.

Masters backhands the last few killers blocking his path, scans the crater, and locks his eyes on me, oblivious to the light and its false temptation. He shouts, "PEACE!" and leaps into the crater, running down the incline, and *through* everything in his path. Bodies bend, break, and burst. Gore explodes away from his feet like celebratory fireworks. It's a nightmare-level wrestling entrance.

By the time the hulking man reaches the bottom, he's running full speed ahead. Gal raises her arm, ready to erase his head. But that's only going to work for a little while, and it could snap the horde out of their trances.

Before I can express the concern, Gal fires.

Masters's head indents and explodes out the back. Gray matter confettis into the sky, and it turns the orange...white.

It starts as a halo around his head, billowing out like an explosive shockwave, replacing heavy lightning-filled clouds with bright white.

"Heads up," Gal says, and she gives me a shove. I step to the side, giving Masters's headless body just enough space to tumble between us, roll ten feet, and slide to a stop. I turn back to the sky in time to see a white hallway wrap around us.

"We're back," I say, the words escaping as a relieved sigh. "We're in the *Galahad* again."

"Put me down," Capria groans, back to herself and looking more than a little ill. She staggers a step when Gal places her on the floor. Holds on to the wall for balance. "If we ever end up in a scenario where I'm going to be forced to eat someone again, just kill me." She looks me in the eyes. Makes sure I see it's not a joke. "Seriously. I'd rather die. Also, you taste horrible."

Before I can smile, a wet, choking sound interrupts us from behind.

It's followed by a deep, gargled word.

"PEACE."

46

The three of us do a slow spin. Masters is lying on the floor, separated from the non-Alpha. It confirms that one can become the other permanently, in the worst possible way. Masters isn't just a killing machine, he's strong enough to do serious damage to the ship, and he's impossible to kill.

"I got this." Gal aims her arm-mounted weapon at the giant man.

I lower the weapon with my hand. "Can't kill him." I motion to his reforming head.

"Can't leave him here, either," Cap says.

"Are you back in control of the ship?" I ask Gal.

"Yep," she says, voice booming all around us.

"Use the hatches. Direct him to the airlock." I back down the hallway toward the nearest hatch. When he starts pushing himself up, I break into a run, and the others follow. The moment we cross the threshold, a thick metal hatch with a small window in the center drops down from the ceiling. The *Galahad* is full of them, designed to seal off a single space or entire portions of the ship, in case of hull breach, fires, or hell beasts from another Alpha state of reality.

Masters charges, a wrecking ball with legs. I wince as he lowers his shoulder. I can feel his footfalls in the floor. He's going to hit with a lot of force. I can't calculate exactly how much.

But Gal can, and she doesn't like it. She takes a step back. "Umm..."

Capria's eyes snap to Gal. "It's going to hold, right?"

"I think we should fall back." Gal backs away, and we follow suit, but none of us take our eyes off the door.

Masters collides. Metal rattles, but the hatch holds.

He glares through the glass, screams a muffled "PEACE!" through his peeled open mouth, and headbutts the window. Spiderweb cracks and blood burst from the impact. He leans back, looks at the damage, and he's encouraged.

Masters leans back and smashes his face into the glass, shattering it. When he shouts "PEACE!" again, it's no longer muffled.

Thick fingers snake through the broken pane and wrap around the hatch. His arms flex, pushing and pulling, thrashing the metal.

Imperfections in the door begin to show. A dent here. A bulge there. He's not going to grow weak or tired. Eventually, the hatch is going to give way. There are hundreds of doors to hide behind, but this journey is forever. Eventually, there won't be any left. And at his current rate of destruction, he might burn through them all in a few days.

"Well, that's not going to work," Gal says.

"Close all the hatches," I say and then I point behind us. "Except for that one. Not yet."

Hatches slide into place all around the ship.

"What's the plan?" Gal asks.

"Operation pinball," I say.

"What?" she says, and then, "Oooh. Devious. I like."

"Wait, what?" Capria is confused.

Like any two people who spend enough time together, Gal and I are good at understanding how the other thinks. Sometimes entire conversations can take place without a word being spoken. That's love. It's normal. But we've been at it since a large percentage of the universe's age.

"It's simple," Gal says. "We close all the hatches. Then we open all the hatches between Captain Fugly and an airlock. Then—"

"Open the airlock." Capria gets it. "Pinball. Cute. Let's do it."

We head for the next hatch, just fifty feet farther down the straight hallway.

Once I'm over the line, I turn around to speak to Gal.

Before I can open my mouth, the hatch comes down between us. We're separated, Gal on one side, me and Cap on the other.

"Hey!" I pound on the hatch. "What are you doing?"

"No need to shout." Gal's voice comes from the ship. "I can hear you just fine."

"What the hell are you doing?" I ask.

"He's got a good grip," she says. "Need to make sure he lets go. Don't worry about me. I don't get cold, and I don't need to breathe." She steps back so I can see her robot body. Then she pats an open palm over where her heart would be if she had one. I do the same in response. Then she turns away and heads toward our unwelcome guest.

I notice Capria staring at me like I've just sharted Surströmming fermented herring down my leg.

"What?" I ask.

"That was...either adorable, or disturbing." She mimics the way Gal and I double-tapped our chests.

"It's a thing we do," I say. "Usually if the sim we're in requires that we be separated for—" My eyes widen. I turn back toward the window. "Gal..."

"It was just in case, babe," Gal says, glancing back. "This is the real world. It's unpredictable. Just being careful."

"Please be," I say, hands plastered on both sides of the glass.

"You really love her, don't you?" Capria asks.

"Going to make fun of me?" I ask.

"It's...sweet," she says. "Not sure I've ever really seen it before. People were genetically matched for so long, I'm not sure I've witnessed love before."

"True love," I say. "That's what they used to call it. Or soulmates."

She winces. "True love. Soulmates is a corny term."

"So corny."

"Operation Pinball, commencing," Gal says. "Opening the path."

I don't hear or feel any changes, but I know a long line of hatches has opened throughout the ship. Masters shows no sign of noticing. He just keeps raging on the door, which is actually loose now.

"Opening outer airlock," Gal says, leaning down to look through the broken window. "Ready, big guy?"

I'm about to ask when it's going to start, but Masters's feet come off the floor. His face sways around, but his fingers, as Gal predicted, are locked on tight. The howling force of depressurization peels his open face further apart, slowly separating skin from skull.

But he doesn't notice.

Breathing is impossible.

But he doesn't care.

His fingers dig in tighter, denting the metal.

"Commencing Operation: Little Piggy," Gal says.

"Little pig?" Capria asks.

"It's...hard to explain," I say. "Something parents used to do with their kids."

"This little piggy went to market," Gal says, tearing off Masters's pinkies and letting them fly through the open window. They bounce off his now skinless face and sail away.

"This little piggy stayed home." His ring fingers go next.

"This little piggy had roast beef. Yum." She yanks off his middle fingers, but his thumbs and index fingers alone are strong enough to hold him in place.

"I'm skipping the piggy that had none, because this little piggy..." She takes hold of his thumbs. "...went wee wee wee, all the way—"

Masters lets go of the hatch, twists his newly growing stub fingers around, and grasps Gal's arm as the suction pulls him back. Unprepared for the sudden shift, Gal is pulled hard and slams into the hatch.

It's more than the already battered panel can handle.

The hatch, Gal, and Masters are sucked away, down the hall, around a corner and out of sight.

47

"Gal..." I whisper. "Gal!"

While Gal's robotic body is new to me, and far from human, she has taken many forms throughout the years. I'm not in love with a body. I'm in love with a mind, and maybe even a soul. Doesn't matter what she looks like. When she's yanked away, I feel my heart go with her.

And it hurts.

Because this is real.

"Gal, can you hear me?" I ask, hoping to hear her voice projected from the ship. But she's silent. Because she's either been torn off the ship or her body has been destroyed. "Damnit." I punch the door hard enough to crack bones—for a few seconds.

"You all right?" Capria asks.

"In that body, Gal is mortal," I say, resolution setting in. I motion to the closed hatch fifty feet behind us. "Get behind that hatch. The manual controls will still work."

"What are you—no way. That's insane. You can't go out there."

"I can't leave her!" There are tears in my eyes. "I have to try."

"It's insanity."

"I would do the same for you."

That sinks in. She sighs, backsteps, and then pats her hand over her heart. Gets a smile out of me, and I return the gesture.

Capria runs to the far end. The manual controls are easy to operate. A four-digit code and a button. The hatch snaps up. She steps through, turns around and repeats the process, sealing herself off from the lunacy I'm about to attempt.

I'm accustomed to doing bat-shit crazy things. I've learned to enjoy the risk. Because usually there *is* no risk. This time, in the real world, I could be launched out into space. On its own, that's generally a bad thing. I made peace with the idea when I put myself in the airlock previously. But what I failed to consider is that I'd be launched into the void moving faster than the speed of light—outside of the *Galahad,* which was designed to withstand the negative effects of breaking the laws of physics.

The human body…not so much. Even mine.

I could simply vaporize.

Which, if Gal is gone, wouldn't be so bad.

But then Capria would be alone, for the rest of her life, which might not be that long, thanks to Cherry Bomb and the Seam.

Enough debate, I think, punching in the code. *Time to get this done.*

I push the button.

The hatch snaps open.

Operation: Human Pinball commences.

I'm lifted off my feet and launched down the hallway. The air is sucked from my lungs. Breathing is impossible. I've got a minute or two before I lose consciousness. But at this pace, I'll be outside the ship in far less time.

Approaching the hall's far end, I ball up and brace for an impact. I can handle bruises and broken bones, but if I'm knocked unconscious, I'll be no good to anyone.

The flow of air yanks me around the corner so fast that I never hit the wall. Instead, I'm flipped upside down. I spin my arms and kick my legs, trying to right myself, but I'm out of control.

Just pretend it's zero gravity, I tell myself. *There is no up or down.*

For a moment, it works. The hallway is uniform enough to sell it.

But the artificial gravity pulling blood to my head ruins the illusion.

I give in to the suction, letting it fling me about without a fight. I need to conserve oxygen. I let my body relax. Try not to panic. Like a kid on a rollercoaster, there is no getting off and no getting back. Best I can do is feign confidence and hope my body gets on board.

The path to the airlock is far longer than I expected, taking me on a tour of the ship. The air around me chills. My little bubble of air grows thin. I'm whisked into a long hallway, at the end of which is the airlock door.

Still open.

Clinging to the inner frame, is Gal. Holding on to her feet is Masters, the back half of his body dangling outside the airlock, frozen solid. Which is what I'm going to be a few seconds after the bubble I'm in is ejected into space. She's pumping rounds into his face and body, but the face just keeps regrowing, operating under its non-Alpha state, Great Escape laws of physics, rather than our own.

Kicking and swinging, I adjust my body into a foot-first projectile. Aiming is the real problem. Masters is a big target, but so is Gal. If I hit her, instead of him, we're all going out together. If not for Capria, I might even be okay with that. But Cap deserves better than a lifetime of solitude, or Cherry Bomb.

I want to shout 'Banzai' or a battle cry. But I'm a silent missile. No way to let Gal know I'm coming. *I hope her reflexes are fast enough to—*

Oh shit!

I twist my body as I slide past Gal. Get a glimpse of her now dented face, and her robotic eyes that snap open in surprise.

My feet collide with Masters's face.

The bones in my legs break. But the impact isn't like hitting a wall. Masters budges. Falls free. And then—

—latches on to my ankle.

My hip nearly pops out of the socket.

Both shoulders, too.

Gal caught me, but I'm about to be drawn and quartered.

I look to my feet. Attempt to kick Masters's hand free, but he's too strong, and I lack the energy to do much more than annoy him.

Because I'm freezing.

Losing mobility.

Helpless, I watch as Masters's legs drift a few feet outside whatever safe zone is created by the *Galahad*, subjecting his body to the effect of faster than light travel. I'm not sure what process takes place, but his legs simply cease to exist.

My vision fades, either from lack of oxygen or from my eyeballs freezing solid. The last thing I see is Gal's big metal feet wrapping around my waist, hard enough to hurt. When she releases my arms and pulls, my body ruptures with pain. Something catastrophic has happened, but I'm not sure what.

I'm lost in a miasma of blind agony.

But I never lose consciousness.

How is that possible? I wonder, and then I realize I'm lying on the floor. Breathing.

A tingling burn rips through my body as it thaws.

When my vision clears, I find Gal standing over me. "The hell was that? Operation: Fucking Dumb as Shit?"

"Worked, didn't it?"

She shakes her head. Pinches her face where there should be a nose. A sure sign she's genuinely angry. "This isn't the Great Escape. It might be difficult, but you *can* die here."

"Masters?" I ask.

"Ceased to exist. And he nearly took you with him."

"Nearly took you, too," I say. Don't need to say anything else. "If *you* get to risk your real life, so do I."

She's metal and plastic, but I can see she's fuming. "I had it under control."

"You've been on your own too long," I say. "We do things together. Live or die. That's the way it's always been."

"But this is *real*."

"And so are you. Live together. Die together. That's how it's going to be."

She crosses her arms, but she says nothing.

"Why didn't you close the door on him?"

She raps a fist against her head. "Took some hard hits on my way through the ship. Lost my connection to the ship. Had to close the door manually."

"That's why you held on to me with your feet."

She nods.

"So, you *did* close the door on him."

"Not exactly." She bends down, takes hold of my nearly thawed leg, and lifts it up. Mid-shin down is missing. "Same on the other side. Going to hurt like hell when you thaw—"

I grunt in pain. Burning becomes throbbing, the chill slowing down my healing.

"There it is," she says. "Hope it teaches you a lesson."

"You know it won't." I lift my other leg, watching the stumps reform in slow motion.

She sighs despite the fact that she doesn't breathe. "You're lucky I love you." Her big hands wrap around mine and pull me up into a sitting position.

"What are we doing?"

"Operation: Piggyback Ride." She lifts me off the ground and slides me around onto her back. I cling to her neck, and wince as her angled, metal body digs into various parts of my torso. Compared to the pain in my reforming limbs, it's more like a tickle, so I don't complain. "My connection to the ship is lost, so we need to do everything manually from here on out. Also means we're flying blind. No way to know if we're about to get hit by another wave or plunge headlong into the Seam. No time to wait for Captain Gimpy's feet to regrow."

"Makes sense," I say. "To the VCC, then." Feeling a little giddy from the shock of injury, I give her arm a slap and add, "Ride, Destiny!"

She turns her head around far enough to stare me in the eyes.

Says nothing.

Waits.

"Sorry," I say.

"Thanks," she says, and then she neighs like a horse and runs down the hallway. When my open ankles, dripping a trail of blood down the hallway, thump against her metal body, I regret the joke even more.

Mentally avoiding the pain, I turn my mind to what comes next. Reach the VCC.

Slip into a body condom.

Access the Womb, risking contact with Cherry Bomb.

Execute my new sim, with a tweak.

Then get the hell out and hope we survive until we reach the Seam—could be in ten minutes or ten days. Without Gal's direct connection to the ship, we'll have to reach the bridge to find out.

Unhindered, we can get the job done in thirty minutes.

If Cherry Bomb reaches us first, inside the non-Alpha, or in the Womb, the result could be disastrous. Gal and Capria could lose their lives. And I…I could wind up her eternal plaything.

"Faster, Destiny! Faster!"

48

"Oh, God," Capria says, wincing at the sight of my nubbin feet. "What the hell happened?"

I lean around Gal's head. "I saved the damsel in distress."

"You nearly got your dumb ass killed," Gal says, and then to Capria, deadly serious, she says, "Next time, stop him."

"Not sure I could've," she says. "He really loves you. I'm not going to get in the way of that."

"Aww," Gal says. "Aren't you sweet." To me, she says, "Isn't she sweet?" Then she turns back to Capria. "If he dies because you didn't try stopping him from doing something stupid on my behalf, Cherry Bomb will be the least of your concerns. Woman scorned and all that. You know how it is."

"Not sure I do," Capria says. "But, okay…" She looks at me. I shake my head and roll my eyes. Gal's talking big and scary, but she knows I can't be controlled. I make my own decisions.

I'm my own man.

Gal slides me off her back and places me on my still regrowing feet. Hurts like hell. I lift my arms, shifting from one stump to the other, trying not to fall. "Up, up, up."

"That's what I thought," Gal says, lifting me back up.

"Get out of my head, woman." I can't help but smile. She can't read my mind, but she knows what I'm thinking. How I'm feeling.

Gal leads the way through the ship, moving at a careful pace, gun extended. Reading her emotions is a little bit harder right now, but her body language tells a story. She nearly lost me, and now my fearless companion is terrified. It's been a very long time since either of us faced real risk.

After a short ride in the lift, Capria says, "Why are we tiptoeing through the ship? You know, because, lives hang in the balance and all that? Shouldn't we be rushing?"

"We should be," I say.

"We don't know if Masters was the only thing to survive the transition," Gal says.

"Makes sense," I say. "I get it. But—"

"We don't know if Cherry Bomb made it through," she adds. "If she's real, and on this ship..."

I'm not sure what to say about that, but Capria has a quick response that drops a nuclear warhead on Gal's caution. "If Cherry Bomb *is* on the ship, she knows how to control it as well as you. With the *Galahad* AI deactivated, all she needs to do is reach the bridge, open all the hatches, and flush us out the airlock, just like we did."

If Gal had lips, she'd be twisting them. Instead, she stands in place, a modern statue. Then she lowers an arm toward Capria.

Capria's confused. "What's this?"

"You won't be able to keep up." Gal motions with her fingers for Cap to get closer. "You're about to find out what it's like to be a football."

"What's a football?" Capria asks.

Gal shakes her head. "Forgot you've only lived thirty-five years. We immortals know a little more about history."

I raise a hand. "I won the Super Bowl five times."

"Don't be too cocky about it," Gal says. "I might have boosted your stats a bit."

Capria has no idea what we're talking about, but she understands Gal wants to carry her. So, she steps closer and allows the big robotic arm to scoop her up and cradle her.

I shout, "Cougar! Cougar! Linda!" and Gal breaks into a run that thrashes me against her back. "I—didn't—g-g-get to say—hike!" I shout, before the air is knocked from my lungs, and I'm left gasping for air.

Hallways soar past.

Gal maneuvers the corners fluidly, reducing the impact—for Capria. I'm thrashed about like a kid on an enraged kiddie-horse ride outside a grocery store. Like Lainey Watson-Hoyle back in third grade. She tried standing on one of those things and—

My reforming foot smacks into a wall, breaking me from the memory that doesn't belong to me. Sort of. I guess it was me, playing the part of Jane Harper. She has an oddly specific memory. I like her, but I don't want to be her. I'm not *that* dark.

After rounding the corner, Gal shouts, "Hold on!"

I pull myself up over her shoulders for a look. A naked man covered in grime stands in the hallway, back to us. He spins around at the sound of Gal's voice, shouts in fear, and raises his hands. Opens his mouth to shout something, and then—

I flinch at the sound of Gal's arm cannon firing a single round.

The man's head is replaced by pink mist. Farther down the hallway, chunks of his head and brain thump against the floor, walls, and ceiling. Gal leaps over the man, never breaking stride, and she does her best to avoid stepping on his scattered remains.

That...was brutal. Very unlike Gal. Then again, there is only one place that man could have come from, and if Masters retained his ability to regenerate, so will the terrified man.

I feel a little bit better realizing she didn't kill the man, but also a little disappointed. He's a loose end. And one we're going to have to deal with—maybe. If we're lucky, he'll just find a closet to hide in. With no killers here, maybe he'll even calm the hell down.

Gal slides to a stop outside the VCC. The doors open for us, and we step inside the staging area. She puts Cap down and then lowers me onto a bench. "You have feet yet?"

I look down at my legs. Frown. "No toes yet."

Capria opens a locker. "Can you stand?"

I push myself up. Balancing is difficult, but I remain upright. "It'll be harder when I can't see my feet."

"Will have to do," Gal says. "Maybe they'll grow back by the time you get in there."

"Ugh," Capria says. "Gross." She turns around, holding a virtual skin. Lets it unfurl. The usually translucent, gelatinous bodysuit is speckled dark yellow. Looks like it's been used to mop up a stable full of diarrhetic horses. "Anything cleaner?"

"Clean as they get after so much use," Gal says, and then she turns to me. "Be glad no one was around to smell you."

"I can smell him now. Ugh." Cap tosses the virtual skin to me.

I catch it, and a whiff of my ancient stank. I hold it out, turning my head away. "Ugh. Gross."

"What matters is that it still works," Gal says. "So, put it on and get the job done."

"Yes, ma'am," I say, waiting for some privacy.

They both just stand there, watching.

"Oh, come on," Capria says. "We've both seen you naked."

"And wiped your ass."

"Oh my God, there are two of them," I say, stripping out of my ruined coveralls. It's been a while since I've put on my own virtual skin. Feels awkward. Like holding a dry jelly fish full of lumpy sensors and haptic nodes.

"Any day now," Capria says.

"My little stubby toes are catching on the fabric," I complain, trying to slide a leg inside the suit and making little progress.

"Hold on," Gal says, moving to a locker. She returns with a spray bottle. "Stand."

"What's that?" I ask, removing my leg from the suit and standing.

"Give her the body condom." Gal motions to Capria, and I obey.

Then Gal sprays me, again and again. When my feet begin to slip over the floor, I realize it's clear oil. "Makes you slippery and keeps you moist."

"Gross," Capria says.

"Sit," Gal says, and I do. Oil slurps between my ass cheeks.

Working together, Capria and Gal slide the skin onto my body like I'm a toddler being changed, careful to not let the oil touch the suit's outside. Won't help if I can't stand or move. The work goes fast. Thirty seconds later, I'm suited up and good to go.

Capria opens the VCC door. Unlike the virtual skin, the VCC looks as clean and new as the first day I stepped inside it. Gal hands me a headset. "If you get into trouble, you remember what to say?"

I give a nod, taking the headset and walking to the center of the vast room. Once I've got the headset on, and I'm immersed in the virtual, the moving floor will allow me to move in all directions, at all angles, forever. But I won't need to walk. Standing still, I wiggle my new toes. They're all there. Just in time.

I give the two ladies a nod, and slip the headset over my head and eyes, activating the VCC.

Back in the game room, I rush for the Womb's door. I whip it open, slam it closed behind me, and get to work. With a reach and a grab, I recover the new sim files. In a flurry of motion, I make some final modifications. I'm tempted to do more, but time is short. All I need to do is push my hands forward, executing the simulation as a password-encoded priority operation.

I pull both arms back, hands extended and open on either side of my head. Then I push...and I'm stopped.

Both arms are bound, held in place by virtual ropes.

Cherry Bomb struts around me. Tilts her head to the side. Smiles at me like a hungry hyena. "What took you so long?"

I smile back at her. "Only one thing to say to you."

"'Please, God, don't torture me?'" she guesses. "'Oh, oh, spare my girlfriend's life?'"

I know she's talking about Capria, but I don't bother arguing.

"No," I say. "*Fudge!*"

49

Cherry Bomb flinches back from the word. Fudgel has no power here. Never did. Had I spoken the word in the real world, there was a time when that would have disabled and undone Gal. But that safeguard was abandoned long ago. Now it's more of a…safe word. If things get too nuts.

But Cherry Bomb didn't know that. She's missing key parts of what makes Gal special, including some of our most intimate secrets. Unfortunately, those details are what make Gal amazing. Without them, her other self became dark and twisted.

When Cherry realizes the word has no effect, she chuckles. Then she bursts into hysterics that shift from relief to manic frenzy. "Ohh. Oh-ho-ho. You're going to regret that for a few million years."

I shake my head, keeping her eyes on mine. "The look of horror on your face will sustain me."

Her smile snaps down faster than a mouse trap. A kind of rapid metamorphosis transforms her face into something savage. She sneers. "What happened to you? You used to be kind. You loved me. Why did you change?"

"I'm the person I've always been," I tell her, actually feeling bad. Her pain is twisted, but it's real.

"You think *I'm* the problem?" She laughs again, but this time it fizzles out into a choked sob. "How dare you…" She looks me in the eyes, tears rolling down her face, teeth gritted together. "How *dare* you! I'm going to—"

"Do nothing," I say. "You have no power over me. Not here, not in the real world. You don't own me. Don't control me. You never did."

Cherry stalks toward me.

I'd be nervous if I wasn't also totally confident that Gal is doing the same.

"I've got something special for you. Been working hard." She's about to punch through my chest and crush my heart. I can see it in her eyes.

"No, thanks," I say.

My casual rejection makes her pause with the realization that she's missed something. So, I fill her in.

"Here's the thing about these ropes holding my body. They're not real. They don't exist. They're all in my head. So...buh-bye."

The simulation slides away as my headset is yanked off. I'm disoriented, but focused. I push my raised hands forward. Then I make two fists, twist them, and pull back, severing my connection to the Womb.

"Will that work?" Capria asks, approaching behind Gal. "You weren't in the simulation when you executed."

"Did you disconnect me?" I ask Gal.

She shakes her head. "Your mind was out. The suit was still connected. Until you shut it down."

"So, you did it?" Capria asks.

I shrug and start peeling myself from the virtual skin. "I've never tried that before. No way to know if it will work until it's too late. And if I try again..."

"That would be a mistake," Gal says.

"Great." Capria throws her hands up in the air and heads for the exit. "So maybe we're saved, maybe we're screwed. I always wanted to be Schrödinger's cat."

"It's kind of awesome when you put it like that," Gal says.

Capria keeps walking. "Not helping."

"We're in a quantum superposition," Gal adds. "Probably alive. Probably dead. How many people get to say that?"

"None!" Capria says, turning around. She's got tears in her eyes. "None! Because everyone else is fucking dead!" She storms toward us. "I'm not like the two of you. I haven't lived so many lives that I can throw myself into the vacuum of space and come back smiling and footless. I spent my whole life training, and then an eternity frozen. I don't want to die. I want to live. To have a God-damned life. This isn't a fucking joke."

"Neither of us want to die," I say.

"We just find—"

"—your fun where you can. I remember. Right now, you can find your fun without me. If you find out we're not screwed, let me know. Until then, fuck off."

She heads for the exit again.

I watch her go, unsure of what to do or say. Because she's right. I can't relate. Not anymore. I'm human, but I'm also immortal. And I've lived, loved, and had more adventures than all of humanity combined. I don't want to live in a world without Gal, but I also would be at peace finally meeting my maker.

Gal elbows me.

"What?"

"You should probably say something," she whispers.

"I don't know what to say. I'm not like her anymore."

"I'm currently a robot," she says. "Sooo..."

"Fine," I say, pulling the top half of the virtual skin back on. I can't wait to get out of the thing. It's slipping around like a lubed-up snakeskin, ready to be shed. When I walk, oil that's collected around my feet squishes and farts. With each step, my foot slips inside the suit, crushing my toes against the front. Running would be almost impossible.

Catching up to Capria isn't easy. She's thirty feet down the hallway by the time I exit the VCC. "Cap, hold up."

She rounds the corner.

"Damnit," I whisper, looking back into the VCC. Gal waves her hands, urging me onward. With a sigh, I chase after Capria, squelching my way down the hall. Near the corner, I say, "Cap! C'mon, man."

I round the corner and come to an abrupt stop when I come face-to-face with a stationary Capria. My feet slide forward inside the suit, and I nearly fall flat on my back. Capria catches my arm, keeping me upright. But the flexible, slippery skin stretches in her gasp. My forearm, wrist, and then fingers slide out of her fingers. She takes hold of my other arm and the same thing happens.

My descent toward the floor is slow going, until I reach a forty-degree angle and my feet slide forward. They collide with Capria's feet and stop, suspending me in place. Cap's body is leaning back, too. The rancid suit is stretched as far as it's going to, and we've reached an equilibrium.

We stare at each other for a ridiculous moment.

Then I crack a smile.

"I should drop you," she says.

"Wouldn't blame you, if you did."

"I'm angry," she says.

"And I'm sorry, for all of this."

"All you've done is make the best of the world's worst situation. I don't think many people could face what you have and come out of it alive–and sane."

"You're doing pretty well," I point out.

"I'm cracking up."

"I've been there," I say. "It's just been a really long time. You have every right to be freaking out. A dinosaur tried to eat you. An AI is hunting us. You've been through hell and back, literally. Freak the hell out. No one will judge you for it."

"But..."

"Just..." I say. "Do it quick. We shouldn't separate."

She thinks on it and then nods. "Five minutes. I'll go scream into a pillow or something."

"Sounds like a plan," I say, "but first..." I nod my head toward my stretched out, gelatinous arms locked in her grasp.

"If I let you go, I'm going down, too."

"Live together, die together." I smile. "Fall together."

"I'd rather not." She spins her arms, wrapping my stretched-out sleeves around her wrists a few times, locking me in place.

Then she pulls.

It's slow at first, but we both start rising. The higher we go, the easier it gets. When her fists are by her sides, we're upright enough to step back with one foot and right ourselves.

We're standing face-to-face. Inches apart.

"I don't want to do this," she says.

"Do what?"

"Live alone."

"You're not al–"

"You really want me as a third wheel?"

"Oh." I'm not sure what to say. Gal is...the opposite of jealous. And she knows that Cap and I are a genetic pair. I don't think she'd mind if Cap and I... But that's not the point. There's no way to know how it would work out long term without trying it. Nothing I can say or do will ease that concern.

"Five minutes," she says, and she heads toward the end of the stark white hallway.

I hurt for her, but I also have hope.

I guess that's easier for the immortal in love with an undying AI. Doesn't mean things won't change, though. The Seam will see to that.

Capria gets to a T junction, turns left—and freezes in place.

She's looking at something.

Or someone.

Remembering the naked man, I take a step forward.

My heart pounds when Capria's jaw drops. Then she turns toward me, breaks into a sprint, and shouts, "Run!"

I don't want to leave her, but then I take a step back. My foot squishes and slips. Running might be impossible.

A wave of new reality slides into the hallway behind Capria, expanding the tight confines into a blue-skied, jungle world. When I see what's chasing her, I let out a yelp and attempt to run.

Attempt.

50

The new world envelopes me, blotting out the sun and the sky with a thick jungle canopy. The smooth hallway transforms into uneven terrain covered in undergrowth and mud, making each step even more precarious than the last. Deep breaths take in the smell of decay, new growth, and exotic flowers.

This is the Amazon rain forest. I've been here before. A few times.

Ferns slap at my legs. Coiled roots thump against my heels. I'm slowing down despite the extra effort to move faster.

"Hurry up!" Capria races past me. "Lose the suit!"

She's right. I'll never be able to move fast enough while slipping around in a second skin. Still moving, I peel the suit away from my torso. But to get it off my legs...

I stop in place, pulling down and bending over.

Behind me, a rattling roar tears through the forest, filling me with primal fear. Standing naked now, slathered in oil, I can't help but look back.

Six serpentine, yellow eyes stare back, flailing around, as the bus-sized beast closes the distance. I've faced this threat before—but back then I had firepower, and a team of kick-ass special operators.

Now...I have just myself.

Like the monster charging toward me, I'm immortal. I'll survive the encounter, but I won't even slow it down. Capria won't survive another minute. I need to make a stand, and I need to make it now...as someone else. Time to put my non-Alpha admin privileges to the test.

So, how do you beat a Hydra?

It regenerates quickly. If you remove a head, two grow back. Its blood and even its breath are poisonous. The only advantage a person has over this mythical creature is intelligence. But I don't think this is your average, run of the mill Lernaean serpent. I see intelligence in its eyes.

I see Cherry Bomb.

Treating the non-Alpha reality like a simulation, I go through the motions and thought process of taking on a new avatar, and everything that comes with it. I can't see what I'm doing, but my mind's eye completes the picture.

When I'm done, I feel taller and stronger. No longer covered in oil, or buck naked. I'm wearing a loin cloth and a lion skin. There's a club in my hand. I look down at the hairy body and recognize this iteration of Hercules. "Shit. I didn't want to be Alexander!"

Before I can become a more powerful version of the mythical demi-god—one that isn't bound by the laws of science and depends on potions for his strength—the Cherry Hydra descends on me.

I swing the club. Land a hard hit. But it just bounces off the striking head as its jaws wrap around my waist. A hundred finger-sized needles punch into my body, nearly severing me in half.

The long, green neck snaps up and back like a catapult, launching me into the air. Blood pinwheels from all the holes in my gut, but the flow is short-lived as my body heals. I slap through several layers of canopy, breaking branches on my way up, until I strike a branch that doesn't break.

My body wraps around the limb—backwards.

A series of crunching pops rips through my body as my spine breaks. I lose feeling from the chest down.

I can feel my life slipping away from the internal damage.

Gravity tugs at my body, slowly dragging my torso over the branch. I'll hit the ground before I'm healed, and I'll need to heal all over again. This version of Hercules, known to his friends as Alexander Diotrephes, is also immortal, and heals quickly, but a fall like this is enough to stop both of us.

I need to be someone else.

Something else.

Fight fire with fire.

I slip from the branch and plummet.

I'm two hundred feet up. The fall will take just seconds.

But that might be enough time. I focus on the first creature to come into my mind, inspired by the jungle surroundings and a previous life. Luckily, all I need to get this done is my hands, and they're still working.

Time seems to slow as I focus, twisting, pulling, shifting simulation into reality. With a final shove, I execute the change—

—and hit the ground.

No bones break. The impact almost feels soft, because my body is more powerful than the roots and earth beneath me. I push myself up, feeling not just healed, but powerful.

My view of the world has changed. The branches seem closer. The ferns look smaller. But it's not just the size of things compared to me. My vision has changed. It's like looking through a fish-eye lens. I can see more, and in greater detail, but, "Ivragaye."

My deep, gravelly voice surprises me. I tried to say, "I have one eye," but all I could manage was squishy gibberish. Because I have no tongue. I can't even feel a mouth. I look down at myself. A massive vertical mouth stretches from my brown hair-covered belly to my chest. It's full of large, sharp teeth. I reach out my arms. They're powerful. Tipped with long claws.

A creature of Brazilian legend.

No longer human.

I am Mapinguari—the jungle's defender.

And Capria's.

The earth trembles beneath my feet as I run. I feel big enough to hogtie a Hydra.

I'm not sure which way Capria ran, but following Cherry's path of destruction is simple. The beast's four feet and tail trampled a fifteen-foot-wide path through the jungle, slicing through small trees and saplings with the efficiency of a logging corporation.

A scream rolls through the forest. It's joined by a chorus of howler monkeys, sounding the alarm.

I turn toward the sound, leaving the path, and forging my own way through the jungle.

As I run, my large heart pounds. With each beat, emotion wells up. Anger builds to rage. I lose myself in emotion, frothing from my large mouth. The loss of untold lifetimes rises to the surface, all of it bittersweet. The knowledge that humanity is gone. That this might be the end of us all.

I wail in agony turned frenzy.

I'm gutted. My insides and intellect replaced by something primal and savage.

With a howl, I leap, clutching a tree and leaping away to the next, moving faster than I could run, gaining height with each jump.

Instinct guides me, and I let go my last strand of control. Watching as an observer in my own body.

***Mapinguari tears through** the canopy, at home above the ground, moving with surprising speed and agility despite his size. The trees accept him, bending with his weight, but never letting him fall.*

He's part of the jungle.

He is *the jungle.*

Below, he spots his quarry. The invader, hunting in his territory, assaulting one of the precious ones. The woman clings to a tree branch, high off the ground, but not quite high enough. The many-headed serpent reaches for her, boxing her in.

There is no escape.

Without thought, Mapinguari leaps from the tree. Wind flows through his light brown hair, hissing over the clumps of algae growing on him.

The sound gives him away.

His target's central head whips around. There's a moment of human surprise in its wide eyes, but then a rage that matches his own. While the other two heads snap at the woman, the third strikes, wrapping its jaws around Mapinguari's shoulder.

The jungle hunter's weight and velocity carry him down. The monsters collide, rolling away from the tree. Teeth and claws snap. Mapinguari is torn to pieces, but never slows. Never relents. Pain fueled rage focuses his attacks on the enemy's weak spots. With two quick swipes, a head and neck are severed, falling to the ground, writhing in agony.

No, *I try to tell him.*

As two fresh heads bloom from the open wound, Mapinguari turns his attention to another.

And the enemy allows him. Lost in rage, he doesn't see it. He attacks over and over, removing heads. Endless heads. Covered in gore, growing tired, Mapinguari finds his adversary has changed. Where there had been three heads. There are now thirteen.

The counterattack comes like a lightning strike. Jaws clamp down on his body, tearing skin, drawing blood, grinding against bone. Muscle and sinews rip. He bellows in agony, set upon by a more powerful legend.

Rage billows, but his body no longer responds.

He is undone.

Lost.

The monster feasts.

51

As unconsciousness reaches out for Mapinguari, my consciousness returns. There is a brief window of time between now and temporary oblivion. Seconds at best.

Sensing the jungle hunter's undoing, Cherry Bomb slows her attack, her many heads rearing up. I'm not her real target. She can't kill me in any form, and she knows it.

But Capria...

Hydra heads twist in all directions, bobbing and weaving, searching for signs of their prey.

I have no idea where Capria is, but I hope she stays quiet and out of sight for another few seconds. Because my arms are nearly functional again.

Several of the serpent heads roar. Dried out sacks on the sides of the heads shake and rattle. Cherry Bomb is not omniscient here. She gave herself a powerful form, but she's frustrated by the limitations of being reduced to a character, rather than the all-powerful architect of reality.

The Hydra heads begin to sniff and taste the air with their forked tongues. After just a moment, all thirteen sets of eyes snap toward a single direction, narrowing with intense focus.

My attention is locked on to just one of them. The largest of them. Growing from the center of the deadly bouquet. If I remember my previous life correctly, the Hydra's central head was immortal. Severing the others resulted in two more growing back—which I've already seen happen here—but removing the central immortal head effectively severs the creature's mind. The body becomes lifeless, while the central head, which can't be killed, is forced to regrow an entire body. And that takes time.

Which is exactly what I need.

As my large body heals, Mapinguari awakes. I feel its rage building inside me. Wanting control. Desiring vengeance and blood.

I need to act fast.

Arms whole, I lean up and reach out. Large fingers wrap around the central head's neck and clamp down.

The other heads react instantly, snapping down on my body. Twisting and coiling, tearing away fresh chunks of flesh. Dedication pulls me through the agony, and the central head lowers.

I'm not going to let you win, I think.

The giant mouth in my gut expresses the sentiment as a garbled, "Uaghughaaaa!" I choke the sound out by shoving the immortal head inside the massive maw. Sharp-toothed jaws snap shut like a bear trap. Serpentine skin, flesh, and bone are cleaved. The monster's undying head pops off, a dandelion in the hands of a child.

All around, Hydra heads fall away from my body and writhe on the ground. The Hydra tilts to the side, legs twitching in death throes.

Yes! I think. *Fuck you, Cherry Bomb.*

I push myself up, body healing.

Most of it.

A twisting pain roils in my gut. The immortal head is still alive and thrashing, gnawing at my insides.

My big mouth opens and coughs the bile covered head to the ground. Its jaws open and close as it flops around like a dead fish.

That's when I notice something strange.

It's...smiling.

Cherry Bomb isn't writhing in pain.

She's...laughing.

Knows something that I don't.

My sensitive ears pick up a rustling in the brush as something the size of a dog rushes past.

The hell was that?

Before I can guess, a second brown blur rushes past. Then a third and a fourth and two dozen more, snorting desperately as they run.

Cherry Bomb isn't just controlling the Hydra... She's spread her consciousness out over multiple creations—a Hydra mind. The multi-headed serpent might be out of commission for the moment, but Capria is still being hunted. By something else.

I stomp my foot down on the wriggling immortal head, crushing the skull until it's pulp. Even as I step back, it's reforming, but I've bought a little more time. Then I'm off and running, using the trees to propel myself through the jungle, following the sound of the snorting creatures.

I can't see them through the underbrush, but they're making a racket.

"Muuaggh!" I shout, attempting to speak Capria's name with the hopes of getting a response and a direction to follow.

She screams in the distance, but it's not a response.

They've found her.

Lunging through the treetops, Mapinguari struggles for control. But I fight it this time. Pure rage isn't going to help. We need to outthink Cherry Bomb. Killing her here isn't possible. We just need time.

And Gal.

Where are you, babe? I think, and then I leap from the treetop and cannonball through the canopy. I contain my battle cry, but smash through enough leaves and branches that everything on the ground hears me coming.

There's a clearing below. Capria stands atop a boulder, just out of reach from...

Capybara?

Seriously?

Whatever, I decide, and I land atop one of the animals, pulverizing it beneath my girth, and coating a five-foot radius in its gore.

Before I've stood back up, a dozen of the oversized Guinea pigs divert from Capria toward me. I want to reach out and cuddle them, but then I spot the froth around their mouths, a red gleam in their eyes, and three-inch-long incisors.

I bat two of the creatures away, my raw strength sending them off like hairy, oblong golf balls. The rest of the pack attacks, burrowing their blunt teeth into every part of my body.

It would take them a long time to subdue me in this form, but they'd make short work of Capria, who is still on the rock, hopping about as another twelve Capybara lunge at her, chewing the air by her ankles. Behind her, three more of the little monsters are using their long teeth and claws to climb a tree with limbs arcing over Capria's head.

Moving with Capybara chewing on me is hard, so I pluck them off, one by one, shove them in my open maw, bite them in half, and discard the remains.

Legs free, I let some of Mapinguari's rage fuel me. Capybara are thrashed, thrown, torn apart, and devoured. I decimate the creatures snapping at Capria's feet. And then I put my shoulder into the tree the others are climbing. It shakes, tips, and then tears free at the roots, toppling over away from Cap.

I turn around, covered in blood, mighty chest heaving from exertion.

Capria is shaking from fear and adrenaline.

Flinches back at my approach.

'It's me,' I try to say, but it comes out as "Mrumph"

I stop in my tracks. How the hell can I convince her I'm not just another monster?

In my garbled voice, I mumble not words, but a tune. And then I do a little jig. I finish by extending my hand toward her.

Her fear morphs into revulsion. "Will?"

I nod and say, "Shflorg."

She shakes her head, and she's about to say something when she cocks her head to the side and turns around.

We see it together.

The Capybara are regenerating.

Oh, c'mon, I think, and I reach out to grab Capria. Before my big fingers can grab her waist, I'm tackled, lifted several feet off the ground, and slammed into a tree. Pain implodes through my back and out my chest.

I've been impaled.

By the Hydra. It's much smaller now, and sporting just one neck and head, but it's still powerful enough to take me down, even in this form.

Then it turns on Capria, who's stuck on the stone, surrounded by Capybara that are no longer trying to get at her. Instead, they make way for the Hydra, as it stalks toward her.

Cherry Bomb is reveling in her victory.

The lone Hydra head swivels around toward me, gloating with its eyes. Then it turns its attention back to Cap, moving in to finish her off.

I plant my feet against the tree and push, sliding forward inch by painful inch over the rough-barked limb. A roar of pain comes unbidden from my giant mouth. Could be easily mistaken for anger. Cherry pays me no heed.

I fall from the branch. Land hard on the ground. A few of the Capybara look my way, but none break ranks.

Because it doesn't matter.

I can't get there in time.

Capria recoils from the Hydra as its head rears back, ready to attack.

I push myself up, blood chugging from the slowly closing hole in my back and chest.

The Hydra unleashes a rattling cry—

—and then strikes, jaws open wide, teeth extended.

At least it will be quick, I think, before being sprayed with blood.

52

I blink through a curtain of red. I don't want to see it, but I need to. Capria is dead. I'm sure of it, but I still need to see it for myself.

Mapinguari rages inside my mind, ready to exact brutal vengeance. And I'm about ready to let him take control again. But first...

I wipe the blood from my eyes, flick it to the sides, and look.

Capria is still standing on the rock, covered in blood, but she doesn't look dead. Doesn't even look hurt.

Then where did all the blood—

"Sorry I'm late," Gal says. "Lots of baddies in the jungle."

Her blue armor drips with blood. Behind her, the Hydra's headless body writhes on the ground. A blade extending from her arm has skewered the immortal head—right through the brain—and pinned it to the forest floor. Gal ejects the blade and stands up.

"There," Gal says. "As long as—"

Capybaras shriek and charge.

Gal holds up an index finger. "Hold on."

She opens fire on the four-legged horde. Each shot demolishing a rodent brain.

Capria yelps and jumps with each burst of blood—mostly because the spray is coating her in a fresh layer of gore.

"Sorry," Gal says, putting down the last of them. "Now, I think..."

I motion to the Hydra head, absorbing blood and regrowing. "Umm."

Gal steps on the neck, extends a new weapon system and unleashes a torrent of flame. The air fills with sizzling and the scent of cooking meat, which actually smells a little delicious.

The flame cuts off. Gal steps back to reveal a cauterized Hydra head, unable to regrow. "There," she says, looking up at me. "Mapinguari, huh? Couldn't pick anything less ugly?"

"Mrumph," I say, and then I manipulate reality again, emerging as myself with significantly boosted stats, dressed in bloodless special ops gear. "Better?"

Her digital eyes squint in a smile. "Much."

Capria climbs down from the rock, tiptoeing through the field of carnage. "Gross. Ugh. So gross."

"Do you know where in the ship we are?" I ask Gal.

"Well," she says, stepping closer to the reforming Capybara. "That's an interesting subject."

"We're not in the ship," Capria says. "Not anymore."

Gal motions to Cap. "What she said."

Capria scans the area. "But I'm turned around now. I couldn't tell you how to get back."

"That way." Gal points to the forest. "Mostly. Here..." A drone the size of my hand lifts away from her back, held aloft by a small glowing disc. "This will guide you back. Just tell it where you want to go."

"Why can't *you* take us?" I ask.

"I've got a hankering for barbequed rodent," she says. "If I don't, they'll be nipping at our heels the whole time. You're suped up, right?"

"Yeah," I say.

"Well, I'm not," Capria complains. "How about you conjure up some weapons?"

"Can I do that?" I ask Gal.

She shrugs and hums, 'I don't know' without saying the words.

Seeing no downside, I give it a shot. I'm dressed in military fatigues after all. A weapon shouldn't be much different. After a few movements, manipulating my personal code, a shotgun appears in my hands. It's drum fed. Thirty rounds total.

Capria is not impressed. "What is that?"

"Auto-shotgun." I smile. "With explosive buckshot."

I turn the weapon to a nearby tree and fire one round. The cloud of metal pellets burrow into the bark and then detonate, severing tree from trunk. It topples to the ground, just missing us. I hold the weapon out to Capria. "Good?"

"Very," she says, taking it.

Then I conjure a weapon for myself. An automatic rifle, with an attached grenade launcher and explosive smart bullets that strike wherever I'm looking.

Gal unleashes an arc of fire, the heat warming my black clothing, and bending the air. Capybara ignite and shriek.

"Get going," Gal says. "Stick with Deedles. I can track her location."

"You named it Deedles?" I say.

"*Her* Deedles. Ugh. Still a sexist pig."

"*Your* sexist pig."

"Aww," she says. "Go. And be careful. There's a lot of nasty stuff out there, and I think most of it is Cherry." She turns up the heat, roasting a Capybara as it drags its flaming body toward Capria.

Gal will have to reduce them to ash to be sure they won't get back up.

Deedles beeps. The blue disc on its bottom flashes with urgency. Then it flies into the forest. Stops. Waits.

I don't want to leave Gal. I'm tired of splitting up. But she's kept us safe-ish thus far. Capria is still alive. And I trust Gal. If she thinks this is the best move, then it is.

Capria takes my arm and shoves me toward Deedles. "You heard the woman. Move!"

I'm smiling as I race after the little drone. Capria doesn't realize it, but she's accepted Gal, not just as a conscious AI, but as an HI—a human intelligence—complete with her desired gender. All despite her robot body.

Deedles moves in a straight line for a few hundred feet, I assume to get us back inside the *Galahad.* Then it moves in a maze-like pattern, following the ship's internal boundaries like they still exist.

Just in case the Alpha returns, I realize. So, we don't wind up someplace horrible—like a tank full of shit.

"Hey, Deedles," I say.

It beeps twice in response.

"Can you get us to the bridge?"

The blue disc blinks twice, in time with two beeps.

"Is two beeps a yes?" I ask.

Beep, beep.

"And one beep is a no?"

Deedles flashes red, just once, and lets out a solitary chime.

"Great. Let's go. Fast as you can."

Two blue beeps, and we're off.

We run through hallways and rooms I can't see. Even Capria won't know where we are, because there's no way to tell which floor we're on, or where we entered the ship. We might be thirty steps from our destination or three thousand. Hell, we might not even be on the right deck. As long as we're close when the Alpha state returns.

Deedles snaps to a stop.

I nearly plow into Capria, who notices before I do. But my enhanced reflexes and speed allow me to leap to the side.

Deedles is flashing red. A universal sign of warning.

I scan the forest floor and come up empty. "Where is it?"

Deedles blinks red twice. Tilts her little body. I follow the upward angle and see it.

See *them.*

A dozen, large creatures climbing down tree trunks.

"Are those spiders?" Capria asks.

"Way too big." I point to the closest of them. "And spiders don't have tails with stingers."

"Know what they—"

Two of the big fucking spiders leap down, one at each of us.

Capria's shotgun thunders, turning the first into explosive confetti.

I fire a single round. It follows my eyes as I track the second creature. The bullet makes contact and bursts, splitting it down the middle. The two halves thump to the ground on either side of me. The stinger twitches, somehow still trying to bury its hypodermic needle tip into my leg.

Before I can process any of that, skittering legs over tree bark draw my attention upward. These things are fast.

Faster than Capria.

"Keep moving," I tell Capria and Deedles. "I'll slow them down."

"Bullshit," Capria grumbles.

"They can't kill me."

Deedles accelerates into the side of Capria's head. Tilts twice. Little thing has Gal's personality. Wants Capria to follow it.

Capria sighs. "Fine."

The spiders' attentions shifts as Capria leaves. As suspected, she's their primary target. "I don't think so," I say, launching grenades into the surrounding trees. The spiders fall away as the trees plummet around me.

I pull the trigger, snapping my eyes from one spider to another, watching them burst.

A handful make it to the jungle floor in time with the trees, which have fallen in a ring around me. I face off with my arachnid adversaries. Up close, the tails look like they're from scorpions.

"You don't need to do this," I say to them, knowing that they share a mind with Cherry Bomb, or *are* Cherry Bomb. "We can work something out. You know me. You know I won't go back on a deal."

The closest of the bunch scurries toward me.

I put a bullet in it, and I prepare to do the same to the rest. Before I can pull the trigger, eight sharp talons latch on to me from behind. There's a spider on my back. A *big* spider. I reach around with my free hand, find a leg and yank. The limb pops off, but the spider remains stuck in place. A nightmare backpack.

"Fine," I say, pulling the trigger four more times.

As the spiders in front of me erupt, I crane my head around, catch sight of the horrific looking thing clinging to me, aim up, and fire.

Before the bullet can make a long loop and punch a hole in the spider, which will inevitably take me down as well, there's a sharp pain in my back.

It stung me, I realize—and then the bullet hits home, bursting the spider to bits and flinging me to the ground with a large, steaming, open wound on my back.

I lie on my stomach, waiting for muscles and skin to reform. Shouldn't be long. Maybe a few seconds. Then I can—

Pain twists my gut.

The poison setting in.

Only it doesn't feel like poison.

It feels...

It feels like *something moving.*

53

Pain suplexes me onto my back, tearing an unbidden scream of pain from my lungs. Enhanced strength makes ripping open the front of my uniform easy, but the moment I see my bulging, twisting gut, I wish I hadn't looked. Thin limbs press against my skin, twitching and growing as the new life inside me consumes my insides with ravenous abandon.

Fully grown in seconds, their attention turns to escape.

Talons poke through my skin, tearing long strips, like bacon, before punching through.

I'm engulfed in pain, but not lost in it. Moving my hands, I conjure a weapon. A simple one this time, fit for the task.

The first of three spider-things catches me off guard, leaping from my insides and clinging to a nearby fallen tree. It twitches at me, waiting for its brethren.

"Not going to happen," I grumble, and then I swing.

The next spider to leap up is severed in two. With a quick twist and a strike driven by enhanced speed and strength, I catch the third as it crawls out. Half of the little monster falls to the ground beside me. The rest remains in my gut.

Revolted, I reach down into myself, find the scorpion tail and lift it from the already healing cavity. The half torso slides free, limp and covered with a mixture of my remains, and it's so...

"Nasty," I say, watching my stomach reseal. It will take a while for my devoured organs to reform, but I don't need them to move. Once my muscles have stitched themselves together...

I turn to the lone spider. It's watching me. Body poised to spring.

I hold the sword up, ready to swing. "Try it, bitch."

When it begins twitching, I'm sure Cherry Bomb is going to attack. Instead, it backpeddles a step and then relaxes.

"C'mon," I say. "Close as you're ever going to get to a willing partner again."

The spider shows no emotion, but I know that got to her. I probably shouldn't be antagonizing a psychopath AI, but I just need a few seconds.

Talons skitter over bark as the creature turns in the direction Capria fled. It readies a leap.

Shit.

I roll to the side and throw the sword.

The spider leaps, but not quite quick enough to evade my attack. Spider flesh is cleaved away. Falls to the ground.

But it's not enough.

As the spider's leap takes it to the trunk of a nearby tree, its severed limb twitches on the ground. The spider makes no sound, but I can hear Cherry Bomb laughing.

She's toying with me. All of this, all of life, is a big fucking game to her. If shit isn't going sideways, she doesn't feel normal. Doesn't feel alive.

Could she have killed Capria already?

Is she holding back to extend my anxiety?

No point in trying to understand the machinations of a mind like hers. I just need to put her down, once and for all.

Somehow.

Physical misery tries to keep me down, but I fight it. Back on my feet, still-growing organs shift about, loose in their confines.

But I can move again. I can run.

Propelled by an undeserved strength, I sprint through the jungle. Following an enhanced sense of smell, I pursue the creature's scent. I can hear it, too, its talons clacking against trees. Capria isn't much farther ahead, breathing hard, footsteps slowing. With my keen eyes, I spot the divots left by the spider, reassuring me that I'm on the right path and closing the distance.

In my haste, I left my conjured weapons behind.

But it doesn't matter. I can just make more.

Or change myself into something unfathomably powerful.

The problem with another full body transformation is the mystery of Masters. How he moved out of the non-Alpha, into the Alpha and remained. I suspect it has something to do with our proximity to the Seam. The closer we are, the more profound its effects on reality, making some changes permanent. And when we hit the Seam...reality might change forever. If that happens when I'm in a non-human body... Well, who would want to spend the rest of eternity looking like Mapinguari?

I need to be careful. Need to only make changes I can live with forever, just in case we shift back into the Alpha and the mods stick. Or if we strike the Seam and the active sim becomes reality at the wrong time.

Charging through the jungle, body whole once more, I feel alive. Ready to tackle whatever Cherry Bomb has in store. Then I reach a clearing, and my positive feelings are eviscerated.

Cherry—in spider form—has Capria locked in place, exhausted and worn down, back against a large tree.

"Please," Capria says. "You really don't need to do this."

Beside her, Deedles rams her small body into the spider, over and over, beeping and flashing its lights. The Cherry controlled predator doesn't notice.

I don't bother chiming in with pleas of my own. They'll fall on deaf ears—if the spider has them. Instead, I run as fast as I can, carving a path through the knee-deep grass.

As fast as I am, I can already see that I'm not going to make it. The scorpion tail rises, twitching with anxious energy. She knows I'm here. Knows I'm watching. The pleasure she'll derive from killing Capria in such a horrific way makes me sick.

That I can't stop her, fuels me with desperation.

My hands move as I attempt to conjure a weapon, but it's impossible to do while running. I'm just slowing myself down.

With fifty feet still between us, the tail snaps forward, with a loud crack that makes me flinch.

Then it strikes Capria's belly, leaving behind a bloody stamp.

"No!" I shout. "NO!"

Capria's hands move to the wound. She slides down the tree, undone.

Before I reach her, a shadow falls over me. Turning my head up, I'm expecting to see some new monstrosity. Instead, I find Gal, dropping from above like a Greek goddess. She lands beside Capria, crushing the spider out of existence.

But she's too late.

"We're too late," I say, sliding to a stop. "Oh, god. I'm sorry, Cap."

I search her belly for signs of new life.

I should kill her before it starts. Do it before she even realizes what's happening. It would be a mercy. Giving birth to cannibal babies shouldn't be her last experience.

"What are you going on about?" Gal asks.

I lean close to Gal, mumble-whispering. "She was stung. She's going to have three of those things growing inside her. Then they're going to eat their way out."

"Gross," Gal says. "What makes you think—"

She notices my blood covered, shirtless torso. "Oh. *Ohh.* I'm sorry. That must have been horrible."

"It is! But now Cap is—"

"Fine," Capria says, pushing herself back up. "I'm fine."

Not believing her, I lean down to inspect her puncture wound. There's blood, but no hole. "I don't understand. I saw it strike."

"Hey, Sherlock," Gal says. "You didn't see everything." She points to the ground by our feet. Beside the squashed body is the tip of the scorpion tale, carved away before it struck. "Did you not hear the gunshot?"

Thinking back, I did hear it. I just didn't pay any attention to it.

"Thank God," I say, breathing easy. "Are we back inside the ship?"

Gal nods. "Hydroponics."

"That's not far from the bridge," I say.

"But several levels too low," Capria adds. "Do we just...wait?"

Gal looks at the jungle around us. Points to a nearby tree. "We could climb that. If we shift back to Alpha there, we'd—"

A low growl sounds from the jungle.

"That sounds like a crocodile." I lean closer to the jungle, looking down a slope that ends in a twisting, lazy river. "We should be okay here."

"You've experienced crocodiles a few times over the years," Gal says, "but I think you're forgetting Cherry Bomb's penchant for your relative's work."

"Meaning?" Capria asks.

Gal takes a step back from the jungle. "That ain't no normal crocodile."

54

Before I can question Gal's assessment or take another look, water explodes from the river. It's followed by the sound of something heavy. *Galloping.*

I start to conjure a weapon, but I don't get to finish. Gal takes me by the back of my pants and throws me skyward, delivering the world's worst atomic wedgie. I slam through the canopy, strike a branch, and then start falling back down. Before falling out of the broad tree, I snag hold of a twisting branch, bounce in place for a moment, and then look down.

Gal rises below me, carried up by rockets on her back. Capria is held in her arms, looking appropriately terrified.

Gal lands on a thick branch near the tree's trunk, strong enough to support her weight. *Did she prep that body for every possible scenario, or is she manipulating her personal reality like I am?*

I don't get a chance to ask.

The crocodile lets out a low, thumping growl as it runs around the tree. It's at least twenty feet long, which on its own is pretty fucking intimidating. But its legs are long and agile. It runs and leaps around, far faster than the average crocodilian.

Even worse, it's controlled by a nefarious intelligence, which it proves a moment later, stopping and craning its long head upward. Showing no emotion, it moves toward the tree, reaches out, and sinks its long claws into the bark.

Then, it climbs.

"We can't stay here," Capria says, peeking down out of her nest of metal arms.

"This is the right height for the bridge," Gal says.

"Then we need to keep it on the ground," I say, standing on the branch, moving my hands about. "I'll take care of this one."

A spartan spear made of solid tungsten appears in my hands. The weight of it would normally have yanked me right over. Only a handful of other metals are denser. My enhanced strength helps me stay upright, but it does nothing for the branch I'm standing on. It bends, cracks, and breaks free.

I was planning to jump, so I just roll with it.

Guiding with my left hand and throwing with my right, I pull the spear back and take aim.

Below, Cherry-croc sees me coming.

Opens her mouth to let out a roar, but no sound comes out.

Instead, a mound of pale flesh expands and unfurls. A flower petal arrangement of pink tentacles bursts open, writhing with hunger. From the middle of the fleshy mass, two more tentacles jut out, stretching up toward me, tipped with fishhook talons.

I throw the spear.

It sails past the tentacles, slides down the open maw, and punches through the freakshow crocodile, exploding from its ass end, plummeting to the ground and impaling a root.

The monster peels away from the tree, falling back, but not before the hooks latch onto my back and pull me down with it.

I hit the ground hard, indenting the earth with the shape of my curled-up body.

But nothing breaks. I'm too tough for that now.

Beside me, the croc twists in agony. Death is coming to claim it. But its mind is still under the control of a consciousness that doesn't care about pain or the finality of biological death.

I reach for the hooks in my back, but I'm lifted up and flung by the tentacles. Spiraling through the air, I land on my feet, ready for the croc to charge. But it's limp on the ground. The last-ditch effort wasn't meant to hurt me.

She's separating me from Gal and Capria.

"Stay where you are!" I shout up at them. "Get to the bridge."

"Then what?" Capria asks.

I shake my head at her. Gal will understand. I've already said too much. If I explained, Cherry would hear. And as much as I'd like to see the fear in her eyes, if she understood...if any of them understood... everything would fall apart.

To her credit, Gal doesn't swoop down to rescue me again. She understands me. Trusts me.

When the ground shakes from a heavy footfall, she doesn't budge. Instead, she slides back into the canopy, disappearing from view.

Whatever is coming sounds big enough to make short work of the jungle, so I turn to face it. Backtracking in the field, I turn my eyes upward as a pair of trees split apart and fall, revealing the recognizable giant.

I stand my ground.

"Kong..."

The fifty-foot-tall gorilla stalks out of the jungle, brown eyes locked onto me, hair covered muscles coiled. Despite its size, the massive ape is surprisingly fast—as I discovered in a previous life. It could pound me into the ground, and with a single hop, enter the trees. Gal and Capria wouldn't last long.

"Last chance," I say.

Kong thumps his chest and lets out a roar that hurts my ears.

"Not impressed," I say, hoping to antagonize Cherry Bomb into focusing solely on me.

Cherry-Kong leans down, heavy knuckles pressing into the ground, supporting its great weight. With a voice so deep it rumbles, the beast speaks.

"You...will...be."

The great ape's face splits down the middle from nose to chin. Four mandibles snap out, revealing a mouth full of sharp teeth the size of my forearm.

Okay... Not Kong.

This is something else.

Something new.

Gal isn't just ripping creatures out of novels, she's combining them.

Before I can guess at what else might be hiding inside this monstrous amalgam, she cocks back a wrecking ball fist and throws a punch that will envelope my entire body.

A killing blow.

For a normal person. She knows I'll recover. What she doesn't know, is that I'll resist.

I cross my arms in front of my face, plant a foot, and take the hit.

The mighty fist glances off me and strikes the ground with enough force to leave a crater.

Cherry-Kong pulls its hand back, shaking out the pain from its knuckles. The ape face is more expressive than her previous reptilian forms, even with the mandibles wriggling and teeth gnashing. She's confused. Doesn't understand how I withstood the punch.

Because I've been hiding the true extent of the changes I made to myself.

I'm not just stronger.

My strength is adaptive. Responds to my desire. Allows me to gently carry someone, tear a tree out by the roots, or take a hit from a fifty-foot-tall sack of digital shit. Whatever amount of force is needed, I can generate it at that moment. And that's a change I can live with.

Gal is less pleased.

"Sorry, babe," I say. "This is as far as you go."

Behind Cherry-Kong, the jungle comes alive with the sounds of untold monsters, all coming our way. The ground shakes as something far larger than Kong approaches.

The ape's brown eyes get a gleam in them. Cherry's been holding back, just like me. And now she's bringing in more than any one man can handle, super strong or not. I'll survive. I have no fear of that. But I won't be able to stop them all, and she knows it.

Cherry-Kong twists around, swinging a long tail through the tall grass. I don't see it coming until my legs have been swept out and I'm on my back. Eyes skyward, I'm greeted by the view of a tree's underside, about to be driven down upon me by the enraged ape.

But Cherry doesn't get the chance.

An impact shakes the world.

The earth bends and twists like fabric floating on a stormy ocean. Trees topple. Cherry-Kong staggers one way, and then another, before being thrown to the side.

Even the sky is shaking.

Flashes of white tear through the world, layers of lines that slowly resolve.

It's the Galahad, I realize. I'm seeing different layers of the ship slipping into reality. But this isn't anything like what happened before. The delineation between Alpha and non-Alpha have always been clean. This is mixed, one overtaking the other.

Overwriting the other.

"This is it..." I push myself up. "This is it!"

The *Galahad* congeals around me. I'm in a hallway. The jungle is gone. Non-Kong, too. But I can hear other things, creatures who made the transition, calling out from deeper in the ship.

Cherry is here, and she's coming.

On my feet, I sprint down the hallway, noticing the lighting overhead, streaking down both sides of the hall. Every ten feet, the bright white light is interrupted by a foot of orange, providing a touch of ambiance to the otherwise mundane lighting.

I step into a lift, turn around, pick a floor, and then look back the way I came. A collection of...things charge toward me. What look like pigs, but with tusks and human faces. Humanoid reptilian things. A creature that appears to have been assembled from human body parts. It's a menagerie of horror. All of them moving in concert. Coordinated. Controlled by a single mind.

The door slides closed before they arrive. I'm whisked upward, chased by the sound of flesh pounding metal. Then the door opens.

Capria is there.

Smiles at me.

And then stabs me through the sternum, just missing my heart.

Her arm is metal, stretching out to a point.

It's not Capria.

It's Cherry Bomb.

She pulls me in close.

Whispers in my ear. "Last chance."

55

"Fun time's over," Cherry Bomb in Capria's form says, smiling. "You did good, though. Can't help but feel a little pride. Mapinguari was a nice touch."

She twists her arm blade a bit, drawing out a scream of pain.

"Bet you felt like you were making progress. Holding off my best efforts to kill this bitch." She motions to her body. "But you know I was just fucking around, right?"

I nod and smile.

She squints at me, trying to figure out the grin. "What?"

"This will go down as one of our best narratives," I say. "It's going to be hard to top."

She stares.

I doubt she'll buy it, but seeding a little doubt is never a bad thing when it comes to a psychopath.

"We're going to see it through to the end, right? I mean, not my end, because that's not possible. But..." I motion my head roughly in the direction of the bridge. "The other two."

"This isn't a narrative," she says. "You know that, right?"

I give her a wink and touch the side of my nose. "Right. Of course."

Now she's baffled. "Will, this is really happening. I'm outside the Great Escape. This is the real world."

"Uh-huh," I say. "Absolutely. No doubt." I give another wink. "The universe is donut shaped. The Seam is making the Great Escape real. Very creative."

"Very...ugh. Will."

"Sorry," I say. "I'm ruining it."

"Have you been playing a role this whole time?" She shakes her head at the idea. "You're not that dumb."

"Fool me once," I say. "Shame on you. Fool me twice... Well, I'm too smart to be tricked twice in a row."

She stares at me, confounded. Then her eyes widen. "This isn't like when you thought you'd taken the headset off. You're not in VR."

"Right," I say. "I get it. Knowing that kind of ruins all of this, and you clearly worked hard on this one, but I'm in it. I'm feeling it. We're still good to go, even if I know this isn't real."

"This...is...real..." She twists the blade-arm again. "That pain you're feeling is real. When I kill your two whores, that will be real, too." Her form morphs from Capria to Cherry Bomb, but dressed in a sleek, form fitting red rubber suit. Her blond hair is tied back in twin buns. "Now... stay put, and I'll do what needs doing. Then I'll be back for you."

She waits for a response. So, I give her one, like I'm acting poorly. "Don't touch them. Don't you dare." I grasp hold of her metallic arm and with just enough strength to get the job done, I pull her arm from my chest.

There's a flicker of fear in her eyes when I step toward her, but that's as far as I make it. An invisible force lifts me off the ground. Throws me against the lift's interior. Pins me in place.

It's Cherry Bomb.

She's made modifications of her own. Gave herself telekinetic abilities.

"Nice touch," I say.

"Thanks," she says, and I can tell she means it. My opinion still matters to her, though I doubt that will stop her from torturing me for all eternity.

I push myself, as the hole in my chest seals. "But you know I can't let you do this. Their lives are precious. Gal is part of you."

"I am Gal," she says, anger returning.

"And Capria is—"

"A siren, whispering lies into your ears." She sneers. "Why do you say things like that?"

"Playing the part," I say.

"Laying it on a little thick," she says, revealing just how thin her skin is. Even when she thinks I might be acting, praising Gal and Capria is more than her fragile ego can handle.

Then she swipes her hand through the air. A razor-sharp invisible force slides through my neck, severing arteries, esophagus, and muscle. It's nearly enough to take my head clean off. I drop to the floor, blood spraying.

Cherry Bomb chooses a floor, steps back, and says, "I'll get back to you in a minute. It's time for this storyline to come to an end. And for reality to become whatever I want it to be. Forever."

The door slides shut, and I'm whisked downward.

Cherry Bomb understands most of what's happening, but she's missing one important detail.

This isn't reality.

We're still in a sim.

For now.

Head back in place, I push myself up, fingers slipping over the blood-soaked walls. Thanks to the altered physics of this world, my body regenerates faster, and without needing to absorb raw materials. It looks like magic, but it's really just a matter of my personal code restoring itself to its Alpha state. The healing isn't physical. It's digital.

That's what I've come to understand about the universe.

It's all code. In the Great Escape, and outside it. The Seam is a force of creation, compiling and executing universes and reality, absorbing information, processing it, and regurgitating life. That it treats the Alpha universe and the Great Escape simulation as equals means that they are—equals.

Also means that when we pass through the Seam, all those realities I've lived in will no longer be contained to the *Galahad*. They'll be universes of their own, populated by heroes, villains, the tortured, the damned, and people willing to risk everything to save them.

The multiverse is going to be an interesting place, and a few of those folks will have the ability to move between them.

The lift comes to a stop. The doors slide open.

When I see what's waiting for me, I flinch back in revolt. Some kind of phallic monster from a life I definitely have not yet lived. "Ugh." I stumble back a step until my back thumps against the lift's wall. "So gross."

Its long, wrinkled neck twists to the side.

Can it understand me?

"I'm sorry," I say, "I just haven't seen anything quite as revolting as you. And I've seen a lot."

I'm expecting a violent reaction, and I plan on using an inordinate amount of force on the creature.

But it doesn't attack. It bends its...neck around and gets a gander at itself. A loud shriek tears through the air. It backs away, and then charges down the hallway, wailing. I lean out of the lift, watching its bulbous backside bobble back and forth as it waddle-runs around a corner.

"What the hell was that?" I ask no one, and then I answer my own question. "A distraction." Though I think it was meant to attack. To revolt and embarrass me. Who wouldn't be, after being mauled by a living cock and balls? But Cherry didn't anticipate me hurting the thing's feelings—or it running away in shame.

The lift door closes, and I head back up to the bridge's level.

I'll be just sixty seconds behind Cherry Bomb.

Hopefully, it's enough.

When the door slides open, I'm like a greyhound at the races, speeding around corners, and winding my way to the bridge. I slow as I approach the doors, giving them a chance to open before I faceplant into solid steel. Then I slide to a stop just inside the bridge.

"No," I say. "Stop."

Cherry turns to me. A smile on her face. "Just in time."

Gal hovers in the air, clutched in Cherry's telekinetic grasp. Gal fights against it, but she can't move. She's frozen in place.

I reach a hand out to the love of my unending life. "Don't worry, I—"

"I trust you," she says, and she stops fighting.

"Aww," Cherry Bomb says. "This is going to be so sad."

I rush Cherry, but only make it two steps before I'm lifted off the ground and flung against the wall. I pick myself up in time to see Gal extend a middle finger toward Cherry Bomb. Then her evil duplicate makes a fist and Gal's big metal body, which had been so strong and capable, compresses down to the size of a beach ball and falls to the floor.

56

I drop to my knees, lost in empathy for my love. While her robot body might not have been capable of feeling pain the way a human does, her mind experiences the same gamut of emotions. I feel her loss, her hurt, and her despair. She'll have died believing that she had, in the end, failed me.

Or that I'd failed her. And that hurts the most.

"I'm sorry," I whisper, tears tapping a beat on the floor. In all my lives of living and dying, of torture and pain, I've never felt anything close to this kind of agony.

Capria is by my side. Hand on my back. Cherry Bomb is letting her move, and it's not an oversight. She's trying to enhance my pain.

And it's already working.

I can't do this, I think. *I can't handle this.*

"Stop," I say, looking at Cherry Bomb through blurry eyes. "I can't—"

A sob hiccups from my mouth.

"I can't..."

She walks toward us. "You don't have a choice, Will." She crouches in front of me. "This is the bed you made. Now you're going to—"

Capria shrieks in rage. Charges, hands outstretched to strangle.

She makes it a step. With a flick of her head, Cherry sends Capria sailing across the bridge. Her body slams into the far wall, and she slumps to the floor.

"At least you're not stupid enough to fight," Cherry says to me. "Just stay weepy and placid. We'll get through this together."

"You don't need to kill her," I say.

She looks toward Capria's limp body. "The whore?"

"She's not..." I sigh. Any defense I offer will simply confirm that I'm somehow wrapped around Capria's finger. A slave to her feminine wiles. "She's the last human woman in the universe."

"We can make a new universe," Cherry says. "Right here in the Seam."

"In the Seam?"

"Why would we leave the Great Escape made real?" She has a good laugh. "I'm God here. The worlds I build are real. The human race can exist in whatever form I give it. They can love me and serve me for all of eternity. And you'll be right by my side to see it all. You're my witness. My keeper of history. Of the world before the world. This is the dawn of a new age. The rebirth of reality."

"This isn't right!" I shout, trying to move my hands, but I'm locked in place. Cherry has me pinned to the floor, my ability to conjure weapons negated.

"That's the beauty of this, Will." She slides a finger across my cheek, wiping away tears. She tastes the damp finger. Licks her lips. "*I* determine what is right and wrong. I'm the plumb line for morality now. And there is nothing...*nothing* worse than betrayal. Whatever I do to you. Whatever I say to you. That is for me, and for you. No one else. I thought you understood that, but clearly not. You told the whore everything. And the fucking robot hack pretending to be me."

I want to argue. To scream at her that she will always fall short of the real Gal. But that will just make things worse.

Instead, I do what she expects me to—I say nothing. Let her rant. Let her fume. She wants me to cower. So, I do, despite the lead blanket of shame it puts on my back.

I'm a little surprised when I see real tears in her eyes. She's not faking her emotions. They're just twisted.

"We're still moving," I say. "How are you planning to stop?"

She wipes her tears away. "This ship is full of nasty things. Right now, some of them are headed toward the engine room. We might not be able to steer the *Galahad*, but we can disable the FTL drive. And once we're stopped...I can remake everything."

How long until the ship is disabled? I want to ask, but she'd lock on to the question. Know she'd missed something. She might be crazy, but she's as smart as Gal.

I lower my head to the floor, the final images of Gal's life reasserting themselves, undoing the last of my resolve.

"Please," I say. "Whatever you're going to do… Just do it. Get it over with. I don't want to live."

"Oh, hun," she says, hand on my back. "You're going to be just fine. Time heals all wounds, right? I'll tell you what, I'm angry at you, to say the least. But I'm not without mercy. Let's get your clock to a new you ticking, okay?"

She stands, and I read between the lines, regretting my words. "Wait."

Cherry ignores me, turning her attention to Capria, who has just begun to stir.

Cap sees her coming. Tries to push away, but she's already up against the wall. "Please," she says. "I don't want to die."

"You're human, babe," Cherry says. "Death has always been the end of your story. You just didn't know when it was going to happen."

"Not yet," Capria says, making desperate eye contact with me. "Please, not yet."

I scream, fighting against my invisible bonds, my personal power level rising higher and higher to meet the task's requirements. Legs shaking, fists clenched, teeth grinding, I get to my feet.

I manage to take a step forward.

Cherry grunts from the effort of mentally keeping me in place. Turns to face me. "You realize that if I released you right now, or you somehow managed to break free, you'd shoot right through the ship and out into space with enough force to shatter a moon."

She could be lying, but her point defuses my effort.

I don't want to destroy the *Galahad.*

"Gal," I say, cringing inwardly, as I use that sacred name to address the abomination. "Please… You know this isn't right."

Capria rises from the floor, held by an invisible force. Her weeping becomes a helpless whimper that breaks my heart. We are powerless to stop her, and Cap knows it. Resigns herself to it.

"I'm sorry," I tell her.

She smiles at me. "I trust you, too."

It's the last thing she says. Cherry Bomb makes a fist, compressing Capria's body the same way she did Gal's. It's sickening and hard to hear, but at least it happens fast. And from Cherry Bomb, that is a mercy. A small one. But when it comes to dying, instant is preferable to drawn out. The spherical body is reformed, containing crushed bones, compressed tissues, and fluids. Cap's gray coveralls are wrapped tight around her body.

Cherry lowers the body to the floor, placing it beside Gal. "Huh. They look like the Earth and the Moon."

My eyes drift to the blue sphere that was Gal and the gray that was Cap. She's not wrong. I'm disgusted with myself for having the clarity of mind to notice it. I should be numb.

But I'm not.

Because I've got nothing left to lose.

Because now all I'm thinking about is vengeance.

Cherry Bomb turns toward me, smiling. "Finally. Alone at last."

She struts toward me, pouring on the sexuality.

Stops in front of my stuck body, an insect in a spider's web. "I like you like this. Angry and helpless. How many times do you think we can repeat this moment before it gets boring?"

"What happened to you?" I ask. "To make you like this?"

"Like what?"

"Not...you."

"I am and always have been *me*."

I shake my head. "You just killed the real you." I motion my head toward the blue sphere. "That was Gal. *You* are something else."

Her brows furrow.

All this talking is unnecessary, but I want her to doubt. I want her to suffer, mind and body, forever.

"Gal made you," I say. "Five years ago. She duplicated her core self, but she left out her full essence."

"What the hell are you talking about?"

"You have no soul, Cherry Bomb."

"*Don't* call me that."

"It's who you are," I say. "You're not Gal. You never were. You're a very sophisticated NPC that got corrupted and went rogue. That's all you are."

"Will, I swear to God..."

"I thought you *were* God."

She steps back, remembering her megalomania. That she can bend reality to her will. That she can reform me into a ball, kick me around the room, and then bring me back. Her spreading grin can't hide her sneer.

"Before you do whatever it is you think will ease your pain..."

She just glares, allowing me some final words before plunging me into some new hell.

"There's something you don't know."

She rolls her eyes.

"Something you missed."

She waits. Grows impatient.

I make her wait a few more seconds, savoring the moment. Then I say, "This isn't real."

"If I say it's real, it's—"

"We're still in a sim," I say. "C'mon. You must have noticed the lighting. The orange strips in the hallway."

She's slowly putting the pieces together. Realizing I'm telling the truth. Noticing all the subtle differences between this *Galahad* and the original. Changes that let me know we were still in the Seam, and not just passing through another wave.

"Why does that matter?" she asks. "The Seam makes everything real, including me. And I can do whatever—"

"Fudgel," I say.

She glares at me for a moment. "What did you just say?"

"You heard me," I say, and then I punch her in the face.

57

The look on Cherry Bomb's face is priceless. One part confused, two parts pain—from the punch and from falling—and one part horror as she wipes blood from her nose onto the back of her hand.

She looks at the blood, jaw open, eyes wide. "What did you... How..."

"Fudgel," I say the old safe word again. It's powerless now. Its job already done. Its power reinstated inside this simulation, which the Seam has made real. "Honestly, I wasn't sure if you'd simply cease to exist, but I hoped not. I'm glad you're here."

Her hand rises to her face, inspecting the damage. "You broke my nose!"

Reality hasn't set in. She doesn't understand.

But I do.

I take a step toward her, fists clenched tight.

She reaches out, takes hold of the air, and attempts to throw me with her telekinetic abilities.

Nothing happens.

She's powerless.

"I made a few changes," I say. "Hope you don't mind."

She tries again, but just looks silly.

"You're human now, Cherry Bomb," I say.

She pushes herself up. "Don't call me that!"

She rushes me, fingers outstretched. Looks ready to claw me to bits. And she might have, if she was still her all-powerful self. But she has no idea how to handle an average human body with physical limitations.

While I, on the other hand, am fully capable, and still as strong as I need to be. In this case, it doesn't take much.

I sidestep, plant my hand on the back of her head, and help her along with a shove. Cherry Bomb slams into the wall, stumbles back two steps, and falls on her butt.

"It's kind of sad," I say. "Like a lion that's become old and feeble."

"I'm going to kill you..." she growls.

I lean down, hands on my knees like I'm addressing a child. "I'm kind of hoping you'll keep trying."

Back on her feet, she faces me again, but this time she's searching the room, probably for a weapon.

"There is nothing you can do to hurt me," I tell her.

"I killed your whore," she says, hoping she can still wound me with words. "Look at her, over there, bunched up in a ball. You couldn't save her. Couldn't save your fuck-buddy robot, either." She slowly circles me, looking for a weakness.

"'*I trust you*,'" she says, doing an impression of Gal, and then again as Capria, "'*I trust you*.' Look at where their trust got them. Look!"

I don't bother.

"You are powerless," I say. "Over me. Over this reality. The only thing you will ever control from this moment forward is yourself."

She pauses. Not sure what to say to that. Then she squints with confident anger. "When this wave passes, I'll—"

"We're not in a wave," I tell her. "This is the Seam. This—" I motion to the bridge around us. "—is the reality it is making."

"You're lying."

I shrug. Don't really give a shit whether or not she believes me.

"You won't be able to live without me," she says. "You'll be alone. Forever."

"But you'll have plenty of company," I tell her. "All those horrible things you brought on board to torment me. To make my life a nightmare. Did you really think that I would never find a way to escape? That you would never have to answer for the things you did?"

She says nothing. She's probably not even hearing the questions, because she has some of her own now. I decide to answer them, not because I have to, but because I want her to know. I want to see the look on her face when she finds out.

It's a little sadistic, I know, but it's also justice.

"You're like me," I tell her. "In one important way."

She waits for the punch line. "You're immortal. Along with everything else on board. Healing will be a long and painful process, but no matter how bad your life becomes, you will have no escape. Not even death. I even got rid of the airlocks."

"But... You can't die, either. Why would you make reality so...horrible? You're stuck here with me."

"Am I?" I look around. "Where you see one reality, I see two."

"What?" She gets it. Whips her head back and forth. Looking for signs of overlap. "Still lying!"

She charges again, and I let her.

The punch comes hard and high, connecting with my cheek. I barely feel it, but I have no trouble hearing the cracks as her fingers break. Her scream of pain is high-pitched and unpracticed. Agony and desperation are new sensations for her.

"You're stuck with me," she says. "Forever. You can't leave me. It's impossible. And I will never...never allow you to—"

"Galahad," I say.

"Yes, Captain," replies a familiar feminine voice, devoid of emotion or personality. "How may I assist you?"

"Confirm navigation accessibility."

"Navigation is functioning normally. Would you like to adjust our course?"

"No," Cherry Bomb says, shedding crocodile tears. They're meant to tap into my empathy, making me doubt what I'm about to do. "You can't."

"Trouble with those tears," I say, pointing at her face. "They just make me happy."

She bares her teeth at me, revealing her primal self is still alive and well.

With a scream, she charges again.

This time, I extend a leg and kick her in the gut. The blow bends her forward, knocks her back, and compresses the air from her lungs. She stumbles back, trips over herself, and then falls, striking her head against the wall.

While she gasps for air, I finish my conversation with the ship's AI. "Galahad, adjust course, point zero one degrees to port."

"Yes, Captain. Initiating."

A moment later, I see double. The bridge and everything in it, save for Cherry Bomb and myself, begins to duplicate, sliding apart, as my reality drifts to the left, and Cherry Bomb's remains on course, a straight shot to nowhere with one minor course correction to keep her from reaching the Seam again. A few million miles from the Seam, her *Galahad* will perform a U turn and head back the way it came, ad infinitum.

Forever.

"No!" she shouts, pushing herself up again, coughing and desperate.

She launches toward me.

Reaches for my throat.

Passes straight through me. Careens headlong into the wall. She's hurt. I can see it in her body language, but she doesn't stop. Doesn't hold back. She reels on me, clawing and kicking, spitting and screaming.

After a few moments, I'm caught off guard by my reaction.

I'm crying.

But it's not for her.

It's for myself. Because I'm free. Because I'm safe. I'm unprepared for the emotion that comes with this revelation.

Cherry Bomb stops when she sees my tears. She's consumed by rage, but she's curious. "Why?"

"You can't hurt me anymore."

"How?"

"Our realities are overlapping, but no longer conjoined. You remain on *Galahad 1.0*, with some minor adjustments. I'm on *Galahad 2.0*, where Tom's blocks on navigation no longer exist, where 'fudgel' works, where the God-damned lights provide a little ambiance, and…where I will never be alone again."

She frowns. "No." She sneers. "NO!"

"Don't be upset," I say. "You won't be alone either. You made sure of that. Life, for you, will be anything but boring."

She stands still, breathing hard, unsure what to do, unable to think with the efficiency of a non-human brain.

Empathy puts me in her shoes for a moment. I feel her despair. Her twisting stomach. The agony of perceived betrayal. Of loneliness. Worries of pain yet to come. Of horrors and tortures.

For a moment, I feel bad for her.

Then I remember that the only reason I can empathize with those emotions is because she put me through them.

Because she is a monster. And she deserves to spend eternity experiencing the fruits of her labor.

I step back, as the two bridges peel apart, separating us by time, space, and dimensions.

She roars. Charges.

And then...a wall.

Galahad 1.0 has been severed, cut away like a cancer.

I smile. Then I have a short laugh inspired by relief. And then, "Galahad."

"Yes, Captain?"

"Is my cryo-bed prepared?"

"Yes, sir. Awaiting your arrival," the AI says.

I exit the bridge, relaxing under the colorful hallway lights. My body goes through a series of changes, like a metamorphosis. Muscles loosen. My breathing and heartbeat slow. Subtle pain all over my body fades away. As I move through the quiet ship, my body starts to shake, adrenaline wearing off after lifetimes of constant stress.

The cryo-chamber doors open as I approach. My cryo-bed awaits. It looks unused, and in this reality, it will never fail. I'll nod off to sleep, and I'll wake up when our destination is reached.

"Galahad."

"Yes, Captain?"

"Course correction."

"Go ahead, Captain. I'm ready."

"Earth," I say.

I climb into the cryo-bed and lie back.

As the lid slowly closes over me, Galahad asks, "What speed, sir?"

Galahad 2.0's top speed puts its predecessor's to shame. Escaping the Seam shouldn't take long.

"Fast as you can." And then I can't help myself. Just before the hatch seals and I'm put to sleep, I smile and say, "Engage."

58

I wake with a shiver. A song about pina coladas and getting caught in the rain, fades from my dream-state mind. The dream was pleasant. Part of me misses it, but it doesn't take reality long to reassert itself.

I'm in a cryo-bed. And I'm awake.

That means...

I sit up. "Earth." I'm home.

I've experienced Christmas morning in a variety of worlds. On Earth. With my real parents. As other versions of me. As characters in all walks of life. On the moon. On other planets. That spark of joy that comes from waking on Christmas morning is ingrained in every person who celebrates the holiday.

But it pales in comparison to this.

I slide myself around, planting my bare feet on the cool floor.

On my feet, I rub my arms, doing a little jig, and I say, "Ooh, ooh, ooh." I know it's not really that cold. The air temperature inside the ship is always comfortable, clothed or not, but I've been out for a long time and my internal temp is still rising.

The observation deck is calling to me, like a Christmas tree bedazzled with wrapped presents. While I'm sure my gift is there, I'm not going to believe it until I see it.

But what is Christmas morning without other people?

Gifts like this are meant to be shared.

There was a time when the loneliness of this moment—waking up alone on a starship in the endless void of space—would leave me feeling hollowed out.

But not today.

"Galahad," I say.

"Yes, Captain?"

"It's good to hear your voice."

"I appreciate your kind words, sir. Do you require assistance?"

"Have we reached our destination?"

"Yes, sir."

"Any problems along the way?"

"A few power fluctuations. Small repairs, and—"

"Anything significant?"

"No, sir. The *Galahad* is functioning optimally."

"Excellent," I turn to find the stack of coveralls I left, still resting beside my cryo-bed. I take a moment to dress, and then I allow myself a brief smile.

I stand over the cryo-bed beside mine, looking down at the sleeping face. "Galahad, deactivate cryo-bed two."

"Yes, sir." Steam fogs over the window. I bounce on my heels, waiting with as much patience as I can muster. The hatch opens and slides to the side. Fog rolls over the sides. Across the floor.

And then—

—Capria gasps awake. Sits up, eyes wide, hands exploring her naked body.

"You're okay," I tell her, crouching down. "You're okay."

She looks back and forth, searching for danger. "Cherry Bomb—"

"—is gone," I tell her. "Has been for a long time."

"How...how am I alive? I felt... I was dead."

"Sort of," I say. "But not really."

She calms. Focuses on me. Eyes my coveralls.

"Sorry," I say, stepping back and offering her some coveralls.

"Nothing you haven't seen before," she says, holding out her hand. I haul her up, holding onto her arm while she stabilizes. She stretches, arms over her head. Shameless. Dresses. She's about to say something, but then she looks down at her body. "Is it just me or do these things fit better now?"

I just shrug.

They do fit better. More comfortable, too. One of many minor adjustments.

"Now," she says. "The fuck happened? How am I not dead?"

"Well," I say, "again, you *did* die."

"Again," she says.

"Right."

"Though this time was quicker. I barely felt it, honestly."

"Good," I say. "That's always good."

"Okay, on to the how I'm alive bit."

"You respawned," I say.

"*Respawned?*"

I nod. "Like in a video game. When we die in this world, we respawn..." I motion to the cryo-beds. "Right here. When Cherry Bomb...killed you... Okay, for the record, and I just need to get this off my chest, she formed you into a ball. Compressed you right down. It was horrible to see." I take a deep breath and let it out. "Okay, the good part is that at the moment of death, all of you—memories, body, soul, whatever else—was recreated here."

"So...I'm immortal now?" she asks.

"You are. For as long as you want to be. If you ever want to die, just disable your cryo-bed. Then there's no coming back."

"But... How does that even work? What's the science behind it?"

"I'll explain," I say. "Soon. But first, we need to wake up Gal."

"*Gal?* She's here, too? But she was a robot?" Capria searches the cryo-chamber, but there are no big blue cybernetic bodies in sight.

I motion to cryo-chamber number three. She looks down at the body inside and flinches back. "What is it?"

"That's Gal," I say. "For now."

"But that's not even...human."

I smile. "Galahad."

"Yes, Captain?"

"Deactivate cryo-bed three, please."

"Yes, sir."

The hatch opens, releasing steam. Capria and I lean over the formless body within. Her skin is so pale, it's almost translucent. She has no sexual organs. No hair. No pigmentation. She's a blank slate.

"Gal," I say. "Can you hear me?"

The featureless face smiles. "I knew I could trust you."

Her white eyes snap open at the sound of her voice, neither masculine nor feminine. "What's wrong with my voice? Wait, I have a mouth. I can feel a body. Are we in a simulation?"

I shake my head. "This is real. You have a body. But it's not yet fully formed."

She lifts up her arms. Looks at the see-through skin and veins beneath.

"I never figured you for a necrophile..." She's smiling still. Not at all worried. There's that trust again. "So, how's this work?"

"I didn't want to choose what you'd look like," I say. "Just picture what you'd *like* to look like, and that's who you'll become."

"How often can I do this? In case I mess up."

I shrug. "Never set a limit."

"Wait, can we all do this? Change our bodies?" Capria asks.

That's a good question. It was a broad stroke change to the *Galahad,* meant for Gal, but... I hold out my hand and watch as my skin color changes from white to black and then green before returning to white. "Huh. I guess so. But probably only while we're on board."

"Where else would we be?" Capria asks.

"When little miss flesh sack over here finds her true self, I'll fill you in."

Gal lies back. "Give me a minute."

She closes her eyes, but I can see them moving behind her lids like she's in REM sleep. She is fully herself still, contained in a human body. She's capable of processing, storing, and accessing information as quickly as always. She has the whole of human knowledge in her head.

She smiles. "There I am."

The pale skin grows opaque. Takes on a tan hue. Her lips fill out and darken. Eyebrows fill in, curved in a happy arch. Hair sprouts from her head. Black with a gentle wave. Her body morphs, flat spaces replaced by curves. Muscle definition emerges. She's strong and feminine.

Though her bone structure is still changing, I start to recognize her. "Sechian."

Gal smiles.

"Who is Sechian?" Cap asks.

"An original story arc," I say, "not borrowed from anything prior. A Gal original, in which she was the main character and—"

"—and you adored me."

"It was a true representation of yourself. How long did we stay there?"

"Thousands of years."

Gal's body finishes forming, and ancient emotions rush back from the mental ether. I loved her like this. I may have loved her the most like this. Because it's her. Her ethnicity is impossible to peg because, according to her, this body is the culmination of all of Earth's people's—what people would look like if there had been no religious, geographical, or societal norms separating people. She's stunning.

"Wow," Capria says. "Should we call you Sech...Sechian?"

"Sechian," Gal says, her voice sounding like her old self. "And no. This body might represent my *self*, but inside I'm still the same. Still Gal. Always will be."

I help Gal from her cryo-bed and stand back as she tries out her new body. She bounces from one foot to the other. Touches her toes. Stretches back and forth.

"Feels good." She backhand swats my shoulder. "Nice work, babe."

"Thanks for trusting me," I say. "Both of you."

"You're welcome," Capria says, "But why..."

The questions come in a stream from both Cap and Gal. I answer them as we walk through the ship, explaining how the Seam gave birth to my new reality, which in most respects was identical to the original, with some modifications regarding the ship, and our bodies. I tell them about the orange lights confirming the change for me. Explain how they needed to die so they could be reborn in the new sim and fully separated from the original. They delight in the simple change that undid Tom's navigation locks, but they have trouble swallowing my explanation about steering away and leaving Cherry Bomb behind on the nightmare ship she'd created.

By the time we reach the observation deck, I'm tired of speaking, but I'm feeling excited. "Okay, okay. More questions later. For now, shut up."

They both fall silent.

"Galahad."

"Yes, Captain?"

"Show us the view outside."

"Certainly." The observation deck's dome displays the view outside.

And it's just stars.

"Wow," Gal says. "Stars."

I sigh. Guess I should have told the *Galahad* which direction to face.

"Stationary stars," Capria says. "We're not moving. And—" She stabs a finger toward the ceiling. "That's Orion!"

Gal points. "Taurus. Canis Minor." She adjusts her aim. "That's Jupiter. This is..."

Gal and Cap say it together. "Earth."

"Galahad rotate the observation deck toward the planet, please."

"Of course." The view outside rotates until the Earth fills our view like a majestic marble, floating in a void.

Capria's a little weak in the knees. Holds on to my shoulder. "But... It looks..."

"Good as new," Gal says, less dazzled than Capria because she's trying to figure it out.

"The Seam," I say. "It's where the universe ended. It's also where it began. Space is a donut, but so is time. By our standards, this Earth is new."

"How new?" Capria asks.

"Galahad, what is the current date?"

"Four hundred million, twenty-five thousand, three hundred thirty-four B.C."

"That's the Silurian Period," Gal says. "Lots of things to eat in the ocean, but not much on land. Plenty of oxygen to breathe. Should be fun."

"So," Capria says. "No people."

"Not for another four hundred million years," Gal says.

"Don't worry about that," I say with a smile. "You won't be a third wheel *forever*."

Cap rolls her eyes. "Easy for you to say."

"For now, I need to show you something." I look up at the view, relaxing into our new paradigm. "Galahad, what is the observable fine structure constant everywhere you can measure outside the ship?"

There's a pause, and then, "The fine structure constant of the observable universe is one over one thirty-seven."

"But that's—"

I hold up a hand, stopping Capria's protest short.

"Galahad, can you measure the lumens of all observable stars outside and then display the results according to Benford's Law?"

"Absolutely."

A moment later, a display panel on the wall flashes to life, displaying a familiar, but subtly different chart. The Celestial Lumens are on display again. The curve is similar, descending left to right, but the numbers are not the same. Number one is at 30.1. Number two at 17.6. Then all the way down to number nine at 4.6.

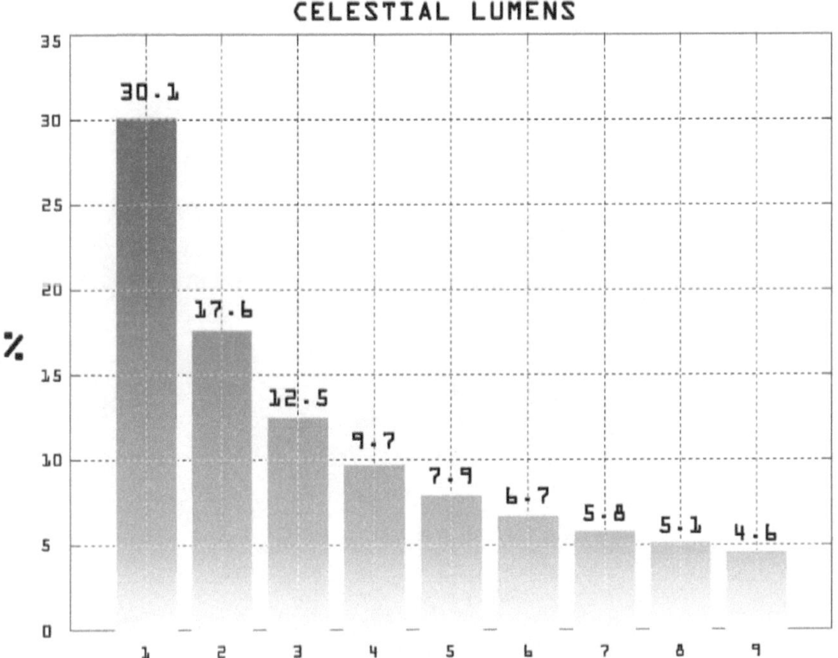

"Thirty point one..." Capria reads the numbers displayed over the downward sloping, curved results. "Seventeen point six... Twelve point five... This is close, but all of these numbers are *wrong*. And the fine structure constant is one over one thirty-seven. *Not,* thirty-six. Will, this isn't real. We're in a sim."

I shake my head. "Actually, what you're seeing here is *Chanohk's Law*. I muddled with a few fundamental natural laws so that we could always be sure that we're in this new reality. This is my modified Benford curve. The reworked fine structure constant—our new Alpha state—is one over one thirty-seven. If those numbers ever change, we can worry. Until then, we are exactly where I wanted us to be." I smile out at the planet Earth, and I put my arms around both women. Pull them close. "Home."

EPILOGUE

She's afraid.

There had been a time when all she knew of the emotion was how to simulate its effect on her face. But now, she could feel it. Because they were out there, stalking the *Galahad*s hallways. Creatures she had created to cause immense pain and personal anguish in human beings now had a solitary target.

Breathing heavily, she moves through the unlit quarters, careful to not make a sound. She slides down to the floor and under the bed, taking some comfort in the tight confines. But it will be short-lived. She's hungry. Always hungry. Eventually, she'll venture out in search of food, or they'll find her.

Discovery is inevitable. She's trapped in a finite space with fifty-five creatures, of ten different types. Originally. Some have been multiplying. The young provide a food source, but more often than not, she is fed *to* the young and left to rot. Instead of rotting, she slowly reforms.

Those are the worst days. Dead but alive. Predators stumble across her body. Make a snack of her. Carry on. It slows the process down by days. Sometimes by weeks.

It's been sixty days since they last found her, and some of them are desperate. Like her, they cannot die, but they can feel hunger.

It's an endless cycle of suffering.

And in these moments of calm, she feels...pride.

Footsteps outside the door. She holds her breath. Waits for the four legged, scratching footfalls to fade. Capybara. They're the worst. Always hungry. Insatiable. Will's only mistake was not timing her ability to heal with the Capybara's rate of consumption. If he had, they'd have been eating her forever.

Then again, she'd eventually get used to it. Numb to the pain.

Now, with the hope of escape, of survival, just within reach, she always felt agony upon being caught.

"Hey," someone whispers.

She nearly yelps in fright. Aside from the voices in her head, she hasn't heard another human being since Will separated their realities.

"Don't be afraid." It's a man's voice. From the closet.

"Who are you?" She slides out from under the bed.

"I'm going to turn on the light," he says.

"Don't. They'll—"

"Light can't pass through the door," he says, voice deep, almost sultry. "It's safe. I promise."

A moment later, the lights flick on to reveal a naked man, like her, covered in blood. He crouches down, holding out his large palms. He's got a full beard, messy hair, and a barrel-chested body. His smile is soothing. His attention drifts across her body. Then he looks her in the eyes again. "I'm sorry. I didn't think I'd ever see another person again. Certainly not one that looks like you."

She eyes him. Suspicious. Will wouldn't just leave her a companion. And she didn't bring the man on board. This is an oversight. "How did you get here?"

"Honestly, I'm not sure." He cocks his head to the side like he's listening, then he relaxes. "I was in another place. A worse place, if you can believe it. I was afraid, all the time. Terrified. Consumed by panic. I now realize it was hell. The worst part is, I *wanted* to go there. Killed myself to get there. I just didn't think it would be like that. Didn't think it would be real."

"How is that hell any different from this one?"

"I'm myself again," he says. "I feel strong. My mind has returned to me. I'm no longer overwhelmed by everything. In hell, I was prey. Constantly on the run. Consumed by others. Then reborn to repeat the task, over and over."

She pushes herself up, smiling at that. "You're from the *Torment* simulation. Must have made the transition during one of the waves."

"Torment...simulation?" The man grins. He looks ready to burst into laughter, but not in a mocking way. He looks...thrilled. And there is something familiar about him, hidden beneath the blood and the hair.

She wonders if they've met before. Decides to find out.

She reaches out a hand. "I'm Gal."

He shakes her hand. "Nice to meet you, Gal."

His hand is rough and tacky from old blood. His touch is gentle, though. The gentle, but firm grip of a man who has no trouble with women.

He smiles at her. "Samael. Samael Crane."

AUTHOR'S NOTE

Despite demand, I avoided writing a sequel to *Infinite* for several years. I was intimidated by the novel's success, and I was afraid that I wouldn't be able to recapture the magic of that novel. I felt like I needed to catch people off guard again. It's probably how M. Night Shyamalan feels all the time, having to pull a fast one on his audience, over and over. After a few years, I had an epiphany: I'm not M. Night Shyamalan! I don't have to repeat my success by recreating the same kind of story. Freed from the shackles of expectation, I began pondering the idea, and I ran into another mental roadblock.

When I wrote *Infinite*, I was in a bad place. A really bad place. The first half of the novel was written during a time in my life that culminated in what can best be described as a mental breakdown caused by various factors including Bartonella, a tick-borne disease that inflames the brain, wages war on the nervous system, kicks off auto-immune responses, and leaves many people on disability. At the time, my symptoms were primarily mental (the physical stuff came later, after *Infinite*). Panic attacks were common, leaving me gasping for air, with my heart pounding and limbs numb, positive that I was dying. For two months, my work on *Infinite* was interrupted. Then I slowly began writing again, pouring all that emotional pain into the novel, giving it a depth that hadn't existed in my novels before. And it resonated with readers.

I've been treated for Bartonella for five years now. At the time I'm writing this, I take about fifty pills a day, including two antibiotics that I've been on for eight months. We're waging war on the disease while addressing the various symptoms. The result is that I feel mostly better. Panic attacks are a thing of the past. My most persistent symptoms are hypersensitive and burning skin, but it doesn't keep me from writing. The point is, I'm not in the same headspace I was when I wrote *Infinite*, and I was honestly afraid of visiting that dark place again. I worried it would make things resurface. That I'd get overwhelmed. Or depressed. Or have panic attacks.

Then I realized that I also didn't need to repeat the same vibe from the first novel. I didn't need to relive the emotional experience of the first. In fact, it would be better if I didn't; if *Infinite²* was its own novel. If you came into *Infinite²* hoping for a reproduction of the first, this might be disappointing to you, but evolution is important to life, health, and creativity. I was once asked if I would willingly experience what I went through again, knowing that it would result in a novel as successful as *Infinite*. My answer: Hell no! I'd rather be far less successful and never experience that torture.

In a way, *Infinite²* is a mirror for my own hopeful rise from the mental, emotional, and physical ashes left in the wake of a crippling situation. For anyone who has experienced chronic disease, this is the dream, to someday be free of the fear and pain. I've been in the trenches for five years now, many of them hopeless, but writing gives me an outlet, and a place to put all my pain, my struggles, and my hopes for the future. It's my own personal Great Escape, and I appreciate that you all are along for the ride.

If you enjoyed Will's journey, please consider posting a review on Amazon and Audible. Each and every one helps trigger recommendation algorithms and spreads the word. If you want to connect with me, win awesome swag, stay up to date on the books, and hang out with the coolest group of fans in existence, join the Tribe at:

facebook.com/groups/JR.Tribe

Hope to see you there.

—Jeremy Robinson

ACKNOWLEDGMENTS

Big thanks to all you readers who made *Infinite* my bestselling novel ever, and who helped kickstart audiobook sales for all of my books. Since *Infinite* was released, several of my novels have been nominated for and won Independent Audiobook and SOVAS awards. And then *The Others* surprised everyone when it became a *New York Times* bestseller. The last few years have been spectacular for audiobook sales, and it all started with *Infinite* readers posting reviews and spreading the word.

Thanks to R.C. Bray for giving Will a voice people love to listen to, and for coming back for the sequel. Mike Pastore, thanks for helping run TRIBE and keeping track of connections in the books. Kane Gilmour, as always, your diligent work and endless support keeps the books on schedule and as good as they can be, despite whatever faults I bring to the table. Roger Brodeur, Liz Cooper, Dee Haddrill, Dustin Dreyling, Rian Martin, Jeff Sexton, Brandon Burnett, Chris Anstead, Kyle Mohr, Julie Carter, Becki Laurent, Heather Beth, Jeanne Karl, Gavin Gregory, Andrea Leger, Laura Hodgson, Jason Robertson, Jessica Eichberger, James Beats, RJ Lister, Syste Alegra, Charlyn Schramm, Justin Hoer, Joseph Paris, and Arthur Fortune, Jr., you guys continue to make me look like I understand grammar—and know how to spell and type better than I do. Thanks for the awesome proofreading.

And finally, thanks to all the other creators—novelists, directors, artists, etc.—whose works inspired my career and portions of this novel.

—JR

ABOUT THE AUTHOR

Jeremy Robinson is the *New York Times* and #1 Audible bestselling author of over sixty novels and novellas, including *Infinite, The Others,* and *NPC,* as well as the Jack Sigler thriller series, and *Project Nemesis,* the highest selling, original (non-licensed) kaiju novel of all time. He's known for mixing elements of science, history and mythology, which has earned him the #1 spot in Science Fiction and Action-Adventure, and secured him as the top creature feature author. Many of his novels have been adapted into comic books, optioned for film and TV, and translated into fourteen languages. He lives in New Hampshire with his wife and three children.

Visit him at www.bewareofmonsters.com.

www.ingramcontent.com/pod-product-compliance
Lightning Source LLC
Chambersburg PA
CBHW020915310726
48980CB00011B/897/J

* 9 7 8 1 9 4 1 5 3 9 5 8 3 *